ALPHA
OMEGA

ALPHA
OMEGA

NICHOLAS BOWLING

TITAN BOOKS

Alpha Omega
Print edition ISBN: 9781789093810
E-book edition ISBN: 9781789093827

Published by Titan Books
A division of Titan Publishing Group Ltd
144 Southwark Street, London SE1 0UP

First edition: May 2020
10 9 8 7 6 5 4 3 2 1

A CIP catalogue record for this title is available from the British Library.

Printed and bound by CPI Group (UK) Ltd, Croydon CR0 4YY.

For JAH

MONDAY

9.30

STEPHANIE BÄCKER lives in a haunted house.

There's a room on the first floor that creaks and groans and sometimes ejects unpleasant-smelling gases from the crack under the door. She can hear what's going on in there first thing in the morning and last thing at night, and is starting to suspect that the ghost doesn't sleep the same hours as she does, or perhaps doesn't sleep at all anymore. In fact it may not even be possible for the ghost to sleep. Every day she enters the room to scavenge dozens of empty cans of highly sugared and caffeinated energy drinks, navigating the detritus by touch alone, only knowing she is approaching the room's inhabitant by a strangely heightened humidity around him. Sometimes he burps softly. Sometimes he wriggles and the synthetic upholstery of his chair rasps against his thighs and then falls silent. She likes the sounds because they remind her of when he was a baby. She'll often stand at the door and listen to him for an hour or more, or will drift around the bedroom, a spectre herself, listening to him burble and groan. The ghost is her son, Gabriel Bäcker, fifteen years old and no longer of this world.

———

Stephanie doesn't realise the package has arrived until she collides with it in the hallway. She goes face-first into the top of it, inhales the rich chemical bouquet of the cellophane wrapping, and then finds herself clinging to the box like a sailor to a shipwreck to stop herself from ending up on the floor.

The most disconcerting thing is not what the package is, or who has ordered it, but how it has ended up inside her house without

3

her knowing. There was no doorbell, no sound of a drone or a DV dropping it off. These are the things that she can hear even in her most death-like sleep. It's just appeared. Her home is one of the few places she can comfortably navigate without her stick, and a new obstacle like this feels alien and intrusive.

Stephanie rights herself and examines the object with her hands. The package is massive, a plastic slab as high as her shoulder and as thick as her waist. It takes three steps to get from one end of it to the other. Its weight is beyond reckoning, but certainly too heavy for her to lift on her own, which again raises the question of how it has arrived in the hallway so noiselessly. The surface is covered with a residue which is somehow powdery and greasy at the same time, and smells like static. As for the contents, she has no idea, and she doesn't want to open it in case it's been delivered in error.

From somewhere in the living room, her PAD *pings* with the arrival of a new message. She walks back, feeling her way along the wall. It's something she hasn't had to do in years, but the package seems to have altered the dimensions of the house and everything seems new. She yells in the direction of the coffee table three, four times until her device hears her and opens her inbox.

"To Stephanie and Gabriel, with thanks for your help," the message says, out loud, in a voice that sounds like Cary Grant or Paul Newman, or some other old-time Hollywood star whose identity has been bought up and repurposed by the company behind the package.

She listens again. There are no details about the sender. The message seems to have been airdropped by the package itself. Perhaps it's from Care? Their housing sponsor does sometimes send promotional and "relationship building" gifts to its residents, but

Stephanie's never been given anything of this size or expense. And usually such a calculated act of kindness would be widely publicised, rather than slipped clandestinely into her house.

She returns to the package and calls up the stairs.

"Gabriel?"

No reply, obviously.

"Gabe?"

She knows she can't reach him in his bedroom, but she likes to say his name aloud occasionally, like a spell that will conjure him back into existence.

Stephanie slices the box's cellophane with a fingernail and opens the top. The packaging is itself precision engineered and the lid seems to open pneumatically. Another tone from her PAD, which is still in communication with the box. Another message from the reverse-engineered Paul Newman:

"Welcome to your new Alpha-ready 8K TruLife Smart TV!" he says. "We can't wait to see you In World, Stephanie and Gabriel Bäcker." Their names are added in a different timbre and accent to the rest of the sentence. "Have fun!"

An HD TV is hardly an appropriate gift for someone with congenital blindness, so whoever has sent the package obviously doesn't know her at all. Or does know her, knows her *very well*, and intends the gift to be for Gabriel and Gabriel alone.

Stephanie decides to hide it, at least for the time being. She clears a path in the hallway, then goes around to the end of the package nearest the door and begins to shove it across the laminate flooring, a few inches at a time. It's tiring, bruising work but after quarter of an hour she's got it as far as the kitchen. From there she manages to manoeuvre it into the cupboard under the stairs and shut the door. For a few moments afterwards, the voice on her PAD continues to describe the machine's technical specs until she shouts at it again and it turns itself off.

She makes herself a coffee and sits at the table, quivering with a mixture of fatigue and low frequency terror she can't quite place. Paul Newman's voice comes back to her.

"With thanks for your help."

Yes, she knows exactly who's sent it, though she won't admit it to herself, much less to Gabriel. She sits in the darkness, fingers laced around the cup. A whisper of pressure on the floorboards overhead. She tells the microwave to play her favourite adverts while her coffee goes cold.

11.35

IT IS HALFWAY through Second Recreational Period, and Josh Pettit (8B), Alex "Peepsy" Pepys (also 8B) and Kiran Ahuja (8W, but generally considered an honorary member of 8B) are looking at a severed human hand. It is the sort of macabre artefact that most boys dream of finding, and always assume they will eventually find if they just search long enough in the empty corners of the school, but now that it's actually in front of them, just enough blackened skin on it to hold the bones together, the reality is difficult to stomach. Kiran has already been sick and is wiping his mouth on his heavy silk tie.

"What do we do?" says Josh. "Should we tell someone?"

"I'm going to pick it up," says Peepsy, crouching and poking it with his stylus.

"Don't! It's probably got diseases."

"Do you dare me?"

"What?"

"To pick it up. We could put it in someone's locker. Put it on Mr De Souza's desk."

Kiran has buried his hands deep in his blazer pockets and is flapping the jacket in a state of extreme agitation, as though he's trying to put out a fire on the seat of his trousers. He walks in several small circles and then goes and hides behind one of the big yellow excavators that are loitering, unmanned, on the edge of the field.

"We should just go back inside," he says, his voice now disembodied. "We're not meant to be here."

Of course, that's precisely why they are there. Year 7s and 8s aren't allowed to leave Recreation Spaces #1–4, everyone knows that. They're forbidden from even setting foot on the playing fields, and the construction site around the school's perimeter is totally off-limits, on pain of Demotion or even Expulsion. The official explanation is health and safety related, but there are lots of rumours flying around the lower years of the school as to what's *really* being built way out in the greenery beyond the football stadium. It was curiosity, and Peepsy's incurably optimistic sense of disobedience, that convinced him, and the others, that this reconnaissance mission was a good idea.

"We can't just leave it," says Peepsy, skewering the hand through its carpal bones and peeling it out of the mud.

"But if we tell anyone about it then they'll know we were here." Josh sniffs long and hard. Everyone is sniffing now. Hay fever is a big problem at NSA all year round.

"We don't have to tell anyone. We can just take it with us."

Kiran suddenly squeals from his hiding place behind the excavator. Josh and Peepsy squelch through the puddles in the tyre tracks, the latter still dangling the dead hand from his stylus point like it's a fish he's caught. Around the other side, Kiran's hands are no longer in his pockets, but under his armpits, as though he is physically holding himself together.

"I've found the other one," he burbles. "And there's that." He nods to the floor so he can keep his arms safely in place. He is rocking back and forth slightly.

Under the giant bucket at the front of the excavator, five more fingers are protruding from the earth, and next to it the smooth dome of a submerged human head, mud-packed eye sockets just visible above the surface as though it's trying to watch them in secret.

"This is too weird," says Josh. "We have to tell somebody."

"No way! I'm not getting put on a Beta timetable. Or worse. What if we get expelled? Then what do we do? Can you imagine Kiran going to Retail Academy?"

Kiran is trying to be sick again, one arm on the rear tyre of the digger to steady himself, but nothing's coming up.

"Let's just go," he says, a cobwebby bit of saliva streaming from his chin. "I'm going."

"Me too," says Josh.

"Oh c'mon."

But the other two are already leaving. Josh is rubbing his friend's back awkwardly. Peepsy watches them take the safe route around the back of the stadium to the Design Technology block, the route that *he* spent so long plotting, which avoids almost all of the cameras but is direct enough to get them to the perimeter and back within the twenty-minute window of each Recreational Period.

Even so, he hasn't got long until he's due back in class. He approaches the bits of body under the excavator scoop and looks at them from various angles. A scream of either pain or triumph drifts over to him from one of the other children scampering around the designated play area.

8

Another loud, satisfying sniff, and he's unzipping his rucksack and pushing his trainers and PE kit right down into the bottom to make room for his new acquisitions. The screen of his PAD gets a great, dirty smear across it in the process. He throws in the first severed hand, with the stylus still attached, and then gets to work digging out the second appendage, and lastly the skull. He sticks his fingers into its eye cavities like a bowling ball, and with a little twisting and straining it slurps its way out of the mud. It's missing its lower jaw, and a few teeth, but otherwise looks pretty well preserved. The head fits snugly into the bag, which he rezips and hoists onto one shoulder.

It's raining by the time he starts back to the main building. The drops are fat and warm, like his shower at home. Josh and Kiran are nowhere to be seen. Behind him the clusters of diggers and drills and cranes and coils of wires and tubing lie dormant, looking themselves like artefacts waiting to be discovered.

Peepsy's rucksack feels much, much heavier than he was expecting.

12.34

MR TOM ROSEN is surveying the crowns of twenty-four living heads, a palette of blacks, browns and blonds with a single fleck of red in the second-to-back row. All faces are angled downwards, so he can't see any of the students' expressions except for occasional manipulations of eyebrows or hairlines to connote concentration, or relief, or sometimes despair. The patter of rain on the window is matched by the patter of twenty sets of fingers on their glassy PAD screens.

Mr Rosen has his own PAD, from which he can see that 25% of the class have finished their primary task and have moved onto the Reflection phase of the lesson. He also has miniature versions of all of the boys' and girls' screens on his device, so he can see exactly what each of them is doing at any given time. If need be, he can then project that live-stream up onto the whiteboard at the front of the classroom, which has made for some memorably humiliating situations for students in the past.

"Five minutes remaining," he says, his voice odd and hollow in his ears after so long in silence. "Project proposals have to be finished by the end of the lesson." He slots himself carefully between desks, arranged in a six-by-four rectangle, turning corners where the whim takes him.

One of the thumbnail images on his PAD is blinking. Carla Le Maitre-Bridge in seat D2 is cycling through pictures and videos of various kinds of turtle. Mr Rosen looks at them for a moment before locking her screen and projecting it publicly.

"Tell me, Carla, how is a detailed understanding of turtles going to help you achieve a Level 9 in your VAC exams? I don't *remember* there being a turtle module in your English and Media Certificate."

Some of the other students laugh and whirl around noisily in their seats. They fix her with gawping, persecutory looks. Mr Rosen watches Carla slump under their derision, then looks at himself from some imagined point on the ceiling and hates himself for taking a shot so cheap and so rehearsed.

"I was just having a look."

"Hang back at the end of the lesson, please."

"But I've got to see Miss Sherratt."

"Then you'll have to explain that to Miss Sherratt. Hang back at the end."

Carla Le Maitre-Bridge huffs, folds her arms and glowers out of the window. The playing fields are only visible as a sludgy green blur through the rain and the condensation.

The class reach 96% completion of the task, and the little boxes on Mr Rosen's PAD light up green as their work is uploaded to be marked. When the bell sounds all the students' PADs are automatically shut down and disconnected, and they slip them into their red NutriStart-branded neoprene cases and file out into the corridor chattering.

Carla is still staring at, or through, the misted window. Her face is pink and swollen, as though she is either about to cry, or is paralysed with rage, or both. The school's central heating is still turned on full blast in November, which has not only made the classroom uncomfortably, soporifically hot, but has also brought a variety of exotic teenage odours into bloom.

"Carla." Mr Rosen perches on the desk in front of her. "I'm going to talk quickly and seriously so you can get to your next lesson."

She looks at him very briefly, and then down at her hands.

"You have a month until your mid-year assessments. Straight after that you're going to have internships to think about. You really don't have any time to waste."

Carla doesn't say anything, just traces her finger in little circles on the tabletop. The desks all have a lavender-coloured synthetic covering, supposedly designed by NASA or MI6 or someone, which can neither be written upon nor scratched into, and is velvety to the touch.

"Why weren't you working on your proposal?"

She strokes the table a couple more times. "I just forgot."

"Forgot? Despite the fact that twenty-three other people are working on it right next to you? How can you *forget* to do something that I set right at the beginning of the lesson?"

11

"I got distracted." Her face has now gone from pink to tomato red, and there is a sheen on her brow and cheeks that makes her look like she's been lacquered. "I find it hard to concentrate."

Mr Rosen slightly downgrades the seriousness of his tone. "That's what these are for, Carla," he says, holding up his PAD. "Change your settings. You can block distractions. It's a *Personal* Administrative Device. The clue's in the name!"

He wanted that to come out as a half-joke, but instead it just sounds patronising.

"It's nothing to do with the settings. It's me. I feel weird."

"What kind of weird?"

"In my head."

Carla now sounds like she has too much spit in her mouth, and her face is very swollen. Mr Rosen's heart does a little adrenaline-fuelled skip as he realises that the situation is straining the boundaries of normality.

"When you say head—"

That's when it starts. Carla begins to have the most extravagant nosebleed Tom has ever seen. Great jets of dark blood come shooting out of both nostrils, spattering the desk's stain-resistant covering and then cascading down the angled surface into her lap. This is accompanied by tears that have been accumulating during the telling-off, giving the impression that all of the fluid is leaking out of poor Carla's body and within minutes Mr Rosen is going to have a shrivelled husk of a girl propped up in his classroom.

He rushes back to his desk, opening and slamming three drawers but finding nothing resembling tissues, only some old bits of graph paper, which he thrusts under her squirting nostrils. The volume of blood means he has to fashion the paper into a crude sort of bowl, which is very quickly filled. Carla is now crying just from pure terror.

"Let's get you to the nurse. Pinch your nose. Come on, tilt your head back." She does so and starts making strange gargling noises. "Forward, I mean forward." Head between the knees? Or was that for fainting? He can't remember.

He manoeuvres her out into the corridor, and they half-walk, half-jog to the medical centre.

The NutriStart Skills Academy is in the shape of a giant hexagon, with spiral arms projecting from each corner like airport jetties. The problem with this very regular geometry is that it is almost impossible to know which side of the school you're on, since all of corridors look identical, and it always takes Mr Rosen twice as long as expected to reach his destination. Today is no exception. They already seem to have turned more than six corners when the blood begins to pour from Carla's ears. She makes a whimpering noise that sounds more tired than scared, now. She tries to stem the flow with thumbs in her ear-holes and little fingers pressed either side of her septum, as though she's miming a telephone with each hand.

Mr Rosen leads Carla, dripping, past two classes of horrified Year 7s, past little Gerald Liu with his wheeled suitcase full of textbooks he doesn't need, who bows and says "Good morning" as though everything is perfectly normal, past a bored-looking porter jangling his keys, past the offices of SMT, whose occupants stir distantly in their ergonomic chairs, and delivers her to the cool blue waiting room outside the nurses' inner sanctum. By this point she looks like the stuff of nightmares, red and wet from nose to chest, from fingers to elbows.

"Oh Lord!"

The nurse on duty appears and takes possession of the girl with the unfazed efficiency of an army field doctor. She ushers the casualty onto a bed inside the surgery itself. Her boyish hairstyle quivers with concern.

"Yes," says Mr Rosen, putting his empty, sticky hands in his pockets, "we've had a bit of a disaster."

"What on *earth* happened?" she says over her shoulder, collecting a range of swabs and bandages and ice packs from different cupboards with amazing speed and fluidity.

"Came out of nowhere. We were just talking."

"What's her history?"

"History?"

"Did you check her profile?"

"Profile. No. I should have done that."

The nurse plugs various bits of Carla's head with foam. She's now woozy and quiet.

"Carla? Can you hear me?"

"You just put foam in her ears."

The nurse somehow manages to glare at him out of the back of her head.

"Carla? What happened?"

"The classrooms are so damn *hot*," says Mr Rosen, more to himself than to anyone else. "Why can't they turn the radiators down?"

Carla's lips start moving, as though she's in secret, silent conversation with herself.

"I think we should probably send for an ambulance," says the nurse, straightening up. "I don't suppose you know which insurer she's with?"

"Ah. No."

"Fine." She puts her hands on her hips and looks him in the eye for the first time. "Thank you for looking after her, Mr Rosen," she says, with the implication that he is now redundant and trespassing on her turf.

"I'll wait out here," he says.

"Will you?"

"Just in case. Let me know if there's anything I can do." Just as he's leaving he pokes his head back around the doorframe. "You'll be alright, Carla." She looks at him like she's never seen him before.

The nurse closes the door to the surgery, and Mr Rosen takes a seat on one of the plastic waiting-room chairs. He realises he has yet to complete and submit his Self-Assessment for the previous lesson, so he takes his PAD from his jacket's inside pocket and syncs it with the school's network. He'll have write up a report on this whole incident, too.

A very quiet, monosyllabic conversation is happening in the surgery next door. Poor Carla. Out of interest, he searches for her profile on the NSA MNet. He finds her photograph, smiling, airbrushed, totally unrecognisable. There is a note beneath *Medical/Other*:

> Insurance: United Transatlantic Snacks standard cover. Policy #889800923B (father)
>
> High blood pressure. Hypertension.
>
> Parents are separated. Carla has taken this badly. Do not mention or discuss with her outside of agreed therapeutic process.
>
> Student can become very anxious. Responds poorly to stressful situations.
>
> Concern level: medium

"Medium," he says, out loud.

While scrolling around the rest of her profile – she's done some hand modelling for Casio, he notes with interest – the room darkens.

There is someone large in the doorway. Something about the bulk of the silhouette tells him it is the Headmaster before he has even opened his eyes.

"Mr Rosen." The tone of the words is too flat to be either a greeting or a reprimand. More just a statement of fact.

"Hello, good morning. Hi," says Tom.

The Headmaster is a monolithic being, who has to stoop to enter the nurse's waiting room. His head belongs on Easter Island, massive, distinctive, and yet totally plain in terms of its features. Tom finds it almost impossible to picture his face when it's not directly in front of him.

"How is everything?"

Again this remark is blandly non-specific.

"Fine, fine," Mr Rosen says. He stands and realises how unconvincing this sounds, given that he is covered with blood. "Just a little incident with Carla Le Maitre-Bridge."

"Year 9."

"That's right."

"Yes. That's right."

A pause.

"She had a nosebleed, so I thought I should bring her down here, hand her over to the professionals, you know, ha ha."

The Head is looking at the door to the surgery, not actually at Mr Rosen. "Yes. Good. That was the right thing to do."

Tom has never seen anything approaching concern on the Headmaster's face – never seen anything approaching any kind of expression, in fact – but his massive forehead wrinkles slightly.

Without knocking, he opens the door into the room where Carla is being attended to. Tom hovers outside.

"Oh, hello Headmaster!" says the nurse with just a hint of terror.

16

"Good morning, nurse." Tom waits for a surname, but it never comes. "May I have Carla for a moment?"

Even from the other room, the pause that follows is heart-stopping. Tom is suddenly acutely aware of how much he has been sweating.

"Nurse?"

"Now is perhaps not the best time, Headmaster. She's very weak. She's lost a lot of blood."

"She will be looked after."

"The ambulance is already on its way. Perhaps you could wait until she's recovered?"

Tom can actually hear the swish of the Headmaster's huge wagging finger in the air.

"There is no need for an ambulance. It has all been taken care of."

"Taken care of?"

"Come with me, Carla."

There are two clicks as Carla's shoes touch the tiled floor. Then the black shape of the Headmaster stoops back though the door, and guides the girl, who only seems to come up to his waist, out into the corridor. Neither of them makes eye-contact with Mr Rosen as they leave. It takes a long time for the sound of their footsteps to disappear.

"What was that about?"

The nurse shakes her head, and points beyond his shoulder. "Look."

The window of the surgery waiting room looks out upon the NSA's car park. He and the nurse watch in silence as a four-wheel-drive vehicle zooms past them, makes a U-turn at the far end, and then comes to an abrupt halt directly outside the school's main entrance.

Tom feels weirdly like he's watching TV as the Head emerges from the glass double doors, not making much effort to support

17

the weakened Carla, and approaches the 4x4. Two other men get out. The polished doors gleam, knife-like, as they're opened. One of the men actually tries to shake Carla's hand. The other offers her a jacket. Then she is inserted into the back of the car, which disappears as quickly as it arrived.

Mr Rosen and the nurse exchange glances but no words. His pocket vibrates. A reminder on his PAD: *Your Period Six self-assessment is now overdue.*

13.00

GETTING EXPELLED is the best thing that has ever happened to Gabriel Bäcker.

He has been In World for approaching one hundred hours straight now, and has already accumulated the kinds of resources that his ex-classmates could only dream of. Page one of his inventory includes, but is not limited to:

Level 99 Diamond Armour
Level 99 Diamond Sword (+ Soul Drain)
Level 99 Ice Bow
Pontiac Firebird
Poisoned Apples x 99
Wheat x 999
Fission Reactor (rare) x 2
Rancid Meat (+ enchantments)
Scroll of Defy Undead
Scroll of Infatuation
Gucci Loafers

Whirlpool Aqua 3500E Washer-Drier
Key to Apartment #1, Highrise
Key to Apartment #1, Emerald Hills
Condoms x 999
Dragon's tooth x 999
Dynamite x 999
Level 99 Plasma Rifle
Level 99 Machete
"Pussycat Club" Membership Card
Nespresso "Flair" Coffee Machine and Steam Wand
Handsaw
Night-Vision Goggles
Lamy E-Z Grip Glitter Gel Pen
NutriStart Protein Power Breakfast Capsules (unlimited)

If he were to visit one of the forums now and exchange his goods, he could easily buy up a terabyte of Sandbox on the Game's fringes, maybe two, to build on as he pleased; to be honest, he could probably just cash in the branded goods and make enough "real" money to move out of his mum's house, temporarily at least, but there isn't much point when the Bit-Pound exchange rate is so low, and when he can double what he already has In World twice as fast as he can Out of World.

Gabriel doesn't think of the NSA much at all now. It makes absolutely no difference to him whether he finishes his internship prep year or not. All of the best jobs are IW anyway, and he's not going to end up in Sales, or Marketing, or even Semiotics, because he's better than that. The reason behind his expulsion is the very same reason he knows he doesn't have to worry. Compromising not just the NutriStart Skills Academy network, but the entire NutriStart

Corporate MNet, was no mean feat and it's only a matter of time before the company, or one of its competitors, comes looking to recruit his technical services. He still considers himself a hero for highlighting flaws in their system, and half expects the school to see it this way too and offer him some kind of reward.

A hand begins to grope at Gabriel's head and he starts to feel the prickling irritation that accompanies being pulled Out of World too quickly, a psychic gear-change that has caused so much distress that the developers have been forced to include regular in-game warnings, and when exiting the game players are encouraged to spend several minutes watching a special "declimatisation" cut-scene that has been designed to readjust them to the real world. Gabriel's mum doesn't understand any of this, and is content to simply tear the VR headset and earphones straight off her son's head.

"Why are you still on this? You promised you were getting ready."

The sound of his mum's voice, which is fuzzier around the edges than the ultra-high-def Alpha Omega soundtrack, and the feel of her warm fingers on his scalp, makes Gabriel almost murderous with rage, and he shoves her with enough force that she stumbles backwards onto his bed, where she stays seated.

"Don't do that, Gabe. Don't push me."

"Then don't just come into my room without even knocking!"

"I did knock, but you never hear anything because you're playing your game."

Gabriel is too angry to speak, and also too ashamed, noticing the saliva that has accumulated on his chin, the stains on his T-shirt, the stink of his body and his bedroom. That just makes him angrier still, angry that his mum should have made him feel this sort of shame.

"Are you dressed?"

"Yes."

Having a blind parent means that lying about something and getting away with it is so easy it's boring. He resents her for that, too.

"I mean *dressed* dressed? For your interview?"

Gabriel puts the VR headset back on, and gives his mum about thirty seconds to fumble her way across the room and locate his head and pull everything off again.

"Gabriel!" He looks up at her and watches her eyes drift around their sockets. Her brow is twisted into a shape that is both assertive and totally hopeless at the same time. "You can't just *not* go to school. You have to finish your Internship prep somewhere. This is a Technical Academy you've applied for. It's right up your street."

"*I* didn't apply for it, did I? You just submitted me without asking."

"At least go to the interview, see if you like it."

"Tech Academies just train you for data entry. That's it. I'm glad you think so highly of me."

"Everyone starts somewhere at the bottom, Gabriel. That's life."

"Your life, maybe."

It's always a surprise when Gabriel sees his mum start to cry. He always assumes that her eyes are 100% broken, and he finds it strange that they should retain this functionality whilst lacking the ability to do their most important task.

"I've made 300,000 Bits in the last six hours," he says. "Do you know how much that's worth?"

"I'm not interested, Gabe." She sniffs and stands. "Please, just go to the interview. Have a wash. Take the bus."

"I'm not going."

"Then I'm throwing out the router."

She's already left the room and is feeling her way down the stairs before Gabriel can disentangle himself from the headset, and the gloves, and the belt, and when he is finally free his legs feel like they're

21

full of cold, wet sand and melt beneath him. He can hear his mum clattering around in the living room as he tries to massage the blood back into his muscles. She is using tools.

"You can't!" he shouts, galloping unevenly after her. "How are we going to get food? And your meds?"

When he reaches the bottom step, she's already got the black box in her hands, and she's tearing the fibre-optic cables out of the back. "I'm past caring. Anything to make you understand." She's pointing an accusatory finger, but not quite in the right direction. "This is going in the recycling."

"Don't be stupid."

"You've driven me to this, Gabriel."

"You're being *stupid*."

"I don't know what else to do."

She tugs at another wire.

She plucks another cable from the back of the box.

"Alright, I'll go!" He has to steady himself on the wall for a moment. "Fuck's sake."

They are both panting a little, and the crumpled profile of his mother's face, her badly styled hair, the drooping cables in her hand, make Gabriel feel unutterably sad, a feeling that the rational parts of his brain have to shout over the top of, for fear that he'll never be able to have another thought, or another feeling, apart from the sadness ever again.

"Please?"

"Yes. I said yes, didn't I?"

She slots the router, disconnected and blank, back into its little alcove in the living-room wall. The plaster is flaking from where she's torn it out. Like all new builds, the black box is one of the first things to go in, and the house is built around it. Gabriel wonders if taking it out has actually compromised the structural integrity of the building. It looks like it's load bearing.

She turns in his general direction and opens her arms, which could be a sign of surrender or an invitation for an embrace.

"I do love you, Gabriel."

"I've got to get changed."

———

Quarter of an hour later, Gabriel is standing on his doorstep, his mum fussing over his jacket, straightening his tie, patting down his lapels. Though neither he nor his mum will admit it, Gabriel has put on a lot of weight since they bought the suit – a functional, funereal two-piece – thanks to the combined efforts of puberty and Alpha Omega. The waistband won't go over his stomach anymore, and has to be slung low, giving his legs a strangely foreshortened aspect. His sleeves have the taut, swollen shininess of black pudding, and when Gabriel needs to adjust his hair or answer his PAD, he has to bow his head a little, since his elbows won't bend much further than a right angle.

While Mum is fiddling and Gabriel is grinding his teeth, their neighbour emerges from the next unit down and waves cheerily.

"Good morning, Mrs Bäcker!"

She stiffens "Oh. Good morning, Mr Carnoso."

"Afternoon, I think!"

"Yes. Sorry. Good afternoon."

Mr Carnoso grins, and his whole head creases. He is fantastically bald.

"Thought any more about my offer?"

"Thinking about it. Certainly thinking about it. Ha ha."

"You won't get a better one, so think quickly!"

23

"I'll let you know in good time."

"Good good. Looking smart, Gabe. You off somewhere important?"

Gabriel doesn't reply.

"He has an interview today," his mum says for him.

"Really? Oh yes, the tech college. My nephew goes there. Chris. You've met Chris, haven't you?"

Gabriel smiles to himself. He has indeed met slobbering, speech-impedimented Chris, In World, many times, and has subjected him to such a rigorous campaign of harassment, from so many cloned profiles, that the boy simply doesn't go online anymore.

Mr Carnoso misunderstands the smile. "That would be something, wouldn't it, if you ended up at school together. You and Chris. We could share the school run, Stephanie? How about that?"

"He has to get through the interview first," his mum says.

"Yes, of course. Don't let me keep you. Good luck, Gabe! Enjoy your days, both of you!" He saunters off down the pavement, and somehow Gabriel can see his smile in the back of his neck.

"What's his offer?" Gabriel says.

"Doesn't matter. You're going to be late."

"What's his offer?"

"Nothing. He just wants to buy something from me."

"What?"

"Just something from the house."

Because of her impairment, his mum has always been particularly susceptible to scams and ruses and unscrupulous people. At his dad's old house she'd been visited by a man claiming to be a member of "Christ's First House of Champions", who'd offered to speak personally with God about returning her sight to her, in return for a small donation. When Gabriel had come home from school he'd

24

found his mum trapped in conversation on the doorstep, while the man's accomplice was calmly and systematically emptying the place of all of its electronic goods via the back door. It really wasn't any wonder that his dad hadn't hung around, after something like that.

Gabriel suspects that this Mr Carnoso business is probably a similar kind of trick, but he doesn't say anything. In fact, he actually hopes his mum goes ahead with it, as though it's a lesson she needs to learn.

"Have you got your PAD?" she asks.

"Yes."

"Do you know what questions to ask them at the end of the interview?"

"Yes."

"Do you have their prospectus with you?"

Gabriel pats the satchel hanging by his hip, loudly enough for her to hear. "Yes."

She sighs, a delayed exhalation from the encounter with their neighbour. "Well, good luck. Don't be nervous. Be yourself."

He couldn't be much further from being nervous. She gives him a warm, dry kiss on the cheek, and waves him off. From the bus stop he watches her waving to an empty street, before she gets self-conscious, runs a hand through her hair, and closes the front door. He can still smell her soap on his skin.

When the bus arrives, Gabriel pays for the journey to the Accenture Technical Academy, just in case his mum works out how to check his travel data, but gets off two stops early, and walks back in the opposite direction, into town, until the high electric whine of the traffic has disappeared and he is surrounded by the faux-marble and chrome of the Heathfield Central Precinct. The sky is the colour of watered-down milk and hurts his eyes; the air is sharp with the smells of espresso and brutally caustic cleaning products.

The neon "AΩ" of the Alpha Cafe is visible from all corners of the precinct, and for a moment Gabriel feels such joy and relief he worries he will actually cry. He swallows hard.

Inside, the cafe is dark and warm and has a savoury-sweet smell about it. He pays for two hours up front, orders a Coke, and once he is settled into his booth retrieves his PAD and his VR set from the satchel, which does not, in fact, contain the school's prospectus.

Once he is In World, he scans the map, checks his inventory, and heads directly to The Party.

———

From: David Graves (MBA), Headmaster, NutriStart Skills Academy 6
To: All parents
Delivered by AIM.

Dear Parents,
Have you tried NutriStart Hi-Fibre Paste Minis? Keep things moving, *on the move*!

In light of the tragic attacks on the Dermacrem: Healthy Glow All Year Round! Training College and the World of Lentils Practical Academy, I am sure a great number of you will have concerns about the security of the NSA site. As teachers and leaders, our first responsibility is always to ensure the safety and well-being of pupils, staff, parents and visitors. Therefore, after last week's events, I have made it the first priority of the school's development plan to review the NSA's security systems and processes, to ensure that our boys and girls can continue with their education and training with total confidence and peace of mind.

The board of directors and myself are currently in consultation with a number of external providers to choose the right security solution for our school. We are looking at a number of initiatives that will improve site safety both internally and externally, and will dramatically reduce the likelihood of damage to school buildings/pupils in the event of a security breach.

Inevitably these improvements will come at a significant financial cost. I feel, nonetheless, that regarding a matter of such seriousness there can be little room for compromise. Discussions with external parties are ongoing, but whatever scheme we eventually choose it is likely that our annual fees will have to increase at a rate significantly higher than inflation. ☹

I realise that this will have a considerable impact on many of our families. Please rest assured that individual cases of financial hardship will be assessed by myself and NutriStart to ensure that no student loses out on the education and training he or she deserves. We expect a decision to have been reached by the beginning of the Autumn Term, when of course I shall be in touch again with more details.

On a lighter note, many congratulations to William Oben in form 9V, who has made it through to the third round of the KPMG Youth Accountancy Olympiad. Well done, William!

With my best wishes,
David Graves
Headmaster (MBA)

13.40

AMONG STRATFORD'S high-rises, the classical facade of the HBO Museum of Britain has the appearance of a souvenir from its own gift shop, something you might find on the end of a key ring. It's not the original building, although it looks identical in virtually every way. The Bloomsbury site was far too valuable a piece of real estate for something as pointless as a museum, and the agreed compromise was to recreate a life-size ersatz model from several enormous 3D printers and ship the whole thing way out east. For Dr Alice Nowacki and her colleagues, the irony of a museum unable to preserve itself is a good source of both amusement and despair.

Alice has just finished her lunch break and is a little late back, vigorously scrubbing chilli sauce from the corner of her mouth. The steps up to the main entrance squeak cheaply under her trainers. She takes a shortcut through the atrium, past the queues for the VR booths and the hologram of Elizabeth II, calls the elevator, and descends to the BIA's offices.

The British Institute of Archaeology, formerly the European Institute of Archaeology, is a skeleton crew of five men and five women operating out of a sub-basement in the museum. They work in twilight and live in constant fear that someone at Home Box Office will remember they exist and sever what remains of their funding. The kind of archaeology in which Alice was trained – i.e. the actual excavation of ancient sites with spades and trowels and brushes – rarely happens anymore and she and her team spend most of their time cataloguing existing finds and adding them to the archive of objects In World. Once they're in Alpha, the punters can examine them in far greater detail than if they were just in a glass case, and without any risk of damage or contamination. The real items are then, supposedly, sealed in a climate-controlled storage facility somewhere near Stockholm, though Alice isn't convinced that they aren't simply being taken to landfill; perhaps there isn't much difference either way.

It's a foregone conclusion that at some point the entire museum – the artefacts, the building, the tour guides dressed as Anglo-Saxons – will be moved In World.

When she arrives at the office, eight of the ten are plugged into their PADs, arranged two or three to a bench. They're all wearing VR masks and making slow tickling motions with their fingers.

"Hello everyone," she says, not expecting an answer, and not getting one.

She takes a seat at her own workstation, fiddles with the elasti-cated band of the headset. She's just about to dive in when Henry appears in the doorway to the "break out" room. Henry's hair is platinum blond today, and under the halogen bulbs of the lab she looks positively angelic. In the breast pocket of her tweed jacket are half a dozen vape pens that each blow a different coloured cloud. Alice hasn't yet made up her mind whether she thinks this is fun and eccentric or attention-seeking and pretentious.

"How was it?" she says. There's just a hint of New York left in her accent.

"How was what?"

"Last night?"

Alice has a cold flush, and then realises Henry's not talking about *that*; no one can possibly know about *that*.

"What happened last night?" More adjustment of the headband.

"Didn't you have a date?"

She slumps with relief.

"That was Friday."

"Right. And?"

"Bad egg."

"Ah, shucks."

Alice nods. "He kept it pretty well hidden until the main course. Then he told me that if women hated the patriarchy so much they should stop using men's inventions."

"That's a good point."

29

"He thought there might be a way to identify feminists In World and cut off their electricity supply."

"I see."

"Then he told me that he still respected me for my role, and that 'women's work' was unnecessarily disparaged because he'd once tried kneading bread and found it genuinely tiring."

There was a time when both of them would have howled with laughter at this. These days, Alice's interactions with Meninists and Masculists and all the rest of them are so frequent and so moronic that they inspire a kind of mental fatigue, which perhaps, she wonders, has been the Meninists' strategy all along – to silence their opponents through sheer boredom.

Henry still has some of the old fire in her, but then Henry has it so much worse.

"Well," says Henry, "onwards and upwards."

"I don't feel like that's my precise trajectory, but yes, I suppose so. Doesn't matter. I have Bertha to keep me company for now."

"Good old Bertha. Now there's a real woman!"

"I'm going to miss her when she's gone. Maybe I'll print a copy of her and hang her in my bedroom."

"Nice conversation starter, when you finally bring a date home."

Bertha has been dead for the best part of two thousand years and is missing her head, hands and one of her feet. Since last week Alice has been examining and logging the remaining two-hundred-ish bones of Bertha's skeleton, before they are uploaded permanently to Alpha and the real things are sent on their final journey to the Stockholm facility. During this time, Alice has had the strangest sensation that she's gotten to know Bertha better than anyone she has ever met. "Loves the bones of her," as her grandmother might have said. On more than one occasion she's been found in the basement late at night, VR headset on, talking animatedly to the woman's remains.

Alice secures the screen to her face, has a brief and unwelcome flashback to her In World activities the previous night. No, that was someone else, she thinks.

She's met by the soothing whiteness of the BIA Hub. She adjusts her focus. The rest of the department are all there, hard at work on their projects. This includes Henry, who is staring catatonically at her feet while the "real" Henry is on her lunch break a few feet away from Alice's chair. Normally this shouldn't happen, but Henry's lazy and has a tendency to just take off her headset rather than exit the Hub properly. The space itself looks the same as the basement would look if someone cleaned it, filled it with expensive equipment, and suffused it with divine light.

Bertha is spread out in pieces on Alice's In World workstation. Alice selects the vertebrae one by one, inspecting and annotating as she goes. Wear and tear around the discs from repeated hard physical labour. More than bread-kneading, that's for sure. Signs of malnutrition, a hairline fracture, early onset osteoporosis. When she reaches vertebra C4 she finds a great, clumsy notch in the bone from a blade that could and should have been sharper. Bertha was decapitated none too cleanly, it seems.

"Hum," she says.

"What?"

Henry rests a hand on her shoulder; the weirdness of this, when Alice can see a whole other Henry at a different workstation (still gazing at her shoelaces). Alice takes off the visor. It takes a moment for her dizziness to subside.

"Did we ever find the other bits of Bertha?"

"Are they in the inventory?"

"No."

"Then I guess not."

"Don't you think that's odd?"

"Not necessarily. They're probably miles away, wherever Bertha fell. It's the heads that were taken as trophies."

"And hands as well?"

"Not so much hands, no."

Alice hums.

"Where did we find her?" she asks.

"We didn't find her. EIA found her, way back. Somewhere in Kent, I think. She's been in storage since before I got here."

"But nothing else was found at the site?"

"Search me. All the info should be in there." Henry points to the headset. "What's wrong?"

"Just seems strange. The missing bits. And if it was some kind of ritual execution, wouldn't there be others nearby? It's not the sort of thing you do as a one-off."

"Maybe there were others. I don't know. Have a look."

Alice goes back In World and nudges the icon for the site report. It spills its contents into her field of vision: inventory, satellite imaging, magnetometer results. She pores over it in silence. It has the usual fuzziness of late-twentieth-century photography, but there's no mistaking what's in front of her. A barrow of some kind, the burial chambers arranged in a circular, almost hexagonal formation. The complex extends off the edge of the image, truly vast. And yet it seems Bertha was the only thing that was recovered from the site, along with a few of her bracelets.

"Well?"

Henry has started vaping again. The air smells of cinnamon and damp towels.

"I don't believe this."

"Alice, I *can't see what you see.*"

"They didn't find anything apart from Bertha."

"How extensive was the dig?"

"There wasn't any dig. Just after they found her the site was bought up by a private company." She scrolls a little further through the document. "Someone called 'Nature's Bounty'."

"Ha."

"But this is ridiculous. I've never seen a burial site like this. It could be the biggest in the country. Someone needs to organise a dig."

"You know HBO won't go for that."

"But *look* at it."

"Who owns the site now?"

"Hold on."

Alice hasn't felt this excited by her work in years. It feels like one or both of the hotdogs she had for lunch might come back up. She exits the BIA hub, opens the Alpha Maps application and enters the location of the site: High Weald, SE90 9HW. She finds herself suspended like a drone over a real-time rendering of the barrow in its current state. The burial chambers have been replaced with the clean lines of a modern building, its grounds so green and well-manicured they look fake.

A promotional video expands to fill her entire field of vision. A ukulele starts playing, accompanied by some whistled melody. An enormous, forgettable face appears and smiles with its mouth but not its eyes. The letters "NUTRISTART" emerge from its lips. The letters are followed by a tick, and the tail of the tick is animated so it turns into two sprouting leaves. Then the leaves turn into two more cartoon faces, which also smile and wink. The whole thing seems very contrived.

"Welcome to NSA!" says the first, larger face, in a voice that doesn't belong to it. "You've just found the safest educational facility in the south of England!"

13.55

TOM ROSEN has his face pressed against the staffroom window. He's almost kissing it. He can taste a slight saltiness in the condensation.

"So when are they going to finish the wall?"

"It's a bit more than a wall," says Mr Barren of the Marketing (Academic) Department, without looking up from the PAD in his lap. He is swishing nonchalantly across the screen with one finger and digging chunks of a gluten-free NutriStart Goodness Bar out of his gums with the other.

"Well, it's not anything at the moment, is it," says Miss Potter, and Tom laughs, even though it's not actually very funny, nor is it meant to be, but Tom is hopelessly in love with the soon-to-be-happily-married Miss Potter and suspects he will be until the day he's put in the earth.

"They haven't done anything for weeks," he says. "I don't think I've ever seen any of those excavators move."

The window squeaks as he wipes it again. The sky and the fields are drained of all colour, like they've been washed too many times, with the exception of a bright orange line on the horizon where the construction site has been cordoned off. "Wonder what's happening."

Tom returns to the seat next to Miss Potter, even though it's further away than the obviously free one next to Mr Barren.

"I still think they're drilling for shale gas," says Miss Potter. "It's all a ruse. Then BP buy the site from NutriStart, Gravesy gets a couple of million kickback, and he can finally buy himself that flat on the King's Road."

"Or a flight back to Easter Island."

"That's all construction equipment out there, there's nothing to suggest anyone's drilling for anything," says Mr Barren with his usual talent for shooting a joke dead between the eyes before it's had a chance to draw breath. "And I actually think that the Academy is possibly more profitable than gas or oil in the very-long-term." He throws the last piece of his Goodness Bar into his mouth and licks all of his fingers and hums. Darren Barren thinks of his gluten intolerance as a sort of evolutionary advantage, and his general air of superiority seems to stem entirely from this one aspect of his diet.

Tom hates Darren Barren almost as much as he loves Miss Potter, more so since English and Media were part-merged with Marketing (Academic), and they were forced to share classes in copywriting and content management. On top of that, he's now taken to sitting in the exact spot where Tom and his lady love come to talk during Recreational Periods.

"If it is just a fence, I'm not sure that justifies, like, a 15% hike in fees." He says this directly to Miss Potter, his shoulder turned ostentatiously to Mr Barren, who doesn't see because he's still hunched over his device.

"Well, it's not just a fence, is it," Mr Barren says. "It's a TASCO system."

"Like the ones they have in China."

"You mean the USA."

"I thought they were Chinese?"

"They *make* them in China."

Tom is momentarily annoyed with Miss Potter for validating

Darren Barren's role in the conversation, and angles his back to be even more obstructive.

"They use them for gated communities," says Mr Barren, finally looking up at them. "It'll monitor everyone coming in and out and be able to track them once they're on school grounds. It's linked to the new CCTV and security hardware, so if there's an intruder he can be isolated automatically with DNATT and face recognition. It's a pretty impressive piece of kit."

"Or she," says Miss Potter.

"What?"

"The intruder."

"The fence itself is electrified, bomb-proof, everything-proof," Mr Barren continues. "The only way anyone'll be able to damage the school is if they organise some sort of airstrike, and I don't think masculists are quite that well-resourced." He does a short, snorting laugh and something flies out of his nose.

Miss Potter looks like she's about to say something else when the Deputy Headmaster comes scuttling into the common room, and she immediately gets up to leave. Darren Barren returns to his PAD with renewed concentration. Only Tom, almost horizontal in the reclinable easy-chair with a half-finished mug of incredibly sweet coffee, looks completely without purpose or motivation, which is bad news in the company of the DHM.

Even though it's called a Recreational Period, the "recreation" part doesn't apply to the teachers and it has long been a mystery as to why the common room should be so lavishly furnished with reclining leather chairs and espresso machines and 8K HDTVs when it is an unspoken rule that no teacher should ever spend any time in there.

"Mr Rosen?"

"Ah, Mr Tooley," he says, struggling to get upright, and watching

Miss Potter's thighs disappear around the corner. "There was something I wanted to talk to you about." There isn't, but Tom knows this is a good way to wrong-foot any member of SMT who has a bone to pick.

"Likewise. Shall we chat in my office?" says Mr Tooley, peering upwards.

When Tom is standing, the Deputy Headmaster's eyes are about on a level with his navel. He is an indisputably tiny man and has a high-pitched cartoon-tiny-man's voice to match. He is also the most feared presence in the school, even more so than the Headmaster, who is unsettling, but in a brooding, faceless way. Whilst the Head is a mythical figure his Deputy is a very real entity, who not only sees all, but makes sure he is *seen* to be seeing all. The disparity in stature between the HM and the DHM has led to the widely accepted theory among the students that they have some sort of symbiotic relationship, that one was created from the other through perverse medical science or perhaps voodoo ritual. Some say that they've seen Mr Tooley actually emerge from inside the Headmaster like a larva.

The staff common room is on the tip of one of the NSA's six galactic arms, which seems to have been a conscious architectural decision to dissuade people from going there. The walk back to the Deputy Head's office is a long one. Mr Tooley's short legs have to move incredibly quickly to maintain even a moderate pace, and his shoes squeak every time he puts a foot down, something that he seems painfully self-conscious about. Mr Rosen, on the other hand, is a long, loping animal, and has to force himself to take uncomfortably small steps so as not to overtake the Deputy Head and appear in any way insubordinate.

The fact that Mr Tooley used the word "chat" suggests that their impending conversation is going to be anything but that.

When they reach the cluster of SMT offices – Headmaster, Deputy

Headmaster, Head of Pastoral, Director of Studies, Director of Teaching and Learning, Head of Aspiration, Head of Marketing (Synoptic) and Brand Liaison Officer – Mr Rosen waits like a chastised boy while the Deputy Head fiddles with his security card. There is a rattle of suitcase wheels. Gerald Liu, class 7B, appears from around the corner and trundles down the corridor to his next lesson. He grins as he passes them.

"Hullo Gerald," says Mr Rosen.

"Mr Rosen," says Gerald Liu, without stopping. "You are very handsome!"

Then he's gone, marching onwards with his luggage to some unknown destination. Tom watches him all the way to the end of the corridor. He is fairly sure that Gerald Liu has been following him in between lessons for the last few weeks.

Mr Tooley is waiting now.

"After you, sir," he says deferentially, and waits for Tom to cross the threshold first.

The Deputy Head's office is vast. A massive peninsular of desk projects from one corner into the centre of the room, L-shaped, with an array of six PADs erected on special stands across its surface. The back wall is almost all window, or rather two-way mirror like the rest of the school's exterior, hence the blueish, sooty light. The other three walls are all adorned with digital picture frames playing slideshows from the NSA prospectus, mostly impossibly happy faces of boys and girls answering questions, performing experiments, formatting data, playing sports, eating their nutritious NutriStart breakfast/lunch, clutching their VAC exam results, shaking the hands of important CEOs, etc., all except one, which seems to be broken and alternates between the text ERROR: NO INPUT DETECTED and a picture of a bear catching a salmon.

In front of the continental desk are three spongy-looking armchairs, a token gesture towards hospitality. Tom knows that in fact they are very uncomfortable, and in the past their bright blue upholstery has left him with a rash on his forearms.

The office is notable for its complete absence of any kind of smell.

"Please, sit down," says Mr Tooley.

Mr Rosen rolls down his sleeves to avoid a repeat of the skin-irritation business and takes an armchair. It is deeper than it looks, bucket-like, which again makes him feel more like one of the students than one of the teachers, enclosed on all sides by an adult chair that is much too big for him. Mr Tooley, on the other hand, goes behind his desk to his executive swivel chair, which makes sophisticated pneumatic noises and launches the sitter several feet into the air, so he is less sitting than roosting. For the first time he is able to look down upon Mr Rosen.

"How's everything going?" he asks without blinking. Perhaps Tooley thinks that this small talk helps put people at ease, but it just makes Tom think of a shark circling something that's bleeding.

"Not too bad. An eventful Period Six, but I think we achieved what we needed to."

The Deputy Head frowns a theatrical frown. "Oh. So you were teaching Period Six?"

"Yes, as far as I remember. Ha ha."

"Right. Well that was what I wanted to talk to you about. Because I think..." He begins to tap on one of the upright PADs in front of him. Still circling, scent of fresh blood in his nostrils. "Yes, there's no entry on the MNet for that lesson."

Tom knows that cannot be true. He entered his lesson report and logged the incident with Carla as soon as he'd received the reminder from the system. The reminder itself was serious enough, and would remain on his record until the end of the year. Not submitting lesson feedback *at all* was unforgivable.

"I definitely entered the report. Definitely. It was a little late, because I was dealing with Carla Le Maitre—"

"There's no entry, I'm afraid." He swivels the PAD around and reveals an empty white box on the MNet interface, in the column headed "Rosen, T O".

"Well, I don't know how that's happened. System didn't save it properly or something." He is aware of how much this sounds like one of his students' excuses.

"The system does what we tell it to do though, doesn't it? What *you* tell it to do."

Mr Rosen shrugs. "Have you spoken to ICT Support?"

"I haven't, and I don't think I will, since they're busy with the new security system integration." He pauses. "Besides, I don't think this is necessarily a technical problem."

But Tom *definitely* submitted it. Without a doubt. He felt compelled to, after the involvement of the Headmaster and Carla's strange departure from the school.

"This isn't my fault, though." A solitary bead of sweat rolls coldly out of his right armpit.

"This isn't the first time you've been a little remiss with your reporting, is it?"

"But I'm *telling you*—"

"It's *so* important, Mr Rosen, that we keep totally on top of our data. If we can't record and track our progress, what chance do we have of professional development? What chance do the students have?"

Tom's heart is beating with such intensity it is obstructing his windpipe. He doesn't say anything because he can't. Mr Tooley takes this as capitulation.

"And I have to say, I find it odd that, while you don't have time to be a reflective practitioner, you do have time to sit and drink coffee during Recreational Periods."

"I'd only been there about five minutes."

The Deputy Head has already rotated on his pedestal, though, and is typing something onto the second PAD. Rosen sits in silence and watches the slow fade of the bear and the salmon on the screen to his right.

"I'm putting a note on your profile, Mr Rosen. It will be public. NSA is going to be putting you on probation for the remainder of this academic year."

"What?"

"Only for the remainder of the year."

"Public?"

"We'd also like you to attend an online training course to ensure you're totally clear on the NutriStart Brand Values."

"But, look, I'm not making excuses, I didn't forget to enter the report!"

"At the end of the Summer Term we'll reassess and consider returning you to your regular contract."

The desk is too big for Tom to jump over and throttle the man on the other side, another deliberate decision in the room's design. Both armpits are now soaked.

"Is there any way I can contest this? Formally?"

Mr Tooley makes a big display of hitting the "enter" key with some finality. "I'm afraid the changes have already been made. You're welcome to voice any concerns in your end of year review."

"Right."

The Deputy Head gives him a smile. "Is that all clear? I hope you understand why decisions like this have to be made."

41

"Very clear."

"Thank you, Mr Rosen. If you could give your formal feedback on this meeting by the end of play today, that would be hugely appreciated."

Mr Rosen nods, and levers himself out of the bucket chair. Mr Tooley is already hard at work by the time he has reached the door and has swiped his access card to escape.

Outside in the corridor, the students have returned from their recreation and are making their way to be registered, their chatter just white noise.

He did enter his report. He said everything. About the lesson, about Carla, about the Headmaster. He was so frightened by the reminder that he submitted it twice by accident and double-checked it after he'd eaten his lunch.

The only other conclusion, which Tom settles upon while staring out of the corridor window into the NSA's organic garden, is sabotage. Someone must've gone in and deleted the report. Someone who didn't want the events reported. Someone above Mr Tooley.

14.08

MISS POTTER settles herself into the chair at the front of the room and takes the 8B register, marking them present or absent on her PAD. Behind them, the grim shroud of sky has been split open, and sunlight pours in through T4's windows. For a moment the room is warm and molten, and then just as quickly the sun is concealed again, as though by an eclipse, and everything reclaims its cold, hard edges.

Peepsy shivers. Something isn't right. His thoughts turn to the items in his locker.

"Alex Pepys."

"Yes, miss?"

"Are you here, Alex Pepys?"

"Yes, miss. Sorry, miss."

"You look flushed, Alex. Everything alright?"

"He's thinking about Miss Munday again."

"That's enough, Amir," says Miss Potter, loud enough to quell the tittering of most of the class.

Peepsy grins to let everyone know he's taken the joke, slumps a little more in his chair and boosts his giant blond quiff with both hands. Josh is making a big show of ignoring him, leaning forward over his desk to talk to Shauna McFeat, stretching himself so much he's practically horizontal to the floor and pawing at the back of her uniform.

When the bell sounds – everyone calls it a "bell", but it's more of a siren, and still makes Peepsy think there's a fire after every single lesson – the rattle and shuffle and hoisting of rucksacks drowns out Miss Potter's best wishes, and Josh shoots for the door without a word. Peepsy follows him to the lockers, where he is bundling up his trainers and jogging bottoms for the last two periods of the day.

"Josh. Hey, Josh."

The other boy has almost climbed inside his locker by now in his efforts to ignore him.

"Josh, you want to see it?" He looks left and right conspiratorially. Most of the class have now trailed away to PE. Three Year 13 girls float spectrally past their backs.

Josh finally withdraws his head from his open locker, and his face is pink and a little damp.

"No!"

"Why not?"

"Because it's weird!"

"That's why you should have a look."

"You shouldn't've done it. I told you to leave it." He clangs the door shut, PE kit under one arm.

"It doesn't matter. Munday didn't even care I was late. And the cameras didn't see me, that was the whole point of the route."

"I'm not talking about Miss Munday, I'm talking about what's, like, *morally* right. It's a *person,* Peepsy. Bits of a person. What are you even going to do with it?"

Peepsy shrugs. "I don't know. Just keep it."

"You should take it back. After school. Or first thing tomorrow."

"No!"

"Your brain's all wrong, Pepys."

"Your mum's all wrong."

Josh huffs in a way that sounds exactly like one of the teachers. "I'll see you in the gym." He half-walks, half-runs to the end of the corridor. They're on the third floor of the NSA main building, and Peepsy can hear the boy's steps echoing right to the bottom of the stairwell.

Then the "T" rooms are silent, apart from a very distant echo of classes on the other floors waiting to begin. For some reason the sound makes Peepsy feel homesick. He's alone again, and also in danger of being late for a second time. But he can't resist another look. He's thought of nothing else since the end of second RP.

He passes his security card over the reader on the locker door, which is made of the same indestructible purple material as the tops of the NSA desks, and the lock *bloops.* There is a cold, damp tomb smell from inside.

The skull is half-illuminated on a shelf at the back, resting on its two severed hands. Peepsy's put a red NutriStart baseball cap on it, peak askew, originally to try and conceal it. It wasn't big enough for that, but he left it on because he thought it looked pretty great. The skull's cavities are still packed with the mud of the construction site, but there are two pupil-like holes in the eye-sockets from where he's put his fingers, giving the skull's face a cartoonish, slightly drunken look.

He hefts the skull with one hand and sets about cleaning it, enjoying the coldness and hardness of its ridges and recesses. He digs the earth out of its nose and the back of its eyes like he's finishing off a hard-boiled egg, picks the worst of the grit out of its teeth. Then he takes off the cap and gives the dome a bit of a polish with his already filthy PE singlet. On its forehead, there's one perfectly circular bit of dirt that won't budge. When he pokes it with his little finger he finds it's a hole that goes right through the bone, into the empty chamber where the brain used to be.

Peepsy knows at least a dozen pupils in the school who have been trepanned, all older than him, though. His eldest sister had it done, too, but he doesn't think about that. It came back into fashion a few years back, and parents were quick to pick up on the fact that it coincided with the introduction of the new VAC exams. For a time, it was a real badge of honour to have that patch below the hairline where the drill had gone through. Sportswear companies did their own lines of luridly coloured Trepan Bands to be worn around the head, like a sweatband but with a little nubbin that slotted into the aperture in the bone, but the school said these contravened uniform regulations and promptly had them outlawed. Originally, it was claimed that the procedure solved everything from anxiety to ADHD to low processing speeds, but it quickly became a symbol of idiosyncrasy and counter-culturalism, until everyone was having it done and, like all fads, it was destroyed by its own popularity.

So. The skull belongs to someone who's died either very recently, or a very long time ago.

"Shouldn't you be somewhere, Alex?"

Peepsy slams the door shut just as Miss Potter is leaving T4. He thinks her angle of sight is oblique enough that she can't see the contents of his locker, but that doesn't stop a flush exploding across his face.

"PE kit, miss. I'm just. This is my PE kit," he says, sounding like there's a golf ball lodged somewhere in his throat.

"Are you sure you're alright? You look feverish."

"Fine, miss. Just tired."

"Aren't we all!"

"I'll take something for it when I get home."

"Jolly good. If it gets really bad I have some ProSustain." She takes a pink blister pack from her pocket. "As long as you log it with the nurses."

Peepsy nods. "Yes, miss."

"Come on, you're late. Nearly second bell."

"Yes, miss."

He rolls his trainers in his dirty T-shirt and loads them into his bag with his PAD, and begins the long trek to the gymnasium, the smell of wet bone still tickling his nostrils.

14.20

TOM ROSEN has a single "free" period before his last lesson of the day, fifty minutes in which to dig up as much information as he can on the mystery of his missing report. He should be using the time to prepare for class, to submit his Proposed Learning Objectives for approval, and to write up his feedback on the meeting with Tooley, but he's feeling petulant and self-righteous and wants to indulge that.

The ICT Department have their own little ecosystem in a square, glassy turret that projects out of the top of one of the NSA building's six corners. In seven years of teaching, Tom has only visited them once before, and was roundly ridiculed for hiking up four flights of stairs for a problem that he could have solved by just running the most basic in-built PAD diagnostic software. All computer and network malfunctions are now rectified remotely before anyone even realises anything is wrong, so most staff can go their whole career without ever talking to a member of The Guild.

Tom feels strangely nervous when he arrives at the ICT reception desk. It's as though he's approaching an oracle, some higher power, for guidance. The glass tower itself has two floors, which give a panoramic view of the whole school and its grounds, fitting for the NSA's overlords.

"Welcome traveller," says a girl from behind a monitor. She's wearing a leotard covered in diamonds of neon-coloured material, topped with spiked shoulder pads. She is also wearing a horned helmet. A staff with a pink crystal ball on one end leans in a corner of the lobby with the umbrellas. "Do you seek an audience with The Guild?"

"Hello. Hi. Yes. I've got a bit of a problem with my reporting system. Something's been deleted, I want to recover it."

"To call back what is lost. Isn't that something we all seek?"

"I'm in a bit of a rush, actually, and I've got to teach Final Period, so if you could just see if anyone's free."

She blinks at him. Her contact lenses are blood-red.

"Please?"

He smiles but she's already registered his annoyance.

"What's your staff number?" she says after a moment, the performance completely gone from her voice.

"54382A."

"Hold on a moment. You can sit down."

There's a light, very rapid thudding as she types something on the touchscreen. Tom takes a seat on the corner sofa. The horns on the receptionist's helmet wobble a little as she scans the monitor in front of her.

The ICT team began referring to themselves as The Guild a few years after Tom joined the school, because of a game they all played within Alpha called *Mage Wars*. The costumes followed soon after. Made-up, slightly Celtic-sounding names, too, which they demanded to have added to their lanyards. No one batted an eyelid. Everyone knew by that point that the tech staff were the real masters of the school, and that by upsetting them you were inviting them to make your life pure hell. The Guild's way of life became sacrosanct, and as a result almost all conversations with the ICT staff now have to be conducted in the affected, faux-medieval register that underpins most of the games they play.

Tom doesn't understand any of it. He is one of about five people in the developed world who doesn't have a profile on Alpha Omega, and one of a few hundred who hasn't played *Mage Wars*. Steers well clear, somehow. It's all very tinfoil hat, but he feels like he's committed to that aspect of his personality, now. In fact, the tinfoil hat and his personality may be one and the same thing.

"All the Network Managers are busy, but you can talk to one of the DAs," says the receptionist at last.

"DAs?"

"Database Architects. They'll have a backup of any reports you've submitted."

"Great. That's great. That's wonderful. Fantastic." He involuntarily makes two thumbs-up, and then hides his hands in his pockets. If he can get a copy of the backup to show the Deputy Head, he'll be off the hook. And Mr Tooley would very much be on the hook, for poor personnel management. The phrase "institutionalised mistrust" loads itself into his brain for deployment later, and he smiles to himself.

The receptionist gets up, grasps her magical staff from the corner, and leads him through the double doors and up to the next floor.

Through a glass door to the right, two men and a woman are sat in a long, trapezoidal space that looks like the bridge of a ship. There isn't an inch of wall that isn't covered with a screen of some kind, and the blue strip lighting along the skirting and the ceiling reminds Tom of a karaoke bar he went to once. The air-conditioning is cryogenic and is recycling fine particles of flavoured dust from the Database Architects' tortilla chips.

One of the men is also in costume. His torso is bare except for two ammunition belts slung over his shoulders, and he's wearing military-style camouflaged trousers with what Tom hopes is a replica pistol strapped to each thigh. He's also got a VR headset on, and his gloved and wired hands are groping blindly but also purposefully in front of him. Tom finds it unsettling that he has absolutely no idea what the man is actually immersed in.

The other two, the man and the woman, are just dressed in jeans and T-shirt, and are both examining some sort of 3D data-modelling screen that looks like an artist's impression of the galaxy. It's as big as the wall of Tom's classroom. The man spins in his chair. His T-shirt says, white on black: *Do I LOOK like a people person?* and has a picture of a zombified stick-man staring at an old-fashioned computer screen.

"Greetings," he says, inclining his head. "And how—"

"Hi, listen," says Tom, quickly enough to stop the DA launching into his archaic spiel. "I entered a lesson report on the MNet earlier, in Period Six, and now it's gone. It's just disappeared."

"Just disappeared?" The DA arches an eyebrow theatrically, and Tom can sense a silent, telepathic snigger being passed around between the three technicians and the receptionist, who has apparently stayed behind just to watch the show.

"Yes. I entered it. I saved it."

"The MNet autosaves anyway."

"Okay. Well. It *was saved*, and I checked it at lunch break, but as of about twenty minutes ago it wasn't there."

"Data doesn't just disappear."

"Well, this did."

"Are you sure you entered it into the correct field?"

"*Yes*, totally sure."

"Intriguing."

"Yes, intriguing, and actually quite serious, because SMT have now put me on probation for data mismanagement. Can you please just check for me? See if there's a backup?"

Tom notices that the other DA is somehow training one eye on her monitor and the other eye on him at the same time. Their stubbornness is starting to give him a headache, compounded by the arctic temperatures and the throb of the artificial lighting.

The technician in the cynical T-shirt puffs himself up as though he's trying to contain the world's most voluminous sigh, and spins in his chair to a smaller, subsidiary monitor that's next to the one showing the 3D modelling.

"Local or corporate?" he says over his shoulder.

"Sorry?"

"Which network did you submit it to? Local or corporate?"

"The MNet. The school MNet."

"Yes, but which *one*?" He obliterates a tortilla chip in one bite.

"Um. Whichever one is loaded onto my PAD."

The DA finally releases a sigh, and, as expected, it's gale-force.

"What colour is the icon in the middle of your desktop? Blue or purple?"

"Blue."

"Right, so you've only got local access. Staff number?"

"54382A."

Tom watches him typing and swiping through various login screens, each getting less and less familiar until he knows that he is well and truly through the looking-glass, seeing pages of code that require a mind-bogglingly high security clearance to access. It's like he's being given a glimpse of the very fabric of the universe. This perhaps explains the ecstatic, otherworldly smile that's fixed on the face of the technician wearing the VR headset.

"And what was the report you submitted?" asks the DA.

"It was a self-assessment report, for Period Six."

"And you saved it in Period Seven."

"That's right."

Tom decides he'll keep a lid on his sabotage suspicions for the time being, even though the tinfoil hat fits a conspiracy theorist rather snugly. With any luck, there'll be a backup that he can restore, Tooley will get a slap on his child-sized wrist, and he won't even need to think about why or how it happened in the first place.

The DA finally turns back to him. "Nothing there."

"I know there's nothing there, that's my point."

"I know that's your point; *my* point is that there is *nothing* there. There's nothing in the activity log. No one's been in or out of that data-field. Ever."

There is a fleeting moment when Tom perceives what it might be like to be mad. For the world inside his brain to bear no resemblance to the world outside it. His headache is much worse now.

"But I did. I'm sure. I put it in there. I checked. I'm not completely delusional."

"Can't argue with the network, sorry," shrugs the DA with satisfaction.

"Could someone have gone in and deleted it?"

"Like I said, there's been no activity in that field."

"But couldn't someone have deleted the activity log itself, or something?"

Off to one side the woman laughs, and it's the strangest laugh Tom's ever heard, a high-pitched *twang* that sounds like a sound effect from a cartoon.

"Even we can't do that," says the DA, also smirking.

"What about the Headmaster?"

The room falls silent. Even the man in the ammo belts and the headset seems to have stopped what he's doing. The DA slowly shakes his head.

"The Head has basically the same network privileges as you. All staff have the same access. Broadly speaking."

Tom gets the urge to stuff all of the technicians' remaining tortilla chips into his mouth, as though it will somehow ground him in reality.

"This just doesn't make any sense."

"You guys do a lot of reporting, right?" The DA leans forward, putting his hands on his thighs. "You might just be thinking of a different report. I can see how they might all just blur into one."

The front third of Tom's head now feels frozen from the air-conditioning. His thoughts are thick like milkshake.

"Can you check one more thing?"

The DA looks at him and doesn't blink.

"I edited the medical log for one of the kids, at the same time. As a follow-up to the report. Can you see if that's there at least?"

"You can check that on your PAD."

"Yes, but, we're here now, so you may as well – in case there's a problem with that, too."

"You know the new security system is coming online this week, don't you? You realise how much work we've got to do?"

"Please. Then I'll leave you all alone."

"What's the name?"

"Her name. Le Maitre-Bridge, Carla."

The woman has by now spun all the way around in her chair and is just scrutinising Tom like he's a laboratory specimen. He tries to ignore her and watches the DA typing in various permutations of Carla's first and second name, which is obviously causing problems with its strange articles and hyphenations.

"Nope," says the DA.

"What do you mean?"

"Not there."

"What, the medical file?"

"No, the kid. She doesn't exist."

14.50

SHE KNOWS she's imagining it, but Stephanie Bäcker thinks she can hear a vibration coming from the cupboard under the stairs. Three times now, since Gabriel left, she's got up and opened the door and run her fingers over the edges of the box to check that it's still there. When she's standing in front of it, it doesn't make any noise at all.

The doorbell rings. She closes the cupboard, goes to the front door, and lets Mr Carnoso into their home. His aftershave is so strong she has to turn away, as though from a blaze. She can still feel it at her back when she leads him to the kitchen.

"Let's get this show on the road!" says Mr Carnoso, and she can hear him rubbing his moist hands together.

"I'd like to discuss the finer details before we go through with it, please."

"Do I smell coffee?"

"I know it makes financial sense, but there are a few ins and outs I need to be clearer on."

"That's real espresso, isn't it?"

"And I keep thinking of Gabriel."

She can hear him clattering around the cupboards, gathering mugs and spoons, scraping chairs over the tiles. He burns himself on the coffee machine's steam wands, screams, tries to turn it into a laugh. There's another gust of aftershave as he sits heavily beside her. She waits for him to present her with her coffee, but it seems he's only made one for himself.

"Gabriel will understand," says Mr Carnoso.

"But you know what he's like."

"You're doing the right thing," says Mr Carnoso. "You have to pay his fees one way or another. He'd be even more upset if he couldn't go to school and see his friends. Right?"

"If he had his way he'd stay in his room and never go to school again."

Mr Carnoso laughs. "These lads!"

"And soon he won't even have his room anymore."

54

Poor old Gabe. She pictures him at his interview, mumbling his way through the questions in his too-small suit. Not a shred of self-esteem. She remembers him on the doorstep. She could smell his body odour through his jacket. She pitied him, pitied herself. Love and shame commingled so intensely as to be indistinguishable.

Perhaps things would have turned out differently if Gabe's father had stayed around, but it's been four years since he walked out of their house, took the Prius and left for the USA to marry a woman – a girl – he'd never even met. He left a message for Gabriel In World, and Gabriel was forced to relay it verbally to his mother.

The girl in question was "Cosmic Whisperer", an ASMR artist who uploaded recordings of herself muttering everything from product reviews to positive spiritual affirmations to tax legislation in her uniquely hypnotic voice. In World, she offered softly spoken eye tests, haircuts and medical exams. Sometimes, for the real connoisseurs, she would just eat a yoghurt or a banana next to the microphone. The whole point of this was supposedly to help people relax, but there was an inevitable fetishy aspect to it, and one that got Gabe's father hooked.

Stephanie had been one of Cosmic Whisperer's most avid subscribers and nudged her husband in her direction when he was suffering from a particularly bad bout of insomnia. The girl whispered directly into his brain every night for a year, so it shouldn't have come as a surprise when he developed an obsession. He was incapable of meeting any kind of challenge or misfortune without Cosmic Whisperer to calm his nerves. He began to contact her directly to request specific scenarios. After she finally agreed to one of his suggestions – he was a deep-sea diver, she a technician readying him for his mission – he decided that he would fly across the Atlantic to declare his love for her. The next morning the Prius was gone, and there was a new message blinking in Gabriel's In World Hub.

She's heard nothing from him since. She's also received nothing in the way of child support payments. Hence her current predicament.

Mr Carnoso leans over and puts a hand on hers. It's cold and sticky like a salamander's toes.

"Shall we get down to brass tacks?" he says.

Stephanie nods. She asks her PAD to begin recording their conversation.

"You'd get the lease on Gabriel's room and the upstairs bathroom," she says.

"That's right."

"And you'd live in it? Or sublet?"

"Sublet, of course. You know Gabriel's room and mine share a party wall?"

"Yes."

"I may knock that through. Let some light in."

She winces. "Okay."

"You were saying something about the garden, too?"

He knows very well what she said about the garden.

"You can have the garden," she says.

"Jolly good."

Stephanie turns in his direction. She can hear the skin stretching around the edge of his mouth, and could swear he's pulling faces at her.

"How much does that make me?" she asks.

"I'm still getting it verified by Care, but they suggested one hundred and fifty thousand."

"That's a lot."

"It's a nice house. That's why I want to get my grubby hands on it! Ha ha!"

Her PAD makes a noise from the kitchen worktop, and she springs up to get it before Mr Carnoso can, because in the past he's taken it upon himself to be helpful and read all of her messages aloud. She finds it and gropes for her headphones, which are in a tangled heap somewhere around the espresso machine.

"Goodness!" says Mr Carnoso. "How old are those? They've still got wires!"

"Excuse me," she says, "it might be Gabriel." She puts the foam rings to her ears and plays the message. It's from the Technical Academy. Her insides settle like sand.

"Good news?" asks Mr Carnoso, and she knows he's grinning again.

15.00

THE PARTY has a near infinite number of rooms and themes, but the lobby looks like the good old pornos of yesteryear – a kind of sterilely opulent LA mansion, all white marble floors, crystal chandeliers and wildly phallic chrome ornaments. Through the enormous French windows Gabriel can see a tropical grotto and peacocks on the lawn; beyond that, a turquoise sea, and the white wedge of his yacht.

He's tracked down the same girl he always goes with, someone who just calls herself "Clodia". She's probably twenty years older than him, but that doesn't matter because today Gabriel is Peter Van Den Hoonaard, a fifty-five-year-old insurance broker from Amsterdam who needs to look more closely at his Alpha profile's security settings.

"Hey Peter," says Clodia, running a finger up the zip of her body-suit. What is she meant to be, exactly? A rally driver? An astronaut? Whatever it is, the outfit has Gabriel practically frothing with lust.

"Hi," says Gabriel, trying to make his voice sound lower than it is.

"Wanna see something neat?" says Clodia.

"Sure I do," says Gabriel, because it seems the sort of thing Peter Van Den Hoonaard would say.

The lobby is crowded now, full of lost-looking women in various states of undress. One of them is currently trying to circumnavigate Clodia's avatar, and it looks like the two are trying to headbutt each other. The other girl, hyperreal in stockings and suspenders and nothing else, sporadically flies ten feet in the air as her AI tries to deal with the obstacle that's been placed in her path. Meanwhile, Clodia is sort of vibrating backwards and forwards, and every time she moves closer to Gabriel it triggers her welcome message.

"Hey Peter... Hey Peter... Hey Peter..."

Gabriel's getting flushed and angry as his fantasy is shattered over and over again. When he tries to step in, the girl in the stockings goes completely haywire and starts whizzing from one side of the room to the other at outrageous speeds, before eventually returning to her default position over by the fireplace and the polar bear rug and starting her whole casual, predetermined stroll around the mansion all over again.

Gabriel breathes deeply and takes a swig from his Coke, a very odd sensation since the bottle itself doesn't appear In World. The bubbles are painful on the roof of his mouth. He finally accepts Clodia's invitation and follows her to one of The Party's bedrooms, whose baroque double doors open onto blackness, which in turn becomes the scenario-select screen.

Whilst the avatars in the lobby are all AI-controlled, the scenarios behind closed doors are very real. Whoever Clodia really is, her uploads are astonishingly numerous and varied. There is apparently nothing she won't do or have done to her, and she must be making a fortune through The Party's "tipping" system. Gabriel does a quick survey of the new content. One scenario is brand new, a thumbnail framed with a red border. The word "hot!" bounces playfully above it. The text reads:

DIRTY COW NEEDS A GOOD MILKING

He doesn't really know what this could mean, but feels the familiar surge of adrenaline that accompanies some new erotic discovery. There's a strange pride mixed in with it, too, like there's something truly pioneering about his tastes. He can feel his palms starting to sweat underneath the stiff VR gloves.

Once he's selected the scenario, he materialises in the middle of a white, minimalist bedroom that looks like the interior of a spacecraft or an upmarket dentist's surgery. There's a circular bed in the middle and a small redundant water feature in the corner.

As it turns out, the title of the scenario wasn't even metaphorical. Clodia is dressed in a stunningly lifelike cow costume. Not sexualised or stylised in any way, just an anatomically correct Friesian heifer, with udders and hooves and a gigantic, swaying head that keeps blinking at him. The more he looks, the less he's sure it even *is* a costume. He circles the cow slowly, like he would a real cow, trying to maintain eye-contact and making sure he doesn't get within kicking distance of its hind legs. He waits for the scenario to start, but nothing happens. She doesn't even speak. She's just waiting mutely on top of the fully made bed, which hints at the erotic subtext but also makes the animal look marooned, as though it's found its way up onto the mattress and now can't get down.

Just as he's about to make contact with the cow, another figure appears spontaneously in the room. Another man. He glitches into existence, then out, then in again, in the opposite corner to Gabriel, next to the water feature.

This is disturbing for a couple of reasons.

Firstly, interactions at The Party are always private. Each scenario is encrypted as securely as a bank transfer. There are two billion attendees at The Party at any one time, a number that includes politicians, celebrities, CEOs, doctors, mothers, fathers, teachers, students, feminists, Meninists, pro-modesty activists and porn addiction clinic staff, all of whom would prefer their predilections to remain behind closed doors.

Secondly, the man who has entered the scenario doesn't have a face. He does have a grey flannel suit, a black tie and a bowler hat, but between them is an empty, colourless oval.

"Gabriel Bäcker?"

The man's voice is painfully loud in Gabriel's headphones, and behind it is a low hum of electronic interference. The cow hovers in between them looking bemused.

"I'm Peter," says Gabriel.

"Peter?"

"Peter Van Hogendard."

"Having some trouble with your name there, Peter?"

Gabriel swallows. The man laughs, a kindly laugh.

"Don't sweat it, Gabriel. If I had a dollar for every cloned profile on here, I'd be a happy man." Another little chuckle. "In actual fact, I get about four hundred dollars for every cloned profile, so I'm a *very* happy man." A pause. "Would you like to be a happy man, Gabriel?"

Gabriel searches through his inventory for something he can throw or fire at the faceless man, but everything's greyed out.

"What do you want?" he says. He hates how high his voice sounds.

"For me, nothing. For you, everything."

"What's that supposed to mean?"

"Well, we can start with the money thing, if you like. Would you like some money, Gabriel?"

"I have money."

"Lots of money."

"Let me guess – someone's left me millions of dollars in their will, but you need a small contribution from me to release the funds."

The man laughs more heartily this time. It looks very odd coming from a blank face. "Ah no. This is a genuine offer of employment."

"Employment?"

"You spend a lot of time playing the Game, don't you, Gabriel?"

"I guess."

"How would you like to get paid to play?"

"Is this about ad hosting? Because I already do that."

Gabriel is prolific enough In World to merit sponsorship by smaller brands, something he regrets signing up to because he has no control over who chooses to advertise through him. Something about the demographic of the people who follow his activity In World means that, more often than not, his avatar is dogged by tiny thumbnail videos selling diabetes pills and acne cream.

"No, this is nothing to do with advertising. We would pay you to try new Alpha Omega content. Exclusive content, not open to regular users. Exciting, new stuff."

"I've tried all the new third-party content. It's always the same as the old content."

"We're not a third party, actually."

"So, what? You work for Alpha?"

"I'm one of the directors, actually."

"I don't believe you."

61

"That's fair enough. Perhaps you'd like to test me?"

"Test you on what?"

"I don't know. I could tell you about yourself. You are Gabriel Bäcker, aged fifteen years, five months and seven days. User for six years and five months. Average play time eleven hours a day, which is considerably above average, and particularly impressive given you're meant to be at school. Most recent session 101 hours and 30 minutes. Yesterday you reached level 910 of a possible 999. You finally completed the 'Any Port in a Storm' mission that you've been attempting since September, and celebrated by shooting most of the employees in the Pussycat Club, under the illegally assumed identity of Peter Van Den Hoonaard – that's how you say it, incidentally – some of whom were not AI and will have to spend a considerable amount of time and money resetting and rebuilding their profiles. Future worlds are your favourites, I think; Fantasy and Historical not so much. You're here at The Party for an average of two hours a day. Your tastes in women have, how shall I say, *matured* of late. This is an interesting development." He nods at the cow. "You have 451,121 followers In World, of which about 100,000 are bots, which, again, is an impressive ratio. A considerable proportion of the remainder are self-described 'Meninists'. You regularly post video and images to Meninist and Masculist hubs, and I have to congratulate you on how well you manage to hide them from the moderators. We still haven't cracked some of your encryption. I'm sure it's all reasonable stuff though, right?"

Gabriel swallows.

"You were expelled from the NutriStart Skills Academy eight days ago for downing their internal network and flooding it with violent and pornographic content. You have ordered six different types of throwing knives in the last three months, In World, again under an illegally borrowed identity – which, I should say, is reason enough for us to close and block your profile. You are clinically obese. You have high blood pressure. You have asthma. You scored a grade points average of sixty-eight in your Pre-VAC exams—"

"Go on then."

"Excuse me?"

"If you can block me, do it. Prove it. If you're a director. Just delete my account."

The room, the furniture, the cow, they all disappear and are replaced with bright white nothingness. When Gabriel stares into it for too long it starts to undulate with colours that he doesn't have names for. The faceless man splays his hands in a magician's "ta-dah!"

"How's that?" he says. "Don't worry, your profile's only been suspended. It wouldn't be in any of our interests to delete the whole thing."

Gabriel tastes the sourness of regurgitated Coca-Cola. His stomach has been squirming since the man mentioned his *mature* tastes or whatever.

"Alright. You've proved your point."

"So what do you say? Want to help us out?"

"I don't want to work for you."

"You wouldn't be working. Just playing."

"And you'd pay me?"

"That's right. If you *did* want to work for us, we can arrange that. There are considerable career opportunities at Alpha for a bright young man like you. You've already shown your technical know-how by getting yourself expelled. You're gifted. We need people like you on the team."

He waits a moment for a reply, but Gabriel remains silent, partly because the white background is giving him a migraine, partly because no one has ever called him "gifted" or even a "bright young man".

"The point is, Gabe—"

"Can you not call me that."

"Gabriel. The point is, you are one of the most active users In World in your age group, or in any age group, for that matter. You know the Game inside out. You're perfectly placed to give feedback on the user experience. The twelve-to-eighteen demographic is key for us, because it prepares you for being a member of the eighteen-to-twenty-five demographic. Which is the most important demographic. You see? We think it's really important to engage with you to produce the next generation of engaging, experiential content."

"So what do you want me to do?"

"To begin with, we'd like you to test-play some new environments. New, totally dynamic content. Just do whatever you want, for as long as you want. Just play. And we'll see what you think."

"And you'd pay me. For my thoughts."

"Exactly. How about we have a meeting to discuss it further? Somewhere else. In World, of course, if you'd feel more comfortable."

Gabriel thinks for a moment. Perhaps the most important factor in his consideration of the stranger's offer is how much it will aggravate his mother.

"Alright," he says at last.

"Fantastic. I'll fix a waypoint on your map, and you can come and visit at your convenience."

"Okay."

"Lovely meeting with you, Gabriel. We're so excited to work with you. Speak soon."

The man's avatar vanishes, and with it the sounds of static. Gabriel is back in the room at The Party, along with the woman dressed as an astronaut dressed as cow. The water feature tinkles pleasantly in the background. He looks into the animal's face for a moment, then tears off the headset and is sick into his chair's cupholder.

15.59

THE FIRST EVER Out of World meeting for the Meninists of Bromley and Chislehurst is taking place in the basement of Taco Crazy, the Mexican restaurant where one of their members is a shift supervisor. Only six of them have showed up, despite reminders. Three are wearing balaclavas and three are not, because Anton Thersites aka "Mr_Red_Pill" only suggested the idea the previous night and no one was sure if he was joking or not. One of those who committed is Anton's old school friend Christian Whitehead, who is only now discovering that the mouth-hole of his balaclava is too small, and has to keep picking tiny black fibres off his free fish taco.

The Meninists haven't yet progressed past the first item on their agenda, which is the late arrival of a shipment of nitroglycerine to one of their mum's houses.

"I asked for *next day delivery*."

"Maybe it has to come through customs?"

"Of course it's not coming through customs! That's the point of the black market."

"Is that what it is?"

"We didn't get it on the black market, we got it through Anton's friend."

"Who's his friend?"

"Not Saleem?"

"He's a Masculist!"

The argument comes to an abrupt halt when one of the waitresses of Taco Crazy comes down in steps. She retrieves several sachets of flavoured syrup from a box that Christian is perched on, digging deep under his backside.

"Oh," says Christian through his balaclava.

"Sorry," she says.

"Sorry."

She smiles at her supervisor and runs back up to the restaurant. There's a brief and intense burst of congas as the door to the basement opens and shuts.

"I thought," Christian says, now they're alone again, "the whole point of this was to show that we're a match for the Masculists. And now it turns out we're borrowing their gear? We may as well be Men's Rights at this rate!"

The road that has brought the Meninists to this point – both in Bromley and Chislehurst and elsewhere – has been long and many-forked. What was once a united front In World has devolved over the last ten years into infighting and factionalism since it became clear that not all Meninists conformed to each other's ideals of masculinity, nor did they share the same views regarding the future of the female species. The biggest split was between Meninists and Masculists. Masculists accused Meninists of being physically feeble, of spending their days playing videogames, of being the polar opposite of what a man should be; Meninists retorted that Masculists were meat-headed and backward. Masculists claimed they loved and respected women, but hated feminists for their damaging and anti-evolutionary rhetoric; Meninists just plain old hated women. The only thing they agreed on was they both wanted to get laid more than they currently were. Somewhere amidst the dust of this scrap between Meninists and Masculists were also the Men's Rights group, who had some comparatively sensible things to say about paternity leave and the gender pay gap, and the mysterious "Men For Women" cult, who believed that women really were another species altogether, whom men had to protect until their mothership arrived to take them back to their home planet.

In the last year, though, a hard core of Masculists have raised the bar and begun committing atrocities Out of World. For Mr_Red_Pill this is a disturbing leap forward in the arms race, and Meninists have lost out on a lot of press as a result. It is time, he has decided, for them to make their voices heard. Assuming, that is, the goods are delivered on time.

"Can you think of a better place to get it?" he says.

"Yes," says Christian.

"Where?"

"Garden centre."

"You think a garden centre will sell nitroglycerine?" Anton laughs.

"Fertiliser. It's an explosive."

"I think you're thinking of something-something-nitrate," says the man to his right.

"If you want to go to a garden centre, Christian, you're welcome to. Go and buy ten sacks of horseshit. I'm sticking with Saleem. Captain Gumbo, can you follow this up?"

There's silence in the basement. The faint throb of the music from the restaurant overhead. Christian picks up another fish taco but stops mid-bite. Anton looks around at the others.

"Captain?"

Captain Gumbo is one of his lieutenants. Surely he's here? No one says anything.

"Take those off."

The three remove their balaclavas. There is a collective sigh of disappointment.

"Wait. Do any of you know what Captain Gumbo actually looks like?"

15.30

ALICE NOWACKI is standing at the main entrance of the NSA. This is the welcome area of the school's In World prospectus. She can turn her head through 360 degrees and see the whole of the DV parking area and some of the fields beyond. The sections of the burial complex beneath the school buildings are a write-off, but there's plenty of ground around the perimeter that looks undisturbed.

Standing in front of her is the Headmaster, beaming, surrounded by the words "News", "Affiliates", "Tour" and "Johnson". Johnson is the name of the cockatoo that is sitting on the Headmaster's shoulder. The bird is a crucial part of the prospectus, chipping in with facts, stats and occasionally risqué jokes.

She's already done the tour, and she's not interested in the school's affiliates. She selects "News". The Headmaster starts to speak. His mouth looks like it's being manipulated by a system of hidden pulleys.

"Fantastic news regarding the NSA 6's new security system!" he says. Now his arms are moving, too. Just like his mouth, they are weirdly dissociated from the rest of his body, flailing wildly in all directions. "The TASCO team have been working non-stop since September to make up for their missed deadline during the summer holidays, and now the hardware is nearly ready for full integration with our internal security system. Once our trial period is complete, NSA 6 will be the most secure educational facility in the UK. If you're not familiar with the technical specifications of the TASCO system, just ask Johnson!"

Alice sighs. She waves a finger over the bird's beak. It squawks and out of its mouth comes a series of technical drawings rendered in 3D, which Alice can manipulate with her hands. The design is hexagonal, the same shape as the school itself. She looks at an elevation view, reading the figures of the height and depth and thickness and voltage of the outer fence. She can also view the completed structure as it will appear in real life. The wall raises the horizon by thirty feet on all sides. Its foundations are just as deep.

"Let it go, Al," says Henry from miles away.

"I can't."

"Even if Nature's Bounty let us on site—"

"NutriStart. Nature's Bounty are a subsidiary."

"Even if they let us on site, we don't have the funding for a dig."

"We might not need funding. We might not even need to dig."

"I don't follow."

"They're doing the digging themselves. They're building some kind of perimeter fence. Or they're about to. Thirty feet, Henry. The foundations. *Thirty feet*."

She can hear Henry shrugging. She removes the headset.

"I think I should go down there," Alice says.

"Out of the question."

"I can be there and back in a day."

"You've got work to do here."

"This isn't real work. It can wait. This can't. Bertha needs her head back."

"As your ex-line manager I cannot endorse this."

"They're already digging, Henry."

There is a sudden fanfare from Alice's PAD. An alert from Smoosh, the dating algorithm that Henry put her onto months ago. It's just about the only one that doesn't require her to take any of her clothes off, and that's the main reason she's using it. It's also the reason that its users have dwindled almost to double figures.

Henry pounces.

"Aha! Well?"

"A match. He wants to meet up tonight."

"Well, then," says Henry. "That settles it. Digging can wait. This could be the first day of the rest of your life."

16.03

ONCE THE last of the children are out of earshot, Tom places his PAD screen-down on the desk, slides it to one side and aligns it perfectly with the corner. Then, bending from the hips, he smashes his forehead into the desk, again and again, until the pain and the swelling are so intense that his brow is completely numb, and he feels like he could keep going all night if he wanted to, until the front of his skull cracked inwards like an Easter egg.

"What are you doing, sir?"

He sits bolt upright and turns to the door. He rearranges his tie. There is a girl hovering outside. He knows she's just seen everything.

"Are you alright?"

"Maggie!" says Mr Rosen, smiling, while Tom Rosen shrinks into the caverns of Mr Rosen's brain and rattles around in the emptiness. "Very well. Very well *indeed*. I've just realised I've forgotten to do something."

The numbness in his forehead subsides and is replaces with a pain so blinding he has to squint at his visitor. He brushes a hand over his brow, pretending to arrange his fringe. The lump is massive.

The girl frowns. Like most children of her age she hasn't yet learned to conceal what she's really thinking. Tom smiles all the more sincerely.

Margaret O'Brien has been a favourite of Mr Rosen's since before he even started teaching her. There's something so old-fashioned about both name and child they've become a kind of talisman for him against the world. He also assumed, at first, that a girl called Margaret would be a ripe target for other children's mockery, and he elected himself her official champion and defender. After two weeks of the Autumn Term, Maggie, with her thick Irish brogue and thicker knitwear, had already been in two fights and broken one of her classmates' arms, and it was clear that Mr Rosen wouldn't be needed in that role. It's looking like Maggie will be expelled before Christmas, which is a shame.

"You're bleeding, sir!"

"What? Oh, yes, so I am."

"Shall I come back some other time?"

"No no. Please. Come in. Leave the door open."

He turns to face her in his swivel chair, and she comes in and looks around the room as if it's brand new, even though she comes here at least once a day.

"What can I do for you, Maggie?"

"Well…" She's staring at the digital photo frame in the "Form Notices" section of the classroom, which displays the grinning face of Y13 Brand Ambassador Jordan Haynes, who looks seventeen going on forty-five. For a moment it seems like she's addressing Jordan rather than Tom. "You know I'm on a Beta timetable now?"

71

"Yes."

"That's why I'm in your class with all the stupid kids."

"Maggie!"

"No offence to you, mind."

"I'm only taking offence on behalf of your classmates. A Beta timetable just runs concurrently with the Alpha timetable. It's not for stupid people, it's just better tailored to your needs."

Maggie laughs. "Right, my *needs*. Like, as in, my *special* needs."

"That's not what I meant, you're incredibly bright."

"I know that."

"Well then?"

"That's my point. I only got put on Beta because I just don't *care* about what we're doing. And I know it was an extra punishment for punching Mel and busting his arm. But mostly it was my grades. I mean, I understand it, and I can do well in it, but I just don't *want* to. Do you know what I mean? So, I was wondering, can I change my options?"

Mr Rosen looks at his hands and takes a deep breath. "It's possible, but I'm not really the man to talk to. Which papers do you want to change? Do you want to focus more on print as opposed to online?"

"No, I mean I want to change my stream."

"Your *stream*?"

"Yeah. I want to do the one with the Creatives."

Mr Rosen looks at her blankly. "You can't do that, Maggie. You've been in the PR and Planning stream for two years, you can't catch that up. Besides, it's all decided on Pre-VAC results."

"But I was ten years old when I did them!"

"I know, but they show us which of your talents we should focus on. It's all about *return on investment*." Tom Rosen, crouching in the

72

corner of Mr Rosen's head, hears the echo of these words from the Staff Handbook and groans.

"They're not my talents, I just did better in the exams. And I don't *enjoy* them. I kind of hate them. I like drawing things."

"You get to draw things on Arts Day."

"Once a term."

Something about the girl's openness moves him unexpectedly. Tom Rosen creeps forward to the front of Mr Rosen's brain.

"What did you get in your Graphic Design Pre-VAC paper?" he asks. His voice has modulated, he realises.

She thinks for a moment. "Um. Sixty, I think."

"And in Data Analysis?"

"Eighty-two." She looks at her feet, as though ashamed by it.

"What about Comms?"

"Ninety."

"There's no arguing with those scores, Maggie. They're bound to put you in Planning or something similar. And chances are NutriStart have already seen them and have your Internship place ready for you."

"Already?"

He nods. "Yep. They're pretty good at modelling student outcomes."

"So you think there's no way to change."

"I can't see how you'd do it. But like I say, it's the Director of Studies who sorts these things out. I'm not the one to talk to."

"You are, because you actually listen to me." She's looking around the walls again, as though she's already forgotten why she came.

"All your teachers listen to you. They should listen to you."

She shrugs. "Okay."

"Maybe get your parents to message Mr Hoffman?"

"Ha. Yeah, sure. Well, I'll see you tomorrow, sir."

Maggie turns abruptly on her heavy, old-fashioned shoes and clomps back to the door. Under her feet is a complex Morse code of bloodstains left behind by Carla, the dots and dashes smudged and dark against the blue carpet.

"Hold on a second, Maggie."

What he's about to suggest almost certainly contravenes the Staff Code of Conduct, but he's still thinking of his "return on investment" comment and feels like the universe needs rebalancing.

"You were friends with Carla, weren't you?"

"LMB?"

"Eh?"

"Le Maitre-Bridge."

"Oh. Yes. Her."

"Yeah."

"Good, so she does exist."

"What do you mean?"

"Nothing. Do you…" He pictures Mr Tooley's face glowering at him from the little eyrie above his desk. "Do you have her number?"

"Why? Is she okay?" says Maggie. "She went home ill, didn't she?"

"I'm not actually sure. I was hoping you could help me find out."

"Were you now?" she says with a little smile. "I thought the NSA had tabs on all of us. That's why we all get a free PAD in Year 7, isn't it? So you can track it with GPS."

"That's very imaginative, Maggie – and very cynical – but not actually true." (It is actually true.)

"I can ring her now if you want."

"That would be very helpful."

Maggie fishes into her blazer pocket, which she wears over her giant fisherman-knit jumper all year round, and pulls out her phone. Technically, Mr Rosen should be handing out a sanction for this, since students aren't allowed personal devices of any kind in the school – only the PAD and PADMicro that they're issued with when they join – but he's too tired and she's doing him a favour.

While she scrolls through her contacts, Mr Barren clicks past the open door in his stiff, expensive shoes. He looks inside just long enough to make eye-contact with Tom and scowl in a way that suggests he's made a mental note of the scene and will be requiring an explanation later.

"Got it," she mutters, and puts the phone to her ear.

Tom waits and watches. Maggie looks at the ceiling, clasping the elbow of the phone-ringing arm in her other hand. Darren Barren comes clip-clopping back, peers through the door again and does another, extra-big frown.

"Weird," says Maggie after about thirty seconds.

"What?"

"It's not getting through."

"She's not picking up?"

"It's not even ringing. Not even going to answerphone."

He sighs and starts to massage his temples. The front of his head is still making convulsive throbs that ricochet all around his skull.

"Are you going to tell me what's going on," says Maggie, slipping the phone back into her pocket, "or is this one of those child safety things you have to keep to yourself?"

Tom looks at her for a moment. He hasn't told any of the other staff about the day's events. He hasn't even told Miss Potter, whose loyalties, he suspects, are to the school rather than their fictional relationship. But good old open, guileless Maggie O'Brien. He reckons he could tell her just about anything.

"I wish I knew what's going on," he says to her, "but it's all a bit of mystery to me. She was ill in my lesson, and she went to the nurses.

75

Then she was picked up by two men in a car, and now she's disappeared from the MNet, apparently."

"Two men?"

"You don't think it was her dad, was it?"

She shakes her head. "She doesn't see him anymore. She moved to live with her mum. He's an eejit."

"Maggie!"

"It's true. And a drunk."

"I don't think that's something Carla would want you to talk about – to anyone, let alone to me."

"So who do you think they were then?"

"Beats me."

"Maybe it's the same thing that happened to your man in Year 12."

Tom looks up from his PAD. At least ten more notifications have arrived over the course of their conversation.

"Who? Which Year 12?"

"You know, the handsome one. Rhys something. Was in a couple of the NutriStart ads before his hernia came back. He got ill last week, and then never came back to school. And now his teachers are all saying he got a place somewhere else, but no one believes them. His friends can't get in contact with him either, apparently."

"This is news to me."

"I mean, I've not heard any of this first-hand. You know what kids are like."

Tom can't help laughing out loud at the comment, and that makes his headache even more acute.

"Yes. I know what they're like."

"Do you want me to call in on her house on the way home?" asks Maggie.

"That's a good idea," he says. He straightens his chair as though it will straighten the world around him at the same time. He feels a little delirious. "I think you and I should conduct a little investigation. You can be my eyes on the ground. My field operative."

"Ha." She shoulders her rucksack, which has been between her feet. "Go on then. But only if you agree to help me change streams."

"I'll do what I can," says Mr Rosen, and the lie feels cold and slimy in his chest. He knows full well he can do precisely nothing to help her in this regard, especially now he's been put on probation by the DHM.

Maggie thrusts a white, braceleted hand in front of him to seal the deal. Mr Rosen shakes it, transgressing yet more guidelines from the Staff Code of Conduct, but he figures what the hell: in for a penny, in for a pound.

"Do I have a lesson with you tomorrow?" Maggie asks.

"Oh. Yes, you do."

"Well, I'll tell you what I know then."

"Jolly good."

"See you, sir."

"Goodbye Maggie. Oh, and Maggie: best keep this just between us."

"Ay-ay," she says and salutes him.

Once she's gone he sinks back into his spinning chair, shivering in the realisation that he's just said probably the most sinister, most dangerous set of words that can be uttered between teacher and student. *Best keep this just between us.* He's committed himself to a lifetime of damage control.

As if to punctuate this thought, Mr Darren Barren marches briskly into the room, overhead lights reflecting off the edge of his receding hairline.

"You haven't seen a USB stick in here, have you, Mr Rosen?"

There is absolutely no reason why Mr Barren's USB stick should be anywhere near this room. He is doing the worst impression of a man who has lost a USB stick Tom has ever seen. Who even has a USB stick these days?

"Nope," says Mr Rosen brightly. "Sorry."

"Ah. Not to worry."

Mr Barren holds his gaze just fractionally too long. Then he taps something on his PAD and marches off to do more important things.

NSA FACILITIES AND INFRASTRUCTURE EXTRAORDINARY MEETING

SMT CONFERENCE ROOM 5

AGENDA

1. Welcome; Thanks; Dinner; Matters arising
2. Deliveries procedure
3. Ants
4. Chairs
5. New security strategy
6. AOB

MENU

Starter
Goat's cheese and caramelised onion tartlette

Main
British beef burger w/chipped potatoes
Mixed salad
Choice of dips

Dessert
Lemon sponge w/vanilla custard
Fresh fruit
Squash

STAFF IN ATTENDANCE

DG	HM	DOP	Estates deputy
RMT	DHM	MF	Bursar
CAM	Estates manager	POS	Brand liaison officer

APOLOGIES FOR ABSENCE
SWR Chief Network Architect

MINUTES TAKEN AND RENDERED IN REALTIME BY
VERBIS SPEECH2TEXT PRO
"We hear you, loud and clear!"

RMT: Well thank you for coming everyone. Mr Swinson, do you want to check your connection? You're coming through a bit fuzzy.

MF: No squash for me, thank you.

RMT: Yes, please, don't stand on ceremony because the Headmaster is here. Do get started on the food.

[*UNIDENTIFIABLE SOUND*]

RMT: Sadly David lost his voice over the weekend. He was rather too vocal at Saturday's fundraiser—

[*LAUGHTER*]

RMT: —so I shall have to be his mouthpiece for items three and four on the agenda, when we get to them. Item four in particular is something I know you feel strongly about – Peter, I believe you have brand-specific messages regarding that – so I'll try to whizz us through the first few things as quickly as possible.

MF: [*UNIDENTIFIABLE*] goat's cheese [*UNIDENTIFIABLE*] delicious!

RMT: So, going forward: the first thing we need to review is our procedure for deliveries, specifically from a Health and Safety perspective. We're all aware of what happened to Tanya in the school office last week—

DOP: Tanya? The one with blond hair?

CAM: They all have blond hair.

DOP: But it's very blond, right?

MF: [*UNIDENTIFIABLE*]

RMT: Tanya lost her thumb trying to catch the drone that was delivering her stationery order. Rotor blade went straight through it, so now the office is under-staffed and we're going to have to enter into legal proceedings with Ryman's, who claim that the drone's navigation system was faulty, and they're entering into legal proceedings with Sony, and the whole thing is proving quite difficult to manage.

CAM: Why the hell was she trying to catch the drone?

RMT: That is a good question, and I think it shows that there's obviously a lack of training when it comes to drone usage. I'll be liaising with JAP about it, see if we can get it added to the compulsory CPD sessions for next year, but in the meantime I think all school deliveries should come through you, Mr Peterson, if you don't mind.

DOP: Sure thing.

RMT: And the Head thinks it's also a good idea if we open all personal deliveries to check for compliance with the Controlled Substances Act – so if you don't mind checking them, Mr Peterson, and letting myself know exactly who's getting what, that would be very helpful.

DOP: Will do.

MF: Actually, I think I would like some squash. Where's she gone? The woman with the drinks?

POS: Can you hear me?

RMT: Good. Obviously we'll feed all of this back to the teaching staff via their MNet profiles. Right. Next two items we can get through briskly.

POS: [UNIDENTIFIABLE] hear me?

RMT: These are mostly directed at you and your team, Colin: firstly, the ants are back in the kitchens.

MF: [UNIDENTIFIABLE]

CAM: Christ. I thought we'd nipped that in the bud. What are we talking

81

about? A handful or an infestation?

RMT: Well, it's quite difficult getting any sense out of the catering staff—

[*LAUGHTER*]

RMT: —but the fact that they've raised it suggests that it's preventing them doing their jobs.

CAM: Not true. They complain about everything. Miserable bastards.

RMT: But worth sending in one of your team, I think.

CAM: Fine. We might have to change the bin rota. They get attracted to the bins. And the sluice. Something might have got lodged. But I'll get some poison down there in the meantime. I'll see what I've got in my arsenal.

[*LAUGHTER*]

RMT: Thank you, Mr Macintosh. And the other thing was a personal request from the Head – he's having trouble getting his chair to recline fully, thinks there might be something stuck in the mechanism.

CAM: Ah.

RMT: Can you send down a porter to have a look first thing tomorrow? Otherwise, can you get together with Mr Freer and submit a funding request to NutriStart to cover a new chair that reclines properly? Ideally the Head would like to achieve a fully horizontal position. Would that be possible? These are the models he would be interested in purchasing.

[*UNIDENTIFIABLE SOUND*]

MF: Oh yes! What a beauty!

POS: Hello?

RMT: Which brings us to the most important piece of business, I think.

POS: Can I just say [*UNIDENTIFIABLE*]

RMT: As you all know, the Headmaster has been in negotiations with a few different security providers. He has also been in contact with a number of other schools, and he plays golf with the Director of the Dermacrem Healthy Glow Academy, so we've managed to get a really clear and wide-ranging picture of the NSA's security needs going forward. At this moment in time, it's looking like TASCO provide the most comprehensive solution. Headmaster, do you want to ping the brochures round? They'll come straight to your PADs. Some bedtime reading for you all.

[*LAUGHTER*]

CAM: It looks stunning.

RMT: It's a system we can integrate with our current CCTV network, and then the monitoring itself can be outsourced, which will save us money in the long-term.

DOP: What is that in the picture? A prison?

RMT: No, that's one of the Transatlantic Snacks Academies in the USA.

DOP: But we wouldn't get a wall like that?

RMT: Yes, the security barrier would run around the NSA grounds, so we can trace anyone coming in or out of the site. It has some clever DNA trace-tracking as well, even if an intruder somehow avoids the CCTV.

CAM: Wowee.

DOP: We don't need an actual wall, though, do we?

RMT: Dermacrem did. World of Lentils did. They just drove a minibus straight through the playing fields and into the DT buildings. In the middle of their "Women in Science" expo.

MF: What's this all going to cost? Have NutriStart given you any kind of a budget? I haven't seen one.

RMT: The final price is at the bottom. Scroll down.

[*UNIDENTIFIABLE SOUND*]

MF: This is an invoice, isn't it? Have you already invested in this? I would have preferred it if you'd kept me in the loop.

RMT: The Head has decided that this is the solution that best fits

83

our needs. He wants the NSA to be renowned as the most secure educational facility in the county. Safety of staff and students has to come first. It's the parents' first priority these days.

MF: But even if we raise fees by 20%, there's no way we can cover this.

RMT: As I say, safety of staff and students has to come first.

POS: [*UNIDENTIFIABLE*] brand [*UNIDENTIFIABLE*]

CAM: I think it's fucking great. Look at it.

DOP: Headmaster?

CAM: He's trying to say something.

RMT: Headmaster, is there something you would like to add?

DOP: What's he pointing at?

CAM: What is that? Martin?

[*UNIDENTIFIABLE SOUND*]

MF: Ants!

CAM: [*UNIDENTIFIABLE*] in my food!

[*UNIDENTIFIABLE SOUND*]

CAM: Bastards are everywhere!

RMT: Shall we adjourn, then?

MF: [*UNIDENTIFIABLE*]

POS: Hello?

[*UNIDENTIFIABLE SOUND*]

[*UNIDENTIFIABLE SOUND*]

[*UNIDENTIFIABLE SOUND*]

[*CONNECTION LOST*]

16.10

THE NSA'S library comprises no fewer than three floors of PADs and PCs, all liquid-cooled, their combined subsonic hum the closest thing to silence you can find in the school. The space has a cold, plastic smell, too, that Peepsy likes because it reminds him of unboxing new electronics. No matter how many students cram into it, the library always feels like it's just been freshly taken out of its cellophane.

Over half of the school come here after lessons have formally ended, some staying as late as eight or nine p.m. before their parents pick them up. A few years back, the school discovered that the way to keep so many boys and girls quiet was not the "shush" of a stern librarian but a piece of software that simply closed the computers down when it registered the frequencies of a human voice above a certain number of decibels. There is no noise on any of the floors, except for a mothlike flutter of fingers on touchscreens.

Whilst everyone else is completing various In World homework assignments, Peepsy has some much more pressing research to do. His search history looks like this:

dead body nsa
dead body high weald
missing person nsa
missing person high weald
burial nsa
murder nsa
unsolved murder
unsolved ritual murder nsa
unsolved ritual murder decapitation nsa

He has five tabs open on his screen. One is the hub for the HBO Museum of Britain; another is a very brief encyclopaedia entry about Druids; the other three all say: THIS PAGE HAS BEEN

BLOCKED – YOUR REQUEST HAS BEEN NOTED AND WILL BE REVIEWED. If he wants to find out exactly what he's got in his locker he'll have to try other sources.

He logs out and heads down the spiral staircase to the front desk. The boy sitting behind it is one of the apprentice librarians, an older student who Peepsy used to play AΩ with. They briefly teamed up In World, Peepsy and the librarian and someone called "Captain Gumbo", whose real identity he'd never discovered. They were close for a few weeks – the Captain had even found a way of sharing resources and XP with Peepsy, which supposedly wasn't possible – until the other two started raping and pillaging and generally making a nuisance of themselves among the other players, and Peepsy decided to go it alone.

"Alright, Adam."

"Peeps."

"Have you got the key to the bookshelves?"

"Year 8s aren't allowed to look at the books." He spins from side to side in his chair with a sedentary swagger. He's wearing one of the old, lozenge-shaped Bluetooth earpieces, an affectation adopted by a few of the Year 12s that isn't catching on.

"What are you talking about? I looked at one of them last year."

"That's because it was last year. Not this year. This year you're only allowed to read the books if you're in the Senior school, and you've got to book ahead."

"You're in the Senior school. You can just send yourself a request, and I can just *happen* to be waiting around the bookshelf when you open it, and *happen* to want the exact same book as you."

"No."

"Go on. It's important." Peepsy tries to push his quiff upwards, but it's becoming limp with sweat.

"You in trouble, Peeps?" Adam says, grinning.

"No."

The older boy taps on one of his three PADs. "You've got a lot of blocked pages open on your profile, says here."

"Come on, Adam, you know the firewall blocks *everything*."

"Druids? You don't even do history. You're in Data Management, aren't you?"

"This is personal stuff. Not school stuff."

"Oh yes?"

"I didn't tell anyone about what you did on Alpha, Adam. I could have got you expelled, but I totally covered for you. You had your ass saved by an eleven-year-old. Whoop. Big man."

Adam's thick, black eyebrows close ranks above his nose. His mouth tightens into a pinprick.

"You're a gobby little shit, you know that, Peepsy?" he says.

Peepsy holds up his palms to protest his innocence. "Just calling in my debts."

Adam opens a drawer under the desk and produces a fob key attached to an AΩ branded key ring with a picture of Princess Elissa on it. She's one of the Daughters of Time from *Mage Wars*, a crucial NPC from Story Mode, but there's also some unofficial content that Peepsy has yet to get his hands on that allows you to have sex with her.

He follows the apprentice librarian through a set of glass doors into the space where the servers and the routers are housed. Something about the throb of the machinery and height of the ceiling, three floors up, makes Peepsy think of the bowels of a ship. Beyond this is a much smaller room with five photocopier-scanners gathering dust, and beyond that a third room, the same size, that he unlocks with a bleep of the fob key.

The NSA library has five metal bookshelves that run on tram tracks laid into the floor, and each one has a crank wheel that allows it to move from side to side, which again makes Peepsy feel like he is aboard a submarine.

"You've got ten minutes," says Adam. "Then I'm going home. If you're not out before then, you get locked in. Have fun explaining your way out of that tomorrow morning."

"Got it, chief."

"You're such a—"

Adam doesn't finish his remark, or if he does Peepsy doesn't hear it.

He goes straight to "H" for "History", and slowly wheels the book-shelves apart so he can slip in between them. The section is only about thirty volumes, maybe even fewer. The library's total collection is probably a few hundred. None of the students have textbooks either, mostly for economic reasons. There's an odd Chinese kid in the year below who was shipped over here by his father with a wheeled, TASCO branded suitcase containing every conceivable textbook he might require, none of which he ever needs to look at, but which he still insists on carrying with him to all his lessons. Everyone else just accesses their learning materials through their PAD.

The majority of the "History" section is a series of books called *History Schmistory!*, slim, brightly-coloured volumes of about fifty pages each. They are mostly cartoons, which isn't what Peepsy is after. At the far end is a book called *Britain Under Rome*, which looks more promising. He slides it off the shelf. It's so heavy he can barely lift it. He sits cross-legged, rests the book on his lap, and turns to the index.

There are ten pages about Druidism, and the first thing he sees when he flips to the relevant chapter is a grainy photo of a skull that looks almost identical to the one in his locker, although in worse condition. It even has the hole in the forehead.

Skull of a Druid priest, trepanned, reads the caption below it. *Possibly sacrificial.*

Peepsy's heart rattles again, and he can feel his saliva turning oddly salty. He quickly reads the text on the opposite page:

Large numbers of both Roman and Druid burial sites in England have come to the attention of archaeologists only recently, as greenbelt land is forced to give up its secrets. Some of these are mass graves, dug in the wake of sickness or battle. Others, though, show evidence of elaborate chthonic rituals including, in some cases, human sacrifice. The most well-preserved of these are the "bogmen" of Ceredigion in Wales, whose dress and appearance suggest they were important figures from Druid society, most probably comprising the priestly caste in whose hands rested settlement of all judicial disputes. The deaths of these men were also, it seems, accompanied by the deaths of up to twelve sacrificial victims, both human and animal. The human victims at Borth, for example, were found dismembered and decapitated, and arranged around the central burial mound, pointing outwards. Some skulls were found with mistletoe seeds preserved in their mouths, others had been trepanned (although whether this had occurred prior to the sacrifice, or because of it, is not known).

Peepsy turns the page.

Stories of "curses" and misfortune dogging the archaeologists who disturbed the site at Borth are of course fanciful; but nonetheless, they are testament to the power the Druids hold over our imaginations today, and perhaps give us some idea of the intrigue and, in many cases, terror that they inspired in their Roman conquerors.

He claps the book closed, neglects to reshelve it, and runs back through the racks of servers to the library's main reading room. Adam says something to him as he passes the front desk, but he doesn't hear it, and he runs up the spiral stairs to the workstation he abandoned earlier. The students wearing headphones turn to look at him with accusatory frowns, unable to reprimand him for fear of being locked out of their machines.

Peepsy sits in front of his monitor, panting. He opens up the Museum of Britain tab with a sweaty finger, scrolls through the staff list until he finds the profile page of the one who looks most like a human being, and then hits "Contact". He stares at the blankness of the "New message" screen for a minute, trying to marshal all the adult words he knows before launching into writing anything. How would his parents start it?

Dear Madam...

He deletes this.

Dear Doctor Alice Nowacki...

The autocorrect feature on his browser changes this to *Dear Dr Alice Nowadays*, and he has to forcibly respell it another three times. Once he's got her name right, he thinks for another minute.

He's pretty sure this is the right thing to do. He can't take the skull back to where he found it. It's too late for that, because the burial site's been disturbed. And what if there's some kind of reward? He doesn't want the construction workers getting it. He also can't tell any of the staff, since he's already on thin ice after being late for Period Six.

He could take it home? No, his family's cursed enough as it is.

This is the best way. Let the professionals come in and deal with it. Until she arrives, skull and hands will have to stay in his locker. He'll just not open it.

He turns back to the message on screen and types a couple more letters. From there the autocomplete software takes over, and he allows it to choose the most appropriate words for him, tapping occasionally to make sure the composition stays on track. When it's done, he submits the entire thing to the thesaurus app, and replaces a few words with longer, more grown-up-sounding alternatives, even when he doesn't know what they mean.

Dear Dr Alice Nowacki,

I hope you are well. I am a student at the NutriStart Skills Academy. I do not wish to give you my name because I desire to remain anonymous. [He's very happy with that as an opening.]

I am contacting you with regards to some items that I found by accident at our institution. Whilst I was playing with my colleagues this morning, I found a skull and two hands adjacent to the recreation area [that's basically true], *which I think are part of a Druid* [not in the autocomplete dictionary]. *I believe them to be a part of a burial ritual, much like the bogmen of Caradigon* [also not in the dictionary, and he has to spell this from memory]. *Maybe you would like to come and observe them and take them for further cogitation?*

I have secreted [he's not sure this is right, but the thesaurus seems happy with it] *the items in my school locker for safety, I apologise if this was the wrong action to take. Perhaps we could convene some-where to transfer the items* [yes, that's *exactly* how an adult would say it, probably the best line in the whole message] *in the near future. You can contact me on my Alpha profile, and my username is #PeepzIsNoScopeGod.*

I anticipate your reply.

With best wishes,

Yours sincerely.

91

He looks from side to side at the other students working silently at their stations, and taps "Send". A little yellow light flashes in the top of the browser, and the word "Sent". Then, immediately afterwards, a green light, and "Delivered: 17:01:21." Now all he has to do is wait.

Peepsy doesn't think of himself as superstitious, but he does have certain good-luck rituals that he's performed for as long as he can remember. One of the most important is as follows: he crosses his fingers on both hands, then crosses his hands – with the fingers still crossed – and then tries to touch a piece of wood with his hands in this position. He refers to this as "The Double-Bind". Unfortunately, none of the furniture in the library is wooden, so when he tries to do it now the rite feels unfinished. This is not a good omen.

From nowhere, Josh Pettit taps him on the shoulder. He yelps in terror, cleaving through the library's silence, and ten computers either side of him simultaneously shut down.

18.00

WHEN GABRIEL finally returns home from the Alpha Cafe, his mum is in the kitchen pressing buttons on the microwave. Something smells like airplane food.

He's had so many cans of energy drink his whole gut from nose to tail seems to be emitting a high-frequency whine. He is not hungry. Whatever she puts in front of him he'll probably pretend to eat, clinking his cutlery around the plate and making masticating noises before throwing it in the bin once she's gone to bed.

Gabriel feels slightly aggrieved that she doesn't call out to him when he comes through the door. Her hearing is so acute that she'll usually hear him getting his key from his pocket while he's still in the street, from wherever she is in the house, and will be there waiting in the hallway when he enters. Not tonight, though.

He makes his way through to the brown glow of the kitchen and finds her laying the table for three. The microwave chatters away to itself.

"What's for dinner?" he asks.

She doesn't reply.

"Aren't you going to ask me how it went?"

He's concocted his whole story on the bus home. He's even familiarised himself with the staff of the Academy from their IW Hub, and has created characters for each of them to give extra richness to his account.

"Why didn't you go?"

The ensuing silence is punctuated by the microwave's *ping*. A thirty-second advertisement for some sort of Vietnamese protein soup plays luridly across its window.

"I did go," he says once the music has finished.

"Gabriel."

"What? I went. Of course I went. And by the way: can you not try and message me on my PAD when you *know* I'm in an interview?"

His mum sighs. She traces her fingers over the tablecloth until she finds the cutlery she's laid out, and she straightens them.

"Please don't lie to me, Gabe. I know you didn't go because the Academy messaged me when you didn't turn up."

"Who messaged you? I don't know what they're talking about, because I was there."

Gabriel knows he's one of the best liars out there. It's a practice he honed while he was still at NSA. This much is true: if you stick to a lie long enough, *really* stick to it, with total, adamantine conviction, even in the face of clear evidence to the contrary, the tide will eventually turn and your accuser will begin to doubt their own mind. It's thrilling to watch. There have been times in the past when Gabriel has even managed to convince himself of his own alternate truth. When this fails – and it rarely does – he has some very long and involved explanation involving quantum physics and multiverse theory to give his lies sound scientific backing. His version of events, he knows, is no less valid than the version of events that everyone else happens to be perceiving in their thread of the universe. Sadly, this held little sway when he faced expulsion from NSA, even among the science teachers.

It works on his mum, though. She seems to be in a state of paralysis, thumb and forefinger around the off-white handle of the butter knife, clinging to it for dear life.

"The interview went well, actually. I don't think I want to go there, though. Didn't like the feel of the place."

"Gabriel," she says quietly. "Stop this."

"But some *good* news: on my way back, I went to an Alpha Cafe and someone offered me a job."

"A weekend job? In the cafe?"

"Sure. I'd love to work behind the till in a cafe. What a dream come true."

"I wish you wouldn't be so sarcastic."

"No, not in the cafe. In Alpha. In World."

"For God's sake, Gabe. I think you need to put that game out of your head for two minutes and think about what's important."

He watches her eyes rolling in frustration. Finds it almost funny.

"Alpha's important," he says. "And it's only going to get more important, for everyone. You don't even understand what Alpha is, because you've never seen it. In fact, you're never going to see it, so I don't know why I should keep listening to you."

The microwave plays the advert again. Gabriel's mum whirls around and slaps at the glass with her palm.

"I don't know what to do with you, Gabriel."

"You can start by sending me to my room so I can actually get on with something useful."

"You can have something to eat first."

"I'm not hungry."

"You're not going up to play your game."

"It's not a *game*. And you can't force me to do anything."

"No, Gabriel, you're going to stay here, and you're going to do real things with real people."

Gabriel hears someone else coming down the stairs, whistling. He looks again at the three place settings on the dining-room table.

"Hello Gabe! Thought I heard someone. How was the interview?"

Mr Carnoso is standing in the plaster fragments that are still on the carpet from when Gabriel's mum tore out the router. His shoes are fastened with Velcro straps like a child's, and his head is a hairless, shrivelled baby-head, and his suit is too big for him, and he looks so mediocre and sad that Gabriel wants to run into another room.

"Are you staying for dinner?" he asks.

"Your mum invited me," says Mr Carnoso, with relish.

"Then I'm definitely going to my room."

"Gabriel!"

"I've just been up there myself," says Mr Carnoso, apparently unoffended. "It's a lovely space. You know we share a wall? You can probably hear me snoring! How embarrassing!"

"What were you doing in my room?"

"Just getting a feel for it."

"Mum?"

"I'm sorry!" says Mr Carnoso. He's either wringing his hands or rubbing them together with glee. "Have I let the cat out of the bag?"

"What are you talking about?"

"Gabe, there's no need to be angry," says his mum. "Nothing's set in stone."

"Your mum's going to sell me your upper floor. The garden, too."

"It's just an idea. You'd still have your own room, but downstairs."

"I think it could look rather nice with a bit of work."

"We need the money, Gabriel, if you're going to go back to school. We can work something out."

Gabriel picks up a chair from under the kitchen table. It feels light, and he feels strong, and for a moment it's like he is In World and everything around him is under his control, to be made and unmade. He swings the chair in a broad arc. It catches the microwave first, knocking it to the floor, then sweeps glasses from the tabletop, before striking the doorframe just in front of Mr Carnoso and splintering. Then he lifts another above his head and hurls it straight down at the laminate tiles. It flies to pieces, which scatter to the corners of the kitchen and roll between his mum's and Mr Carnoso's feet. They're both saying something, but he's not sure what. He pulls the tablecloth off the table, watches the pleasing cascade of plates and cutlery, and then strides out of the kitchen, past the cowering Mr Carnoso, and up the stairs, feeling like every step could crush bone.

In his bedroom, he wrestles his body out of the constrictive suit jacket, tearing the seams around the shoulders as he does so, happy to hear and feel the fabric come to pieces. He puts on combat pants and a sweatshirt and the trench coat that his mum hates so much. He grabs his sunglasses, too. Then he packs a bag with his AΩ hardware: headset, gloves, belt, baton, twin replica wireless submachine guns (from South Korea, banned there as well as in the UK), along with a pair of socks rolled into a ball and as many energy drinks as he can fit in the holdall's pockets.

When he emerges onto the landing he hears the tentative rustle and clink of someone trying to clean up in the kitchen. Immediately the headphones go on, and he selects the soundtrack for his departure on his PAD – AΩ "Industrial Theme" feels like a good choice – and he comes back down the stairs feeling serene. His mum is saying something but he can't hear her over the music.

The door slams behind him and Gabriel sets off down the street, past the rows of identical, cubic houses. His trench coat billows pleasingly behind him. It's past sunset but there's an odd violet glow about the clouds, which is reflected in the concrete.

Just as he's leaving the boundaries of the estate, the brooding, mechanical pulse of his music cuts out and interference floods his head. The sugar and caffeine and adrenaline are subsiding, and he feels like he's dragging his body like an anchor. He stops and checks his PAD to see if the 7G network is down. When he pulls it from his coat pocket, the AΩ track select screen is gone, and has been replaced by the faceless man in the flannel suit and the bowler hat.

"Is now a good time to talk?" he says.

"Not really," says Gabriel. "What do you want?"

"We were hoping you would have found the way-point by now. Do you have enough Bits for Fastravel?"

"Yes. Stop bothering me. I want time to think it over."

"If you're not interested, just let us know and we can find somebody else."

"No, that's not what I said."

"How about we give you a quick demonstration? Can you get In World where you are?"

"Not really. I'm in the street. I've just left home."

"Bear with me a moment."

The screen of his PAD goes blank, but the hiss of interference remains maddeningly clear in his earphones. He's already walked far enough to be in the adjoining estate. This one's sponsored by a completely different brand, something to do with DIY or power tools or something, and already he can see sales reps in electric-blue zip-up jackets starting to close in on him from various corners of the neighbourhood.

The faceless man reappears. "We've dispatched a DV. Please just make yourself comfortable and it'll take you where you need to go."

Gabriel looks up and down the street. His mum's house is out of sight. There are no vehicles in the road.

"Hey, I'm Mike from PowerGrip!" One of the reps holds out his hand, and Gabriel shakes it limply, still staring at his PAD. "Great to meet you. Can I ask you where your permanent residence is?"

"I'm from the Care estate," he mumbles.

"What a *great* place to live," says Mike enthusiastically. "Can I ask what benefits your brand offers residents on their estate?"

"Dunno. Something medical. My mum's blind, she gets something from them. Discount or something."

"Hiya pal, I'm Sophie from PowerGrip!" A second rep has ambushed him from behind. She rests a reassuring hand on his shoulder. "Are you thinking at all about a future residency in the PowerGrip estate?"

The first rep's smile twitches like there's a fish-hook caught in it.

"Maybe you'd just be able to fill out a very quick questionnaire?"

"I'm sure you're thinking of getting your own place in the not too distant future."

"It's never too early to be thinking about property ownership."

"Sign up now and you'll receive a free PowerGrip Multi-Tool!"

There's a low electric hum as the Driverless Vehicle appears at the side of the pavement. It is completely black, no advertisements on it at all, which takes all three of them by surprise. The door opens automatically and announces: "Gabriel Bäcker."

"This is mine," says Gabriel. "Bye."

He gets into the front seat and the door closes behind him. The two reps watch the car drive away, and then go their separate ways, without talking to each other. The DV drives itself into the hot darkness of the evening, and the estate disappears in a stream of neon.

20.05

"YOU DON'T mind if I record this, do you?"

"Record what?"

"This. Us."

Alice Nowacki does mind, in fact, but it would be odd and improper of her to object since everyone else in the restaurant is currently recording themselves, or their food, or themselves together with their food. The young mother next to her is trying to console her son, who is sobbing because he can't find the right kind of cat ears to superimpose on his photo. She stares as he throws his PADJunior into his ramen, spattering her sleeve, but doesn't say anything. Alice doesn't know what the opposite of broody is, but that's what she feels right now, in her bones.

"No, please," she says. "Go ahead."

"Oh God. You do mind, don't you?"

"Really. It doesn't bother me."

"You're sure?"

"Sure."

"Bless you."

Her date smiles and lays his PAD on the table between them. Its camera captures a 360-degree view of their dinner. He looks into the screen and fiddles with his hair.

"Have you tried these?" he says, not looking up. His voice has a slight transatlantic twang that she hadn't noticed when they first met.

"Tried what?"

"Smoosh's diagnostic tools," he says.

"I haven't, actually."

"It just means I get alerted if I'm going off track."

"Off track?"

"If you're losing interest in me."

She wonders why it isn't beeping right this moment. Must be broken.

"Then later," he says, pushing his hair in a different direction, "I can review things and try to do better next time."

"Oh."

Alice is already keen to get away. Back home. Back to Bertha. She knew the date wasn't going to work out from their exchanges on Smoosh, but Henry talked her into it. The first question he asked her was what piece of music made her cry. She found the question odd, but obliged and sent him a video. He sent back a video of himself, crying.

She takes a swig from her glass of soju. It tastes like kerosene.

"Is it nice?" he says, seeing her wince.

"Nice isn't really the word."

"I can order you something else." He looks mortified. "I mean, you can order *yourself* something else. Of course."

"Nope, this is exactly what I need."

"You're sure?"

Such pain in his face!

"Dead sure."

He nods and goes back to calibrating his diagnostic whatsits. Alice scrutinises him properly for the first time.

Her date's name is Jet. She supposes he's about forty years old but she can't be totally sure. Up close his face looks like it's been digitally manipulated. He could be a twenty-year-old who's added lines and facial hair to make him look rugged; equally, he could be a fifty-year-old who has had work done, or is wearing a lot of make-up. Either way there's something off about it.

He looks up at her. "Shall we start, then?" he says.

"Start?"

"The date."

Alice laughs, and the sound reverberates around her head like she's standing in an empty room. How quickly can she get through a bowl of noodles, she wonders. She scans the restaurant, awaiting the food like the arrival of a long-lost family member.

Jet catches her eye. "Ready?"

"I was born ready." She has another mouthful of rocket fuel.

"I'd like to start by saying how grateful I am to be here."

"I'd like to… echo that sentiment."

"I really enjoyed reading your profile. You sound so interesting!"

"You too. You're an artist, right?"

He looks sheepish. Are those tears again? "I guess," he says. "Do you think I'm a hipster?"

"No. Not at all. I think it's great. What do you make? Do you paint, or what?"

"No, not paint." He frowns. "I'm an imagineer."

"What's that?"

"I imagine things for people."

"What kinds of things?"

101

"At the moment, animals. New types of animals, that people might want as pets."

"Oh right."

"I think of them in my head."

"That's where I do the bulk of my thinking, too."

"And then I describe them to people."

"That's it?"

He looks affronted for a moment.

"Yes. But, Alice, when I reveal my work to my audience, you should see their faces. Such light! Such joy!"

"So it's like performance art?"

Jet shakes his head vigorously.

"Not performance, no. It's very private. Very intimate."

"Do people commission you to think of them? These animals?"

"No. It's a gesture. It has to be spontaneous." He looks coy again. "I thought of one for you, earlier today."

"Wow! That's very kind."

"Would you like me to describe it to you?"

"I would love that so much, Jet."

"I think, Alice, for you—" he puts his hand on her bare forearm, in a manoeuvre that feels unexpectedly predatory "—a tiny horse. And the horse has paws, Alice! Little, soft paws! But her teeth are ever so sharp. Can you imagine? And her tail is a hundred miles long, golden, golden…"

Jet suddenly breaks from his reverie and peers at his PAD. Alice draws her arm out of range of his.

"Oh God."

"What is it?"

"I've lost you. Look at your readings! Oh Jesus, why do I always end up just talking about myself?"

"You were talking about my horse."

"Stop. Stop. Please." He watches back the last five minutes of their conversation, sucking his teeth and cursing inaudibly. Alice can't bear to hear her own voice played aloud.

"It's really okay," she says.

"It's not. I apologise."

"There's no need."

"Can we talk about you?"

He looks at her imploringly. She looks back. Surely, thinks Alice, she must be able to meet someone, somewhere, on the continuum between Jet and the Meninist she met the previous week. There *must* be some middle way. She drains her cup of soju.

"Me."

"What do you do?"

"Good question. Well, so. I work at the Museum of Britain."

Jet shakes his head in wonderment. "Incredible," he says, and then glances at his PAD to make sure he's said the right thing.

"It's a little bit tedious, actually. At the moment we're just cataloguing everything and creating 3D models for Alpha Omega. Quite what will happen when we're finished with the catalogue, I don't know – it feels distinctly like we're working ourselves out of a job. I doubt the museum itself will last more than a few more years. Everyone will be able to see the exhibits from their homes. HBO are talking about mocking up historical scenes In World, so you can see the items in their original context. Which is fine, I suppose. It just makes what I'm doing feel a bit futile. I mean, what's the point of studying the past if you can just *go* to the past whenever you want? Why expend the effort? It's almost like there's no such *thing* as the past anymore. Do you know what I mean? I know that sounds mad."

She's babbling, and Jet has tensed up. Perhaps the diagnostic software isn't calibrated for this kind of dramatic monologue.

"I'm not supposed to fixate on the past," he says.

"I think we're all told that. That might be part of the problem."

"My therapist told me."

"Oh."

"Do you have a therapist?"

"No."

"No?"

"No."

The silence is mercifully broken by the arrival of the food. Their waiter is a pale, androgynous entity, both of his cheeks pierced with something that looks like a pair of bicycle handlebars. The adornment passes right through one side of his face and out the other.

"Hey there, guys," he says. "Boshintang and a Gogi bap?"

Most of the words are unintelligible, and there's also a weighty glob of saliva hanging from his lower lip, because his face piercing is obstructing his tongue from scooping it back in. He throws down a bowl of spiced soup in front of Alice, and Jet gets a very smooth, very white bun that looks suspiciously like it's made of polystyrene.

"It's beautiful," says Jet, examining his dish. "Would you mind if I took a moment to be appreciative of this?"

Alice already has her face practically in her soup bowl, and gestures with her spoon. Jet goes very quiet, and stares at his bun with great concentration. He still hasn't started eating by the time Alice has finished. She sits and watches him, belly straining like a water balloon.

"Everything alright?" she asks.

He nods. There's the sound of a PAD *pinging*, but this time it's not the one on the table. It's hers. Under any other circumstances Alice would think it rude to check her messages in the company of someone else, but since Jet doesn't seem all there at the moment she fishes her device out of her rucksack to check if it's anything important. The first thing she sees are the letters "NSA" in the message title, and she can feel her blood warming.

The message is from a student. The wording is odd, but earnest; and if it isn't a joke then there's hope that the NutriStart site isn't completely lost. "Human remains," the message says, amongst some vague and not totally germane references to Druids and bogmen. By end of the letter she's grinning, and Jet's diagnostic romance software is going haywire.

Jet looks up with such forlorn hope she almost considers staying.

"I'm sorry," she says. "I have to go. Emergency."

"Have I done something wrong?"

"What does the software say?"

"It says…" He looks at the screen, pulsing with all kinds of beautiful data visualisations. "You're excited. And flirtatious. And perhaps considering going home with me?"

Alice laughs. "Sorry," she says. And then: "You're nice."

The faces of both Jet and his PAD light up simultaneously. Alice pays the whole bill, shoulders her rucksack, and hails a DV to take her back to the museum.

21.55

TOM ROSEN has finished his day's work. He has written up his assessments of the day's lessons, booked an online appointment with the Head of Pedagogy to discuss his missed Year 7 targets, submitted the lesson plans and Learning Objectives for the following morning, completed his own daily Performance Management Review, updated the Risk Assessment for Wednesday afternoon's Universal Positivity Workshop, chosen from next week's lunch menu, and has reviewed and graded sixty identical, autocorrected essays about Millennial Web Copy, using grading software developed by the same company who make the autocorrect software, which seems to render the whole process circuitous and futile.

He sheds Mr Rosen like old skin and leaves him shrunken and desiccated in the empty English, Media & Marketing (Academic) office. He'll try to wear him again tomorrow, and a few more tears will appear at the knees and the elbows, and again the next day, and the next, and in a few more years Mr Rosen will be little more than a looped and tattered shawl, with poor Tom visibly naked beneath it. He wonders whether he'll even realise when that day comes.

Across the hexagonal central garden, he can see a handful of classrooms and offices still have lights on, but the NSA's ground floor is silent and dark as he walks to the pick-up/drop-off point. The corridor is haunted with luminous apparitions of students and staff, drifting across the HDTVs that line the walls. They greet him as he passes. Some give him a finger-and-thumb "okay" hand signal.

Tom breathes as deeply as he can, listening to the echo of his heels. The air is sharp with artificial citrus and bleach. This is the only time of day when the school doesn't smell faintly of sewage, arising from the myriad digestive problems of everyone who has spent more than a few days on the site. It all started when they installed the new high-speed routers last year, whose signals are widely believed to interfere quite intimately with the human large intestine. Nobody has actually raised the issue, though, because firstly they're too embarrassed, and secondly the routers were eye-wateringly expensive and are a real feather in the Headmaster's cap.

The Head pops into Tom's thoughts just as he's approaching his office. From this side of the NSA hexagon he can just see across the garden and through the office windows. There are two men in there, silhouetted against a light that is much softer than the fluorescence in the classrooms and the corridors. Tom stops. One of them, he is sure, is the man who tried to shake Carla Le Maitre-Bridge's hand as she was helped into the car earlier that morning.

Does he care? Isn't it Mr Rosen who cares, the figure who was left in a heap in his office? He must care, Tom Rosen must, because he's not making for the building's exit, but is now creeping round the corner and up to the door of the Headmaster's office. The door to his reception is open, but the second, inner door is closed. The voices of the two men are low and inexpressive, like machinery.

"There are always going to be anomalies," one of them says. "Even the anomalies are worthwhile data."

"The thing is," says another, "we *are* tweaking things. We're always tweaking."

Tom tries to get closer to the door. The carpet in the HM's reception is so thick every footstep feels like crunching through deep snow. When he's near enough to see one of the men's ankles through the crack – he's sitting one knee on top of the other, trouser leg riding up to reveal his sock, patterned with pictures of sausage dogs – Tom is suddenly aware of a massive presence behind him.

He turns to see the Headmaster – a giant, a golem – standing in the darkness of the corridor. He's holding a tray of cocktails. Two of them have little umbrellas; one has a too-big wedge of pineapple perched on its rim.

"Mr Rosen," he says, again in a tone so devoid of cadence it almost expresses no meaning at all.

"Headmaster," says Tom.

Neither offers anything else. They stare at one another for a moment, and then Tom goes awkwardly out into the corridor, and the Headmaster nods as if in approval. The mountainous man strides into the reception with his drinks, ice clinking in the glasses, and shoulders open the door to his office. Tom is distracted by the size of the Headmaster's feet, like a pair of black German U-boats, and forgets to look at the other two men before the door is closed.

After the heavy *clunk* of the lock, there is a moment when Tom wonders whether the thing actually happened. Just as he did when Carla was taken away. Yes, it must have. The HM's footprints are still in the carpet. Just like Carla's blood is still staining the floor of his classroom.

There's no sound coming from the office now, just a strange extra-sensory throb that's telling him to turn around and leave. He does, confused. He goes to the staff exit, swipes his access card, and the doors hiss like an airlock releasing him into outer space.

The pick-up/drop-off point is still busy, and the atmosphere is hot and tense. One of the Driverless Vehicles seems to be having problems with its navigation and is driving in circles round and round the DV rank. Some of the kids who still haven't gone home have decided it's a great game to try and balance things on the car's roof as it zooms past. The other DVs don't seem to have any idea what's going on, and are unleashing a chorus of horns and alarms and automated voices declaring in tones somewhere between soothing and authoritative: "Child on board. Please drive considerately. Child on board. Please drive considerately. Child on board. Please drive considerately."

After all the day's events, and the run-in with the Headmaster, this is all too much for Tom's tired brain. Everything feels horribly disjointed. He decides to walk. At least he'll be home by midnight.

As he leaves the main gate and turns onto the tree-lined avenue, he notices, on the perimeter of the school, beyond the stadium and the Recreation Spaces, the jerk and swing of diggers and cranes. The construction site has been floodlit, turning the warm November fog into a rainbow haze. There are figures in luminous jackets pacing between the machines.

Within the last few hours, they've started building again.

TUESDAY

8.18

PEEPSY'S SISTER can't feed herself anymore, which means that every morning he and his parents have to sit patiently probing her mouth with a plastic spoon loaded with baby food, most of which she doesn't actually swallow, and nobody feels like they have the right to get on with their own lives until she's been fed and cleaned up and safely stowed in the DV that takes her to the Activity Centre, where she goes about her own secret daily routines. As a result, Peepsy is regularly late for school through no fault of his own, but he just can't be bothered explaining all of this to his teachers, and so finds himself regularly in detention and forever teetering on the cusp of Demotion.

Today is worse than usual, though: he's over fifteen minutes behind schedule and he's in danger of missing the start of assembly. All of the seats in the auditorium are numbered and named with little LCD screens, so it's always obvious if someone is missing, and who that someone is.

Peepsy's original plan was to go to his locker first to check on the artefacts, which he's been thinking about all night, but there's no time now. He runs across the pick-up area to the students' entrance, where the concrete is lit red by the huge LED NutriStart sign affixed to the front of the school. It looks volcanic and barren.

It turns out he's not completely alone. When he approaches the students' entrance, which he refers to as "The Tradesman's" (a joke he's stolen from the Year 12s and still doesn't properly understand), there's another boy outside, older than Peepsy.

The boy isn't wearing anything. A prank, perhaps? Locked out of the changing rooms? The strange thing is, the boy himself doesn't seem to mind, or to notice. His naked flesh is doughy and very pale. He's got his back to the automatic doors and is watching Peepsy closely as he crosses the concrete. Peepsy stares back, trying to work out if he recognises him.

"What happened to you?" he ventures when he's a few yards away.

The boy doesn't respond. He's much bigger than Peepsy, and his silence is intimidating.

"Are you one of the Year 11s?"

The boy opens his mouth. At the same time, Peepsy gets a spontaneous attack of tinnitus and his blood starts short-circuiting around his head.

"Ow. Can you hear that?"

Nothing.

"Do you want some clothes? I've still got my kit from PE yesterday. It doesn't smell great, but."

He digs into his rucksack, ears still ringing, acutely aware of precious seconds ticking away. When he looks up, the boy has gone. He's not in the car park. He's not gone into the school. Peepsy spends several seconds spinning on the spot. Looks like the prank was for his benefit, after all. It's not appreciated, given how on edge he already is.

Once he's through the automatic doors he breaks into a run. He has a lot of excess adrenaline to burn off. Even from the far side of the NSA main building, he can hear the rumble of the assembling students and staff, a vast migration of bodies from all corners of the school. Thankfully he's not the last person to arrive. He can see Mr Rosen approaching the auditorium from the other end of the corridor, still doing up his tie and looking like he needs a shower.

The assembly hall is a bulbous, circular growth on the side of the school, attached by one of the umbilical, airport-style passageways. Peepsy joins the back of the three thousand children all trying to force their way through this impossible bottleneck. Up ahead, it transpires, a Year 7 pupil has dropped her access card and older, taller students are going down in their dozens, tripping over her as she scurries around between their feet looking for it. When Peepsy finally gets to the end of the passageway, she's being hauled unconscious from the crush by a porter. Two Year 12 boys are fighting because one claims the other touched his crotch when they fell over. A protein milkshake has exploded in a Year 10 girl's pocket, and she and her friends are now dripping wet and strawberry-scented. Someone is crying, somewhere.

Peepsy finds entrance "H" and files in with the rest of his year group. The tiers of seats curving above and below him are very disorientating, so he tries to keep his eyes on the floor. He follows the numbers and letters until he finds his own seat. When he gets there, Josh Pettit's face looks up from his PAD.

"What the hell were you doing on Alpha last night?"

Peepsy's still thinking about the naked boy.

"Uh?"

"You just sat in your Hub the whole time. We kept inviting you to do the new missions in Highrise, but you just ignored us."

"Oh. Yeah. I reckon my connection was broken or something."

In actual fact he was waiting to see if Dr Nowacki would make contact with him, and digging into Alpha's Omnipedia to find all the worst stories about Druid blood rites. He hasn't heard anything back from the museum yet.

"Get this," says Josh. "Kiran's sponsored now."

"I thought Kiran's dad had banned him from the Game?"

"He did. Kiran's found a way to connect to the Alpha servers through his blood-pressure monitor."

"What? Really?"

"Really!"

115

"How the hell did he work that out?"

"Because he's committed, Peepsy. Some of us *want* to put in the work because we want the Clan to be successful."

"Sure."

Peepsy's been finding it harder to care about *Mage Wars* in recent weeks. He hardly cares about Alpha at all, in fact. He knows that Josh has already got an inkling of this heresy. He turns away from his friend and looks over the tiers of seats.

The auditorium is full now. Voices at various stages of puberty clash and overlap and produce odd sub- and super-frequencies that make it difficult to think clearly. Way down below in the orchestra pit he can see rows of teachers: Mr Rosen digging into his eyes with his knuckles; Miss Potter smiling bravely through the chaos; Mrs Day from Statistics looking, as ever, like a week-old corpse; polished and manicured Señor De Souza with his spray-on hair; Miss Munday, perfect, unflinching, a marble statue of herself; and Mr Barren, surveying the whole space as though he is personally in control of all three thousand pupils. Above the trenches is the no man's land of the stage, dominated by a projector screen that must be at least forty feet wide. It is ominously blank.

"What did you do about the things?" asks Josh. He has to shout it into Peepsy's ear from inches away.

Peepsy shakes his head. "Nothing."

"You're an idiot," says Josh, sitting back in his chair. "You can't just keep them."

"It's fine," says Peepsy, "I've got a plan. I might even make some money from it." The boast sounds totally empty, even to his own ears.

"You know they've started work on the building site again? Where we were yesterday? So you can't take them back."

"I wasn't planning on it."

116

"Then what are you going to do?"

"Wait and see."

"Are you going to tell the teachers?"

"No."

"Then what?"

"God, shut *up*, Josh. I thought you didn't want anything to do with it?"

"I thought of something. Last night."

"Good for you, Josh, throw a party."

"I reckon I know what to do with what you stole."

"I didn't *steal* it," says Peepsy, looking over his shoulder to see if anyone's listening in on their conversation.

"You did steal it. Kiran was looking at what you get for grave-robbing, and if you're found guilty you can go to prison. Remember that mad guy who tried to dig up Queen Elizabeth's body? He's in prison."

"That was totally different."

"Not that different. Anyway, doesn't matter. I thought of a way to get rid of the evidence."

Peepsy doesn't really want to give Josh the satisfaction, but he rises to the bait anyway. "Well? How?"

"The incinerator. Under the school. The one they use for getting rid of non-recyclable waste."

"Are you allowed down there?"

"You weren't allowed to go out to the perimeter fence, but you did that."

The giant screen down on the stage suddenly becomes a square of solid blue light, so bright it floods the entire auditorium. The tint on Josh's face makes it look like he's in an aquarium. Peepsy's stares down between his knees. He can't stop thinking about the boy on the steps.

117

Tier by tier the conversations stop, although "silence" is a statistical impossibility. With so many students in one place there's always at least a hundred people scratching themselves, or coughing, or sneezing, or gurgling with hunger, or surreptitiously breaking wind. Add to that the ripple of reaction around each of these bodily events, and in actual fact only about 30% of the audience are quiet at any one time.

Peepsy notices that the two boys who were fighting and the girls who are covered in milkshake have been forced to stand with the teachers.

A timer appears in the bottom of the screen and ticks down from twenty to zero, and the tension in the auditorium becomes almost unbearable as every boy and girl restrains themselves from chanting like they're launching a rocket.

At zero, the blue is replaced with the broad, terrifying face of the Deputy Headmaster. Something has gone wrong with the resolution of the broadcast. His features have been stretched to fit the screen and he looks grotesquely wide and amphibious. Even on a screen of this size, the picture is infinitely brighter and clearer than real life, and Peepsy can see every glistening hair in his nostrils, every delicate, purpling thread-vein, the slightly receding gums above his canine teeth when he tries to smile.

"GOOD MORNING EVERYONE," says Mr Tooley's cavernous mouth. The volume is instantly adjusted by a techie somewhere up on the balcony.

"Good morning," he says again. "Thank you for your patience." Peepsy can see and hear the saliva sluicing between his teeth when he forms his words. It's hypnotic. "There are several important announcements to make this morning, but as you know we are delighted to welcome back one of the NSA's most prestigious alumni for a very special assembly." His eyes roll downwards and it's obvious he's reading something off a screen. "Jess Goldie has been the star of twenty of the highest-grossing NutriStart feature films, including *The Huntress, Zero Hour, Dark Web, Dark Huntress, The Spider, Dark Spider, Rogue Female, Rogue Female II: Daggerfall, Dark Dagger, Shadow Web* and *Entropy Calling.* She has also been lead singer for the multi-platinum-selling NutriStart grime collective Runnaz, and some of our older students may remember that Jess was one of the original influencers behind the '101 genuinely life-changing salads' mini-series."

There's a general whispering. Mr Tooley looks up.

"Now: this is a fantastic opportunity for us, and I have no doubt that you will all take something from Jess's presentation. Can I ask, however, that your PADs are disabled and put away. NSA will be recording this for the In World portfolio, so there is no need for anyone to record their own, private version."

Barely suppressed groans, the sounds of PAD cases being zipped.

"Well, then. Without further ado. Please welcome: Jess Goldie."

The auditorium breaks into applause as a girl who can't be twenty years old strides onto the stage with pneumatic brio, flicks her blond hair over one shoulder, and scans the crowd like it's a presidential rally.

"Hiya NSA!" she laughs. Her voice is deep and goddess-like. She must be wearing a tiny headset microphone, because her NutriStart all-in-one is too slight and figure-hugging to conceal wiring of any kind. "It's so great to be back!"

Mr Tooley's face is still there, a permanent backdrop to the presentation.

"Let me start with a quotation," Jess says, turning serious very suddenly. "Listen to this: 'No one can construct the bridge upon which you must cross the stream of life. No one, but you yourself alone.' Do you know who said that?"

Peepsy tunes out, partly bored by the talk, partly mesmerised by

Mr Tooley's gigantic visage. The Deputy Head seems to have forgotten that he's on screen at all, and has a lobotomised, thousand-yard stare that drifts unsettlingly over the auditorium from left to right and then back again. Sometimes his nose or his eyebrow twitches independently of the rest of his face.

"We tell ourselves unhelpful narratives. I'm not clever enough. I'm not beautiful enough. I'm not happy enough. Only it's not *really us* that tells us these things, it's our subconscious. Now, our subconscious is the bit at the *back* of our brain…"

Jess is still going strong, strutting noisily in her heels up and down the stage. There's something soft-focus about her that's difficult to place. If it weren't for her thundering steps, Peepsy thinks, she might be a hologram.

"…and before you know it your teenage years are behind you and you realise you've *wasted* all that time…"

The incinerator might work. He's always wanted to see the incinerator. For most of Year 7 he thought the idea was so old-fashioned it could only be a myth, but it really does exist. In the summer term some Year 11s posted a video on Alpha of them throwing rats into it. Their expulsion caused shockwaves through the student body, since it was the first hard evidence that the school was reviewing and policing behaviour In World, or at least had a mole. Peepsy starts planning a possible route into the sub-basement and loses all track of time and space.

Everyone has started applauding again, because Jess has apparently finished, and the dormant face of Mr Tooley is roused into action.

"Thank you, Jess, once again," he says, "and good luck with the new album."

"Thank you everybody!" she booms, skipping off to the side of the stage. "Think big! Dream big! Love yourself!"

Mr Tooley also claps, too close to his microphone, and it sounds like the assembly hall is under sustained mortar fire for a few seconds.

"Very good," he says. "Now. There are several routine items of business to relay to you, but before that there is a very important announcement from the Headmaster."

The atmosphere in the hall is unbearably hot, but the mention of the Head sends a shiver of anticipation through the audience.

"As some of you may have noticed, the construction teams have returned to the perimeter site, where they will be working for the remainder of the term. It goes without saying that this area of the Academy remains strictly off-limits to all staff and pupils."

Peepsy picks at his fingernails. He can feel Josh's eyes on him.

"While the full integrated security system will not be operational until next term, we will be trialling new security hardware and software in the NSA main building this coming week, to check for any bugs prior to full roll-out. It's vital that we familiarise ourselves with the system internally before we synchronise it with the systems on the perimeter, so we need to see *lanyards*—" he holds up his own to the screen, the plastic reflecting his office lighting and blinding everyone in the auditorium "—without fail from tomorrow morning onwards. You will need your lanyard to get in and out of *any* area of the main school site. The ICT team will be pressing the button at midday tomorrow and will be monitoring high footfall areas throughout the week."

Muttering ensues, but whether it's dissension, or slightly piqued interest, or boredom is impossible to tell.

"Next, regarding this afternoon's football match, you are reminded that attendance is compulsory and you must be present for registration *in the stadium* before Period Seven—"

There's a scream. About ten rows in front of Peepsy, some Year 7 students leap to their feet in an almost perfect circle, like an asteroid has landed among them. In the centre of the uproar is a red cloud, and in the centre of the cloud is a boy.

Mr Tooley is still talking.

It takes a moment for Peepsy to realise that the cloud is blood, spraying from the boy's nostrils as though from an aerosol. A handful of his classmates, who weren't quick enough in moving, have blazers that are now dark and glistening.

Most of the Year 7s are clambering over each other to escape. Nobody seems inclined give the boy any help, and he's just spinning in panic like a garden sprinkler. Down below, the teachers are on their feet, and Mr Rosen is the first to set off, leaping up the stairs with his weird stork legs, two or three at a time. The Deputy Head has finally realised that something is amiss and has disappeared from the screen.

Despite Mr Rosen's best efforts, it's actually another teacher who reaches the boy first, Mr Briggs, ex-Royal Marines and now Head of Resilience and occasional 1st XI football coach when his drinking is under control. He throws off his suit jacket and wades into the squirming children, and even from where Peepsy is sitting you can see the knotted vein pulsing on the side of his forehead. The intense, slightly lost look on his face suggests he's having some kind of flashback. By the time he's hoisted the stricken child and flopped him over one of his shoulders, Mr Briggs's cheeks are wet with tears and it's obvious that in his head it's a decade ago and he's on a battlefield in Syria or Russia or Korea and the weight on his back is a corpse. Mr Rosen has only just reached the edge of the row, and is standing redundant, not knowing what to do with his hands as the boy is carried away, down the stairs and out of Exit A.

The hall is in uproar. Those students who brought their PADs in with them have been filming the whole episode, and you can be sure that by first Recreational Period someone resourceful will have found a way to get the incident smuggled out and posted on Alpha. Form tutors are desperately trying to keep the children seated and calm, but the river has already burst its banks and there's nothing they can do to get it under control.

Normally Peepsy would find this exhilarating, but something is nagging at him.

"Alexander Pepys," says Josh, holding up his PAD to Peepsy's face and speaking like a news anchor. "Thoughts on today's extraordinary developments?"

"Turn it off," he says.

"Our reporter Alexander Pepys, there, traumatised by the terrible events we've seen here at the NSA."

Peepsy swipes at the black tablet and knocks it out of Josh's hands.

"*Hey!* What are you doing?" He shoves Peepsy, who falls back into his seat. "What the fuck am I meant to do if that's broken?"

Josh Pettit never swears, which only makes the situation feel more uncanny. The projector suddenly fires up again, and instead of Mr Tooley's face it starts showing a three-and-a-half-minute promotional video for the school with a deafening ukulele soundtrack that momentarily silences the students. It opens with a shot of the Headmaster, Mr Graves, pacing around a sunlit wheat field with a benevolent expression on his face that Peepsy is certain has been added in post-production.

The teachers are all looking around and mouthing things to each other, which is never a good sign.

The fire alarm comes as a relief, a single, solid, piercing tone that summons the school to the Recreational Spaces. The auditorium thunders under thousands of dragged feet. Under the guidance of Miss Potter and another teacher who Peepsy doesn't recognise, class

8B filter away either side of him. Josh is still examining his PAD, even though it's obvious the thing isn't broken. He huffs and frowns and polishes minute scratches on the screen with his finger.

Peepsy is the last to leave. He watches the promo video to its end. When the hall is finally quiet, he can hear the seats below him are still dripping.

8.50

"THIS IS WEIRD, isn't it? Is this weird? It is weird."

"It's only as weird as you make it, sir."

"Okay. Fine. Fine."

"It is fine. You wanted somewhere private. This is as private as it gets at NSA."

Tom Rosen and Maggie O'Brien are standing a couple of feet away from each other in one of the cleaners' cupboards. The light is dirty and yellow, and there's a damp wool smell that's either coming from the mops hung on the wall, or from Maggie's thick sweater.

"Sorry to drag you away from the fire drill like that," says Tom. "Just thought we might not get another opportunity."

"That's alright."

"So, what have you got for me, Agent O'Brien?"

He smiles and sways a little on his feet. After a sleepless night he's doubled his dose of ProSustain, and everything on the edges of his vision has started to take on a faded, sun-bleached look. His hands are shaking, and Maggie's definitely noticed. She clears her throat.

"Well, I went to Carla's house."

"Yes."

"And her mam was in."

"Yes."

"And her mam said that Carla wasn't there because she'd gone on a school trip, and she wasn't sure when she'd be back but it was definitely for a few days."

"School trip? What school trip?"

Maggie shrugs. "Dunno."

"And no one else was there?"

"No." She frowns and picks at something that looks like soup or toothpaste clinging to her jumper.

"What?"

"Carla was never very well-off, was she? Even with her posh name and all. Like, that was why we got on. But her mam – she was watching this great big TV in her front room that I'd never seen before. Massive it was, one of the curved TruLife whatsits. And she was wearing all this fancy make-up that I've never seen her wear. The house just felt different, y'know?"

"Like she'd come into some money."

"I suppose."

"And you still haven't been able to contact Carla?"

"Nope, her PAD and her phone are still dead."

Tom sighs.

"That's a big old lump you got on your forehead, sir," Maggie says, pointing. "You want to get some ice on it."

"Thank you, Maggie." He touches it gingerly. "You'd better get back to lessons."

"Eh? I'm not done. Come on, sir, if you're going to play spymaster, do it properly."

"Oh. Right. Sorry. I mean, yes." He checks his PAD for the time. His own lesson will be starting in two minutes. "What else?"

"So Carla and your man Rhys, they aren't the only two. Lots more kids are getting sick. Three more boys from Year 9 didn't turn up this morning, no reason, but someone was playing Alpha with one of them and he reckoned he heard him foaming at the mouth over his microphone. And apparently there was a Year 11 girl – Marta something – who went blind in her PR lesson and thought she was being attacked by birds."

"Did she—"

"*And* Cian in the year below – Irish, prick – had the nosebleed thing *and* was sick in registration and apparently the sick was all brown and thick like gravy, and someone said you could see things moving in the sick, like little insects or something—"

"But is that—"

"*And* now you can add Small Paul to the list after this morning, too."

"Small Paul?"

"Paul Winkler. The boy who exploded in assembly. Smells like mince."

Tom blinks at her, his head ringing like someone running a finger around a wine glass.

"Do you think they're all related?"

"Well it's your job to work that out, isn't it, sir? I'm just relaying the information."

"Right. Well. I see. Then, keep up the good work, I suppose."

"Okay. Cheers, sir." Maggie picks up her old rucksack and pulls down the fraying sleeves of her sweater so they cover her hands completely. "Maybe see you at lunch." She opens the door to the cleaning cupboard and trudges out.

Tom waits a few moments before leaving, fully aware of how utterly creepy it would look if they were to emerge from the cupboard together. It's not like it's in a particularly public place – at the top of the old stairs that lead to "the Underground", the NSA's catacombs – but still better to be safe. He perches on the edge of a mop bucket, thinking and massaging his thigh where he pulled it running up the tiered seats in the assembly hall.

When he finally opens the door, it turns out there is somebody there. It's not Maggie. It's not, thankfully, another member of staff. It's Gerald Liu, and it looks like he's been standing there at the top of the stairwell for several minutes, waiting for Mr Rosen to come out.

"Mr Rosen!" says Gerald, beaming. "You are not a cleaner. Why are you in the cupboard?"

"Just looking for something, Gerald."

"Maybe you have a secret?"

"Aha." Tom scratches the inside of his palm, as he always does when he's nervous. "No, I just wanted to clean up something that was spilled in the classroom."

"You and the girl are good friends?"

The pause that follows is taken up with Tom's brain screaming at his mouth, telling him to say something, anything to fill the silence.

The noise he finally makes is something like *"Gluh"*, and then he swallows, and comes back with the old faithful: "Don't you have somewhere to be, Gerald?"

"I am going to the Underground to pick up shirts for sports."

This doesn't make any sense, but in the circumstances Tom is happy to let it go.

"Right, then off you go. First period is about to start!"

Gerald Liu nods and continues down the stairs, choosing not to lift his suitcase of books off the floor, but letting it drop down every single step and echo noisily around the building. To Tom it sounds like a death knell.

From: MF
To: DG
Re: Security costing

Dear David,
Just a quick message about the shortfall we discussed. Anything from
NutriStart about this? Just spoke to Freya and she seemed to think
we have to find it in the current budget. Would be good to get this
wrapped up before EOY accounts.

Thanks

M

_____

From: DG
To: MF
Re: Re: Security costing

Martin,
A solution is forthcoming.

Best

David

Headmaster

_____

From: MF
To: DG
Re: Re: Re: Security costing

Dear David,
Any movement on this? Pretty large hole in the spreadsheet! Looks like

NutriStart won't budge on funding, but I guess that's to be expected. Spoke to Suryan at NSA 2 and he seems convinced that we won't get anything else out of them. He said something about the Head being ultimately responsible for fundraising initiatives?? They probably do things differently there, though!

What about a consultancy? Very happy to look into it, if you want? (Not suggesting you need help!)

All very best wishes

M

———

From: DG
To: MF
Re: Re: Re: Re: Security costing

Martin,
A solution is forthcoming.

I was sorry to hear about your wife.

Best

David

Headmaster

———

From: MF
To: DG
Re: Re: Re: Re: Re: Security costing

Dear David,
Thanks you for your thoughts re: Chrissy (not actually wife – never got around to it!!)

Looking a bit desperate now!! No pressure, obviously, but paying for new system + construction really of paramount importance. Are there cheaper options, maybe? Loved what I saw in the brochure, obviously, but maybe we could mix and match options to bring the price down??

Do let me know.

With grateful thanks and warmest wishes for the future,

M

From: DG

To: MF

Re: Re: Re: Re: Re: Re: Security costing

Martin,

My apologies. My secretary told me she was your wife.

Best

David

Headmaster

9.01

DAN BRIGGS'S office as Head of Resilience is next door to the NSA's five psychotherapists, which is either a thoughtful gesture or a cruel joke on the part of whoever does the room allocations. If he is making use of their services, it's not doing him much good. Tom finds him standing in the middle of the floor, staring at an interactive whiteboard which is displaying a formation of coloured circles. He's changed his shirt, but his hands and one of his cheeks are still rouged from carrying the bloodied Paul Winkler. His frown looks like a landslide over his eyes.

"Dan?" said Tom, knocking with a single knuckle on the office door.

He doesn't reply. As if to reinforce the concept of "resilience" to visitors, everything about the room is stiff and cold and highly uncomfortable. No beanbags or fish tanks here, just bare, white-washed walls and a small metal desk and two folding metal chairs that look like they've been borrowed from an airbase. Pinned to the noticeboard behind Mr Briggs are a variety of military insignia and photos of football teams he's coached in the past.

"Dan?"

"Tom," he says without turning to him. Lt Dan Briggs, ex-Royal Marines, is one of the few members of staff who doesn't refer to Tom Rosen as *Mr* Rosen. He finds this extraordinarily meaningful.

"Dan, where did you take Paul Winkler after assembly?"

Tom checked the school roll on his PAD immediately after the assembly. Small Paul was gone, erased, just like Carla.

Mr Briggs steps up to the whiteboard and moves one of the coloured circles up and left. It looks like he's strategizing for this afternoon's football match, which adds to the overall military HQ feel of the room.

"Nurse." He stands back and folds his arms.

"Was anyone else there? Was the Headmaster there?"

"Nope."

"Did someone come to pick him up?"

"Who?"

"I don't know, parents or… someone else."

"No."

"So did he go back to lessons?"

"Suppose."

"But you don't know for sure?"

Mr Briggs has no neck, which means that in order to face Tom he has to turn his entire body, and it looks a bit like he's squaring up for a fight.

"You ever killed a man with your bare hands?" he asks.

This is the third time this year that Briggs has put the question to Tom.

"I've not killed anyone, ever, actually."

"An animal?"

"Only by accident."

"By accident."

Briggs turns and moves a midfielder a little further towards the opposition goal. Tom waits for a follow-up question, but nothing comes.

"Do you know what lesson Paul should be in now?" he asks. "Do you have your PAD here?"

Briggs twitches his giant, breeze-block head towards the desk. Tom picks up the tablet, which has as its background a photo of Lt Dan Briggs in a desert somewhere, surrounded by his brothers in arms.

He wonders when it was taken. Lt Dan Briggs is a weathered, age-less lump of granite, probably somewhere in his fifties. The boy smiling back at him from the PAD screen is a teenager.

"What form was he in?" Tom asks, opening up the application and navigating around the MNet's 3D timetable. "7B? 7E?"

"7E."

"Right, then he should be in Graphics. I'll go and see if he's there."

Dan Briggs's frown doesn't so much deepen as change character.

"You're teaching," he says.

"Correct."

"You're on probation."

"Also correct. But I'd quite like to get to the bottom of this. Or the top of it."

He's on the verge of telling Dan Briggs everything about the previous day – Carla, the ICT team, the Head's office – but stops short. The man seems to have enough on his mind as it is. The whiteboard looks like no football team formation Tom has ever seen. The players are arranged in a circle like they're besieging a city.

"You alright, Dan?"

"I've pulled something in my calf."

There are a few moments of silence.

"No, I mean…"

Dan pounds at his temples with both fists. No, this isn't Tom's job – the man's got five therapists across the corridor.

"Doesn't matter," he says.

He leaves and takes the stairs up to the Graphics and Imaging Department. There is a residual smell of oil and acrylic paints that makes him feel pleasantly nostalgic. When he reaches Graphics Suite 28E, he finds the lights turned off, and the room lit from the IWB at the front, which is playing a video of a woman marching up and down in bright red stilettos with a python curled around her neck.

The students are all wearing VR headsets, engaged in a simulated photoshoot with the girl on the screen. Their slight torsos drift and slump under the weight of the helmets, like seaweed underwater. He watches the rows of hands, wire-bound, grasping at nothingness, and can't help thinking of souls trapped in limbo.

There doesn't seem to be a teacher present, but the students aren't in any way bothered by this. Tom could watch them for the next thirty-five minutes and no one would even know he was there. In the past, teachers have found themselves with black eyes and broken noses for interrupting VR sessions too abruptly, so he's wary of tapping anyone on the shoulder or removing their earphones.

A spindly figure uncurls himself in the dark corner of the room and stands squinting in the high-intensity beam of the projector.

"Oh. Hello Mr De Souza." A couple of the students nearest the door twitch slightly, as though distantly roused from a dream.

Señor De Souza looks at him as though he is a figment of his imagination. "What are you doing here?" he says.

"I'm looking for Paul Winkler. Did he ever make it back to class?"

"No. Never made it back…" the Graphics teacher says wistfully.

"Do you know where he ended up?"

He shakes his head. "No," he says. And then: "Aren't you on probation?"

Tom doesn't hang around to answer him. The ProSustain's modified caffeine is doing strange things to his head. It feels like his brain is trying to fight its way out of his eyes and nose. He heads back down the stairs to find the nurse. His own class have now been abandoned for eight minutes, he notes.

On the ground floor, he has to take the long way around the

building's hexagonal perimeter, for fear of walking past the SMT offices and bumping into Tooley or the Head. When he finally turns the corner into the nurse's corridor, he's surprised to see the woman herself walking briskly towards him. They both read the non-verbal cues on each other's faces.

"Have you seen him?" she asks, breaking into a trot.

"Paul?"

"Yes, the little chap with the busted nose."

"I was going to ask you the same thing."

"He's gone." She looks up and down the corridor, panting. "Ran off."

"*Ran off?*"

"Poor thing's delirious. Lost so much blood. Hallucinating, too. I turned around to get an icepack and he'd gone. I've been looking for him for twenty minutes."

"And the Head? Has he been in again? To pick him up? Like yesterday?"

"The Headmaster's there."

She points out of the window that looks into the NSA's organic garden. There he is, the hulking Mr Graves, drifting slowly, inexorably through the greenery like an unmoored ship. He stops and bends at the waist to examine a tomato plant.

"The car is outside again, though," the nurse adds.

Tom manoeuvres past her and continues down the corridor to the medical room. The usually sterile air has been replaced by Small Paul's unmistakable whiff of meat and onions.

The plain black car is indeed outside the window, in front of the DV rank. There are two suited men waiting by the passenger door, but they are not the same as yesterday's visitors. This pair look more anxious. Tom watches them walk to the NSA's main entrance, wave manically in search of a sensor that might let them in, and then return disconsolate to the car. They do this twice more in a sort of ritualised dance until they finally give up, get back in their vehicle and drive silently away.

When he goes out into the corridor, the nurse is still watching the Headmaster. Tom stands at her shoulder.

"Is he alright?" she whispers, as though he's a wild animal she risks disturbing.

Tom doesn't answer, and together they watch him disappear into the undergrowth, tomato in hand.

"We need to find him," says the nurse.

"Who?"

"Paul. Go and get Mr Tooley."

"Really?"

"Well, it doesn't look like the Head is going to be much help, does it?"

"But what if Tooley's in on it?"

"In on what?"

Tom doesn't know. He's feeling quite faint now. Somewhere on the other side of the school are twenty-five abandoned children to whom he should be giving an introduction to semiotics.

"I'll get him."

He walks to the end of the corridor and looks into the DHM's office. There's nobody in. Tom tugs nervously at his lapels. If Tooley isn't at his desk, then he's at large, in the building, patrolling.

Tom is jogging by the time he turns the corner into the EMM Department. At the far end, standing next to the open door of his classroom, is a tiny figure in a suit. It looks like a ventriloquist's dummy. As Tom approaches, contrary to the rules of perspective, the figure doesn't get any bigger.

"Mr Rosen," says the Deputy Head.

"There's a boy missing, Mr Tooley," Tom says immediately, to forestall any castigation.

"There's a teacher missing, too, Mr Rosen." He raises his eyebrows.

"I know. I'm sorry. But I've been looking for him. For Paul. Small Paul. Paul Winkler. From the assembly. He's gone."

"Now that you're here, I think you should get your lesson under way."

"I will. But Paul. I really think someone needs to phone his parents."

"If there is a narrative to be managed, I shall manage it."

"But the *boy*."

"If there is a narrative to be managed," Mr Tooley repeats, "I shall manage it."

Then he walks away tutting.

Mr Rosen puts his head into the classroom. All twenty-five of his students are there, silent and pale with fear.

10.00

GABRIEL SITS atop his customized Panzer IV tank and watches the orange sun sink over the bay. Below him the waves lap lazily at the sand, but he can't hear them over the sound of the engine. He tastes salt and diesel on his lips.

Experimentally he lets rip with the 7.5cm cannon, sending a shell arcing over the beach and into the sea, where it impacts dully on the surface and disappears in a cloud of white spray. Disappointed, he rotates the turret to face the spur of land jutting into the water to his left, and fires another couple of shells into the jungle. Parrots and macaws disperse madly into the air as the explosion rips through the silence of the bay and sends the trees and the creepers up in flames. Gabriel, bored out of his mind, continues to pound the shoreline until the forest is one giant firestorm and the beach is crowded with terrified wildlife.

With this accomplished, he puts the tank in gear, turns it on a sixpence, and levels the cannon at the tiki bar behind him and the bronzed, naked girl serving drinks. He's just got her in the crosshairs when he hears a voice from down on the sand.

"Mr Bäcker?"

He turns off the engine.

"There are better ways to start an interview," says the voice, "than destroying the interview room with artillery fire."

Gabriel drops down from the turret and lands next to the faceless man. To their left, the barmaid is cheerfully, interminably pouring drinks, despite the fact that she is still staring down the barrel of the tank's cannon.

"Thank you for agreeing to meet us formally," says the man, his head and bowler hat silhouetted against the burning jungle.

"You didn't say this was an interview," says Gabriel. "I thought you just wanted to do a demonstration."

"Ah yes, this is just an introductory session."

"But you said 'interview', just now."

"I did, indeed."

"But I've already got the job, right? Because I'm not going back home, and you did sort of promise me."

"Just a joke."

A pause, filled with the usual static that accompanies the faceless man.

"Shall we take a walk?" he says at last.

Gabriel follows the faceless man around the back of the tank. Here a path leads past the tiki bar and through parts of the jungle that haven't been destroyed. Up ahead, a deer sees them approaching and disappears into the trees. The undergrowth sings with crickets.

"What is this?" he asks. "I can't get onto any of the other maps."

"It's yours. Your own private Alpha space. This is where we'd like you to test-play some of our new scenarios."

"Sandbox."

"In a way. But this area doesn't exist anywhere on the Alpha Omega world map. You won't be interrupted by other players. It's designed for you, and for you only. At least, it will be."

There's a puff into the faceless man's microphone, like he's laughing or dislodging something from his nose.

"That sounds the same as Sandbox."

"Not quite. The new scenarios we're trialling are procedurally generated. That's where—"

"I know what that is."

"Of course you do. But here's where things get really fun. The algorithm we're using to generate your private world is itself created and altered by your preferences. So if you like something, and respond well to it, you'll get more of it. Stuff you don't like will get filtered out. Until every moment of your In World experience is tailored to you and your enjoyment."

"Okay."

"Pretty neat, right?"

None of this sounds like anything new. The whole of Alpha Omega is built upon ratings already. You can give feedback on practically anything from a section of the map to another player's facial hair, an illusion of democracy that Gabriel is not alone in trying to undermine. For a time in Year 10 it became a running gag among NSA students to track down as many of the teachers as possible In World, find any content they'd posted, and give it all one-star ratings from multiple accounts. That was the reason why Mr De Souza's virtual dog-show never took off.

The path climbs upwards through intensely green trees and flowering bushes, the faceless man a few paces ahead.

"So I've got to keep reviewing stuff?" Gabriel sighs. "Is that all this is?"

"No no, it's nothing as old-fashioned as that. Just play. That's all we want. We can track your behaviour and work out what's turning you on and what's turning you off. So to speak."

Over the crest of the hill is a secluded bay, much smaller than the one he parked the tank on, with a collection of beach houses clustered like sugar cubes in the greenery, and a pier extending out into the shallows. The water is so bright and blue it looks phosphorescent. The sunset is apocalyptic, a supernova of light that stops Gabriel in his tracks in a way that hasn't happened in years of playing.

"Sorry if this all seems a bit clichéd," says the faceless man. "These are just default parameters that we start all of our players off with. Bog-standard paradise. But, hey, it's not bad, is it?"

Something about the frequency of the light coming from the sky is producing an acute pain in his forehead, as though someone is injecting him with a syringe between the eyes.

"It's okay," he says.

"Yes. It is okay. You'll test play this area for a twenty-four-hour period, and then we'll move you on to something else."

"And what am I meant to do for those twenty-four hours?"

"Like I say: play."

"What is there to do?"

"Everything. Let's head down to your Hub and I'll show you what's what."

The trail down to the beach houses is lined with tropical flowers and attendant birds that add to the orgy of colour. A warm mist softens the edges of everything. Gabriel can feel himself perspiring pleasantly.

At the bottom of the hill they emerge from the jungle, to be greeted by the girl who was manning the tiki bar on the other side, having somehow made it over before them. And then, as they approach the complex of buildings and swimming pools, Gabriel sees that there are more women loitering on its fringes. None of them has any clothes on.

"Aloha," says the girl, and as she waves, her breasts lift as though they're filled with helium. Each sphere is artistically lit by the setting sun.

"Wonderful," says the faceless man. "Really wonderful. Look at that, Gabe. It's learning already."

"What?"

"The algorithm. It's pulling things from your historical data and using it to populate the area."

Gabriel regards the girl's flawless body and then punches her in the side of the head. The smile on her face never falters, and she staggers over to the right as though caught in a strong wind.

"She's an NPC?" he says. "Not a real player?"

"Well," the faceless man laughs, "that very much depends on your definition of the word. She's controlled by AI, sure, but she's based on behavioural data from real female players you've interacted with in the past, so basically indistinguishable."

"Can I do whatever I want to her?"

"Pretty much, yes. Let's leave that till later, though. Come inside."

141

The living quarters of the beach house complex look a lot like The Party, only a little less kitsch. One side is entirely glass, offering a panoramic view out over the sea and the exploding sunset. Another wall is a giant screen for streaming movies; opposite that, neatly displayed on racks, are all Gabriel's favourite guns: M-16, SS09, EM-2, Colt CM 901, T-91, a rare Grossfuss Sturmgewehr, a Kel-Tec PMR-30, an Auto Assault-12, .44 and .45 Colt Anacondas, Glocks 38, 39 and 40, all meeting the technical specifications of their Out of World counterparts. There are also antique muskets, crossbows, buckets of grenades, and some sort of alien weapon that's curved and organic and looks a bit like a squid.

"Do you like it?"

Gabriel doesn't reply.

"Stupid question, I suppose!"

"So," says Gabriel, selecting an assault rifle from the collection and aiming it at the faceless man's blank head, "you'd pay me to test this place?"

"Per day. In Bits, if you don't mind. Just makes everything easier if we can pay into your Alpha account instead of an Out of World bank account."

"I don't mind."

"Wonderful."

"Do I need to sign a contract or something?"

"No, no, nothing as formal as that! You're only fifteen for goodness' sake."

Gabriel only now notices that while they've been speaking a dozen naked women have appeared in the shadows of the room, in a circle, giving the impression that he is at the centre of some kind of ritual. They're all muttering in breathy, alluring voices, but they keep interrupting each other so he can't hear what they're saying.

142

"I'll do it," he says.

"Perfect." He can hear the faceless man smiling through his microphone. "You're going to be so happy here, Gabriel!"

11.25

ALICE IS half walking, half running through one of the cool white tunnels under London Bridge Station. There's a mermaid swimming alongside her. It passes from one LED screen to the next, trying to get her attention. She does her very best to ignore it. When Alice reaches the escalator, the mermaid calls out to her:

"Stamp out bad breath *for good*!"

Alice watches the mermaid somersault and disappear into a turquoise liquid, which is not, it turns out, the sea, but an expensive oral gel that the mermaid is promoting. Alice self-consciously tastes the inside of her cheeks and roof of her mouth. The advert is tailored to her, because the smart screen can take data from the PAD in her rucksack. How her PAD knows she hasn't brushed her teeth, though, is a mystery. Two men in suits pass her in the opposite direction and the mermaid singles one of them out, which makes her feel a little better.

Alice emerges from the top of the escalator onto the platform, which is housed inside a cavernous, cylindrical space like a submarine. Cinema-sized ad screens arch thirty feet over her head, all the more intimidating for the fact that she's the only person there. It feels as though she's being brought to account before a council of gods.

One of the screens simply says, black on pink: "EVERYONE'S GONE TO THE PARTY."

Alice turns her back on the ad, but there's another one behind her telling her the same thing. She tries looking at her feet, but the floor is trying to sell her some trainers that are cleaner and more expensive than hers.

She digs into her bag and checks the student's message again. A head and hands, he says. It's probably too much to expect they'll belong to Bertha. It's probably too much to expect anything. The whole thing is probably a goof.

She connects to Alpha Omega, ignoring the hundred or so private messages that have agglomerated in her inbox, and searches for the boy's avatar. There he is. He's obviously spent a lot of time and money cultivating his look. Displayed on a podium is Alex Pepys: pale, blond, skinny as a rake, wearing sunglasses and a medieval suit of armour. He's leaning on a sports car and holding a bazooka that's as big as he is. There's a list of his marksmanship awards down the left-hand side of the screen. Occasionally he fires coloured bursts of energy into the air and says in a pubescent voice: "Yeah baby!"

It's a relief when the tube arrives. The air-conditioning is on full blast in Alice's carriage, and only when she's sat in its currents does she realise how heavily she's sweating. She unzips a couple of layers and bundles them onto the seat next to her.

There's a message from Henry.

You coming in today?

She replies:

Nope. Things to do.

What kind of things?

Secret things.

Are you going to the school? Is this a joke? What the hell are you thinking?

She's not sure what she's thinking. She knows she's trying to prove something, but what it is, and to whom, remains unclear. It's a feeling she's had for some time, possibly since birth.

11.30

MR TOOLEY has his own special box that he stands on to give announcements to the staffroom. It's a movable podium with a plush, carpeted top and wheels that collapse inside it when under a person's weight. Tom Rosen can't see Tooley or the box, but he can hear the casters squeaking as it is manoeuvred between the teachers towards the huge digital noticeboard. Finally, the Deputy Headmaster climbs aboard and his little pink head pops up above the audience, silhouetted against the screen. Tom sinks lower in his chair.

"Many thanks for assembling so promptly. The Head and I are obviously aware that you all need your Recreational Period for planning and self-assessment, but after this morning's unexpected events we thought it prudent to address you as a staff body re: strategy re: these problematic students."

Tom squirms and looks at Miss Potter sitting beside him. She silently grimaces in reply, but he's not sure if they're grimacing about the same thing.

"As you will probably be aware, a number of boys and girls have fallen ill today, and the disruption to lessons has been significant. At the moment it is proving difficult to find any sort of pattern in symptoms, so neither I nor the Head nor the school nurse will speculate as to a diagnosis or a cause."

Somebody over by the espresso machine drops a cup and says, "Fuck," very loudly and clearly. Mr Tooley pauses before continuing.

"What I will say is that the situation is far from ideal in terms of optics."

Tom turns again and looks incredulously at Miss Potter, but she is listening very carefully. The whole common room is. The place is never this full, and there aren't enough seats for everyone, so clusters of teachers arranged broadly by age and social milieu are standing in corners or around the PAD charge-points, sagging onto one hip or the other as their feet get tired. They make it look and feel even more like an airport terminal than usual. The group in front of him is mostly young, newly qualified teachers, who all come to school on electric scooters and wear vintage clothes that are a whisker away from what used to be called "fancy-dress". Lots of them have badges on their lapels with references to obscure Alpha Omega memes. Tom doesn't understand the memes, or the people wearing them.

Darren Barren is standing closer than anyone to Mr Tooley, head bowed as though he's listening to a funeral eulogy. Occasionally he nods in agreement. His hands are clasped in front of him respectfully. Tom knows he is actually doing this to make his sleeves tighter around his biceps.

"It goes without saying," Tooley continues, "that an academy full of sick children is very much off-brand." Slow nod from Mr Barren. "And it's absolutely crucial that whatever is happening here is communicated in the right way at the right time." Very rapid nodding. "As a result, can I ask that, if any of your students find themselves getting into any kind of medical difficulty, you send them to the Sports Centre where the nurses can deal with them on-site, without fleets of ambulances turning up on the Academy's doorstep. Obviously, the necessary restrictions will be put in place on the students' PADs—" single nod "—and staff are expected to refrain from any comments to press or loved ones until the school has had time to formulate an official statement on the matter." Back to regular nodding.

Tom looks around. Everyone's taking this without question or complaint. It may well be that they're anxious that ten minutes of the Second Recreational Period have already passed, and know that they don't have time to cause a fuss or start a discussion.

He, for his own part, is enjoying his delirious ride towards self-destruction and puts his hand in the air.

"Mr Rosen?" says Tooley, looking faintly annoyed from atop his podium.

The young teachers turn to look where he's sitting. One of them is wearing a top hat and a monocle and is having trouble getting them both to stay on his head at the same time.

"Wouldn't it make more sense to close the school?" Tom says. "I mean, if it's contagious?"

"The loss of revenue from a day's closure would be unacceptable," says Mr Tooley. "Purchases and click-throughs at lunchtime alone amount to several thousands of pounds. And there's no need to add to the hysteria, Mr Rosen, by suggesting that this is some sort of infectious disease. As I have said, there is no pattern in the symptoms."

"But you quarantined Carla Le Maitre-Bridge, didn't you?"

Everyone else in the common room – there must be at least two hundred people in there – seems to be holding their breath. He can see Miss Potter gripping the leather armrest next to him. He notices she's not wearing her engagement ring, and that puts him off his stride a little.

"There's no suggestion of any student being put in quarantine."

"She was taken away in an unmarked car. And none of her friends can get in contact with her." The ProSustain is all but gone from his system now. He opens his eyes as wide as they'll go in an attempt to stay clear-headed, then realises this makes him look demented.

147

"If you want to discuss individual cases," says Tooley, addressing everybody but keeping his gaze on Mr Rosen, "please do book an appointment with me through the usual channels."

"Paul Winkler's gone as well."

"Like I say, individual cases can be discussed in private."

"In private," Tom echoes.

"I am keen to allow you all to return to your work," says the Deputy Head. "I hope what I have said makes sense re: protocol."

Tom makes a noise like he's dislodging a hairball.

"If you are unsure of anything, please do not hesitate to ask me or a member of the Senior Team. The most important thing is that you continue the fantastic work you all do in a calm and professional manner. The school timetable will carry on as usual, including the 1st XI football match this afternoon." He waits to see if anybody has questions, but everyone is checking the time on their watches and their PADs and seem to drift to the exit without actually moving their legs. "That will be all, then. Any further updates will be sent from SMT via the MNet. Have a good day, everybody." Mr Tooley dismounts from his box.

Lots of the other teachers are looking at Mr Rosen as they leave the common room. He stays in his chair and lets them ogle him. One of the young Copywriting teachers gives him a mock salute and smiles a smile that has so many convoluted layers of irony that its meaning is lost. The man's lapel badges *clack* against each other as he raises and lowers his arm.

"Are you alright?"

Miss Potter has her hand on his shoulder.

"Yep."

"Sure?" Her face looms in front of his. "You're very pale."

"I'm just tired. More tired than usual, I mean."

She reaches into her handbag and produces the familiar foil packet, over which is stencilled a cartoon sausage dog giving a thumbs-up. "You want one?"

"I probably shouldn't. Already had too many this morning."

She shrugs, pops one out of the packaging and swallows it with one of the tiny capsules of juice she carries with her. "I don't think you should bait Tooley like that."

"I wasn't baiting him."

"Especially when the situation is as serious as this."

"When you say serious, do you mean because of the sickness thing, or because of the optics thing?"

"Well. Both." She pauses. "The poor kids, though."

"It's true what I said about Carla. She's gone."

"Gone?"

"Look her up on the MNet. She's not there anymore. The Head took her away."

"What? The Head? Why?"

"Same with Paul Winkler this morning."

She gives him exactly the same look that he gives his students when they're spinning him a very long and unbelievable excuse.

"Are you saying they're covering something up?"

"I don't know what they're doing."

He considers telling her about what he saw in the Headmaster's office, the cocktails, the sausage-dog socks. About Carla's mum, watching her new TV, plastered in expensive make-up. He doesn't know where to start. He feels like he's having to dredge energy from somewhere in his bowels just to stay awake.

"I don't know why they can't just let them go home," says Miss Potter. "Are they going to keep them in the Sports Centre overnight?"

"I suppose."

"Can they do that?"

"I suppose," he says again.

Most of the other teachers have filtered out now. Through the thinning bodies he can see Mr Barren and Mr Tooley having an involved conversation.

"Strange that it's just the students, isn't it," says Miss Potter, putting things back in her bag. "None of the teachers have come down with anything, have they?"

"That's a point," he says, and stares at her. "You're right. It's only the children."

"Wonder why that is."

With Herculean effort he sits up in the chair.

"Are you going to watch the football this afternoon?"

"Yes. We have to, don't we?"

"In theory. I might try and nip away and pay a visit to the Sports Centre. Have a chat with some of the patients. Gather some intelligence."

Barren and Tooley both look at Mr Rosen simultaneously and turn their backs like gossiping teenage girls. They're obviously talking about him.

"We should go," he says.

He rocks backwards and forwards a couple of times to give him the momentum to get out of the recliner, then follows Miss Potter through the staffroom's automatic doors. He feels a bit better with the hard floor of the corridor beneath his feet.

"Don't go and leave me by myself at the football," says Miss Potter. "It's dull enough even when there's someone to talk to."

"What do you mean?"

"I thought you were going to go and gather evidence."

"Oh. Yes. You won't be on your own, will you? Doesn't Clemency get a complimentary ticket?"

"He does," says Miss Potter. "But won't be coming. He'll be at work."

"Work? Didn't you say his job was In World?"

"It is. He does high-end real estate."

What a dweeb, thinks Tom. Who works *in* a computer game? And what kind of a name is Clemency?

"But he's not coming."

"No." A few more paces. "Things didn't work out between us."

Tom stops. This is spectacular news. Every nerve in his face wants to broadcast his delight and he doesn't have the stamina to conceal it.

"Jesus." He tries to recalibrate his mouth. Can you grin with surprise? With shock? Is that a thing? "When? What happened?"

"I don't really want to talk about it right this minute."

"Yes. No. Of course. I mean. I'm sorry."

"Are you doing anything after the match?"

"Working."

"I mean after that. Have you got an hour free tonight? For a drink. And a talk."

Tom opens his mouth to agree with more conviction than he's ever had about anything in his life, when there's a scream. It comes from the end of the staffroom's connecting tunnel, where it meets the NSA main building.

He and Miss Potter run ahead, where a group of young children – Years 7 to 9 or thereabouts – are gathering around something on the floor. Rosen recognises a few of them. Gerald Liu is there, he notices, climbing on top of his suitcase to get a look over the taller boys, who are obviously trying to screen him out. He keeps tapping them on their shoulders and saying "Excuse me", over and over again.

Even from some distance away, Tom can hear that their voices sound odd and thin. None of the loud brashness of overconfident teenagers. They're scared.

The children turn and part when they notice him and Miss Potter approaching. He can see blood immediately, and Miss Potter rushes to a very white, crumpled-looking girl on the floor.

"He went up there," says someone.

"It stinks," says another.

The girl's leg has a ragged, oval bite-mark in it. Tom looks to where one of the boys is pointing and can see a section of panelling dislodged from the ceiling, exposing great, muscular bundles of fibre optics overhead.

"He went up there," says the boy again.

"Who?"

"I don't know his name."

"How?" says Tom.

"He jumped."

"Jumped?"

Tom looks at the faces of the other children. They nod solemnly. Who can jump that high?

He goes to the nearest classroom and grabs a chair from under one of the desks. The moment it passes the threshold, a tiny alarm starts sounding from *inside* the chair itself, and a recorded message – *PLEASE RETURN TO SEATING AREA!* – which he ignores. He places it under the hole in the ceiling, climbs on top, and sticks his head into the cavity. It's dark. He sniffs. Mince and onions.

13.45

THE SITUATION in the dining hall is one of absolute noise. It's as

152

though someone has recorded the sounds of a thousand children shouting and eating and banging cutlery at the same time, subjected it to extreme compression, and then pumped it back into the hall through low-quality speakers at maximum volume. Peepsy is in the middle of it, drowning. He wants to drag himself out and away from his peers' conversations, but the hall is full and there's nowhere else to sit.

"Paul Winkler, Rhys Prince, Ben Weir—" Hugo Raffi is counting on his fingers "—Ahmed in the year above, Tilly Taplin, fit Carla. Who else?"

"Shauna."

"*Shauna?*" Hugo's eyes bulge. He can't believe he's at the centre of such a sensational story, and nobody is telling him to shut up, or that he's a liar. "That's at least seven people."

"What happened to Shauna?"

"Shauna's got warts."

"Shauna's always had warts. I saw one of them burst once."

There's a collective groan and a couple of people throw down their spoons in disgust. The impact splatters custard across the tabletop.

"Oi, and you know James McBride," says Hugo.

Amir is scooping up the custard with his access card and wiping it on Josh Pettit's jacket without him noticing.

"Oi, James McBride, in the year below."

"What the *hell*, Amir!"

Josh pours most of the contents of a salt cellar on Amir's dessert.

"James McBride, yeah, the skinny kid in 7C." Hugo keeps up his attritional style of conversation. "Apparently he shat himself in Analytics."

Josh laughs out loud, and while he's distracted Amir decides to up the stakes and dump the entirety of his now very salty sponge pudding onto Josh's plate of spaghetti. There's muttering all round in anticipation of escalating hostilities.

Kiran Ahuja pipes up quietly, almost inaudibly: "That's not actually fair, since you started it, Amir…"

Thankfully, Josh is the bigger man and pushes away his food in defeat.

"Seriously, though, what d'you reckon it is?"

"I think it's the WiFi," says Alastair McQuade from about four seats down, where he's taking up two place-settings and has so much ketchup around his mouth that he looks like he's just been devouring a raw carcass. "I read a thing. It's like radiation. It's basically like going to school in a nuclear reactor."

"Nah, it's a disease or something," says Amir.

"Maybe we'll all get super-powers."

(Peepsy thought of a better version of the same joke but chose not to say it.)

"It's not that kind of radiation, though," says Kiran. "Everything gives off radiation of some sort. Sunlight is radiation."

"These are new routers, though, aren't they?"

"I reckon Carla had an STD and she's been passing it around."

"What does STD stand for?"

"The earth itself gives off radiation, all the time."

"Really?"

"Has anyone noticed the security settings have been changed on everyone's PADs again?"

"Yeah, I saw that."

"Doesn't gonorrhoea give you nosebleeds?"

"Amir, I'm *eating*."

"What's up with Peepsy?"

"He's thinking about Miss Munday again."

Peepsy doesn't look up at the mention of his name. He pushes a bland, perfectly rectangular piece of chicken around his plate and doesn't say anything.

On top of his anxiety about the artefacts, and the ghost boy, and the possibility of a Druid curse, the dynamic of the group is bothering him. He'd normally be at the centre of conversations like these, as curator and ringleader. That role now seems to have fallen to Amir, who doesn't really let the quieter ones talk, and whose jokes are too loud and too crude. Even Hugo Raffi seems to have attached himself to this new tribal leader. Peepsy's starting to feel confused, and a little scared, too. Maybe this is how it will be forever. He'll never get the old Peepsy back. Everything's changed for good.

"Is he in trouble?" says Hugo.

Everybody else gets back to what's left of their lunches.

"Oi, Amir, is he in trouble? Is Peepsy in trouble?"

They're already talking about him in the third person.

"Oi, Amir."

"Oh my God, just fuck *off*, Hugo." Peepsy slams a palm onto the table and feels something cold and sticky beneath it. "I'm not in trouble. I've not got a boner for Miss Munday. I'm just eating my lunch."

Hugo Raffi's eyes go huge and bulbous, and his lips disappear inside his mouth.

"I wasn't even *talking* to you Peepsy. I was talking to *Amir*. Oi, Josh? Wasn't I talking to Amir?"

The others have taken the hint and are stacking their plates and glasses and bowls of salty-spaghetti-custard onto the bright red NutriStart dinner trays. The trays have little diagrams on them explaining the importance of a balanced diet, and what the elements of that diet should be, and where you can buy those elements. There's a sprightly cartoon kid winking in the bottom right-hand corner, whom Peepsy hates, and always covers up with his dessert bowl.

Somewhere over by the vegan hatch somebody drops their entire lunch, and the hall erupts into jubilant applause and whistles.

"Kiran, wasn't I talking to Amir? Not Peepsy?"

Hugo's moment in the limelight has ended, and suddenly everyone's ignoring him again. His eyes dart uncertainly from one boy to the next, and he looks more frightened than disappointed, like he thinks he might be a ghost and no one can see or hear him. Peepsy feels a bit sorry for him.

"Oi, Kiran," he says one last time, but to himself.

Amir is the first to leave. "Boys," he says, standing and nodding to everyone apart from Peepsy. "I've got to go finish that demographics thing for De Souza. See you at the football. Good luck avoiding the Carla disease."

Hugo Raffi dutifully follows him. Ally McQuade leaves too, and the whole dinner table springs upwards about six inches, but Josh and Kiran stay behind. Peepsy still hasn't touched his food. The chicken breast has *corners.*

"Are you alright, Peeps?" asks Josh. "Why are you being such a snowflake today?"

Peepsy presses down on the meat with the back of his fork and watches the warm, clear fluid pooling around the salad leaves.

"Peepsy?"

He finally looks up, at Kiran.

"You're clever," he says. "What do you actually think is happening?"

"What do you mean?"

"With everyone getting ill."

Kiran leans forward on his elbows and adjusts his executive-looking wire-framed glasses. It suddenly strikes Peepsy that his friend has a very old face. Not mature, exactly, but worn-down. In fact, he can't remember ever seeing him smile. He imagines Kiran and his dad standing in front of the mirror together in shirts and ties, practising serious, adult expressions before bedtime.

"I mean... They're just ill, aren't they? It's a virus or something."

"Viruses don't give you nosebleeds."

"True."

"They don't make you hallucinate."

"Who said anything about hallucination?"

Peepsy looks at both of them and knows he shouldn't keep talking.

"I think it's all my fault," he blurts.

"Eh?" says Josh.

"Because of the *stuff*. The stuff we found yesterday. Because we took it—"

"You took it."

"I took it, and I shouldn't have, and I looked up about it and it's probably from a Druid burial site, like a sacrifice thing, that we shouldn't have disturbed, but the school started building the fence and now the *stuff* is in my locker and I've probably cursed the school and all of these people are being made ill by, like, evil spirits or something, and it's *my* fault it's *all my fault* and I think it's making me insane, because I saw a boy this morning outside the entrance and he wasn't wearing anything, and I think he might have been a ghost."

Peepsy looks up and down the table and can see that a group of Year 9s have been listening in and are laughing at him.

Josh is not laughing, and neither is Kiran.

"Alex," says Josh – he hasn't called him by his proper name since they first met at the beginning of Year 7 – "you're being weird."

"You shouldn't joke about it," says Kiran. "It wasn't right to dig up those things. We said so."

157

"I'm *not* joking, I'm being totally serious, I really think I've fucked up here."

"Where's the skull?"

"It's in his locker," says Josh before Peepsy can reply.

"*Still?*" says Kiran, his disappointment making him look and sound even more like his old dad.

"Curses aren't... *real* though, are they?" says Josh.

"No," says Kiran. "Rubbish."

The boys look uneasily at each other, until a pea hits Peepsy on the side of his head. The Year 9s laugh again and load more projectiles onto their forks. He turns his back to Josh.

"I'm going to get rid of them. The things. Today."

"How?"

"Like you said, with the incinerator. You've got to come with me, though."

"No, we don't," says Josh. "Kiran's right. We told you not to. This is your problem."

"Does it really have to go in the incinerator?"

"I don't know what else to do. I sent a message to the archaeologist woman."

"And?"

"I said she could meet me in Alpha to arrange handing over the artefacts, but she didn't reply."

"Right."

"I mean, I know the best thing is to put the bones back where they belong, but I *can't* do that, can I? Especially not now they're building out on the perimeter again. I just want to get rid of them."

Peepsy feels another pea strike the top of his ear. He looks at his friends' faces and realises they're actually embarrassed to be with him. Josh is scratching at a non-existent stain on his thigh, and Kiran is wriggling with discomfort like he's suddenly been afflicted with an all-over rash.

"Go on. Come with me," he says. "We haven't got lessons. We can go during the match."

"But we still have to be registered," says Kiran. "We're supposed to be in the stadium."

"We can get away. I'll think of something."

His companions are already on their feet.

"I'm out," says Josh.

"Sorry," says Kiran.

"Alpha tonight?"

Peepsy doesn't answer, and the other two don't so much leave as very gradually blend into the surrounding noise. When Peepsy looks up again they're lost in the sea of business wear that's surging around the waste disposal hatches.

The spaces beside him have already been filled by a group of Year 13 boys and girls, who are having a working lunch and are comparing graphs and pie charts on their PADs. They all have tiny earpieces in, black wireless buds, which suggests that the meeting involves more people than those who are physically present. One of the boys, who has a tiepin and some of the worst acne Peepsy's ever seen, accuses another of being "ineffective", and the other one simply nods and makes a note of it. The girl immediately to his right has her elbow in the remnants of Amir's custard and hasn't noticed.

The hall is busier now the older students have been allowed in. The pile-up around the food hatches is exacerbated by the complex series of transactions that take place between the students, as everyone quickly and surreptitiously tries to swap the meals they've been recommended with the things they actually want to eat. Lunches are always pre-ordered via MNet, and the options that a student is allowed to select are dictated by: a) daily and weekly performance data (identifying lapses or surpluses of energy on particular days or in particular lessons); b) feedback from the PE Department; c) nutritional value of previous meals ordered that week. Hence Peepsy's only option, after his atrocious showing in the PE lesson on Monday and Miss Nangle's obsessive remarks about his lack of muscle tone, was this protein-rich "chicken" slab and a dessert that is literally just a bowl of seeds. To eat what you want every day involves either trade-offs with your classmates, or incredibly precise monitoring of your nutritional intake and minute adjustments to your daily routine, to try and second-guess the NSA's catering algorithm. Amir's lemon sponge and custard was the result of about two weeks' work.

Today everything seems even more manic than usual, though, as if the hall is moments from a riot. This morning's events and the ensuing rumours have brought the place to boiling point. It's so hot in here. And the smell – not so much of food, but of the sweat that comes off food when it's left out at room temperature for too long.

Peepsy spots Mr Rosen ineffectually marshalling the queue around the water fountain. He's not even trying. He's looking in the other direction, doing something odd with his eyebrows and sinking his chin down into the hollow of his neck. Peepsy follows Mr Rosen's eye-line and sees that he's communicating with the Irish girl in Year 9. What's she called? "Big Paddy" is how she's known in Peepsy's circle, but he can't recall what her actual name is. She's winking and smiling back at Mr Rosen. Then, immediately behind him is Gerald from the year below, luggage in one hand, carton of soy milk in the other, staring euphorically between Mr Rosen's shoulder blades. No one else seems to have noticed this odd triptych, including Mr Rosen and Big Paddy themselves.

Peepsy pans around. A group of Year 7s are huddling mute and lamb-like on the end of the table, some seeming too small to even lift their trays of food. The Year 9s to his left are no longer firing peas at him and are building a tower out of their own geometric pieces of meat.

And then the boy is suddenly back again, standing there in his nothings, between Peepsy and the Year 7s. He's within arm's reach.

"It's you, isn't it?" Peepsy says, thinking of the artefacts in his locker.

He turns around to see if anyone else has heard or seen him, and in doing so knocks over his water glass. The Year 9s fall about laughing again. He leaps up as the water spills over the table edge and onto his crotch. He spins a full 360 degrees. The boy has gone again.

Everyone in the dining hall is looking at Peepsy now. The Year 13s have put their meeting on hold for a moment, fingers to their earbuds. Even Mr Rosen is staring at him. There's a swelling tide of laughter. Peepsy buttons up his suit jacket, glad, for the first time, that it's several sizes too big for him and can hide the spreading damp patch between his legs.

14.13

TOM AND MAGGIE, in a cupboard again, this one on the NSA's third floor and piled with old IT hardware – flat-screen monitors, printers, keyboards, two VR headsets, all greying and worn. The smell of hot dust, their faces greasy and white and high-contrast under the LED lighting.

"That's, what, twelve people?"

"Thirteen," says Tom. "If you count the boy in the dining hall."

"You think?"

"Didn't you see the way he got out of his seat? Like he was seeing things."

"Have you asked about my timetable swap?"

"So it seems like the symptoms are psychological as well as physical. Carla didn't seem quite right in the head, either. I wonder how she is. Where she is."

"Sir?"

"I haven't had a chance to ask about your timetable yet. Apologies. I will when I see him."

"But do you think it's possible?"

"Possibly."

"Right."

"Paul Winkler's symptoms were physical to begin with, too, but something's obviously happening in *here* as well." He taps his sore head.

"What's Paul Winkler been doing?"

"I don't know. But maybe stay away from the ceiling."

"What's wrong with your eye, sir?"

"What do you mean?"

"It's doing a weird fluttering thing."

"I get that when I'm tired. The boy who ran out of the dining room, do you know him?"

"No. I've heard some of the other Year 8s talking about him. He's got a nickname, Snoopy, Snoopsy, something like that."

"He looked like Carla did. I think I should talk to him, before he ends up in the Sports Centre."

"The Sports Centre?"

"That's where the Deputy Head wants you all to go."

"What?"

"When you get ill."

"They'll lock us in?"

"I think they'd rather the wider world didn't know." He peers at her. "Are you alright Maggie? You're feeling hale and healthy?"

"I suppose."

"Well keep it up. If I were you, I'd stay at home tomorrow."

"Don't think my mam would stand for that. And my grades are bad enough without my attendance dragging everything down even lower."

"This is more important than your IPR, Maggie. The school isn't going to close because it'll play very badly from a PR perspective, so you'll have to take matters into your own hands. Encourage your friends to stay home too, I think."

"I don't really have any friends apart from Carla."

"Oh."

"Can I go now, sir? It's nearly registration."

"What's the *link* though, Maggie? They're all children, that's obvious. None of the staff have been affected."

"Well, there aren't any real superstars on that list, are there?"

"Meaning?"

"I don't know all of them, but they seem pretty low achievers. Academically, I mean. Rhys was a pretty boy, but thick as shit."

"*Maggie.*"

"Oh I'm sorry, sir, are you my teacher again now?"

"…"

"It's true. Carla was failing at everything. The other Year 9 boys who stopped coming in were all bottom set data entry, Beta timetable."

"Paul Winkler was weak too. What about this Snoopy person?"

"Dunno. I said, I don't know him. Can I go, please?"

"Yes. Go. Sorry. Thank you, Maggie."

163

"No problem. See you at the football, I guess."

"I guess."

"Are we always going to meet like this, sir?"

"What do you mean? In secret?"

"In these… small spaces."

"It's difficult to find places that aren't monitored."

"It's okay, I don't mind. It's just, if we are… can you buy some gum or mints or something?"

"…"

Maggie checks her PAD and curses under her breath. When she opens and closes the cupboard door the world beyond is bright and loud. Tom would like to stay here all day, all year. Just sit out his probation in silence.

Something scampers over the fibreglass panels of the ceiling. It's too heavy to be a rat or a pigeon. Not heavy enough to be someone from maintenance. It's *fast*, too. Tom leaves as quickly as he can, regardless of who sees him.

14.30

GABRIEL CAN'T see the sea anymore, even when he's standing on the beach house terrace. The sand, the waves, the pier are all obstructed by a rippling expanse of flesh that stretches from one end of the bay to the other. Procedurally generated women are popping up in their thousands, fungus-like. Apart from those in Gabriel's immediate vicinity, the women only have themselves to interact with and each individual's behaviour has been algorithmically reduced to four or five animations. Watching them all from above reveals the patterns in their programming. All at once they'll perform the same subtle flick of the hair, the same cock of the hip, and the whole beach will undulate and glitter like a shoal of fish changing direction

Gabriel himself is tired and sore and from a practical point of view it's now just very difficult to get from A to B. He has to slowly, stubbornly barge his way between their bodies, like an icebreaker through the Arctic, a haunting chorus of sweet nothings pounding his ears from all directions. To add to his feelings of disorientation, the Game has obviously picked up on how much he liked the sunset, and has frozen it above the horizon, injecting the sky with ever more lurid and hallucinogenic colours.

A couple of other things have changed: the wall of guns has vastly increased and now covers most of the living quarters' interior. When the women first started multiplying he tried culling them like rabbits, and it was entertaining for a while to cut bloody swathes through them in order to get to the seafront. Now it's become apparent that the bodies won't disappear, and the dead women are even more of an obstruction than the live ones.

The other new thing is the portraits. In the few areas of blank space not taken up with weaponry, oil paintings of Gabriel have started appearing, usually with his top off, baring a torso that's in much better shape than the one he actually has. He's not sure what data the Game is calling upon to create this new content.

From where he's standing on the terrace, he tries to force his way down to the water's edge, where he's sure he saw some jet-skis when he first arrived.

"Hey Gabe," say ten of the women, not quite simultaneously, giving the impression that their voices are drenched in reverb.

"Wanna fuck?" say another ten, and the invitation is echoed down the beach.

165

They part in front of him and close behind him. Gabriel might be imagining it, but some of their faces look sort of shocked by his presence, like he's an unwanted anomaly.

"Wanna fuck?" A thousand scattered voices.

"Hey Gabe."

"You can put it anywhere you want."

"Wanna fuck?"

"Wanna fuck?"

Gabriel stops walking, and lets their naked bodies enclose him.

"This is boring," he says, out loud, to no one in particular.

14.45

"WHICH ONES are ours?"

"Red-and-white kit."

"There are hundreds of them."

"Red top, white shorts. White top *red* shorts are the NutriStart reps. Those are our boys, in the corner."

"Jesus, they're *huge*, aren't they? You don't notice when they're wearing their suits, do you? Look at their thighs!"

The 1st XI begin their warm-up under the LED lights of the stadium's ad banners. Tom feels irrationally jealous, as though, in this tiny window of opportunity, one of them might sweep the newly single Miss Potter away from under him. Their thighs *are* very impressive.

"Where and when do you want to have this drink tonight, then?" he asks.

"Hmmm?"

"Tonight. When do you want to get together? For a drink. Like you were saying earlier."

"Oh. I don't know. Eight or something. You can come to mine if you want."

There's a lot of chatter from the children behind them.

"What?"

"I said, you can come to mine if you want."

Miss Potter continues to stare at the football team. Tom is flustered. He turns around and is met with row after row of pink, pubescent faces from Years 7 and 8, and almost as many hovering black rectangles, as they hold their PADs up to record the game and each other. Way, way back he can see that two Year 9s are holding up spherical LifeStream cameras, which are swiftly confiscated by the ever-vigilant Mr Barren.

The girls immediately behind Tom grin and look at each other. They've probably just captured a video of his awkward exchange with Miss Potter. He pretends he hasn't seen, or doesn't care, and turns back to the pitch.

"Well, let me know," he says.

"I just did," says Miss Potter. "Eight at mine."

"Right. Yes. That's what you said."

He pretends to watch the team practising, and experiments with several different configurations of hands-in-pockets.

The NSA 1st XI football team are not only impossibly muscular, but also very, very handsome. On top of this, every available surface around the pitch and the seating is taken up with animated digital banners advertising products for NutriStart and a few of their affiliates. The glow from these screens makes everything – players, spectators, grass – look shiny and plasticised.

"Is this a particularly important match?" asks Miss Potter.

"Don't you read your weekly staff briefing?" he jokes, and feels relieved when she tosses him the smallest of smiles.

"I must have missed that bit."

"It's the semi-final. Wait, quarter-final. No, semi-final. The inter-something-something cup. Sponsored by the heartburn people."

"Happy Tums?"

"No."

"Gastrozole?"

"No…"

"Not Mrs Dalton's Charcoal Soothers?"

"No."

"GerdEaze?"

"That's the one. GerdEaze Inter Academy Cup. I think."

"And who are they playing?"

Tom checks the online programme on his PAD. "Samsung Academy West 501. In blue."

"Then who *are* all the other people in red and white? They're not all NutriStart sales reps, are they?"

"No, some of them are from GerdEaze. Apparently we have to sit through an exhibition match of GerdEaze reps versus NutriStart reps before the actual game starts. The GerdEaze people get to play whoever the sponsors of the home team are. Some content generation thing."

"Oh."

The girls behind them are taking photos and giggling again, and he turns and fixes them, briefly, with a frown.

"Where's everybody going?" asks Miss Potter.

It transpires that the warm-up match is more of a spectacle than anticipated. When they return to the pitch, the GerdEaze team are all dressed as giant anti-heartburn lozenges and the NutriStart team are staggering around in man-sized foam smoothie bottles, and they do a couple of shambling laps of the stadium, some jumping and spinning, most just waving, endlessly waving to the baffled crowd. The awkwardness is partly smothered by deafening electronic music, which sounds like Bruce Springsteen played on a hundred thousand synthesisers. It's being pumped out of speakers at only one end of the stadium, and the echoes from the three facing stands are all out of sync. This nauseating soundtrack continues for the entire match, which in the end only lasts about ten minutes: a practical decision, since the lozenge and smoothie-bottle costumes are so cumbersome that everyone is completely exhausted and disorientated after a few passes of the ball.

All of this is too much for Tom's brain to comfortably digest. He stares up into the sky and watches the flightpaths of twenty or so drones that are filming the match and the audience. Above everything, scrolling around the roof of the stadium in six-foot-high letters, is the new NutriStart slogan, white on red:

Good is good!

Every year he has to teach a lesson to the Year 10s explaining why this, after a decade of tweaks and iterations and simplifications, is the perfect brand slogan.

The crowd makes a noise somewhere between cheering and jeering as the costumed players leave the pitch, still waving. Then their tone changes as the school teams emerge from the tunnel and return to the pitch.

"Can I open my eyes now?" says Tom. Miss Potter laughs.

"Yes. All over. Thank God."

"Phewee."

"So are you going to disappear once the game starts? Are you still planning on going to the Sports Centre?"

"Maybe." Tom scratches his cheek and surveys the children behind him. "Say, you don't know what form that Snoopy kid is in? He's Year 8, isn't he?"

"Snoopy?"

"Yeah, Snoopy. Snoopsy. Blond, big quiff. Bit of a handful. He had a sister…"

"Oh, *Pepys*." She laughs. "Alex Pepys. He's one of mine. Where the hell did you get Snoopy from?"

"Doesn't he have a nickname or something?"

"Peepsy. Obviously."

"Ah yes. That makes more sense. Is he here? He had a bit of a moment in the lunch hall. I wanted to talk to him."

Miss Potter raises her eyebrows. "Did he? Interesting." She stands and scans the boys and girls chattering in the three rows at their backs. "He was here. I registered him. I mean, he was absent *mentally*, but physically all here. I wonder where… Josh!" She calls to the end of the row. "Where's Alex? Wasn't he sitting with you?"

The other boy, who has mousey hair and tanned skin that doesn't suggest foreign extraction so much as lots and lots of expensive holidays, looks blank for a moment. Suspicious, as far as Tom is concerned.

"He got ill."

"Ill?" says Miss Potter. "What kind of ill?"

"Just said he didn't feel right." Tom and Miss Potter exchange a glance. "He's gone to the Sports Centre to see the nurses."

"Why didn't he tell me?"

"He didn't want to bother anyone."

"Why didn't you tell me?"

Josh shakes his head.

A strange kind of noisy hush suddenly descends on the spectators as the players make their way to the centre for kick-off. In this lull, Tom can hear the whine and rattle of the construction machinery working on the security perimeter.

Miss Potter opens her mouth to press Josh further, but the match starts, the crowd erupts, and the boy is lost in the roar.

Each passage of play lasts fifteen minutes, after which the game is paused for messages from the sponsors. The smoothies and lozenges reappear, marching around the edge of the pitch throwing antacid tablets and nutrient bars into the crowd. The largest of the stadium's screens also displays promotional videos for the players themselves, usually a montage of their best goals, interspliced with footage of them just *hanging out with their friends*, being *normal, well-adjusted kids*, laughing and horsing around Out of World, beautifully lit and meticulously edited and making no reference whatsoever to their gruelling daily regimen of physical training, intravenous nutrition and steroidal injections.

Miss Potter turns to Tom during one of these promotional breaks.

"I'm worried. What if Tooley checks my register? He'll kill me." She pauses. "And Alex. Of course. Poor Alex. Do you think we should go and look for him? I don't like the idea of him just wandering the school."

Tom gets up. This might be his last chance to ask questions, before Alex Pepys is whisked away in an unmarked car, or is locked in the Sports Centre with the other patients, or disappears into the school's ventilation like feral Paul Winkler. Getting away from Miss Potter would also limit the opportunity for making a complete idiot of himself in advance of their date. Can he call it a date? He already has.

"I'll track him down," he says confidently. "Maybe you should stay here."

"I will. I need to be here to look after the form."

That's a shame, he'd hoped she would show at least a slight inclination to accompany him.

"Josh…" Miss Potter beckons the tanned boy over, and he fights his way past six or seven sets of legs that are all trying to trip him over.

"Yes, miss?"

"How long ago did Alex leave?"

"Dunno. Just after you registered him. He's not in trouble, is he? Isn't that what he's meant to do? Go to the Sports Centre?"

"Yes. No, he's not in trouble. But we need to make sure he's alright. When you say ill… how ill are we talking?"

"Just a bit sick."

"How did he seem… in the head?" interrupts Tom.

"Um. Fine."

"So how was he ill?"

"Um."

"What happened at lunchtime?" Rosen presses him, and he's aware that Miss Potter is watching him. "Did he talk to you about it?"

A flicker of recognition passes over Josh's face, and his long eyelashes twitch.

"Um. I didn't sit next to him at lunch."

"But did he *mention* anything to you?"

Miss Potter rests a hand on his arm. "It's alright, Mr Rosen. We can just talk to Alex about it when we find him. Yes?" Her voice sounds like she's addressing an elderly, slightly deranged relative.

"Yes. Of course. Right. I'll go and look for him." He sighs. "I couldn't take you up on that ProSustain offer, could I?"

She reaches into her bag and produces the foil packet. He swallows two of the hard little pills without water.

The GerdEaze reps make one more lap of the pitch before the next quarter of the game starts. Everyone on the bottom tier of seating is now ankle-deep in heartburn medication. The drones move into formation above the centre circle. The teams return.

"Go now, before they start playing again," says Miss Potter once Josh has returned to his seat. "It'll be less obvious."

"I'll see you later. Eight, was it?"

"Please, Mr Rosen."

"Yes. Eight. Right. Goodbye."

He makes his way to the tunnel that leads out of the corner of the stadium and back to the main NSA building. Just as he reaches it, all of the digital screens illuminate at once, no logos or graphics of any kind, just very bright white. Tom is reminded of archive footage of nuclear tests. The pitch looks bleached, and around all of the cowering players the screens cast complex, cruciform patterns of shadow.

The light is accompanied by an electric mosquito whine, which gets amplified by the speakers. The spectators are starting to shout and groan, and just when the experience is becoming unbearable there is a hot fizz and all of the lights and the screens go out. The mid-afternoon sky is like cement overhead.

There is a cry of pain from somewhere on the pitch. Tom thinks: what if someone were to get very publicly ill here, now? Watched by drones and streamed live to the world? Does Tooley really think he could manage that narrative?

While his eyes are recovering, he thinks he can see something moving around from one player to another. In the gloom he could swear it's a chimpanzee – humanoid, but much smaller than the people wearing football kit, and it seems to move on its arms as much as its legs.

Two of the players are rolling on the ground. The rest look like they're being herded around the pitch, like sheep before a sheepdog.

No one in the crowd knows what noise to make. Some of the students are laughing uproariously, others sound much more concerned. Even amidst the confused chatter he can hear that the chimp-creature is making hissing noises.

The power returns, the LED screens pour a low blue light onto the pitch, and suddenly Tom can see what's happening out there, along with the rest of the stadium.

It's not a chimpanzee, it's Small Paul Winkler, who is foaming at the mouth and snapping at the calves of the football players. Of the two who are rolling on the grass in pain, one is missing a hand. The hand is about fifty feet away, resting on the goal-line. In the blue glow of the screen's default background the trail of blood is black. The boy's wrist looks like it's pumping crude oil out onto the ground.

All of the spectators scream at once.

Small Paul is unbelievably fast. He scuttles from one set of legs to the next, grasping and biting. His sleeves and trouser legs are rolled up and his highly polished business shoes are still on his feet. His face and shirt and the lapels of his tiny suit are smeared with gore.

Groups of players from both teams vault the barriers around the touchline to escape from him. He catches one of the NutriStart reps who can't keep up with the rest, throws him or her to the ground, and in his frenzy crawls *inside* the giant foam smoothie-bottle costume, and there's a cartoonish few moments while their fighting causes the costume to bulge and distort into the shape of various body parts. Then Small Paul emerges from the lid, licking his lips, and leaves the motionless carcass behind him.

Tom looks back at Miss Potter, who is trying to stop her class running off in all directions. In the tier above, Mr Barren has insisted that all Year 9s sit in complete silence with their eyes closed. On the opposite side of the stadium, old war-torn Mr Briggs, who was coaching the team from the sidelines, is just staring up at the sky and rocking backwards and forwards on his heels.

Tom adjusts his jacket sleeves and readies himself to take action, but what action he hasn't yet decided upon. At the same time, Small Paul leaps from the pitch into the seating area. The stampede is instantaneous. Hundreds of bodies of children and adults are up and surging towards the nearest exit. Tom is borne backwards, down the tunnel, the opportunity lost. The last thing he sees before he is forced out of the stadium is the fleet of drones, still hovering above the pitch in anticipation of the match restarting, remote and passive amid the carnage.

15.12

PEEPSY BUNDLES the skull and the hands into his rucksack and closes his locker door. From the top floor of the NSA building he can hear the crowds at the football match like a distant sea. He hopes that Josh and Kiran have covered for him. Josh is reliable enough, but it would be just like Kiran to buckle under pressure and tell Miss Potter everything.

Peepsy's head is lit, but behind and ahead of him is darkness. NSA has installed energy saving halogen lights that only turn on when they sense somebody is nearby, and since the school is empty they illuminate the route for him alone. It all adds to the slightly numinous feeling of a pilgrimage. The artefacts clack wetly in the bag as he runs down the stairs. He can imagine the skull's teeth hitting the other bones, and for some reason it makes his own teeth hurt.

On the ground floor he turns left and has to make his way past both reception and the SMT's offices to get to the basement, and from there to the waste disposal area and the incinerator. He marches confidently through two sets of automatic doors. This is no time to be skulking. At the main entrance the receptionist is weeping quietly to herself, watching a video of what seems to be either her own wedding or the wedding of someone who looks a lot like her, and doesn't even notice him.

He passes the nurses' rooms, which are locked and dark since they shut up shop and moved all their operations to the Sports Centre. Beyond that, the offices of SMT are also closed. Although the door to the Headmaster's office is shut, at a certain angle Peepsy can see across a corner of the organic garden and into Mr Graves's private chamber. There's some very low mood-lighting inside. He can just make out the Headmaster lying almost horizontal in something that looks like a dentist's chair. Odd that he's not at the football match, Peepsy thinks.

He slips past the offices and reaches the corner where a corridor leads to the mythical "staff common room". Just next to it are the stairs down to the basement storerooms. They're called "The Dungeons" in a way that is meant to be funny and ironic, but is also a truthful admission that everybody is inexplicably terrified of what's down there.

As soon as he sets his foot on the top step, there is a *clink* and a shout below him.

"Ah! What are you doing?"

It's one of the cleaners, emerging from a store cupboard. She's only visible because of the red piping and monogram on her overalls.

"I'm going to the Dungeons, obviously," says Peepsy.

"It is locked."

"Well, can you unlock it?"

"Why? You're not allowed underground."

"Oh come *on*."

"No."

"But I've been told to come down here."

"By a teacher?"

"Yes. Mr Briggs. He's sent me to collect some bibs."

"Bibs?"

"A bib. Like a vest. You wear it for football. It's for the football team. They're meant to be playing, like, now."

"Ah. Football." The cleaner smiles.

"Yeah. Do you not get to watch the football match?" he asks.

"No." The smile disappears and she shakes her head sadly. "We have to stay here. To guard. To look for boys like you."

"Guard?"

The cleaner taps the name embroidered onto her overalls, and in the circle of the first "a" in "Maria", Peepsy can see the glint of a tiny camera lens.

"I see you!" says Maria with glee, and laughs.

"Well," says Peepsy, trying not to visibly panic, "if they're watching me then they're watching you too, aren't they?"

The cleaner shrugs. "No problem. I'm doing my job."

"You're going to hold up the whole football match if you don't let me get into the Dungeons. Mr Briggs really needs those bibs. They're for the substitutes. And he needs... a pump. To pump up the ball. The ball is totally flat."

The cleaner narrows her eyes. "I don't believe you."

"You'd *better* believe me, or you're going to be responsible for cancelling the whole match. Everyone's waiting."

Peepsy wonders what the likelihood is of the footage from Maria's camera ever being seen. Maybe Tooley's looking at it right now, live, in his office. The very fact that he's been caught wandering the school unsupervised is probably an expellable offence, so he may as well push on.

"Okay. I will take you there. But I will wait for you, and we go back to football together."

The pair of them descend to the bottom of the stairs. The Dungeons are three floors under the main building, not a basement but an infernally deep sub-sub-basement. There are rumours, too, of a sub-sub-sub-basement where there's either the school's main server array, or a mass grave of low-performing students, or the laboratory where Mr Graves makes clones of himself, depending on who you talk to.

At the bottom of the stairs the cleaner produces an old-fashioned fob key and opens the door. Inside is a tomb, utterly dark, a smell of dust and cobwebs and damp concrete. Peepsy reaches for three grimy switches just inside, which cause half of the strip lights to ping and strobe, while the other half stay resolutely blank. The detritus from incalculable years of school life is heaped in the shadows.

"I wait here for you," says Maria.

In Alpha, Peepsy has played countless missions in environments such as this, and there's a confusing moment when he instinctively tries to check his Head Up Display, before realising that his brain doesn't have a Head Up Display.

"Do you know where to go?" calls the cleaner behind him.

"Yes," he says, although he doesn't. He has no idea where the incinerator might be.

He grips the shoulder straps of his rucksack tightly, his fingers already stiff and white from the cold, and sets off into the flickering darkness.

There's no discernible order to the artefacts that are stored down in the NSA's catacombs. In fact, it doesn't even seem like they've been consciously "stored" at all, more just pushed underground under the weight of the new school. The shapes are all brooding and indistinct. There are piles of old audio-visual equipment, televisions, speakers, amplifiers, mixing desks, lighting rigs; upright tanks of something highly flammable, their red warning triangles flaking and concealed in dust; several canoes and mouldering lifejackets; bent and jagged music stands in a tortured heap; a single sad photocopier with its paper tray open, as though waiting to be fed; a minibus too, a proper old minibus that a teacher could drive, with a tarpaulin over the top of it. When Peepsy looks underneath he sees two crushed and faded juice cartons on the back seat from its final outing. How they drove the minibus down here is anyone's guess – there must have been a ramp out of the underground at some point, now built over. And on either side of the partially illuminated main strip, more concrete caves, going God knows where, filled with more ancient trash that no light ever touches.

Around the corner, deeper into the labyrinth, boxes and boxes of documents. When Peepsy opens them the wet cardboard disintegrates. Inside are thousands of old printouts of student IPRs, graphs and figures tracking boys and girls who have long since left NSA. All this data, all these people, turning to mulch. He wonders whether his sister's reports are in here, although they probably predate even her. She probably wouldn't want to be reminded of her stellar NSA career, anyway, given that she can't even dress herself these days.

His tinnitus suddenly returns. He looks up.

The boy is there again, standing quite still behind a stack of old textbooks. He is still naked, and from this proximity he can see he's covered in stains and marks that look like tiny bruises.

"What are you doing?" he says stupidly. He blinks.

Again the boy opens his mouth, but nothing comes out.

"These are yours, aren't they?" Peepsy rattles the bag of bones.

The boy flickers in and out of existence, then vanishes completely.

Peepsy exhales very slowly through his teeth and perches on top of the piles of reports. The walls and the ceiling of the Dungeons suddenly seem to be moving independently of each other. He waits for the boy to come back, but there's no sign of him.

Onwards he goes, through the towers of boxes, sweat collecting in his palms. The Dungeons seem to be warming up. He thinks he can smell his own body odour. Up ahead gigantic steel pipes, wide enough for him to fit inside, have wormed themselves into the earth and through the basement ceiling, where they are connected to one of six of the school's boilers. The lights and dials on the heating system beat a fast counter-rhythm against the irregular flashing of the overhead lights, making him even more disorientated.

And then, beyond the hum of the boilers, another corner and a concertinaed metal shutter that opens and closes horizontally, the gateway to the waste disposal area. Right now it is closed, but not entirely – there's a foot-wide gap between the end of the shutter and the concrete wall, and there's a burnt orange light coming from inside.

Peepsy pushes his rucksack through first, and then squeezes himself through. It turns out he wasn't imagining the heat or the smell, although the odour isn't from his body but from the mountain of waste piled up down here. Three mountains, actually: one of recyclables, one of electronics and large items, and another – prime culprit for the stench – of decaying food. All of it comes thundering down huge metal slides from somewhere up above, and down in the darkness of the sub-sub-basement it is sorted and despatched by support staff whose working hours don't bear thinking about. Amir once claimed that he went into the school kitchens after a parents' evening and found the staff bedding down in sleeping bags under the sinks and the dishwashers and the conveyor belts for the students' trays, still wearing their hairnets and protective blue gloves.

In the corner, next to the pile of recyclable material, is the incinerator. It looks like a pizza oven. Its door is open and it's spewing heat into the room, causing the food waste to putrefy and stink even more vigorously.

Peepsy holds his breath and walks towards the incinerator with his rucksack held before him like a sacrificial offering. He stands in front of the inferno, sweat pouring in rivulets down the sides of his nose and over his upper lip, and digs the skull and the skeletal hands out of the bottom of the bag.

The whine in his ears again.

He whirls around and the rucksack goes skimming across the floor. There's nobody there. He turns back again and the boy's standing between him and the incinerator door, flesh hanging off him like wet clothing. His eyes are foggy and roll lazily in his face.

Peepsy licks his lips, and the sweat tastes of iron. It drips red between his feet. He pinches his nose hard and it takes only a few seconds before the blood is backing up down his throat and making him retch.

The dead boy opens his arms in an imploring gesture. Peepsy sways forwards and backwards three times – he counts it – before he passes out and collapses into the phantom's chest.

15.30

IT'S BEEN nearly twenty-four hours since Gabriel stormed out, and Stephanie's heard nothing from him. An absence of communication isn't unusual – there have been periods of silence two or three times as long as this in the past, when he has locked himself in his bedroom and played his game – but she could always hear the telltale cough or sniffle or creak as he shifted his heavy frame in his chair. She orbited quietly around those sounds. Even when Gabriel decided he wanted nothing to do with her, she still knew where he was, knew that he wouldn't, couldn't leave their home. Wouldn't survive without her. In this respect he had hardly changed since he was a baby.

But Gabriel has gone, now. The silence in the house is maddening.

Safeway Security Ltd have been predictably unhelpful. They're able to tell her that he left the Care housing estate on foot, but because the brand of the adjacent estate, PowerGrip Electronics, is in no way affiliated with Care, there'll have to be some high-level negotiations between both brands to get the CCTV footage released from PowerGrip's data centre and delivered into the hands of Safeway Security. PowerGrip Electronics have their own private security company, Streetwize Security, but Streetwize and Safeway don't even talk to each other, let alone exchange security information, firstly because they both want the edge in an increasingly competitive marketplace, and secondly because the founder of Streetwize is Safeway's CEO's ex-wife. The result of all this is that it will take another two or three days before Safeway can even begin to trace Gabriel's movements beyond the boundaries of the estate.

She's checked his travel data on her PAD, which in itself took several hours because her device has to read every option aloud to her. But Gabriel hasn't used his travel card since he pretended to go to his interview on Monday. Then she thought she'd message the other parents from his year group, but she can't remember a single one, and she can't find the "New Parents" pack that was sent to her four years ago by the NSA. If she were on Alpha Omega, of course, she could put out a general message, but she doesn't have a profile anymore, and even if she signed up now she wouldn't have any followers and wouldn't know where to start looking for them.

If she doesn't hear anything by this evening, she'll have to go looking for him herself. "Looking" for him. Ridiculous!

Delivered by AIM.

Dear Mr Graves,

Thank you for your reply to our enquiry – we've been overwhelmed with the positive response from almost every educational institution we've contacted.

As you say, the arrangement sounds more than a little serendipitous from your point of view. Be assured, our financial contribution is the very least we can do in return for your assistance – it even seems a little on the niggardly side! I really cannot overstate how important your cooperation is, and we are all looking forward to working with the NutriStart brand values.

A meeting In World would be preferable for us. It would be good to discuss specifics and hopefully get something finalised before the New Year gets under way. Let me know which scenario you would prefer and we can get a date in the diary.

Yours with utmost sincerity

AΩ Dev Team

15.35

THE NSA'S pick-up/drop-off area is in complete chaos, and even with his walkie-talkie and high-visibility marshal's jacket, trousers and hat, Tom is finding it difficult to bring the situation to order. He is in the middle of the DV parking bay, stranded by swirling currents of students and parents, neither moving nor speaking for fear that he'll be swept away or trampled or accidentally hustled into a car with somebody's children.

Tom is, unfortunately, one of thirty deputy fire- and traffic-marshals at NSA. It's not a role he actively chose, but along with every other member of staff he is obliged to "contribute to the extra-curricular life of the Academy" and marshalling was the only activity left by the time he got round to filling out his extracurricular interests questionnaire. About once a term, in times of great crisis, the deputy marshals are scrambled like fighter pilots to manage a particularly complex DV parking scenario. Tom had only just made it safely back from the stadium to the EMM office when the call came through, and he was forced to dig out the jacket and trousers and luminous conical headwear and hurry to the pick-up point. In doing so he pulled his groin again, and arrived the latest of anyone, massaging his inner thigh.

Predictably, his line manager for the marshalling duty is Mr Darren Barren, who is the only one who actually uses the walkie-talkie, and who insists on using the NATO phonetic alphabet and ending every transmission with "over".

Tom can hear him now, squawking something from his beltline.

"Tango Oscar Romeo. Tango Oscar Romeo, please respond, over."

He lets him continue like this for a minute or so. The children

184

continue streaming past him, some in tears, obviously upset by what they witnessed in the stadium. Students and parents huddle in groups having quiet, urgent conversations. In front of the concrete island where Tom is standing, dozens of DVs are queuing, trembling slightly, backed up from entrance to exit.

"Tango Oscar Romeo, come in, over."

"Hi Darren."

There is pause in which he can hear Mr Barren's slightly panicked breathing.

"Is that transmission over, over?"

"Yes."

"Tango Oscar Romeo, please clarify your transmissions by saying over *when they're over, over."*

"Will do. What do you want?"

Another pause.

"Transmission over, over?"

"Yes."

"You've got to say over, *or I won't know that you've finished, over."*

"You will know that I've finished because I'll stop speaking. When there's no more sound coming out of the walkie-talkie, that's because the transmission is over."

Mr Barren takes a moment to work out whether what he's just said obeys protocol or not.

"Is that all you wanted to tell me? That I have to end everything with *over?*"

"Negative. Tango Oscar Romeo…"

"You know you can call me by my name?"

Mr Barren ignores him. *"Dignitaries and brand ambassadors have been escorted from the site but the visiting team are having trouble reversing their coach near exit C. There's been a mini-scooter collision near the pedestrian crossing, three dads and one of their daughters, four scooters in total, please investigate and advise, over."*

Tom doesn't answer this time. In the middle of the churning crowds, framed by two stationary DVs, he has seen a ghost.

"Tango Oscar Romeo, please respond. Tango Oscar..."

He turns the little knob on the top of the walkie-talkie to zero and Mr Barren's voice disappears.

The ghost looks lost and a little bemused. She's standing on the other side of the DV rank in a sweater, jeans and trainers. She's got a rucksack, too, which he recognises. It has a few more holes in it than the last time he saw it. When she bends down to dig something out of it, he notices a group of Year 12 boys filming her on a PAD. Tom can guess what they're up to. There are quite a few inexpensive apps that run on the PAD that can render a fully clothed man or woman completely naked and insert them into any number of "adult" situations. The impossibly beautiful Miss Munday gets the worst of it. She's on her second marriage and third nervous breakdown after all the starring roles she's had in the students' videos.

He walks in front of a spasming DV, triggering its pedestrian alarm but ignoring it. The group of creepy boys disperse. When she raises her head again, she sees him. That smile! His first thought is how lined her face is, around her lips, her forehead, the corners of her eyes, and this is followed very quickly by a worry about how old he must seem to her. It's like he's looked in a mirror for the first time in over a decade.

"Oh my God," he says.

"It's you!" Her voice is loud and cheerful and not at all ghostlike.

"Oh my *God*," he says again, and then eventually smiles. "Nowacki?"

"Hi Tom. Nice hat."

He quickly swipes the luminous cone from the top of his head, then smooths and ruffles his hair, then smooths it again.

"I don't normally wear this."

"Sure you don't."

"I'm not a traffic marshal."

"You look a lot like one."

"I mean I am right now, but that's not my job normally."

"Part-timer, huh?"

"Right."

"Probably a good thing." She surveys the mayhem in the parking area. "It doesn't look like you're very good at it."

She laughs, and it sounds like the first sincere laugh he's heard in years. His face feels very warm. He's probably falling in love again. What's she doing here? Does this count as cheating on Miss Potter?

"I didn't know you worked here," Alice says. "In fact, I don't think I know anything about you anymore."

"Me neither. I mean, I don't know anything about *you*." Although the other interpretation is also true.

"It's so nice to see you."

"Yes!"

There is a pause. It seems like they're both trying to assess whether it really is nice to see each other. The last time they saw each other was their graduation day, and fifteen years later they can instantly read all of the wasted time and missed opportunities of the intervening period in each other's faces. Maybe that's why she's here, Tom thinks, wildly. Maybe they can pick up where they left off.

"You teach English here?"

"Amongst other things. When I'm not directing traffic, of course."

"Good on you," she says. It sounds a little patronising, and Tom thinks, on the basis of that: no, he's not falling in love. "My brother's

187

teaching now at one of the big Samsung Academies. I think he hates it."

"It can be trying."

"How are things going? In general, I mean."

"I don't know. I've not decided yet. Give me another fifteen years."

She gives him a familiar, knowing smile. Maybe he does love her? Gosh, what a rollercoaster!

"How come you're here?" he asks. "Don't tell me you're thinking of sending your kids to NSA."

Tom clocked the lack of wedding ring at the same time as he was making a mental note of her wrinkles, but it's good to make sure.

"Kids!" Alice snorts. "No. I don't really know why I'm here. It's to do with work."

"What's work, these days?"

"I stayed at the museum. Remember my internship?"

"Oh yes." He doesn't remember.

"I'm with the BIA now. Institute of Archaeology. I got a message from one of the students here about something they'd found on the grounds. It's a bit stupid. It was probably a joke. But here I am."

She looks around the pick-up point. It's still gridlocked. The hot, red light from the NutriStart banners is doing nothing to keep people calm.

"What's going on?" she says. "Do you always finish this early?"

Tom's tiredness returns in a single hefty wave. "No. You've not picked a good time."

"What's happened?"

"Officially…" He reads from a press release, hastily disseminated after Small Paul's frenzy in the stadium. "'The NSA's fourth-round Inter Academy Football League match, sponsored by GerdEaze, fast-acting and long-lasting double-action relief for heartburn and reflux, was unfortunately cancelled due to the illness of a non-NSA-affiliated spectator. The incident was logged and dealt with in accordance with the NSA's Health and Safety handbook. The [insert name of event] will be rescheduled for a convenient time in the near future.'"

"And unofficially?"

"Something's making the kids ill. Really, very ill. I'm not supposed to tell you, but… Well, I just told you."

"Oh dear."

"I don't think they've quite grasped the seriousness of the situation. A few press releases aren't going to keep everything under wraps. All of this, it's way outside their usual protocol. I think they'll have to close the school tomorrow."

Alice slumps a little.

"Oh. Shucks. I was hoping to have a look around."

"Even if it was open, I doubt they'd let you go snooping. My security pass basically restricts me to my classroom and the common room. Everything else is out of bounds. And I *work* here."

He notices, as he's speaking, that she's lost eye-contact with him and is now looking over his shoulder. She's doing an odd combination of smiling and frowning.

"What?" he says.

"You're wanted."

Tom turns and sees Maggie. She's a picture of cheerful composure. She crosses the road without looking, nearly causing another DV pile up, dragging her school bag by its strap behind her.

"Sir!"

"Hello Maggie. You made it out alive, then."

Maggie screws up her face. "Eh?"

"I mean, you got out of the stadium okay."

"The stadium? I wasn't in the stadium. I was doing that *extra work* you set me." She taps the side of her nose.

"Ah. I see."

"And I reckon I've had a breakthrough."

"Good. Jolly good. Well, then, come and find me tomorrow morning, and we can go through it."

Alice Nowacki suddenly pipes up: "Oh don't postpone it on my account. I'm not hanging around here much longer."

"This your girlfriend, sir?" says Maggie. "Jesus, she looks like she'd eat you for breakfast."

Alice snorts with laughter. Tom shrinks into his high-visibility jacket like a tortoise.

"She's not my girlfriend, Maggie."

"You want to find a cupboard or something?"

"Maggie, that's not appropriate."

"Not for you two, I mean for me and—"

"That's enough."

"Please, do what you have to do," says Alice. "I'm going to come back tomorrow. On the off-chance this place is still open."

"Oh, it'll be open," says Maggie. "Always open for business, that's the NSA."

"Well. That's good news for me, if not for you." Alice turns to Tom. "Can I get your number?"

"Here we go, sir! She's into you!"

Tom ignores Maggie and holds out his PAD. Alice places hers on top of his, a strangely intimate gesture, he always thinks, to share their contact IDs.

"Great. What a treat to see you!" she says.

"You hear that, sir? A *treat*."

"Speak soon," says Tom.

Alice tightens her rucksack around her shoulders, waves, and sets off for the exit. The pair of them watch her go.

"Reckon you're in there, sir," says Maggie. "Reckon it's the vest and the trousers that did it."

"Hush. Come on, let's get inside."

He abandons his post at the DV parking bay and follows Maggie, still dragging her battered school bag by its shoulder strap, around the corner of the NSA building to a side entrance. He looks over his shoulder a couple of times, but Alice is lost in the crowds.

What are the chances! After such a long period of bachelor-hood it's unbelievable that he now has two women waiting upon him. Within the time it takes to cross the lower-school Recreational Area #1, he's already constructed the Tom–Alice–Miss Potter love triangle, envisaged first dates/birthday presents/Christmas presents/ Valentine's Days, worded exactly how he will break up with either/ both of them, then gotten anxious about the whole situation and decided it probably isn't worth the hassle.

"Where to, sir?" asks Maggie, holding the door for him.

He emerges from his daydream. "Auditorium."

"Really?"

"We can go under the seating."

"Did you get those mints?"

Oh God! Was that why Alice was standing so far away from him? He breathes onto the back of his hand and sniffs.

In the auditorium there's a solitary young woman scrubbing Small Paul's blood from the seats in the upper circle. She doesn't notice them enter the storeroom beneath the tiers, or she does notice and doesn't care.

"This is the best one yet," says Maggie in the darkness. "Better than a cupboard. Very roomy. Ow! Jesus!" She stumbles over something.

Tom turns on his PAD, and the blue light turns him and his marshal's jacket into a fluorescent beacon in the middle of nothingness. The space should be filled with scenery for school plays, costumes, props, instruments for the orchestra, but it's just a black void.

Maggie floats towards him as though through deep, still water, only her face visible by the light of the screen.

"What's the new discovery, then?" he asks.

"Not really a discovery. Confirmation."

"Of what?"

"What we said earlier. I got into the Sports Centre while the stupid football match was on. There's a way through the swimming pool to the viewing gallery."

"You're not allowed in the swimming pool."

"There's a way into the swimming pool through the canteen."

"You're not allowed in the canteen."

"So I stole Mr De Souza's ID card, big deal."

"…"

"Anyways, I found my way into the Sports Centre, to the viewing gallery, above the big clock. You know? So. All of the kids are laid out in these rows of bunks, with the nurses wandering around them. Some of them had been restrained."

"And? What did all this confirm?"

"I made a list." There's a rustling of paper. "A list of all the people I could see. Must be nearly a hundred now. And they're *all* eejits."

"What?"

"They're all the stupid ones, far as I can tell. Like we said. Look!"

She puts the balled-up paper into his hand, and for a moment her face disappears while he angles the screen's light down onto the list. Tom recognises about three quarters of the students on there. He'll have to cross-reference them with the MNet IPRs and medical histories to prove the theory conclusively, but for the time being, yes, they do all look like eejits.

"Doesn't look good, does it, sir? All of the Beta timetable lot. Maybe I'll be next."

"This is really useful, Maggie."

"You're welcome."

"I'll double-check these on the network."

"Right-o."

She's not moving.

"Anything else?"

"Well. How are you getting on with *my* extra task?"

"What's that?"

The girl's face becomes distorted and ghoulish in the blue glow.

"About changing timetables. You promised."

"Oh, Maggie, I'm sorry. I just haven't had time. I will ask. But I've been teaching, and we had the football match, and things just got away from me."

"Come on, sir." There's a seriousness in her voice that leaves him cold.

"First thing tomorrow, I'll send a message to the Director of Studies."

"That's brilliant. A message. I'm sure he'll get right on it."

"You don't have to be sarcastic with me, Maggie. I told you it wouldn't be easy."

"I'm starting to think you don't actually give the tiniest shit about me."

"What's that noise?"

He can hear something by the door, a rolling of wheels. Possibly a vacuum cleaner. Possibly a suitcase.

"Don't try to change the subject."

"I'm not, *listen.*"

193

The rattling stops, then continues, then stops again. Little blobs of shadow are moving along the crease of light under the storeroom door.

"You're pathetic, sir, you know that? I thought we had a deal. I'm not going to do your dirty work for you if you're going to wriggle out of what you promised."

"I didn't *promise* anything, Maggie."

But she's gone, melted into the void, and when she opens up the door to leave there's nobody outside, no vacuum cleaner, no wheeled suitcase. She slams it behind her, dislodging a shower of dust from the scaffolding above him.

He turns off his PAD and waits in absolute darkness for a few moments. When he leaves the storeroom the auditorium is still completely empty, save for the one cleaner doggedly scrubbing at Paul Winkler's seat. He goes past the EMM office without looking in – it'll be full of teachers, Darren Barren perhaps, or Miss Potter, whom he still feels he has betrayed in some way – and returns to his classroom.

Tom sets up his PAD on the desk but spends the best part of an hour staring at his own reflection in the window. He checks his breath twice more.

He wakes up, looks down, taps the central MNet icon. It winks and expands and offers him the search bar. He starts entering the names on Maggie's list, and their profiles are presents to him. Many of them he doesn't recognise at first, because the parents have paid to have their children's faces touched-up.

Along with their photos are historical Individual Performance Reviews and medical data. Maggie was dead right. Every one of them has a little red flag above their name to signify a Special Educational or Medical need – Asperger's, hyperactivity, dyslexia, dyspraxia, dysgraphia, dyspepsia, slow processing speeds, colour blindness, anxiety, hypertension, hyperextension, flat-footedness, oversized fingers, you name it. Their grades and performance reviews are uniformly poor.

Why any of this would make them more susceptible to illness, though, is beyond him. It's a pattern, but it isn't any kind of an explanation.

He's examining the end-of-year IPR graph for Shauna McFeat when he's made aware of something hovering outside the door, a pale, pink moon rising and setting in the little porthole. It bobs up, sees that Mr Rosen is staring at it, and sinks down again, muttering to itself. He goes and unlocks the door.

"What are you doing here, Gerald? School's over. You should be in the library or on your way home."

Gerald Liu nods. "Do you like computer games, Mr Rosen?"

"No, I don't. Is there something you want? You know it's rude to spy on people."

"I'm James Bond!"

Sometimes Tom thinks that Gerald Liu operates by some higher logic than other human beings. It takes him a moment to catch up with his non sequiturs. "You mean you *were* spying?"

The boy looks immensely pleased with himself. "Yes!"

Tom pauses to digest this.

"Have you been spying on me for a few weeks?"

"Yes!"

"Why?"

"If I help, I will not go back to Beijing."

"Help? Help who?"

Gerald shakes his head. All he says is: "I don't want to go back to Beijing."

"Gerald, *look* at me. Who has been asking you to spy on me? Was it one of the other teachers? Was it the Headmaster?"

"No, no. I apologise, Mr Rosen." His face takes on a look of stern self-reproach, his mouth almost disappearing completely between his cheeks. "Very sorry to interrupt."

"Gerald. Tell me. You won't be in trouble."

"I don't want to go back to Beijing. I have many new friends here. We are friends. Very sorry, Mr Rosen."

"*Gerald.*"

"Very sorry. Very, very sorry."

He nods again and grabs the handle of his suitcase. Tom snatches at his arm as he tries to get away, and Gerald tugs and grunts a couple of times before Tom realises that he's a *teacher* and this is a *kid* and he's way, way out of line here. Before he comes to his senses Gerald tears himself free and runs off down the corridor. He's not entirely sure, but under the sound of the suitcase's wheels he thinks Gerald might be sobbing.

Tom goes back to his chair and closes his eyes. He needs to go to sleep, maybe forever.

He's about to call off his drink with Miss Potter when a message appears in his inbox. It's from the Deputy Head.

Dear Colleagues,

Please note that in spite of the disruption to the GerdEaze Inter Academy League match, the NSA remains open as usual tomorrow. Please continue to plan your lessons and upload your performance reviews according to your individual timetables.

Investigations are under way to apprehend the intruder, and whilst we deeply regret the injury and inconvenience caused, we also feel it has been an important demonstration of the need for heightened security on the NSA site and a validation of the ongoing construction work around the Academy.

*I would also like to take this opportunity to remind you that the trial
of the new internal security systems will take place at 1200hrs tomorrow,
and you must bring and display your lanyards to allow a fair test of the
system's functionality.*

Regards

RMT

Tom laughs. Clever, clever. He'll grant Tooley that much.

He starts to compose a message to Miss Potter again. The PAD
pings a second time as another missive arrives from Mr Tooley. This
one's directed specifically at him.

Dear Mr Rosen,

*Please note that you have failed to comply with the terms of your proba-
tion, and your contract with NSA will be terminated with immediate effect.*

*You will be able to return to the Academy tomorrow to collect your
property and to conduct your exit interview with RMT, but you are
required to be off-site before 1200hrs. At this time, the new security
network will no longer recognise you as a NutriStart employee.*

Thank you for all you have done for the school.

Regards

RMT

He doesn't laugh this time.

18.30

THE MENINISTS of Bromley and Chislehurst, now down to three
members, are standing around a Driverless Vehicle in Mr_Red_Pill's

darkened garage. One of them is poking around in the glove compartment. The other has a can of spray paint and is stencilling an insignia onto the side of the car. He steps back and folds his arms.

"What do you think of that?" he says.

The man looking around the passenger seat withdraws his head and comes around the side.

"It's alright."

The man with the spray paint nods in satisfaction, and coughs. The other one starts coughing as well. The garage is tiny, and the smell of paint fumes is overwhelming. When Mr_Red_Pill finally joins them they are both still doubled over, heaving into their fists. He swings the door to the kitchen back and forth, back and forth, to try and clear the air.

"Where is everyone?" he asks, once the coughing fit is under control.

"I don't know."

"Cold feet, I guess."

"I don't think they like meeting Out of World."

"Has anyone heard from Captain Gumbo?" says Mr_Red_Pill. "At all?"

They shake their heads.

"I think," says the one with the spray can, "he had his account suspended. I haven't seen him on Alpha for ages. Probably because of some of the stuff he was posting on our Hub."

Mr_Red_Pill tuts. "Another victory for free speech!" he says.

The three of them stand around the car, hands on hips, not saying anything. Mr_Red_Pill examines the insignia on the rear window. Some of the paint has been sprayed on too thickly and is starting to dribble down the glass. He does his best to tidy it up with his finger.

"Well, this is a problem."

"Why?"

"Turns out Saleem sent the nitro to him. Said it would be safer."

"Does the Captain know?"

"I don't know."

"What now, then?"

Mr_Red_Pill sighs and wipes his finger on his trousers.

"I'll have to talk with Saleem again," he says. "Get him to deliver some more of the stuff."

"*More?*"

"Yes, more!"

"Does that mean we have to… pay again?"

"Yes, obviously."

"I'm not sure I can afford that."

"What do you want me to do about that?" Mr_Red_Pill shouts. "Listen. It's November the 19th *this Friday*, and all we currently have is a car with a broken GPS, and no explosives. So, yes, we'll have to pay Saleem again, and this time I'll go and pick up the stuff in person, if I have to."

Silence again. There's the sound of someone using a food processor in the kitchen adjacent to the garage.

"And we're still going for the school?"

"Yes. That's the whole *point*."

"What's the point?"

"They're feminist, liberal propaganda machines! You read what Captain Gumbo said."

"It's true," says the one with the spray paint. "My son had to go to a seminar on Gender Neutral Content Generation a few weeks back."

"But… I mean… they are children."

"That's *also* the point," says Mr_Red_Pill. "No one cares if you blow up adults anymore."

"I just feel like we could make a similar gesture In World."

"*Gesture*? We're not going to achieve equality through *gestures*, my friend. I'm starting to wonder whether your heart is really in this. What's your name again?"

"Richard."

"*Richard.*"

There's a shout from inside the house, summoning all three of them to dinner. Mr_Red_Pill starts salivating – his mum promised them macaroni and cheese tonight.

"Don't think I'm done with you," he says. "You need some *serious* educating, Richard."

22.45

JUST AS Alice is about to climb into bed, her PAD screen illuminates. She thinks – hopes – it's a message from Henry, but no such luck. It's from Tom Rosen. He's asking her to come and visit him.

She sighs as she pulls on her cold jeans. She doesn't know what is more predictable, the message itself or her response to it.

WEDNESDAY

07.20

AT A CERTAIN altitude the lush, tropical forest thins out and the terrain becomes unexpectedly alpine. Gabriel stops and looks back the way he's come, surveying the empire he's built along the shoreline. The complex of villas has grown tenfold and now looks part military installation, part theme park, with machine-gun nests and surface-to-air missiles erected among the log flumes and rollercoasters.

The sunset is still fixed in the sky, an alternating palette of reds and golds and violets. Beneath it the beach is crowded with people. After he got bored of all the women, Gabriel created some alien-type enemy characters to play against, but within minutes of them arriving the women were already making amorous advances, and the alien-type enemies were happily accepting them, and every-where Gabriel went there were aliens and tiki girls flirting with each other in the bushes. Now the beach has the feeling of a party he hasn't been invited to, so he's taken the hint and headed inland. The algorithm is still half-heartedly trying to keep up and places a different iteration of a woman in front of him every few hundred paces.

Somewhere in the foothills of his domain he encounters the faceless man. Gabriel can't quite work out when he last saw him, whether it was minutes or days ago. The sunset seems to have ended time altogether. He similarly can't remember the last time he ate or drank anything, or went to the toilet. And sleep? Has he slept? He raided the drinks cabinet in his beach house, he remembers. Didn't he have a nap after that?

"How are we doing, Gabriel?" says the faceless man.

"I'm alright."

"Something wrong?"

"No."

"Your serotonin is low."

"My what?"

The man pauses. "We just noticed that you're leaving the area. Are you unhappy with your experience?"

"I just want to explore. It's getting crowded down there."

"Yes, we saw. Love what you've done with it, incidentally."

"I'm bored, too."

"Interesting."

"What's interesting?"

"That you've already had enough of this place. Interesting, but not unexpected."

Gabriel looks back at the bodies swarming on the beach. He has the vague memory of watching the Recreational Spaces of the NSA, from up in The Guild's turret. He was a member, briefly, until they found out what he'd done to the school's network.

"I think your algorithm's broken," he says.

"How's that?"

"Because I hate talking to you, but you keep coming back."

"Aha. I'm afraid I need to operate independently of the Game, Gabriel."

"Then it's not a fair test of the system, is it?"

There's a moment of silence. A girl and her tentacled lover appear from the undergrowth looking embarrassed.

"I wonder if we need to change environments. Perhaps this wasn't the right one for you. How about we mix things up a bit?"

"Do I have a choice?"

"Gabriel, this whole *place* is your choice!"

8.01

MARIA DA SANTOS MARTINEZ has had a frustrating morning. She was up out of her bunk under the ventilation tower at 5.30 a.m. to sweep and polish corridors G1–6, only to find that they were already full of men in overalls, nicer overalls than hers, black and close-fitting, who were carrying laptops and spools of wire and suitcases of expensive precision tools. They'd taken the digital screens off the walls and removed the black orb-shaped cameras from the ceiling and were poking around inside them. She knows that something important is happening at midday, and her supervisor keeps telling her to put a "lamb yard" around her neck, but whatever they were up to seriously disrupted her routine, and she had to mark all areas as "incomplete" on her progress form. After that she was supposed to clean the male and female staff toilets, but one of the stalls was locked, and she knocked politely three times before its occupant furiously opened the door, eyes red and raw, some kind of powdery narcotic smeared around her lips and nostrils. Again, she had to mark the section as incomplete, all of which will come back to haunt her in her Performance Review on Friday. At 7.30 a.m. she was supposed to have her break, but it so happened that Student Brand Ambassador Jordan Haynes, who seems to have more authority than a lot of the staff despite still being a pupil, had spilled some juice in his DV on the journey to school, and Maria was summoned to the car park to clean and fumigate the vehicle immediately.

Now, her breaktime fully squandered, she has to attend the compulsory Wednesday Wellness seminars, which are for all the support staff, in which they extol the virtues of probiotic diet management, mindfulness and meditation, the Power of Yes, etc., whilst never addressing more pertinent issues, such as the lack of natural light in the sleeping areas and the toxicity of the cleaning products that's turning a lot of Maria's colleagues' skin a ghastly shade of yellow.

They're sitting in rows on cold, foldable metal chairs in the support staff common room, listening to a man in a red baseball cap talking about the Law of Positive Attraction. She doesn't understand most of it. There's a slideshow behind him which features a homeless man, then a man in a smart suit holding lots of cash, then a rainbow, then a circle with "YOU" written in it, with lots of arrows pointing inwards to emphasise its centrality to the message. The presenter's face is a permanent waxy grin, and he keeps winking at one of the dishwashers in the front row, a wiry and tattooed Hungarian man who, Maria knows for a fact, killed someone in the old country.

"Remember in week six when we talked about mindsets?" says the man.

A cartoon brain appears on the screen, making what looks to Maria like a "shrug" gesture. The sound of the word "mindset" is familiar to her, but she doesn't know what it means, any more than she did in week six.

"The fact is—" the waxy man laughs "—a lot of our *negative* mindsets appear *positive* at first glance! They're comfortable, they're reassuring! Right?"

He shows a picture of a lamb on one slide, and then on the next a wolf climbing out of a sheep costume.

"We need to look *closely* at our mindsets to work out if an *unhelpful* thought pattern is actually *disguised* as a helpful one. See?"

She can see, and the image is faintly disturbing. Maria once went to visit her grandfather and saw a wolf, not a proper wolf but a *lobo-*

guará, tearing their chicken coop to pieces. She can still remember the scent of the animal. That was a very long time ago, now; a different life.

While she's reminiscing, the wax man opens a plastic tub and starts distributing brightly coloured vests to the room.

"Now," he says, his grin tightening around his teeth even further, "let's get some blood pumping around your bodies! Right? On your feet!"

The chairs scrape and clang as everyone drags themselves upright.

"We're going to play a little game! Reds, you're going to play *bad mindsets*." He does a comical frowny face. "Greens, you're going to be *good mindsets*. We're going to see how you all interact! Now, all of you take a bib."

The last syllable suddenly raises the temperature of Maria's blood. That word, that word…

She left the boy in the Dungeons. She waited and waited at the door, but after an hour they notified her on her PAD that she was needed in the stadium as a matter of urgency, and she'd gone to the changing rooms to mop up something that looked suspiciously like blood – not suspicious, actually, not nowadays, since she seemed to be cleaning up bodily fluids all the time – and forgotten all about the kid.

He'd be alright, wouldn't he? The door to the Dungeons was an old one; it probably wasn't on the same timed, automatic locking system as the newer parts of the school.

What if it was? What if he was still down there?

Maria reassures herself: kids are resourceful. He'll be fine.

What if he tells his teachers I locked him in? What if he tells his parents? She has a son of her own, in Retail College, who's already ashamed enough of his mother. Fired from a cleaning job!

She thinks about running out of the seminar now to look for him, but that'll only land her in more trouble. Someone hands her a green bib and she forces herself, despite her thumping heart, to listen extra carefully to the instructions of the exercise.

8.10

TOM ROSEN stumbles out of the back of the DV like he's drunk, although as far as Alice is aware he's ingested nothing but ProSustain and ice cream wafers for the last twelve hours.

He leads her to the NSA's main entrance, walking a few feet ahead, and the bright morning sunlight brings every crease and stain on his clothes into sharp relief. The years have not been kind to him. He probably hasn't been kind to himself. She hasn't quite made up her mind whether she feels sorry for him or not.

On the steps beneath the giant revolving glass door, he stops and gobbles down another couple of caffeine pills.

"I'm not sure you should keep taking those," she says.

"I've got to. I need to be on the absolute top of my game for this exit interview with Tooley. He's not going to know what's hit him."

"He'll know what's hit him if you *actually* hit him."

"Damn straight!"

"I really think you should take a moment."

"Absolutely no way. Come on. Cross your fingers that I can get you in on my security pass."

"What if you can't?"

"You'll have to sit tight and I'll go and get Alex myself. See if I can get Miss Potter to smuggle him out of his lessons."

At about midnight the previous night, after listening to him bewail his fate and the NSA's fate and the fate of the world in general, she finally told him about the message she'd received from Alex Pepys and immediately regretted it. By then Tom was in a feverish state and got very excited at the mention of the boy; he said he was also looking for the very same child, that he might have some valuable information regarding the unpleasantness at the school; then he latched onto the Druid curse narrative and started forming all kinds of bizarre conspiracy theories about the school's management, and the illness among the kids, and the resulting cover-up, none of which made any sense to Alice.

For her own part, she'd like to just see the artefacts and get away as soon as possible. Tom is proving difficult to be around. She also needs to make things up to Henry, whose messages are becoming increasingly terse and dismissive.

The NSA's main entrance looks like a futuristic portcullis, all clad in sheets of opaque, blue glass. Beyond the revolving door, the foyer is hospital-white and seems to have no edges or seams, like the building was ejected whole from a 3D printer. The reception desk is monolithic. Behind it are three receptionists, one of whom has obviously been crying very recently, blackcurrant-coloured trails of mascara dribbling down both cheeks. Tom picks the one in the middle.

"Good morning, Mr Rosen," she says. Alice finds this strange, a bit like when her parents referred to each other as "Mum" and "Dad". Strange and sad, too, that they wouldn't use each other's real names. "Are you here for your exit interview?"

Tom twitches. "You know about that?"

"Yes. There's a note on your profile here. Your security pass will be valid until midday, then you'll have to be off-site. Okay?" She beams at him.

"Okay." He drums on the top of the desk. "Listen, Jenny—"

"Gilly."

"Your name tag says 'Jenny'."

The receptionist checks it, the pin tugging on her lapel.

"Oh yes, Jenny," she says. "That's me."

"Jenny, I don't suppose I could have a visitor pass for the morning, could I? I have a friend here who's… thinking of sending her son to the school."

"Does she have an appointment for a tour?"

"No," says Alice.

Tom rolls his eyes. She can't tell if this is just another symptom of too much caffeine in his system.

"I'm afraid you have to book ahead for an OW tour of the school, and they take place at weekends," she says, tapping at the monitor in front of her. "Next available tour will be in March of next year."

"Can't I just let her have a look around?" asks Tom, his voice tissue-paper thin.

"I can't give her a lanyard without an appointment, and I can't give her an appointment without background checks. I could start the checks now, if you want?"

"Don't worry about it," says Alice.

"Oh dear," says Jenny/Gilly, fingers fluttering over the touchscreen. "You're Alice Nowacki?"

"Yes."

"The data they're giving us on your salary doesn't seem to match up with NSA minimum requirements."

"You know what my salary is?" says Alice.

"You're *Doctor* Alice Nowacki?"

"Yes."

210

"As I say, minimum salary is one of the first criteria for admission, and it looks like your application wouldn't be accepted for the next two financial years."

"Yes, but how—"

"It recognises your face," interjects Tom. He rubs his cheeks and opens his mouth like a cat yawning. "How about that? It's the only reason she knows who I am. I've never seen Jenny or Gilly before in my life. Never seen any of these three. They change them about once a week."

One of the other receptionists starts weeping again, and Jenny/Gilly beams again.

"I think I should go," says Alice.

"*No*," says Tom. He whirls around and leans over the desk on his elbows, face a little too close to the receptionist's. "Please, just let her through, for half an hour."

"I can't do that, Mr Rosen. She's welcome to look around our In World prospectus, though – it's identical in design and facilities to the real NSA building, and we've populated it with some of our best students' profiles. For the full immersive experience we recommend you experience the prospectus in VR, or you can use one of the visitor PADs." She points to the side of the desk, where there are five devices displayed on rotating stands that look like bar stools.

"She doesn't want to see the In World version," says Tom, "she wants to look around the actual place, here and now."

"Tom, it's fine."

"If you have any questions, you can just ask Johnson."

"I *hate* Johnson!"

Tom snatches one of the PADs from its home, snapping the charging cable, and hurls it at the wall-sized screen behind the receptionists. One of its illuminated panels cracks and goes dark, decapitating the picture of Brand Ambassador Jordan Haynes that's being displayed. The third receptionist, a very tall, very young man, also starts to cry.

"Can we have one of the cleaning team and a technician to main reception, please?" says Jenny/Gilly, to no one in particular.

"Tom!" says Alice. She grabs his forearm, which is vibrating like he's sitting on top of a washing machine. "Calm down. This is not a problem."

"I'll call Mr Tooley," says the receptionist. "He's our Parent Liaison Officer."

Alice takes Tom to the corner sofa, but he wrestles himself free, tearing his jacket at the shoulder.

"Don't call Tooley."

"It's no trouble," says Jenny/Gilly, and then immediately: "Hello, Mr Tooley? We have a prospective parent at reception, and Mr Rosen is here for his exit interview."

"*No.*" Tom tries the automatic doors to the left and right of the reception desk, but they don't open. The sensor makes a sad little *bloop* when he waves his pass in front of it.

"Tom!"

Alice stands paralysed in the middle of the foyer, between the frantic Tom Rosen and the sobbing receptionists, lit by the screen that now reads "*Go d is good!*" because of the broken panel.

She starts for the exit, but as she's hoisting her rucksack onto one shoulder an unimaginably small man appears behind her, apparently without using any of the doors. There's something very odd about his dimensions, as though he's not *meant* to be small: it's like he used to be a normal-sized man but he's been shrunk in a washing machine. He appraises the situation and prioritises Alice, coming forward with his creepy doll-like hand extended.

"Ms Nowacki? Good morning. I'm Mr Tooley. You have some questions about salary criteria, I'm told?"

There's a clinking sound as Tom tries to use his PAD to lever the doors apart.

"Not really, I was actually just wondering if I could have a quick look around the school."

"I'm afraid that—"

Tom swears, hisses, and sucks on his finger.

"—you'll need to—"

Tom hurls himself shoulder first into the door, and the glass booms like the skin of a drum.

"I'm sorry, Ms Nowacki, would you excuse me for a moment? Perhaps have a look at our In World prospectus—" he gestures to the row of PADs, notices the damage and convulses slightly "—while you're waiting? I just need a quick word with one of our staff, and then I'll come back to talk you through our fee options."

Tom is now speaking very quickly to the tall, male receptionist, attempting to convince him to hand over his security pass. Even from where she's standing, Alice can see the dry fizz of spittle exploding from Tom's lips.

"Please, don't worry, I can see you're busy. I'll just come back another time."

"Please take a seat," says Mr Tooley.

"It's fine."

"Please take a seat."

She perches on the arm of the sofa, and Mr Tooley takes a moment to decide whether this is satisfactory or not. Then he nods, wheels around, and goes to collect Tom from the reception desk.

"Good morning, Mr Rosen."

"He's here for an exit interview," says Jenny/Gilly helpfully.

"Thank you, Jenny."

Tom straightens up, and Alice watches him pop two more Pro-Sustain into his quivering mouth. He adjusts the frayed sleeve of his jacket.

"If you'd like to accompany me to my office, Mr Rosen."

"You're the worst," says Tom.

"This way, please."

"Just the worst."

"Please refrain from giving feedback until the interview is under way."

"I've got some questions for *you*, Tooley, actually."

"Rest assured that the interview will be dialogue-modelled. This way, please."

"Don't touch me."

Mr Tooley tries to guide Tom to the door by the elbow, but Tom jerks his elbow away and the torn seam gapes like a fish's mouth.

"Sorry, Alice," he calls over to her. "I won't be long. Wait here."

The automatic doors *bleep* and sigh and he disappears through them, followed by Mr Tooley.

Alice Nowacki sits a moment longer on the arm of the sofa. She feels punch-drunk. What an excruciatingly unhappy place.

Her worry is that once Tom has been dismissed, he'll become attached to her. He'll see her as some serendipitous lifeline provided by the universe. Everything falling into place. That would be just like him. She should leave while she has the chance, but then she imagines returning to the museum empty-handed, apologising to Henry, skulking back to her apartment. The evening plays out before her. Out comes the Jelly Cola multipack, on goes the headset, another night in paradise, oh boy!

She picks up her rucksack and heads for the revolving door.

"I'll be back shortly," she says to Jenny/Gilly.

"Thank you so much!" say all three receptionists in miserable chorus.

8.30

PEEPSY IS ROUSED by the sound of an elevator. He has no idea what time it is because there are no windows and because no one has yet turned off the basement's grimy, casino-ish strip lighting. He's hungry and thirsty and badly needs the toilet.

At some point overnight it seems his nose stopped bleeding, but all of the tubes that normally keep his head working are blocked and swollen. There's a thin crust of blood over his face that he can feel cracking and flaking when he moves his jaw, and the floor around him is a dark, dusty red-brown.

Somewhere behind the three gigantic piles of garbage the elevator clangs to a halt, and he can hear the tramp of feet. He opens his eyes and gets up, his shirt and trousers stiff and creaking. He stumbles about for a bit and then hides himself behind a golf-buggy-type cleaning vehicle in the corner of the room. Only once he's there does he realise he's left his rucksack and its contents in the middle of the floor.

About twenty support staff emerge from around the corner and crawl like ants over the heaps, sifting and sorting and removing erroneous items. No one talks. They are silent, purposeful, like scavengers on a battlefield.

Peepsy watches from behind the cleaning-buggy's bonnet. Twice in their shift a loud buzzer sounds, accompanied by a red light, signifying that one of the huge, colonic pipes overhead is about to make a new deposit. The support staff scuttle away to safety and there follows the Russian roulette of waiting to see what will come raining down on them. Both times it's food: mostly milk and oatmeal and uneaten fruit. Breakfast stuff, so the school day must have started, Peepsy thinks. He can't help feeling that the men working on the pile of food waste have a much ickier job than those who are sorting the recyclables and electronics, and he wonders if there's a separate pay scale to reflect this.

After about half an hour of drudgery, one of them spots the rucksack near the incinerator and picks it up. The man – he looks like he could be Kiran's dad – deals with it as efficiently as he would anything else. He unzips the bag, puts Peepsy's PAD into the container of electronics, throws the skull and the bones – a *human* skull and bones, which doesn't seem to bother or surprise him in any way – into the "organic/compostable waste" pile, and the bag itself goes into "mixed unrecyclables". Then he goes back to raking through the main heap.

It soon becomes clear that their shift isn't going to end anytime soon. Peepsy looks on despondently as the buzzer sounds again three times, and each time another hefty bolus of old food is sluiced on top of the artefacts. He's not sure if that's better or worse than putting them in an incinerator, but it's probably not good news from the point of view of the restless dead. The buzzer goes for a fourth time, on comes the light, and something that looks like a dialysis machine comes hurtling out of the "non-recyclable" pipe and nearly crushes two of the sorters.

While he's watching, Peepsy becomes aware of a presence at his shoulder that definitely isn't one of the support staff. His tinnitus returns. He covers his ears and crawls under the buggy.

8.40

BEHIND MR TOOLEY'S monumental desk there is a mechanical rodeo bull, its body saddled and dismembered and impaled on a pair of steel pistons. Its head has a pair of painted-on "crazy" eyes, a pink lolling tongue and two very straight horns that you can use as handlebars. Tom has never seen it before, and there are bits of foam and cardboard packaging strewn around it, suggesting that it's only been delivered very recently. A gift.

Mr Tooley really, really likes cowboys. Every year the NSA has a fundraising "dress-down" day, and every year the Deputy Headmaster has come in wearing the full get-up: Stetson, waistcoat, bandolier, chaps, spurred boots, everything. It's not a joke, because Mr Tooley doesn't like jokes and certainly wouldn't turn himself into one. Nobody laughs, nobody says a word, as he clanks heavily around the corridors in all his gear. When he reprimands the students, his fingers tickle the handle of his revolver, which may or may not be fake.

So the rodeo bull is not totally out of character. But its presence in the room throws Tom off his stride when he is admitted through the door, and his stride is already erratic given how overcaffeinated he is.

"What's that doing here?" he says.

The DHM ignores him, settles into his executive chair and launches himself above Tom's eye-line. "Shall we get this underway?"

"A present to yourself?"

"I notice you haven't filled out the self-assessment form that was sent to you."

"Or from an admirer?"

"So this will take slightly longer than usual."

"Can I have a go?"

"Mr Rosen."

Tom finally looks Mr Tooley in the face. "Yes."

"Perhaps you don't understand how serious the situation is."

"No, I understand."

"Then you understand that it is in your interests to respect the process."

"The process?"

"Yes."

"The *process*."

His mouth is incredibly dry, his spit like dust as it showers the desk in front of him. He runs his tongue over his teeth. They're furry, and taste sour. His breath must be truly abominable.

Mr Tooley nods. "Yes."

"That's all this place is, isn't it? Process."

"Mr Rosen, I have a meeting with a very important vlogger in twenty minutes, so I'd encourage you to make the most of this opportunity while you can. I will not be postponing the meeting on your account."

"What's the meeting for? To tell them that everything at NSA is totally fine? Business as usual, right? Will you be showing them the bloodstains in room 8? Or in the auditorium? Are you going to give them a tour of the Sports Centre, get some footage of the students you've locked in there?"

"Mr Rosen."

"*What*."

"I will be the first to admit that the current situation at NSA 6 is unprecedented, but we are simply following all the protocols detailed in the Safeguarding and Welfare section of the School Development Plan. If you think it should be handled differently, you are welcome to feed that back – but you really should have made your voice heard during the consultation phase."

"Why is it only the ones with low test scores?"

"Mr Rosen."

"Where's Carla?"

"Carla had to be withdrawn from school."

"Withdrawn to where?"

"Once a student has been removed from our database, I'm afraid we no longer have a right to know their whereabouts or circumstances. Our duty of care ends at the school gates."

"You're totally fine with all this, aren't you?"

"I'm not sure I understand what you mean."

"This all makes sense to you?"

"The School Development Plan makes sense, yes. It was created in consultation with several internationally renowned pedagogy strategists, at some expense, so I would have hoped that it made sense, at the very least." His smile makes a wet sound, like an amphibious eye opening and closing.

Tom can see where all of this is heading. It occurs to him that the matter of *truth* is really just a matter of *stamina*, i.e. who can maintain one's assertions the longest, until all opposition is simply too tired to challenge them. If he'd ever spoken to Gabriel Bäcker about this, he would have realised they had a lot to talk about.

Tom is already too tired. There is nothing to be won here.

"Shall we just get this interview done, and I can get on with packing my stuff up?"

"That is what I have been suggesting, Mr Rosen."

He tries to slump in the bucket chair, but when he's not sitting bolt upright its rigid, high sides force him to curl up and put pressure on his heart and other organs.

219

"Well. Go on. Fire away," he says, straightening himself out.

"Good. I'll read you a series of statements, which are designed to help you reflect upon your career, and upon the school itself. To each statement you'll be required to give a response out of sixty, with zero meaning strongly disagree, and sixty meaning strongly agree."

"Why is it out of sixty? Why not ten?"

"Sixty is the scale that gives the most meaningful responses, we have found."

"How many questions are there?"

"Ninety-five."

"In twenty minutes?"

"In sixteen minutes, now."

Tom rubs his eyes and looks at the mechanical bull again. What the hell is it doing here?

"Fine."

"Statement one: NutriStart has a clearly defined set of brand values that have been communicated effectively, and that prepare students for life beyond the school."

A pause.

"There are at least three different statements there," says Rosen.

"Please just give a response out of sixty, with zero meaning strongly disagree, and sixty meaning—"

"Sixty."

"Sixty? Are you sure?"

"Sixty."

"Alright. Statement number two: What is more important to you, NutriStart products, or NutriStart brand ethos?"

"That's not a statement, that's a question."

"Please just give a response out of sixty."

"Sixty."

"Sixty? Are you sure?"

"You know, we're going to waste a lot of time if you repeat my answers and ask me if I'm sure every time."

"Statement number three—"

"We're also going to waste a lot of time if you say 'statement number whatever' before every single statement."

An intercom suddenly sounds on Mr Tooley's desk. He looks at Tom for a moment, his mouth open. His chair releases a jet of compressed air, and he descends about a foot to answer the call.

"What is it, Jenny?"

"Good morning, Mr Tooley," says Jenny/Gilly's voice, even though she's only just seen him in reception. "Just to say, the prospective parent has left the building and won't be requiring a meeting with you."

"Left the building?"

Left the building? thinks Tom with a jolt, but then he remembers he has Alice's contact ID now, and she left some things in his flat, so she can't go far.

"Where did she go?" says Mr Tooley. "Did you try and stop her?"

"She went out to the pick-up point, Mr Tooley. Shall I go and fetch her back?"

"No, thank you, Jenny. Let me try and talk to her."

Another hiss and the chair returns to floor level. Mr Tooley almost disappears completely behind the desk. When he emerges from around the corner he hands Tom the PAD he's been using.

"Please stay here and complete the questionnaire. I will come back for the results in twelve minutes. Give your answers as much thought as you can, so we can improve the NSA experience for future staff and students."

Tom takes it without replying.

"Once the questionnaire is complete you'll have to stay in the room until our legal team arrive."

"Legal team?"

"Yes, they want to ask you some questions about your relationship with Maggie O'Brien."

"With *Maggie*?"

"Yes."

"Why? What relationship?"

"That's what we need to clarify."

"When were you going to tell me about all this?"

"We felt it was rather too sensitive a topic to discuss over AIM."

"Sensitive?"

"Yes."

"Who's said anything about me and Maggie? That's horseshit."

"We have two witnesses."

"I thought I'd just forgotten to fill out another form or something. I thought that was why I'd failed my probation. Maggie? Me and Maggie? Come on!"

"Please complete the questionnaire, and I will be back shortly."

Mr Tooley leaves his office and locks the door behind him.

8.50

"I'M GOING to use up three of my Far Sight points, and I'll play my Mage Storm against your Cavalry Charge."

"You can't play Mage Storm, you haven't built up enough adrenaline points."

"You don't need adrenaline points to cast Mage Storm. It's an active spell, if you've got a necromancer in your deck."

"I think we need to check the codex."

"I've *read* the codex. It's an active spell that can be cast at any time in the magic phase, regardless of adrenaline or health stats."

"Then how come you wouldn't let me cast Command Undead last round?"

"Because that's a scroll, not an active spell. Two adrenaline points and five intelligence points required to cast."

"Are you sure?"

"Um, do plague warriors worship the Great Gnarl?"

Laughter all round.

"Yes, I'm sure. Those are the minimum stats, and you don't got 'em, my friend."

"I'd still like to read the codex myself."

"Should someone check on the migration?"

"Wise."

"Don't start the next phase without me."

Arturius Ironbound, real name Anne Brant, age forty-eight, husband, two children, exits the *Mage Wars* arena and allows Alpha Omega to play her the declimatisation cut-scene, which lasts for exactly two minutes thirty-five seconds, until it's safe for her to remove her headset. Even after this, the ICT offices still look and sound blurry and indistinct, like she's viewing everything from the bottom of a swimming pool. She leaves the other members of the Guild in the darkness of the break-out room and returns to her workstation. Her shoulders are aching from her custom-made Shadow Knight costume. She didn't realise how heavy real metal armour would be when she ordered it In World, and she can't change out of it now because she's got nothing else to wear.

Her PAD is lying face-up on her desk, surrounded by cans of energy drink and a pot of marshmallow fluff with a spoon sticking out of it. She unlocks the device, and the screen is illuminated with a green status bar and a flashing triangle with an exclamation mark inside it.

Network mapping complete, it says. *Begin system migration?*

Anne removes a gauntlet and taps "Okay". Another exclamation mark appears.

Existing security software will be disabled during migration period. Proceed?

Tap tap. "Okay."

Starting transfer.

As soon as she puts the PAD back down amongst the detritus of her breakfast she can hear the click of doors unlocking around the ICT centre. Everyone knows that this has to happen before the new system can go online at midday, but that doesn't make the sound any less disconcerting.

She goes back to the break-out room and nestles down into the leather beanbag that still retains the concave imprint of her armoured backside. It's good to take the weight of the costume off her feet. The short walk to the workstations has left her out of breath.

She puts on her headset and returns to her fellow players, who are waiting patiently in the *Mage Wars* arena. She scans the cards in her deck.

"Welcome back, Arturius. How's it looking?"

"All fine. Migration's started, and the old system's offline."

"Yikes."

"It's fine, it'll only be a couple of minutes. If that."

"Would you care to move on to the magic phase?"

"Does the Vampire Brood-lord need a suntan?"

Everyone laughs again. Anne couldn't be happier with her job.

FW: Autocue for Rian/Jin Ae
[APPROVED, DO NOT EDIT]

(I know you don't need me to tell you this, but make sure you study in advance for cadence, pacing, colloquialisms, etc. Long pause = 4.5 seconds, short pause = 2 seconds. Enjoy the adulation!!)

Thank you, thank you. [Short pause] Wow. That's very kind of you. [Short pause] Wow. [Short pause] Thank you. [Long pause] Thank you so much for coming to our home, and showing your support, and drinking all of our booze. [Long pause for laughter] No, seriously, we'll be taking this out of your pay cheques, so steady on there, Jorge. [Short pause for laughter] Jin Ae has a few words to say to you all as well, and she will no doubt be infinitely more articulate and interesting than me, so I'll keep this short. As you all know, this... well, what can we call it? Partnership? Friendship? Love affair? [Short pause for laughter] Somebody said the other day that we should call it a "triumvirate", and I'll admit I had to look up the word "triumvirate". I quite like it, although I think historically triumvirates aren't very successful and usually come to some horribly violent end... [Short pause for laughter] Anyway. As I was saying, you all know that this triumvirate has been a long time coming. Some of you at the back have been presiding over it since the beginning – Kim, Jorge, couple of others – and you've watched this thing come together over the course of, what, a decade? And now, here we are. The deed is done.

You know, when I first started designing games I always knew they could, and should, be about more than just entertainment. I think any artist, novelists, screenwriter, whatever, agonises over the same question: just how *useful* is their work? What are the responsibilities of art in terms of entertainment on the one hand, and didacticism on the other? Do we, as artists, have any loyalties to anything besides diverting our audience for an hour? Or ten, or twenty, in the case of Alpha. [Short pause for laughter] Well, I've always felt that games should be fun, but that they are capable of doing so much more than that. That they could *help* people, that they could be a positive, progressive force in the world.

We always knew – me and Jin Ae – that Alpha had enormous potential to improve lives, and there was a moment around about the 500-million-player mark when it really hit me, hit us, just how privileged we were to be helping so many people. Now we're looking at 6 billion people whose lives are enriched daily by the ability to go In World and live out whatever fantasy they could possibly imagine. [Long pause for applause] And then, I guess, there was this kind of brutal come-down [Short pause for laughter] when I realised that what we were doing was only ever a quick fix, like, sticking a band-aid over unhappiness. Because, guess what, people have to leave Alpha Omega occasionally – yeah, it's true [Short pause for laughter] – and once they're Out of World they have all the same problems they had when they went in.

And I was thinking hard about this, about how to make Alpha's service more meaningful – more profound, you could say – when Jared got in touch and said Good Day were interested in working with us. Let it be known, people, he called *me* first. [Long pause for laughter] And what was so amazing was how simple it all was. Jared was asking about whether we could use In World behavioural data to diagnose health issues, specifically mental health issues. And I said, well, sure we do – we already do exactly the same thing with our friends at BFF marketing, who look at the same datasets to make their campaigns more targeted and more effective. And hey, shopping is a kind of medicine, isn't it? Retail therapy, right? [Short pause for laughter] So in the future, we're going to be able to diagnose Alpha players' problems *and* treat them, so they'll not only be happy when they're In World, but also happy and productive and effective citizens Out of World. You know how difficult it is to get an appointment with a health specialist, no matter how good your insurance? This bypasses all of that. It's like you've got a doctor watching you, and treating you, twenty-four hours a day, so you can just get on with your life. And the super-interesting thing is, now we're working together, we'll be able to work out just how In World Therapy and medication interact with each other. We'll be able to find the perfect balance of VR scenarios and old-fashioned meds. Not saying that Good Day products are old-fashioned, sorry Jared. [Short pause for laughter] Then add in a bit of retail therapy, thanks to BFF, and you're looking at 6 billion – well, 7 billion, we're projecting by end of the year, isn't it, Kim? – Alpha users who literally – *literally* – couldn't be happier. Now that's a triumvirate I'm excited to be a part of.

So. I'd like to propose a toast. What do you reckon? To health and happiness? [Long pause for laughter, applause]

8.52

THE NSA'S GROUNDS remind Alice of a golf course. Pools of flat, uniform green that look like they've been cut from the same piece of paper and glued to the surface of the earth. The fields and pitches are neatly bisected by concrete pathways the colour of Caribbean sand. These paths are lined with benches that broadcast NutriStart affiliate advertising into empty space, and drooping glass bulbs that look like cute, old-fashioned streetlamps, but on closer inspection turn out to be cameras.

Off to the right is the NSA's stadium. She can't believe how big it is – almost the same size as the school itself. There are unmarked vehicles parked outside it and a handful of men in black combat gear, walking with a wide, John Wayne gait and posture so upright it looks like they might topple over backwards. It's off-limits after yesterday's incident. Alice still doesn't fully understand exactly what happened there because Tom's account was very confused in the telling.

She tacks left over the grass. Ahead she can see the silhouettes of cranes and excavators, and among them evenly placed shafts of scaffolding that look like the guard towers of a prison wall. They extend across the entire horizon, and half of them already have sections of grey-green corrugated metal erected between them. The site is cordoned off all around with bright orange tape.

The skeletal outline of the wall, or fence, or whatever it is, passes between two low hills that she can see from here are likely sites for a barrow or a tumulus. The nearer of the pair is churned with the tracks of construction vehicles and piled high with excavated soil. It does not look at all promising.

Alice has worked up a sweat by the time she reaches the site.

She can see a group of men in high-visibility overalls huddling around the corner of a prefab cubicle-type building and laughing. It's a loud, mirthless laugh that sounds like a challenge, a raising rather than a lowering of defences. There is the combined whir of several generators, and, distantly, the hiss and spark of welding. In the middle of the encampment, piled up next to a row of chemical toilets, is a heap of human bones.

She stops. "Holy Jesus Christ," she says.

When she reaches the orange tape she tries to stoop underneath it. One of the men in the group sees her at once and wanders over. He has the curiosity of someone approaching a stray animal.

"Hold on, my love," he says. His neon overalls and helmet remind her of a character in a pre-school children's TV show, a big green bear or something, but she can't remember its name. "You need to get back behind that line there."

She keeps walking.

"Have all of those been dug up from the site?" she says, gesturing at the pile of human remains.

"Site's off-limits. You're going to get hurt wandering around here. You work at the school, do you?"

"Weren't you going to tell anyone about all that?"

The men next to the cubicle building seem well attuned to the frequency of her voice. They've all looked up from whatever it is they're crowding around.

"We're here to build the wall, my love. That's all. If something's in the way of the foundations, it's got to go."

She stops short of walking into his arm, which has been raised, in a calculated way, to breast height. "I don't work at the school, I'm from the BIA."

"BIA?"

"I'm an archaeologist."

"A what?"

"I just want to have a look at the site before you go ahead and do your thing."

"Nope."

"A look. A quick look."

The other construction workers are all waddling over in their bright green jumpsuits to investigate the altercation. She realises that the thing they were all watching and laughing at was a rude movie. It's still playing loudly from the PAD which one of them is holding at his side. She can tell they've deliberately left it on. They might have even raised the volume.

"If you want access to the site, you'll have to apply to the site manager at TASCO, but I'll be honest with you, it's not worth their while given the health and safety risks. If you get hurt, it's us that'll get the rap. You don't want that, do you?"

"It's about ten feet away. I'm not going anywhere near the actual wall, so I'm obviously not going to get hurt."

"You can't go anywhere beyond the tape, my love."

"Just let me through."

"Can't you hear me?"

"You don't have to be quite so officious."

"I think you need to calm down."

Alice breathes deeply. The woman in the video is whimpering in a strained approximation of someone who's enjoying herself.

"Look. If I go to the other side of the tape, can you at least bring me some of those bones to look at?"

"I've got a bone you can look at!" says someone else.

She ignores this.

"Please?"

"We've got work to do."

"You're not working, you're watching porn."

Sharp intakes of breath and laughter from the other ten or so workmen – and women, she notes – gathered in a luminous green crescent.

"Well, that's not very polite, is it?" says the first man, visibly entertained. "What finishing school did you go to? You could do with some manners, my love."

"Fuck's sake."

Whistles all round.

"Just tell me what I have to do for you to let me in here."

The man holding the PAD lifts it up. "This?"

He points at the screen, and she only sees it for a fraction of a second before looking away, but knows instantly that it's etched into her long-term memory: the upturned buttocks pulled taut across the ridges of the girl's pelvis, something huge, black, glassy inserted between them, much bigger than a baby's head, the skin around the object red and rubbery and smeared with a clear jelly.

They all laugh again and for a moment the sound mines something deeper inside her than just anger. Sadness, despair maybe; for them, for the girl in the video, for herself.

"Ah, go on, at least give it a try!"

"We'll start you off with something smaller."

The first man is trying to usher her away from their camp, now.

"Time to go. Show's over."

She looks at the pile of bones. There must be the remains of at least a hundred bodies there, all pretty well preserved. She digs her own PAD out of her bag and starts trying to take photos, but the man puts his gloved hand in front of it.

"That's a criminal offence, that is."

"Oh give me a *break*. Just let me take one photo."

"On your way." He manhandles her by the shoulders back towards the orange boundary tape. Every time she raises the PAD's camera, he swats it back down again.

"Can you take your hands off me."

"Oh, here we go," he says. "You going to go and say I assaulted you now? I'm trying to keep you from getting hurt."

"No, I just don't need to be physically *thrown* off the site."

"Well, don't even try it, my love. You call it assault, we call it trespassing. Everyone saw what happened."

She squirms a little to get away from him and ducks under the tape. From there she watches the luminous, alien workforce troop back to the hut and congregate around the video again. One of them hollers something to a man operating an excavator, but her blood is so hot and noisy in her ears she can't hear it.

Once upon a time, Alice and Henry had attempted hiring electric scooters to get from the museum to the station. At the first set of traffic lights someone in a DV shouted something at her of dubious intent, and at the second set Alice watched as Henry dismounted, opened the DV's bonnet, removed its battery with her bare hands and threw it in the Thames. She wishes Henry was here now. She would have thought of something good to say, something rather more intelligent and devastating that "give me a break".

She treks back across the grass and re-joins the path to the main building, ready to pick a fight with someone. Anyone. Maybe one of the kids? Some of the younger ones are tiny, they wouldn't stand a chance!

When she approaches reception she can see tiny Mr Tooley scanning the drop-off point in front of the school, looking like a lost school-boy waiting for his parents. She jogs up the steps quickly and quietly while he's looking in the opposite direction and slips back through the rotating door.

"Good morning, can I help you?" says Jenny/Gilly, as though she's never seen her before. Behind her a maintenance team are already replacing the screen that Tom broke earlier.

"I'd like to see the Headmaster. Now. Please."

"Do you have an appointment?"

"What? No! You know I don't have an appointment. We spoke about ten minutes ago."

"Are you a prospective parent?"

Alice stares into the receptionist's eyes. They seem very deep-set. Her face is buried under so much make-up it looks like she's wearing a Chinese opera mask.

"No. Can you just tell me where the Headmaster's office is? This is urgent, it doesn't need an appointment."

"If you need information urgently you can speak to Mr Graves's avatar In World. Of course, Johnson can answer most Frequently Asked Questions."

Alice's hands, resting on the polished white desk, curl silently into fists. She looks around the reception. Something has changed since she was last here: the double doors on either side of the foyer are wide open.

"Miss Nowacki?" the receptionist says. "You're already on our database, have you visited NSA before?"

"Are you joking?"

"Would you like to book an appointment?"

"No. Don't worry about it."

She sets off towards the door on the left, the one Tom was directed through, and Jenny/Gilly calls after her:

"I'm afraid you can't go through there without a lanyard."

"Yes I can," says Alice, and crosses the threshold into the corridor.

The inside of the NSA is unbearably smug and only makes Alice more determined to raise hell. The corridor is one long gauntlet of trumpeting TV screens, displaying the achievements of its most handsome staff and pupils and playing very low-volume pretend folk music. She's sure she can also detect, beneath the soundtrack, a hum that's either too high or too low to hear. The whole place smells of shit and heavily perfumed cleaning products.

She follows the corridor to its end, past what looks like the infirmary, above which is another digital screen that says "IF YOU ARE FEELING UNWELL PLEASE GO TO THE SPORTS CENTRE J and shows a picture of a clam with a thermometer in its mouth. There's a window opposite that looks into a lush, green garden, which apparently has no entrance or exit. Beyond this she finds the offices for the bursar, admissions, and for something called the "Aspiration team". At the far end is the Senior Management Suite. All the doors to these offices are wide open, just like those in the reception.

The Headmaster's office has an antechamber with yet another receptionist acting as gatekeeper. She looks young enough to be a student at the school. "Oh…" she says, when Alice interrupts her line of sight, but otherwise does nothing to stop her.

Stepping into David Graves's private office feels grossly transgressive in a way that Alice isn't prepared for. She expected it to be executive and minimalist with perhaps a few carefully curated family photos or personal knick-knacks. She expected him to be seated and suited at a desk near the window, PAD in hand, greeting her with a practised face of professional concern.

In reality, the place is more boudoir than office. It's dim and musky, and the Headmaster isn't even aware that she's come in because he's got a VR helmet on. He's lying fully horizontal in a recliner,

234

wearing a shirt and tie and tracksuit bottoms. There is a very low groan escaping from his lips, which lasts such a long time that Alice thinks it must be coming from a refrigerator somewhere, or maybe it's the air-conditioning, but eventually it stops and David Graves inhales deeply and begins the noise all over again. There is a desk, in a corner behind him, on which is a cage containing a sick-looking cockatoo. Its beak is nuzzled into what's left of its plumage, and it seems as catatonic as its owner.

The Headmaster gurgles, and Alice Nowacki suddenly finds the experience of watching him voyeuristic and obscene. For some reason she can't bring herself to remove his headset, out of fear of what might be beneath it. She backs out of the office into the foyer area, and yelps when she treads on someone's toe. It's Tom, looking even more manic and strung-out than earlier.

"What's going on?" he says. "Why're all the doors unlocked?"

"I don't know. The main entrance is open as well. Have you seen your Headmaster recently?"

"Mr Graves is busy at the moment," says the PA, who's still sat at her desk.

"Did you come to find me?" says Tom, hopefully. He's mangling his packet of ProSustain with his fingers.

"I came to find him," she says, pointing into Mr Graves's office.

"So did I! That's a coincidence."

"I don't think he's going to be much use to either of us."

"Would you like to make an appointment?" (The PA.)

They both stand in the doorway and watch the Headmaster's chest slowly rise and fall. His nostrils are enormous, Alice notices, dark and cavernous, like twin entrances to the Underworld.

"How was the exit interview?" she asks.

Tom twitches.

"The interview is ongoing."

"Oh."

"It's taken a few unexpected turns."

"Oh dear."

"They think…"

Tom looks up into his forehead and seems to carry on speaking, silently, to someone floating above him.

"They think what?"

"Nothing."

"Really?"

He shakes his head and his eyes take a moment to refocus on her.

"I thought you'd left."

"I went out to look at the site."

"And?"

She doesn't want to tell him. Not Tom. She's not sure why. Perhaps because he'll try and comfort her.

"Doesn't matter. The long and the short of it is that I'm not going to be able to do what I want out there. I thought your Headmaster might be able to weigh in, but apparently not."

"Mr Graves's schedule is full for the next month or so." (The PA again.)

Alice pulls her PAD out of her rucksack to review the attempted photos from the site. She scrolls through about six blurred images of the man's green hand. In one of them you can see the rest of the construction team laughing in the background, and her simmering blood returns to a rolling boil. She can hear the girl whimpering as clearly as if she were in the room.

"Shall I go and find Snoopy?"

"Snoopy?"

"Snoopsy. Peepsy. Alex."

Alice has forgotten all about him. That might be some consolation. "I suppose so. I don't want to come away from here with nothing."

"Exactly!"

"Where is he?"

"Well, let's have a little look-see."

She follows Tom out of the Headmaster's reception area, where the PA is still searching for available slots in his schedule, and through a door headed with "Mr R. M. Tooley, Principal Deputy Headmaster". Tom snatches a PAD from the desk inside and swishes over the screen.

"He's still on the system," he says at last. His grin is slightly off-centre. "They haven't deleted him. But he's not registered for any classes today."

"So where's he going to be?"

"We could try the Sports Centre. That's where he said he was going yesterday afternoon. He said he was feeling ill. I want to go there, too, anyway. I'm not leaving without finding out what's happening."

"I thought you'd decided on the Druid-curse explanation? That's what you said last night."

"Well. We'll find out, won't we? Maybe Snoopy will reveal all."

"Maybe." Alice is already dreading accompanying him across the school. "I think you should have a glass of water, Tom."

She's halfway to the water cooler in the corner of the room when she sees the dark, bovine shape behind the desk.

"What's that doing here?"

9.00

"I'M TIRED."

"Then sleep!"

"Won't that end the test?"

"No siree! This scenario lets you sleep In World, Gabriel. Alpha will know when you need to recharge your batteries and make all the necessary adjustments to your display. You'll wake up naturally when it knows you've come to the end of your sleep cycle. You don't need to leave the Game at all!"

"I don't think I want to do that."

"Did you like the Nazis?"

"Did I *like* them?"

"Not the Nazis themselves, but the scenario? You said you were bored, so we thought we'd introduce a bit of jeopardy. Did you like it?"

"It was okay."

"How did it feel to be the hero? Did it make you happy?"

"I guess. It was good to have something to do. Like, a task."

"Perfect. You prefer a goal-based approach. We get that, we just needed a bit of time to calibrate your preferences in a neutral environment. So you prefer completing missions to an open-world, Sandbox scenario?"

"I don't know. Both, I suppose."

"And environment-wise, which was your favourite? The beach? Martian surface? The mountain lodge?"

Gabriel shrugs, but obviously the faceless man can't see him do it.

"They're all quite similar. And it's boring not having any other players to interact with."

"I understand, Gabriel, but other users would skew the results of the test."

"You're here."

"I just have to jump in occasionally, we've factored that in."

"But do you have to be here?"

"I'm just interested in the reasons behind your choices."

"I'm all out of choices. I think I just want to go home."

Gabriel's pretty sure he can hear the faceless man licking his lips behind the mic. Then the ever-present white noise is fragmented by the sound of other voices, like there's a busy call centre in the background. He has to wait a few moments for the man's voice to return.

"Home. Interesting. You'd be happy there?"

"Why do you keep asking me if I'm happy?"

"Home could be tricky, Gabriel. But we'll certainly consider it for a future scenario."

"I mean, I think I might want to end the test."

"What about school?"

"School?"

"If you're after familiarity. We could easily recreate the NSA for you. The Headmaster there has been very cooperative with us. We can duplicate the In World model they use for tours, and you can edit it however you want. Obviously it will naturally converge on your preferences, as usual. What do you say?"

"Will it be like the beach again? All those women?"

"No no, we can populate it just like the real thing. We can borrow behavioural data from users and replicate them just as accurately as the buildings. It'll be like all your classmates are there. Teachers, too. And again, if they show positive behaviour, from your point of view, it will be reinforced through the algorithm. Pretty neat, right? No more teachers telling you off!"

Gabriel thinks of the NSA's staff and students. The prospect of personally putting a bullet between their eyes makes him positively giddy.

10.00

TOM ROSEN is marching a few paces ahead of Alice, trying to look determined and proactive, but he's tripped over his own feet twice already now and he's fairly sure she saw it. He can't walk or think straight. Tooley's talk of "relationships" and "witnesses" and "legal teams" has added another burden to his overworked brain, causing his head to list violently to one side. He's trying to recall who might have seen him with Maggie, and whether he said anything incriminating, to her, to anyone.

Gerald! Of course, there was Gerald. Another child he needs to trace!

They're halfway around the circumference of the ground floor, and it's obvious now that every door in the school has been unlocked and thrown open. They pass five or six lessons that are in progress. The classes are only about half full, and the teachers look a bit lost in front of such a small audience. One of the teachers is Miss Potter. Tom sees her before she sees him.

"Wait," he says to Alice.

"What?"

"This is Alex's class. They'll have Goal Setting all morning."

"Goal Setting?"

"You bet. Worth seeing if anyone knows anything, I reckon."

"We can't just go into a lesson, can we?"

He doesn't answer that. He slips into the back of the class, which like the others only seems about two-thirds full. There's no sign of Alex Pepys. Alice follows him behind the back row, her hands forced awkwardly into her pockets. At the front of the room, Miss Potter's brow contracts mid-sentence into a brief, minute frown, then she goes back to addressing the class.

"So. Before we get started. Can we recap what we're looking for from your goals? Three things." She holds up three fingers. A few students raise their hands.

"Amir?"

"Actionable, measurable... and something else. Something-able."

"Anyone want to jump in and help him out? Ella?"

"Reasonable?"

"Right!" Miss Potter counts them off on her fingers. "Reasonable, actionable, measurable. Keep those three in mind when you're doing your presentations." Then she looks up. "Seems we've got a couple of extra audience members, too – make sure you impress Mr Rosen!"

Tom hates watching other teachers teach, because it makes him realise that he uses exactly the same shtick as everyone else and he's nowhere near as unique and engaging as he thinks he is. It's embarrassing.

The children chatter among themselves for a moment while Miss Potter works her way to the back of the classroom.

"Hello," she says, a little mystified. "You look awful." She and Alice exchange uncertain smiles.

Tom parts his dry, tattered lips. "I'm sorry about last night."

"Last night?"

"We were going to go for a drink?"

Some of the kids in the back row are staring at them.

"Yes. Thank you, Mr Rosen. We'll discuss later." She looks at him incredulously and then throws her voice over the heads of the class again. "Okay, Alysa, you're up first. Everybody else: let's be quiet and professional and think about the kinds of feedback we might want to give on her presentation skills."

A very slight girl gets up and goes to the IWB at the front of the room, squinting in the powerful beam of the projector. She says something apologetic that Tom can't hear, and spends a few moments fiddling with her PAD, until the screen behind her is suddenly animated with brightly coloured text that reads: *Alysa Mohammad 8B – Personal Goals Autumn H2*. The title sequence rolls like cinema credits. In all four corners of the slideshow she's put a cartoon cat with bulging, heart-shaped eyes. Alysa herself watches the animation as though she's never seen it before. Once her name and the presentation objectives have disappeared, the cats leave the corners and whizz in circles to herald the next slide. She giggles to herself.

"Good morning, everyone," she says. "So. I'm starting with the goals that I set myself last term. Um. Maybe you remember them, but. Um. So, but, these were what I had to improve. Wait. These."

She taps her PAD screen, and the rest of the class are already heads-down and entering live feedback on their own devices.

There's more elaborate animation on the IWB, as the cat prances its way from the top to the bottom of the screen, revealing five bullet points as it goes. They read:

- *Identify leadership opportunities*
- *Greater contribution to class discussions*
- *More memorable and exciting online presence*
- *Widen experience of PAD functionality*
- *More "me" time*

Tom glances to his right and sees that Alice has her hand over her mouth as though she's just witnessed a car accident.

Alysa forges ahead.

"So. The first one I actioned by applying to be head of Year 8 student council... I did that. I didn't get any votes, but. It was... useful I guess?"

She looks to Miss Potter for reassurance, who nods and adds: "A useful learning experience."

"A useful learning experience, yeah. Also I think people maybe saw my name on the list, so maybe more people know who I am now? I don't know. I might try again next term. I don't know."

She looks around her classmates, but most are still tapping furiously on their PADs. Tom suspects the feedback isn't hugely positive.

"Um." Alysa's face suddenly brightens. "Oh yeah! I got a nine for participation on my IPR last week. And the week before that I got a five. I don't think I've got above a five ever. So that's good. Um."

She slumps a little in her trouser suit. It's a couple of sizes too big and it looks like her head will disappear completely if her posture gets any worse. She stares up at the board again, her back turned to the audience, gyrating nervously. This prompts another flurry of typed comments from the rest of the class.

"And then. Well. I don't really know what to do about the online presence thing. My mum doesn't let me go on Alpha on school nights, so it's quite difficult to keep up with what everyone's doing. My granddad sent me some money, and I bought some new clothes for my avatar. They're quite cool. Like… a bright green Nike track-suit thing. And it's a real one, not fake. Um. Also. Someone said it wasn't really clear what my brand message was. Like, they didn't know what I was for. So I thought maybe my thing could be that I'm the funny one, and I should just put up funny and sort of silly videos and things. So I made a video. It was like a puppet show I did in my living room…"

Someone groans from the side of the room.

"Excuse me?" says Miss Potter sharply. "Amir, can you listen politely please?"

"I've seen it though, miss, it's rubbish."

"Amir, you've got your PAD for giving feedback."

"It's so *bad*, miss, it's not even funny."

Some of the other students start laughing. Alysa is trying to look like she's also in on the joke, but her smile is sad and desperate and her huge brown eyes are shining too much.

"You can go next if you like," Miss Potter says to Amir. "I'm sure Alysa will extend you the same courtesy you've shown her."

"That's not fair, miss!"

"Then be quiet and let her finish."

Tom watches Alysa limp through the rest of her presentation. Particularly unbearable is the final section, in which she pledges to try and stop being so anxious. Her mum has bought her a voucher for a spa weekend as an early Christmas present, and she's enrolled in a pilates class. By the end her voice is hardly audible, and the class have grown hot and restless, squirming and rustling in their executive office-wear. The windows of the classroom are fogged with sweat. The slideshow ends with the return of the cartoon cat, who winks at the audience and emits a speech bubble from his mouth that says: "Thanks for listening!" It's met with a smattering of unenthused applause and Alysa returns to her seat, staring at the screen of her PAD so as not to make eye-contact with anyone.

"Thank you, Alysa, I hope that was useful for you," says Miss Potter.

The girl nods without speaking, without looking up. She lets her curtains of very black, very straight hair conceal her face.

"Next up…" Miss Potter looks down her list. "Shauna?"

"Ill," the class say in chorus.

"Oh. Yes. Of course. Gregor?"

"Ill."

"Golly. What about Jess. Are you here?"

"Yes, miss."

"Do you want to go and get set up?"

The second girl picks her way between the desks to the front of the class, and everyone takes the opportunity to start talking very loudly to their neighbours. Miss Potter doesn't try to stop them. She turns to Tom.

"Sorry, Mr Rosen – is there a reason you're here?"

Tom is still staring at Alysa. It takes him a moment to realise someone is talking to him.

"Yes. Alex Pepys."

"Do you know where he is?"

"I was going to ask you the same thing."

"I thought he was with the others in the Sports Centre?"

"I didn't get that far. I was wondering if he'd checked in with you since yesterday."

"I haven't heard anything."

"Right."

"And he wasn't in registration."

"Have any of his friends seen him?"

"I haven't asked."

"Do you mind if I do?"

Tom notices that Miss Potter is very gradually leaning away from him as he speaks. He forcibly tries to conjure some saliva to coat his furred tongue and teeth.

"Do you have to?" she says. "It'll only start more rumours. You know what Tooley said about keeping this thing under control."

"Tooley's a—"

Two boys on the back row are gaping at the conversation. Miss Potter shakes her head.

"I think I'd like to get back to teaching my lesson, Mr Rosen. I'm sorry."

"You know he fired me, don't you?"

One of the students picks up on this. "What? You got fired."

"Mr Rosen. I think there is a better time to discuss this." She turns to Alice, who's hugging herself with awkwardness. "I'm sorry. I don't know why he's brought you here. We'll have to talk later."

The whole class is now looking at the three of them.

"Is that your girlfriend, sir?"

"Why'd you get fired?"

"Is it because you brought your girlfriend into school?"

"Where's Peepsy?"

"Tom," says Miss Potter. "You're not helping me. You might have been sacked but I still have a job here—" sharp intakes of breath from the other students "—and I need to teach this lesson. How's this going to look on my self-assessment?"

Tom is too tired to put up a fight. His head feels like a bag of sand when he nods. "I'm going to the Sports Centre. We'll talk later?"

"Maybe. I'm sorry."

"No, *I'm* sorry."

"It's fine. Sorry," Miss Potter says again, but to Alice, not to him.

The pair of them leave and continue in silence along the corridor. Behind him, Alice keeps inhaling sharply as though she's about to say something. Tom can feel he's no longer propped up by the ProSustain. His blood is thick and cold. Besides the tiredness there's something else, something like a deep embarrassment, that's stopping him from speaking. In fact, the thing he wants to talk about is the embarrassment *itself*, something so large and intrinsic to his being he can't think of a way to even begin discussing it.

He fumbles in his jacket pocket and retrieves the foil packet. Only two left. He'll have to ration them.

As he's popping the pill from its casement, there's an irregular thump of feet, the sound of someone whose feet and shoes are too big for the rest of their body. He looks up to see a student who was in Miss Potter's lesson hurrying towards him. It's the tanned boy who spoke to him in the stadium the day before.

"Sir."

Tom swallows the pill painfully.

"I don't actually think you need to call me that anymore, Josh."

Josh pauses, unsure of how to continue.

"Shouldn't you be in Miss Potter's lesson?" Tom prompts.

"I told her I was going to the toilet."

"I see. Good trick."

"You're still looking for Peepsy, aren't you?"

"Alex Pepys? That's right."

The boy looks like he might cry. "I know I shouldn't have… I mean, I should have said yesterday. I shouldn't have told you he was ill. But I said I'd help him. But now I know I shouldn't have. I should have told the truth. I thought, maybe it wouldn't matter, you know? But now I'm just worried. I wish I'd told you. Yesterday. At the football match. But he asked me to cover for him. Me and Kiran. But it's not Kiran's fault."

"Let's skip to the end, Josh."

"He didn't go to the Sports Centre. He was going to the Dungeons. He wanted to use the incinerator. And he hasn't come back."

"The incinerator? Why?"

"He wanted to burn something."

"I gathered that much."

"I can't really say anything else. I don't want him to get into trouble."

"I'm not a teacher here anymore. As of yesterday afternoon. I couldn't get him into trouble if I wanted."

247

"Oh yeah. Why did they fire you?"

"Long story."

"Someone said you punched Gerald Liu."

"That's completely untrue."

"Oh, okay."

Tom hopes everyone else is as easily convinced as this.

"Well. If you're not teaching, then…" The boy looks at Alice, who smiles back at him as though being brought out of a deep sleep. "…can you and your girlfriend look for Alex?"

10.55

PEEPSY IS thigh deep in the slurry of several thousand unwanted school meals. His trousers are rolled up and his shoes and socks are in a neat pair at the edge of the heap, like he's gone paddling in the sea. The food waste is a mixture of the students' breakfasts, things that the kitchen staff have thrown away from the previous night, and the contents of the "compostable" bins that are dotted all over the school and only get emptied every few days. There's gallons of porridge, yoghurt, coffee, protein shake, vitamin smoothie, juice, almond milk, oat milk and the slightly grey lactose-free milk substitute "M20", all mixed into a rich broth with half-eaten vegetarian sausages, chicken breasts, jerky, scrambled eggs, raw eggs, a variety of beans and pulses, three different types of NutriStart paleo-bars that the students are given for free by the Academy's sponsor, along with an infinite number of other, unidentifiable lumps. Peepsy lowers his forearms into the depths and splays his fingers. He moves slowly, like a trawler, hoping he'll snag the things he's looking for. He thought he'd find this experience more disgusting, but he doesn't mind the smell anymore and the sensation against his skin is cooling and quite pleasant.

The other support staff have finally gone on their break, or they've been called away to deal with some other waste-management emergency, but he doesn't know how much time he has until they're back. Nor does he know how long he's got until the next load of slop is released on top of him, but for the last ten or fifteen minutes the buzzer has been silent.

"So once I've found them, then what?"

He knows the other boy is still there, watching him, because of the whine in his inner ear.

"Come on, pal, give us a clue. They're your bones, what do you want me to do with them? Do you want me to bury them again somewhere? I can't take them back to where I found them, they've dug that whole place up."

More tinnitus. He rattles a finger in his ear and accidentally plugs it with rice.

"Eurgh. Why am I doing this?"

Peepsy straightens up. When he turns around, he sees the dead boy looking at him with something like longing.

"What? You feeling sorry for yourself? Nope. You did well to get out when you did. Bet you didn't have to go to a school like this. Bet you didn't have to go to school at all. And looks like they fed you better. You're pretty chubby for a ghost."

The boy disappears for a fraction of a second and then reappears. Again Peepsy notices the hole in the middle of his forehead, dead centre between the curtains of his hair, which despite his spectral nature still looks very greasy.

"At least the hole in the head killed you. Did it? Was that it?" No reply. He turns back to his work. "Could have been worse. You should meet my sister. You'd have loads to talk about. If she could talk. Ha."

As he wades into the deep end, two thick, black droplets of blood plop into the pool, which is now up around his waist. He wipes his nose on the back of his hand.

"Ah, c'mon man. Don't give me a nosebleed again. I'm trying to help you, aren't I?"

The blood continues its slow ooze. Peepsy alternates between sniffing and blowing for a few seconds, but neither does any good.

His shin suddenly knocks against something as bony as itself.

"Oh, hello!"

He plunges his arms back into the stuff and feels around his ankles, dredging up the skull and a couple of finger bones. The skull's eye sockets are compacted with something gelatinous. He tucks it under one arm and after a few more moments fishing around he finds the rest of the hands, clutches all the artefacts to his chest and returns to the shore.

"Here you are," he says to the ghost. "Got 'em. Sorry they're not very clean."

He lays them carefully down next to his shoes and socks, and then tries cleaning his legs with his suit jacket. It's scratchy and non-absorbent and leaves a sticky, sweet-and-savoury residue on his skin. There are bits of rice and potato between most of his toes, which he scoops out and flicks across the floor towards the incinerator.

"So what do you want me to do with them?" he says, rolling his socks on and off again, deciding he needs to give his feet time to dry out a bit. "Nothing? What is this: you don't *want* to talk, or you *can't* talk? No? Fine. Suit yourself."

He gets up and goes over to the container full of electronics, where his PAD is now buried under a layer of laptops, hard drives, obsolete tablets, fragments of circuitry and bundles of cables, which have all found their way there since Peepsy regained consciousness. When he finally retrieves it, his hands are grazed from digging among all the sharp edges, and the PAD itself is cracked across the screen. He wipes his index finger on his shirt and presses it onto the scanner. It turns on, but a message appears, refracted by the broken shards of the screen: *Connection lost.*

Peepsy hasn't contacted home since the previous morning. Even on a good day he worries about his mum and dad, who are in a constant state of fatigue from their daily outpouring of care for him and his sister. They're now all constructed in such a tense and fragile balance that even trivial things – a lost bag, a low IPR grade, a dropped fork at the dinner table – can precipitate Total Familial Collapse for a week. Recently he's been trying to give them both a break by staying in his room, but whenever he tries this they start worrying that he's becoming withdrawn, or that he's addicted to Alpha Omega, which wears them down even more.

Not coming home for the night, no call, no message, might just be enough to kill them.

He tries reconnecting the PAD without success, and realises that it might not even be that the device is broken. He's possibly so deep underground that not even the new high-speed, wide-coverage, bowel-tickling routers can reach him with their signal. Another blob of blood, thick like jam, spatters the screen.

"I just want to say," he reprimands the boy, who has moved into the corner of the waste disposal room apparently without walking, "that I think you're being completely unfair about this. It wasn't even me who dug you up. It was the builders. If anything, I saved you from the diggers. And just because someone moved your bones around a bit, doesn't mean you have to take it out on the whole school. What's your problem with Carla? She didn't do anything. I actually think you're way out of line, pal. Ugh, God, I *stink*."

The boy watches him from the gloom.

"Say *something*, if you're so pissed off. I'm trying to *help* you."

"Alex?"

The voice is not a child's voice. It's deep and old and has a slight quiver to it.

"Oh. So you can talk."

"Alex?"

"What?"

Then he realises that he's being spoken to from behind. He turns his back on the boy and the incinerator and the heaps of garbage. Stepping through the horizontal shutter that partitions the waste disposal room from the rest of the Dungeons is a man in a torn tweed jacket. He's wearing the official blue lanyard of a member of staff, but he looks too trampy and malnourished to be a teacher. He takes a few steps forward before Peepsy recognises him as Mr Rosen. A woman follows him through the gap in the shutter, whose face rings a bell, but from where he can't remember. She's not wearing a lanyard of any description, which is very odd indeed.

"Alex," Mr Rosen says for a third time.

"*What?*"

"Who are you talking to?"

11.30

STEPHANIE HAS been in the atrium of Alpha Omega HQ for two hours. It feels like she's at a busy airport terminal. She's now with her fourth customer services representative, though, in truth, they've all sounded very similar and might have been the same person. Someone keeps trying to offer her sparkling water.

"I'm fine, really."

"Are you sure? We bottle it on site."

"No, thank you."

"We put in our own electrolytes."

"Who am I waiting for?"

"Farris will be here any minute."

"Who is Farris?"

"He's part of the player liaison team. Out of World. Say, you want to go In World while you wait?"

"Are you joking?"

"Not at all. We've got scenarios for the partially sighted. Everyone's welcome in the Game!"

Stephanie knows exactly the sorts of scenarios she means.

"I'll pass."

"Sure?" The girl is humming slightly under her breath, like she's impatient. Or maybe she's just enthusiastic. "We've just had a whole load of new content made for us by Cosmic Whisperer. Have you heard of her?"

Stephanie shakes her head and tunes the girl out while she keeps talking.

First thing this morning, Safeway Security Ltd finally produced some meaningful information on Gabriel's whereabouts. They announced with some fanfare that they'd managed to unlock his PAD, and had traced its movements to the Alpha Omega headquarters not far from King's Cross Intranational. Combined with the arrival of the parcel on Monday, this information was enough to put Stephanie on edge, and she was in a DV before she'd had breakfast.

When she arrived at their offices they welcomed her with open arms, but claimed they knew nothing about Gabriel. They hadn't heard of him. They weren't allowed, they said with regret, to release user data without the user's consent. Stephanie tried pointing out that he was under sixteen, that surely the consent of his parents was enough. Her consent had been enough for them in the past, she said, not wanting to elaborate. This caused some confusion, and in the following two hours she was passed from James to Erin to Clarence to Rain, the girl with the sparkling water, each of them greeting her by her first name like she was an old friend.

"Hey there, Steph!"

"Stephanie."

"I'm Farris."

Rain gives Stephanie's arm a squeeze.

"It was so nice to meet you, Stephanie!" she says. "I hope you find your son!"

"You're looking for Gabriel Bäcker?" says Farris.

"Have you found him?"

"Captain Gumbo, right?"

"Excuse me?"

"He's Captain Gumbo? That's his name. In World."

That's a name that she hasn't heard in years. It was a series of audiobooks Gabriel used to listen to when he was very small. It was about a pirate, who was also a chef, who sailed the high seas solving disputes by cooking delicious food for everyone. In every story he had to find just the right dish to solve whatever problem had come up. He never seemed to have any time for pirating, but he didn't mind, apparently. Gabriel loved those books.

"I didn't know that," she says.

"He's kind of a legend round here," laughs Farris, and Stephanie's heart feels like it might explode.

"So he's been here?"

"I mean, he's a legend In World."

"Oh. Apparently he was here yesterday evening. Here. Physically."

"I don't think so."

"But his PAD—"

"PADs give out a lot of screwy data. It probably *thought* he was here because he was playing Alpha."

"And was he? Playing, I mean?"

"Sure he was. One of our people spoke to him In World last night, and this morning."

"So do you know where he is?"

There is a tiny pause, just long enough for Stephanie to think that something is awry.

"Can't say for sure, but he mentioned something about going back to his old school. Does that sound right to you?"

Odd. Why does *this* guy sound like he's grinning too?

11.40

FROM WHERE Alice is standing, Alex Pepys looks like he's covered in papier mâché. He's shoeless, sockless, with his trousers rolled to the knee, urchin-style. Underneath all the other stains his nose, upper lip and shirt are caked with blood. His tie is bound around his head and knotted at the back, for reasons Alice can't discern.

"What do you want?" he says. His voice is thick and nasal, like he has a bad cold.

"Your friend said you'd be here," says Tom. "We were all worried about you."

"Which one?"

"I think his name is Josh."

"Oh, *Josh*. He's such a snake!"

"You don't have to get annoyed with him, he did the right thing telling us. You look like you could do with some help."

"I'm fine," he says, blowing black snot onto the concrete between his feet. There's something stoic about him that moves Alice unexpectedly. She also feels guilty for thinking about kicking a child a little earlier. "I just came down here to get some bibs," he adds.

"You don't have to make excuses," says Tom. "You're not in trouble."

"I'm not making excuses. I was sent down here by Mr Briggs. Then, I don't know, I guess I got a nosebleed or something and I must have fainted."

"Alex. We know what's going on. You came here to use the incinerator. We know you found something on the building site. This is Dr Nowacki. You sent a message to her, didn't you? She's here to talk to you about the things you discovered."

Alice watches Peepsy as he squints, blinks and glances quickly behind him. She follows his eyes and sees the skull and bones lying on the floor in the nest of his suit jacket. Bertha? Difficult to tell from this distance.

"You're not in trouble. I promise," says Tom. Those last two words don't sound at all convincing, to anyone. "We just need to speak to you. You're ill, aren't you?"

"I'm alright."

"You don't look alright. And you didn't seem alright in the lunch hall, yesterday."

"I'm just tired."

"Amen, brother."

"What?" says Peepsy.

What? thinks Alice.

A pause.

"Can you remember when you first started feeling unwell?" asks Tom. "What does it feel like, precisely?"

"I don't know."

"Mr Rosen," Alice interrupts. "I think, after everything that's happened, we should all just get out of here, get poor Alex cleaned up, and ask questions later." Tom looks at her dumbly. She looks at Peepsy. "Yes? How does that sound, Alex?"

"I'd quite like a shower. But I haven't got any other clothes."

"That's alright. We can sort something out."

"This is it, isn't it?" he says. "You've got to expel me now, haven't you? Now I'm going to be doing data entry for the rest of my life. Or working in Taco Crazy."

"No one's getting expelled," says Tom. "Well, apart from me."

"Can teachers get expelled?"

"Oh yes."

Alice walks past them and squats by the pile of human remains. She turns them over in her hands. They're in superb condition, under the smears and lumps of old food. Looking into the skull's empty eyes is thrilling. Her first thought is to send a message to Henry. A video call would be nice.

Peepsy's stopped talking and is looking at her nervously.

"You've got to be careful with them," he says. "He's easily offended, I think."

"He?"

"The bones…" He looks around the waste room, as if checking to see if they're being spied upon. "Nah. Doesn't matter."

"No, go on."

"Nope."

257

The boy seems very confused, his brow softly furrowed under his makeshift karate headband. The stench coming off him is quite extraordinary. Alice suddenly knows for sure that this won't simply be a case of taking the artefacts and leaving: Peepsy needs looking after, and she's not going to leave him in Tom's quivering hands.

"Look," she says, "let's get these things bagged up. You get your shoes on, and clean yourself up best you can. Then we can get you to the nurse. In the Sports Centre? Have I got that right, Mr Rosen?"

"Right."

"Okay then." She unzips her rucksack and places the head and hands carefully inside. "Let's be quick. Don't we have to be out of here by midday?"

11.50

AT THE REQUEST of Mr Tooley, Mr Barren is composing Tom Rosen's farewell message for "Eye on NSA", a weekly electronic publication that doubles as a newsletter and a marketing brochure for the school. Whenever a member of staff is dismissed, standard procedure is to release a valedictory statement, always at least in part fictionalised, to pre-empt any gossip that might arise from their sudden disappearance from the school.

Mr Rosen leaves us after fifteen happy years at NSA, during which he oversaw the exciting transition from State Academy to full Sponsored Academy status. His contributions to the life of the school have been countless, from...

Mr Barren rubs his exceptionally close-shaven chin. This piece is actually much harder than expected, even when he can just make it up, because there's nothing that sounds believable.

> *...from his effective guidance of Pre-VAC students to his inspirational leadership of the traffic marshalling team. He has also been a beloved colleague...*

He deletes this.

> *He has also been a dependable colleague...*

Delete.

> *He has also been an expendable colleague...*

He laughs to himself, and then quickly hammers the backspace button again. He sighs and tries to slump in his chair, before realising that his chair is specifically, ergonomically shaped to prevent his relaxation.

The archive photograph of Tom Rosen, which was apparently taken when he first joined fifteen years ago, stares out from the screen. His hair is a darker brown and almost reaches his shoulders.

"Mr Rosen. He is a rock star!"

Gerald Liu's voice is loud and brassy in Mr Barren's ear, and his breath smells strongly of barbecue sauce. The boy's head is directly over Mr Barren's shoulder, and when he turns in surprise their cheeks touch in a way that feels tender and not quite appropriate.

"Gerald, please *knock* before entering a member of staff's office."

"The door is open."

"Yes. So it is. Even so, please knock. You might be interrupting something important. Do you understand?"

Gerald frowns. "The door is open," he repeats.

Mr Barren closes his PAD and get up out of his seat. "I suppose you're here to collect your reward?" he says, with a smile that looks like somebody's pulling back the skin around his ears. "As well you should. Another outlaw rounded up."

"Mr Rosen is very angry. Yesterday, I made him very angry. Today, he didn't teach the class."

"Of course Mr Rosen is angry, you caught him doing some very bad things."

"Mr Rosen and I are friends."

"Mr Rosen was your teacher. Not your friend. And he did things you're not allowed to do when you're a teacher."

"Will he come back?"

"No, Gerald, he's not coming back. And that's a good thing – for the school, for everyone."

"Did you tell my father?"

"Of course not!" He claps an awkward hand on Gerald's shoulder. "Mr Rosen might be leaving, but you're staying right here, at NSA, where you belong. You've done excellent work."

"I don't want to go to Beijing."

"No one's sending you back, Gerald. You kept your end of the deal, so, as promised, you can have your pick of any of these."

Mr Barren unlocks a drawer behind him and produces a sheaf of brightly coloured cards in cellophane packaging. They are download codes for additional Alpha Omega content. He lays four of them on the desk next to the PAD: *Number Shape, Toxic Event V, Euro Dog Simulator* and something just called *You've Got Lice!*

"I didn't know what you were interested in, so I got a few. Take one. It's yours. And there'll be another one for you if you don't mind taking on another job."

But Gerald Liu doesn't look at all pleased. He's staring down at his feet, jowls hanging heavily from his face, picking at a thread that's come loose from the lining of his suit jacket.

"Gerald?"

Without even casting his eyes over Mr Barren's stall, he takes *You've Got Lice!* in his little fingers and shuffles out of the office with his suitcase creaking behind him.

11.55

THE NURSE — her name is Etienne, but no one, apart from one other nurse, knows that — stands in the "D" of the basketball court surveying the devastation. Sports Centre #2's linoleum is a complex web of coloured lines, boxes and circles and boundaries, layered one on top of the other to delineate various different sports. On top of these is another, less ordered layer of roll mats and blankets and sleeping bags, strewn violently across the floor, and among them small piles of swabs and tissues, mops and buckets, and in one corner a saline drip, horizontal and leaking. The final layer on top of all this is the children themselves, though there aren't many left. They fall into two camps: those who have hallucinated themselves into unconsciousness, and those who are on the road to recovery. The latter were, unfortunately, sane and lucid enough to watch the carnage unfold, and are now huddled under the giant LED scoreboard while one of her colleagues tries to reassure them. In accordance with Mr Tooley's diktat they've had their PADs taken from them, to ensure that the scene doesn't find its way into the outside world.

All the others – about 60% of her patients – have now escaped, and are roaming the NSA at will, driven by God knows what. Sometimes she hears them shrieking, on the balcony, outside the windows.

Whose bright idea was it, thinks Etienne, to open all the doors?

11.56

THE HEADMASTER and his recliner sigh, one after another. He rolls to one side, then to the other, like a seal sunning itself. Then he freezes, his thumbs quivering over the VR control sticks. Some gas escapes his lips.

"A solution is forthcoming," he murmurs, but nobody Out of World can hear it.

11.57

SOMEWHERE IN a ventilation shaft above the auditorium, Small Paul has eaten seven, going on eight feet of high-speed fibre-optic cable. The last few inches he slurps into his mouth like a piece of thick spaghetti, then crunches and swallows it greedily.

A noise below. He hoops the second and third spools of cable over his shoulder and scurries off to investigate.

11.58

MISS MUNDAY is waiting patiently in the lobby of the ICT Department, holding her PAD face down. She won't turn it over because the screen is showing an edited video of her having sex with a horse, which is playing interminably on a loop, and it won't let her access any of the PAD's other applications.

"Can you come back at lunchtime?" says the receptionist, who is dressed as a dragon.

"Not really…" says Miss Munday.

11.59

MR BRIGGS is in one of the therapists' suites next to his office. He doesn't have an appointment. He's trying to tell the therapist a joke about landmines, but she's just not getting it.

12.00

"IT'S FINISHED compiling. It's coming online… Now. Hold onto your butts."

"What?"

"I said, *hold onto your butts*."

"What's that?"

"It's from a film. An old film."

"No, I mean what's that noise? Did you hear that?"

"No."

"Sounded like the doors locking."

"Guess that means it worked then."

They clink their cans of energy drink.

12.01

THE DOOR to the Dungeons is still twenty feet away when it closes, as though slammed by an unseen hand. The shutter that leads to the waste disposal area also begins to grind, and by the time Tom and Alice have run back there it has closed and sealed them into the middle section of the basement, surrounded by the years of detritus.

"Card's not working," says Peepsy when they return to him.

"That's because you've only got student access," says Tom.

"No, I mean it's not doing anything. Look." He clacks his lanyard against the reader. There's no red light, nor does it make the *bloop* noise to signify 'access denied'."

"Let me try." Tom waves his pass, at varying distances, but the reader remains blank.

Peepsy looks at Alice. "What about you, Professor?"

"'Doctor', actually. And I don't have a security thing, I just walked in here."

"Bold. Very bold."

Alice smiles at Peepsy, and for the second time in twenty-four hours Tom feels envious of a teenager. Not even a teenager, this one. Christ, what's wrong with him?

"I'm sure we can break it down with something," he says. "There are plenty of blunt objects down here we could use."

"I don't know, sir. Sounded pretty heavy when it closed. What do you think it's made of?"

Tom raps the door with his knuckle, not knowing what to listen for. It's solid and synthetic, like the stuff the children's desks are made of.

"Some kind of polymer," he says confidently.

"What does that mean?"

"It means he doesn't really know."

"Yow! Shots fired!"

They're both grinning. Tom isn't entirely happy with this new alliance but he says nothing. He stares at Peepsy for a moment, then goes looking around the basement for something to ram or prise their way out.

The other two sit back and watch the show as Tom brutalises the door with a music stand, a fire extinguisher, part of a trampoline frame, an old computer monitor bowled underarm, and lastly one of the photocopiers. He gives it a run-up of several yards, but its tiny, skewed wheels give it a top speed that's slower than walking pace. After all this he tries his outdated security pass again.

"Well," he says quickly, to pre-empt their mockery. "Looks like we're stuck down here."

"I really, *really* need the toilet, sir."

"You mustn't call me that anymore."

"And I'm hungry."

"Yep. Definitely trapped."

"Don't worry," says Alice. "It'll just be a temporary thing. They're installing a new security system, right? This'll just be teething problems. The tech people will be up there fiddling, I imagine." She looks meaningfully at Tom, encouraging him to be a bit more reassuring.

"Oh," he says, "they'll be fiddling alright!"

He's not sure what he means by that. He pulls his PAD from his jacket pocket and starts prodding at it.

"Can I message my parents with that?" asks Peepsy. "My PAD got broken."

"Nope." There's a sad-face icon at the top of the device's screen. "No WiFi, no 7G. We're off-grid down here."

"Oh."

"Don't worry, they'll be trying to fix it," says Alice. "We won't be waiting long. I've got—" she unzips the back pocket of her bag "—an orange you can eat, if you want it."

Alice tosses Peepsy the fruit, and he sniffs it.

"All I can smell is myself." He dangles his arms awkwardly at his sides, still clutching the orange. "Right. What do we do now?"

"Wait, I suppose," says Alice.

"Okay. Well. That'll be a laugh, won't it? Plenty to talk about."

Peepsy wanders away from the door and jumps up onto the top of an old industrial oven. The inches of dust form a wide crater around his backside. He looks expectantly at Tom and Alice, his bare heels clanging against the oven door, and attempts to peel the orange.

The grown-ups look at each other, then both follow his lead and take seats on their own pieces of abandoned catering equipment. Everyone waits for someone else to start talking. Outside of the classroom, Tom feels just as self-conscious and uncomfortable speaking to children as they do speaking to him. He wonders if the children themselves ever realise this. Maggie was different, of course. Good old Maggie.

Next to him, Alice opens the main compartment of her rucksack and exposes the skull. "So, Alex," she says, "how did you find this?"

"Um."

"It's alright. Like Tom says, we're not going to get you into trouble. Tom doesn't work here anymore. I *never* worked here."

"You sure? This isn't, like, a trap? You're not wearing a wire?"

Alice laughs again. "No. I promise. Anyway, with everything else that's going wrong here, I think your Headmaster's got higher priorities than punishing you for wandering off the site."

"But that's the point, Professor."

"Doctor. Alice. Just call me Alice. What's the point?"

"Everything else is going wrong *because* I wandered off-site."

"I'm sure that's not true."

"It is. It's all my fault." Peepsy puts down the orange, whose skin is dented but as yet unpeeled. He's been attacking it so hard it's now almost cubic in shape. "I only wanted to go and have a look, because Tooley had been telling everyone we *definitely* weren't allowed to go and watch the wall being built, and we *had* to stay in the Recreation Areas – and, I mean, come *on*, if you're going to tell kids there's something secret being built outside the school then of *course* they're going to try and find out what it is."

Tom looks at his feet and nods. Peepsy's argument is compelling.

"Anyway. I went out there to have a little look. And I found that—" he points at the skull "—in the mud. Well, I didn't find it. Kiran found it. But I picked it up and brought it back. And that's when everything started going wrong."

"I don't see the link," says Alice.

"Come on, Professor. I read a book about Druids. Look at the hole in its head. I saw pictures of them. All those Druid places are cursed. I took the bones from where they were meant to be buried, and now there's all this voodoo stuff happening to the school."

"I don't think there's anything voodoo about it. Your classmates are just getting ill. It's a virus or something."

"Even if it *is* a virus, where's the virus come from? The curse started it. The book said that bad luck followed the people around who dug up the other burial sites."

"Alex, that's just coincidence. There's no such thing as curses."

"But the boy."

"The boy?"

"Doesn't matter." He has another go at peeling the orange and in his frustration he hurls it into the darkness. It makes no sounds as it disappears. It's like it's been tossed into a bottomless well.

Alice turns back to him. "No, go on. Which boy?"

"There's no boy. It doesn't matter."

Tom watches him carefully, before interjecting: "Are you seeing things?"

"I'm not seeing things, sir, he's actually there."

"*He* being…?"

Peepsy sighs in defeat. "The boy. *That* boy." He points to the skull and bones. "They belong to him. He's been following me ever since I moved them. He never says anything, but he's always just there, and I know he's pissed at me."

"Is he here now?" asks Tom.

Peepsy swivels around on top of the oven, looking over each shoulder. "No. He comes and goes, though."

"Was that what you saw in the dining room yesterday?"

"Yeah."

Tom and Alice exchange a look, which Peepsy picks up on.

"I'm not insane," he says. "He was here when you found me."

"You were talking to him. We heard."

"Didn't you see him?"

Alice shakes her head.

"I'm not insane," Peepsy repeats.

"We're not saying you are."

"But you think it."

Tom remembers the pattern he and Maggie discovered, the link between the sick children and the low grades, and asks: "What's your IPR like, Alex?"

"See!" Peepsy's eyes go wide and astigmatic. "You think I've got mental problems!"

268

"No, it's not that. This is important. All the other students who are getting ill are low-functioning, low-potential children."

Both Peepsy and Alice look at him in disbelief.

"Not my terminology," Tom says in his defence. "Those are NSA descriptors. Are you on a Beta timetable, Alex?"

"No. Come on, sir, I'm not that dense."

"Please don't call me 'sir'. Do you have any special educational needs?"

"No."

"Any medical problems?"

"Well…" Peepsy picks some dried porridge oats from his temple. "They thought I had that blood thing. The blood thing that makes you tired. Because you don't have enough iron."

"Anaemia?" Alice chips in.

"That's it. They thought I had that, because I was tired all the time, but I was just spending too many hours on Alpha Omega and it was fucking up…" He corrects himself. "…it was doing things to my sleep cycle. And anyway, I'm not allowed to *not* have enough iron, am I? Because the school monitors what I'm eating. What we're all eating." He points a finger accusatorily at Tom. "I found a cheese ball in that big thing of food waste. I almost ate it. I've never been allowed to eat cheese at this school. The nutritionists always say it's too fatty, and it'll affect my concentration."

Tom feels like there's something very important about this information but he can't figure out what it is. It just sets his spider-sense tingling, nothing more.

"Interesting," he says.

"How is that interesting?" says Peepsy. "It's irrelevant, anyway. Why would a curse target only stupid people? Or people with medical problems? Jesus, I *have* to go to the toilet, sir."

Tom blinks forcefully to stay awake. "Just go somewhere out of sight, Alex. Find a corner to do it in. And tell us which one so we know not to go there."

Peepsy leaps off the top of his oven, wincing, and shuffles off amongst the mountains of rubbish until they can't hear him anymore. Alice watches him go.

"He's great," she says.

"He's okay."

She turns back to him.

"This place is awful, Tom."

"I know."

"Then why are you still working here?"

"It's difficult. Making decisions."

"Ha! Don't I know it."

Tom tries to take a deep breath but his lungs feel too heavy. He knew she'd bring this up. Suddenly it feels like its fifteen years ago. "You're not allowed to criticise me for it now. We're not together. I made my choice. I embraced it, to be single and indecisive. That was my decision."

She shakes her head at his joke. Now Peepsy's disappeared, there's a coolness between the two of them. Tom can feel that strange numbing embarrassment that followed him down the corridor after Miss Potter's lesson.

"Anyway," he continues lamely, "all schools are like this now."

"There must be somewhere better than this."

"Wouldn't have thought so."

They both stare at the floor for a moment. The silence is broken by Peepsy tripping over something around the corner, crying out in pain, and then saying, "Oh cool!"

"So what's your theory?" Alice says at last. "About the sickness?"

"I don't know. I thought I knew. But I'm too tired to think. Maybe we should just call it a curse and be done with it."

He reaches instinctively into his jacket pocket and pulls out the packet of ProSustain. Last one. He pops it out of the foil into his dirty palm. The branding on the packet is a grinning sausage dog, and suddenly all he can think of is the sock, half obscured, belonging to the visitor in the Headmaster's office.

"If we're locked in here," says Alice, "now might be a good time to get some sleep, Tom."

Tom stares at Alice, then at the cartoon dog, then at the pill in his other hand. Somewhere in the darkness, Peepsy is muttering to himself.

12.05

GABRIEL'S VISION of the NSA is laid out as follows:

The main auditorium is where he's corralled most of the women. Some of these are NSA's Year 13 girls, including the Deputy Brand Ambassador and NSA Dance Team leader Abigail "Savage Abs" Savage, who once laughed at him when he tore his trousers picking up some chips from the dining-room floor, and is now paying for it by being brutalised on an almost hourly basis on the auditorium's main stage. Miss Munday is also here, and a handful of the younger female staff, who also receive his attention. He originally planned on taking them all down to the Dungeons, but found he preferred the frisson of engaging in this kind of activity in a very public arena.

In the classrooms, most lessons continue as normal. The AI of the school's students is set up so they continue with their daily routines and parents who are given the tour will be able to experience a normal

NSA day. Gabriel likes it like this. He enjoys the experience of being able to watch everyone else suffer their usual grinding timetable while he is free to go about his business. The bells still ring at the end of every period, and he takes great pleasure in watching everyone trying to navigate the mayhem he's caused elsewhere in the school. Occasionally he will enter the class of a teacher who disliked him and start shooting at their limbs. The Game has learned quickly how much Gabriel appreciates the panic of the younger children, and they scream and scatter and sometimes jump out of the windows, even on the third floor.

The staff common room has also been left untouched. Gabriel, like all NSA students, was never allowed into this holiest of holies, and even now, even in his current state of mind, there's a sanctity to it that he feels the need to preserve. In quieter moments he will drift among the common room's recliners and browse the brands of tea and coffee laid out for his teachers.

The school's main entrance has been repurposed as a prison, because Gabriel thinks this will send a message to any visitors. Using his Sandbox tools he has redecorated the foyer with an appropriately medieval aesthetic. Confined to the cages and strapped to the various instruments of torture are: Will Oben, who in Year 8 threw all his clothes into the changing-room showers; Claire Bostridge and Sacha Turnbull, who circulated doctored naked photos of him In World the week before he was expelled; Joe Steiner, runt from the year below who pulled on his tie so hard the knot became an impossibly tight little stone that needed to be cut out with scissors, and who got Gabriel put in detention because the teachers thought, unbelievably, that he'd *done it to himself*; all of the student librarians he could find who got him banned from the library computers or enforced the ban once it was in place; Mo Ghanem, one of the prefects who'd been passing off Gabriel's hacks as his own; Maya someone-or-other, who kissed him at the Year 9 networking event for a dare; a boy in his year whose real name he doesn't know, but who operates in Alpha Omega with the username DoNkEyInSoUp and uploaded a video that made fun of his mum; and Mr Tooley, who was the principal instigator of his expulsion. Mr Graves is obviously a prime target, too, but Gabriel hasn't yet seen him around the school and his office is locked and strangely impervious to gunfire.

There are two students he's singled out for preferential treatment. Alex Pepys was a laugh back when they used to terrorise Mr De Souza. He and Peepsy hung out In World for a while with a boy called Adam Mackay, another librarian, who later dobbed Gabriel in to the moderators and got his account suspended. Adam is also hanging up somewhere in the school's foyer. There's also Gerald Liu, who in his desperation to make friends became Gabriel's hotline for acquiring obscure oriental snacks and, occasionally, weaponry. Gerald also gave him access, ill-advisedly, to that strangest and most forbidden of fruits: "Shi Mo", the Chinese incarnation of Alpha Omega, which has provided a rich new seam of mischief in recent months. Gabriel never spoke to either Alex or Gerald in person, but as far as he's concerned these were meaningful relationships, so he's allowed them to escape his grim reprisals for now.

The SMT office suite now serves as Gabriel's armoury. His Panzer IV is parked in the organic garden. He had to drive it through the south side of the school to get it in there, demolishing the nurses' room (and the nurses) in the process.

The Game continues to set him optional tasks. Apparently there's a loot box somewhere in the NSA's basement. He takes the stairs, more interested in the Dungeons themselves than what's in the box.

In the sky above the school, the sun sets interminably.

13.30

"SO ARE THERE points? How do you win?"

"No one really wins. The aim is just to do the best throw you can. To do something new. To push the boundaries of the sport. The winner is always Binball."

"I see."

Dr Nowacki smiles but Peepsy knows she hasn't really grasped the idea, because she's a grown-up and no grown-up has ever understood the simplistic beauty of Binball. In fact, there are plenty of children who have never got it, either, or who get it but think it's stupid.

Peepsy crushes another sheet of paper – an IPR report for someone called "Chino Masters", a name he laughed at for a good ten minutes before he was able to compose himself and get the game under way – turns his back on the empty plastic crate that they're using as a "bin", and nonchalantly tosses the compacted ball over his shoulder. It hits one rim, then the other, and finally lands in the bottom with the others.

"See, that one's called an 'Easy McDifficult'. It's like the 'Easy McRanger' but it's more difficult. See? But you've got to make sure it doesn't *look* difficult.'

Dr Nowacki nods.

"Right. What if you do make it look difficult? Is that a 'Difficult McDifficult'?"

"Good question," says Peepsy, thinking how easy it is to be a good teacher. Patience and praise. That's all there is to it. Why don't they get that? "That's actually called a 'Riggers Technical', after Jane Rigby, who *always* makes things look more difficult than they are. Every shot is like rocket science. You can do it like this, too…"

He balls the paper extra-tight, allowing the sweat from his palm to add an extra density to the projectile – an advanced technique – and then throws it underarm as high as it will go without touching the ceiling. The crate rattles as it lands.

"That's called 'Drone Strike'. Or 'Tooley's Revenge'. He's the Deputy Head. He came into T4 while Amir was mid-throw – the thing was *in the air* – and it hit him right in his bald spot. We all thought he was really, actually, literally going to kill someone."

Dr Nowacki throws her own paper ball, which lands in the bin but then skips out again and hits Mr Rosen where he's sleeping, curled up on the floor like a dog among the boxes of old documents. He doesn't stir.

Peepsy crosses himself solemnly, as the rules of Binball dictate.

"What are you doing?"

"You need to pay your respects when that happens," he says. "When it goes in and out."

She laughs, and makes the sign over her chest.

"But you get another go," he says.

She throws another one but this one misses completely, and again hits Mr Rosen just below the eye. His nose twitches. Peepsy thinks Rosen looks very odd when he's asleep. A totally different person. It makes him feel uneasy to see him so unguarded, like he's watching him through his bedroom window, or spying on him in the changing rooms.

"Wow, Professor," says Peepsy, going to collect the errant paper balls, "you're really bad at this. Why can't adults throw?"

"That's not fair," says Nowacki. "You've obviously had a lot of practice at this."

Peepsy tiptoes around the sleeping Rosen and comes back. "I'm not really match fit, though. Miss Potter had a crackdown. There actually isn't a whole lot of paper in the school, anyway. What's the time?"

"Just gone half past one."

"*What?* But we've been down here for *hours!*"

Peepsy initiated the game of Binball (an unofficial meet: he'll have to update the Binball almanac when he sees Josh again) to try and distract himself from the thin, papery feeling in his stomach, and to banish the awkwardness of having to hang out with Mr Rosen and his girlfriend (yet to be verified). He likes the Professor, but it's not like they've got anything in common they can talk about. There have been some suffocating lulls in conversation. Sometimes the school's bowels resonate with clicks and gurgles from the central heating system, but the doors themselves have remained silent and locked.

"How long would you have to wait down here before you thought about eating someone else?" he asks. Alice does a double-take.

"'You' as in 'a person', or 'you' as in 'me'?"

"'You' as in you."

"Wow. Well. I don't think I would. I don't think it would cross my mind." She holds another ball up to her eye, squints, and launches it with a flick of her wrist. This one goes in and stays in. "There's not much meat on either of you, though, is there? Tom would be all gristle. Trust me, I've seen what's under those clothes."

"Gross."

"Sorry."

"What's the story with you and Mr Rosen anyway? Are you going to get married?"

"Oh my God, no," says Dr Nowacki, sitting on one of the boxes and zipping up her fleece, a deliberate gesture to end the game. "We're just friends. Were friends. A long time ago. I haven't seen him for fifteen years."

"But you've seen him without his clothes on."

"Okay, fine, we were boyfriend and girlfriend. For a bit. That's all I'll say on the matter. Don't judge me."

Peepsy considers this. He has difficulty applying the words "boyfriend" and "girlfriend" to either of them. In fact, he can't imagine either of them being a "boy" or a "girl". Both seem trapped in a stasis of grown-up-hood, like they've been forty years old their whole lives. Forty? Thirty? Fifty? He has no idea.

"So, what, you met at school?"

"University."

"University? Really?"

"Really." She points at herself. "*Professor* Nowacki."

"Why?"

"Why what?"

"Did you go to university?"

"Why not?"

"Seems like a waste of time to me."

"It was fun."

"Do you get paid?"

"I wish!"

"You don't even get *paid*?"

"But you get to learn things. And meet interesting people. It's where I met Tom." She nods at the foetal Mr Rosen. It's *very* strange hearing someone refer to him by his first name.

"You think Mr Rosen's interesting?"

"In his own way."

Peepsy lets the matter drop. It's unfathomable. She and Mr Rosen exist in some dark and unknowable country that he doesn't want to explore, and perhaps Dr Nowacki doesn't want to explore either.

"What about you?" she asks. He realises he's staring longingly at the locked door again.

"What?"

"Would you eat another person to survive?"

He shrugs. "Yeah, probably."

"Well, you've got me worried now. I take back what I said about Tom. He's the one you should eat first."

"I heard a story," says Peepsy, "about a mine that collapsed, in Venezuela, and there were three miners that got trapped, and when the rescue teams got to them they found that two of them had killed the other one, and had started eating bits of his leg."

"Really?"

"Yep. You know how long they'd been trapped underground? Six hours."

Dr Nowacki laughs and covers her mouth.

"Like, that's shorter than the normal time between lunch and dinner isn't it?" says Peepsy. "Amazing."

Mr Rosen finally rolls over, disturbed by all the hilarity, and mutters something that sounds like "bag".

"That's great. I really hope that's true. I mean, I don't, but I do, you know?"

"Bag," burbles Mr Rosen. "Bag."

"We should be quiet and let him have his nap," says Nowacki. "Come on. Let's go and look for another way out of here, this can't be the only door."

"Really?"

"Yes. The torch still works on my PAD, even if nothing else does. Let's have a little explore. You don't want to hang out with your teacher and his ex-girlfriend for longer than you have to, do you?"

She pulls her PAD out of the rucksack, and briefly blinds Peepsy with its tiny torch bulb.

"No," Peepsy says, blinking hard. "I guess not."

Nowacki is already on her feet. She starts clambering over the mountains of trash, the blue light held before her, until she blurs with the darkness and disappears.

14.00

DAVID GRAVES (MBA) has to connect one more pink balloon to his line of four other pink balloons, which will cause the balloons to pop and release any number of bonus tokens, including extra lives, a "freeze" balloon, a triple points accumulator, or even a piece of fruit that he can add to his collection and trade in for Bits at the end of this round. That would be the perfect outcome, seeing as he already has two pineapples.

The next balloon is yellow, though, not pink, which produces a tiny surge of dread. There is a small area of yellow balloons in the bottom left-hand corner, but his thumbs are too sweaty and he places it incorrectly, causing the whole nexus of coloured balloons to shift further down the screen and bring him closer to losing the round completely. The helpful pirate who oversees the balloons cackles his derision from the top corner. Graves tries to ignore him. One pink balloon is all he needs. With three pieces of fruit under his belt he'll have enough points to level up and reach the next round.

Somewhere outside the Game he can hear a tidal sound of children shouting and crying. He doesn't know if it's coming from the simulated children in the simulated school or from the actual children in the actual school, but ultimately it doesn't matter, it's all the same and he wants nothing to do with it. He's here specifically to avoid them.

He just needs the balloon, that's all that matters, one more juicy pink balloon, that'll shut the stupid pirate up!

14.30

THIS GIRL looks even more ill than the others, and is behaving very oddly, down on all fours and arching her back like a cat regurgitating a hairball. Sometimes she presses her face down towards the floor, as though she's trying to see something very small on the linoleum; sometimes she rolls her whole head around to look at the ceiling. And she's talking, endlessly talking. There's a brown-red pool under her, too, but it's unclear whether the girl is its source, and, if she is, which part of her body the fluid is coming from.

Maria Da Santos Martinez has nearly finished her midday shift and knows better than to get involved, especially after the business with the boy she let into the basement. But she's been around all six sides of the NSA's third floor since lunchtime, and this is maybe the fifth or sixth student who's not in lessons and who's acting in a way that's difficult to ignore. A group of boys have been running laps of the building, naked from the waist up. They're still going now. They pant like wild animals every time they pass her, trailing the scent of hot blood and cheap teenage deodorant. She found another girl standing at the top of the stairs, looking very closely at the texture of the wall.

"What is this?" she asked when she saw Maria, pointing at one of the breeze blocks. Then she moved on to the next one. "And what is this?" She traced her finger along the cemented cracks. "And what is this?"

Maria didn't answer. She kept her head down and got on with the vacuuming.

Maybe these are all things that their teachers have asked them to do. Of course, it's not for Maria to question any of it. She has her own job to be doing. It's none of her business.

She reaches over her shoulder and removes the telescopic mop from

280

her MultiClean backpack, extends it, and very gently nudges the girl on all fours until she falls over sideways. She squirts the pool of liquid underneath her – it looks like some sort of sauce, but Maria's quite sure it can't be that – with a disinfectant gel, waits for the pleasing "fizz action" to take place, and then cleans up the residue with the sponge end of the mop. Then she prods the girl back into her original position, although she can't get her upright again, and continues to the end of the corridor.

Maria looks back the way she's come. There are "CAUTION: WET FLOOR" signs erected at intervals of about ten feet, amber warning lights rotating slowly and seriously at their apexes. The girl has stopped talking but is still prostrate and retching. The group of racing boys appear around the corner again, and sprint wildly towards her. If they slip and hurt themselves she's not sure if she's liable, even if she's put the signs up. They come and go without incident. They're chasing something, but not each other.

Her goal is achieved. On her PAD, Maria marks the section "Level 3, T-Corridors 1-6, Communal" as "Complete". The screen turns green and she gets a thumbs-up, which temporarily soothes her anxiety. Then the school bell rings out, a melancholy siren, and she looks around for somewhere to hide while the students swarm to their next lessons over her beautifully mopped floor.

Nothing happens. There's no sound of doors opening, no ominous drone of adolescent voices, no herd-like trudge. The girl continues to squirm on her belly.

It strikes Maria that the corridors have been practically empty since she started her rounds at midday. With the exception of these few errant, distracted children. She can't remember seeing anyone going to lunch, staff or students. And now, again, the place is quiet. She doesn't mind it at all, the quiet – it would be a relief, were it not for her worry that something might have changed about the school timetable, about her roster, and she shouldn't be there at all.

"Hey! Hello?"

The voice is coming from the round glass porthole in one of the classroom doors. It's followed by a rattle of the door handle and three regular thumps from the other side. The glass is very thick, and the man who is trying to get her attention, his face creased and purpled with what is possibly rage, sounds like he shouting through a cushion.

"What's going on?" he says.

She shakes her head and stows the collapsed magic mop in her backpack. Not for her to get involved. Not for her to interfere with the running of the school. They've made that clear.

"Can you open the door?"

Maria checks where she's heading next, hoping that when she looks up his face will have gone.

"Hey! Can you *open the door*?"

His eyes are wide and white. He looks like he's putting all his energy into catching and holding her attention.

"Open the damn door!"

If she leaves now she'll have a seven-minute break. She might have a chance to get a drink of water before her next shift.

"Hey. *HEY!*"

Maria walks back over where she's cleaned, pleased to see that the chemical sheen on the floor is now dry, and collects the flashing signage as she goes. The running boys pass her one last time, wheezing with exertion. She glances out of the windows that overlook the NSA organic garden, and can see a group of students, boys and girls, digging in the earth with their bare hands. Others are trotting around the perimeter like caged animals. At the top of the stairs, the girl is still counting the bricks in the wall, interrogating each of them.

"And what is this? And what is this? And what is this?"

15.10

THE LED beacon above the NSA's main entrance rotates its motivational messages in the same order as it has for at least a year. Stephanie Bäcker has obviously never seen them, but she can remember the exact rhythm and intensity of each throb of light from the last hundred times she's stood here. It's like a homing beacon. Maybe it drew him back. Gabriel. Gabe. Captain Gumbo. God, she hopes he's here.

The sonar-like *ping* of her SeeingStick matches the pulse of the promotional screens overhead. Along with the in-built motion and obstacle sensor, her stick has a soothing, faintly Irish male voice that directs her towards the lobby. She doesn't particularly like the voice, but it's a default setting and she doesn't how to change it. When she reaches the steps it quickly becomes clear that she is one of several people waiting outside the NSA in a state of anxiety.

"It's locked. It's not budging."

"It's just stuck, push it again."

"It's not *stuck*."

"Bang on the glass, get someone's attention. Wave at them."

"What am I meant to be waving at? All I can see is my own reflection."

"Do any of you work here?"

"Not like that, like this. They won't see you otherwise."

"Were you here yesterday for the football match? Maybe they've stepped up security because of that."

"Wave harder!"

"Do you work here? I've come to pick up a drone."

"Log in to Alpha, dear, see if they're answering direct messages."

"I've *already* sent them a message."

The chatter stops abruptly as Stephanie approaches, out of respect, or awkwardness, or curiosity, which is always the last thing she wants because it makes her feel like her navigation of the world is some kind of compelling spectator sport. It sounds like there are several sets of parents, the delivery man, and a few others whose presence she can feel, but who until now have kept quiet. The recorded Irish voice continues to coax her gently towards the entrance.

When it becomes clear that she isn't going away, they begin talking again, but not to her.

"Are you here about the evening classes?"

"Evening classes?"

"The night school."

"I'm here about the Management Consultancy trip."

"I'm going round the back."

"They took Alfie on a Management Consultancy trip on Monday, no details, just said he'd be away from school for a night. I can't get him on his phone or his PAD."

"That's *exactly* what happened with the evening classes. Suddenly Shauna has to stay overnight for obligatory pre-VAC induction. I mean, that's fine, I want the best for her, but why couldn't they give us more notice? I haven't been able to contact her, either. Neither has her father."

"A trip?"

"What?"

"Did you say there was a trip?"

"Yes. For Year 11s."

"What about Year 8s?"

"I don't know."

"Shauna's in Year 8."

"And she has night school?"

"Apparently."

"I've not heard from Alex since yesterday. He didn't come home. But I didn't get anything about a trip or night school or anything."

An entirely new voice suddenly interjects: "The NSA is an outstanding school, and its commitment to the security and pastoral care of its students is unrivalled in the area. I'm sure our children are being well looked after."

"Are you missing someone, too?"

"An outstanding school."

Everyone goes quiet again.

Stephanie is aware of a change in the light, which suggests the LED display on the front of the school has been changed. There is music playing, too, someone on an acoustic guitar, amplified by speakers nearby. Above them all, in the NSA's standard promotional video, a six-metre-high Mr Graves walks through a sunlit field. To Stephanie Bäcker it is no more than a surge and flicker of grey and black ghosts.

16.00

ALICE IS LOST, but she won't tell Peepsy that because he's enjoying himself too much. In the last alcove they explored he found a surplus of several thousand packets of glucose tablets, ordered in bulk by the PE Department, now dusty but within their expiration date. He guzzled five of them, straight off the bat. Now he is positively buoyant, demanding to hold the torch and pioneer the expedition. Besides, he already seems to know that they're lost. That might, in fact, be the reason he's so upbeat.

"So, Alex," she asks, "what do you want to do when you leave NSA?"

"What do you mean?"

"What do you want to do? What do you want to be?"

He momentarily flashes the PAD's light in her face. "Dunno. Whatever's right for me. Whatever I'll do well in."

"But in a *perfect* world, what can you see yourself doing in, say, ten years' time?"

"Well, at the moment I'm doing okay in Conversion Optimisation. So I'll probably carry on with that."

"No, I mean, what do you *want* to do. If you could do *anything*."

"I don't understand."

"Like an astronaut, or a plumber, or a chef. Or a teacher. Or an archaeologist."

"They're not real jobs, though, are they? Real people don't do those things."

"I'm a real person! So's Mr Rosen."

"I suppose."

They reach another dead-end. It's impossible to tell if the passage-way actually stops, or if it's just blocked with rubbish, but in either case they can't go any further. The deeper into the tunnels they go, the more the discarded items seem to be ordered – as though over time they have coalesced and ordered themselves – according to broad categories. This particular pile is sports and exercise themed, made up of hundreds of racquets, crash mats, shorts, T-shirts, socks and trainers (singly and in pairs), segmented rubbery rings that Alice thinks are called "quoits", balls of all sizes, engraved medals and trophies.

Peepsy does a three-sixty with the PAD.

"Which way?"

"Up to you," says Alice. "You're team leader."

"I never go right."

"Ever?"

"I mean, yes, of course I have to go right sometimes. But I don't *like* going right. Because it's the 'right' way. And the right way. You know? It's like the word's always trying to *trick* you into going that way, because right is always 'right'. Like, it's the way you'll go if you don't *think* about it. If you let yourself be tricked. And I don't like the sound of the word. Sounds so pleased with itself. 'Left' sounds nicer. Sort of calmer."

"Sounds good to me," she says. "Left it is."

"Hold on. I'm going to steal some of these first."

He rummages in the heap of sports equipment and finds a holey but clean-ish T-shirt, and a pair of voluminous tracksuit bottoms. Alice looks the other way as he peels himself out of his food-and-blood-encrusted shirt and trousers. His torso is so pale it's almost luminous. The karate bandana finally comes off too, and when she turns back to look at him she can see a deep red line in his forehead from where he tied it too tightly.

"Okay," he says, hitching up his waistband and tucking the T-shirt inside. "On we go."

There's a serenity that comes from being surrounded by the darkness. It's quiet, too, and the air is cool and damp. There's no smell of decay. Just a stillness, like being on the seabed. Alice listens to her breathing, matches it with her footsteps. Peepsy was right, left is calmer.

They march on in silence, until the torchlight starts to pick out the sharp edges of doorframes lining the passage. The doors are closed, but have round windows at head height, like the classrooms in the main school.

"Hello," says Peepsy, and veers over to inspect them. He rests his nose on the little sill of the window and raises the torch to the glass. "Holy shit."

"Alex?"

"Sorry."

"What is it?"

Alice follows him and looks herself. After a couple of shoves the door gives way, breaking the seal of scum and dust around the jamb. Peepsy steps through ahead of her.

"Creepy."

The classroom is laid out as though it's ready to receive its next cohort of children. As though it's been ready for the last fifty years or so. Individual desks are arranged in rows, some slightly out of alignment, as though knocked by a bag or a foot when the last class left. All seats face the whiteboard, which is a regular whiteboard, not an IWB, whose pens have long gone dry and are still arranged neatly on a shelf at the bottom. There's no projector, no PC, which dates the room fairly conclusively. There are still pieces of work on the wall – reviews of books that Alice has never heard of, written in very large, round handwriting, mounted on coloured paper. The basement has been largely odourless, apart from the occasional striking whiff from Peepsy's dirty uniform, but this room is thick with the smells of paper and wood and varnish.

"How strange."

Some old instinct drives her to go and sit at one of the desks in the front row. Peepsy perches behind her. The layer of dust that covers the furniture is not as thick as expected. Alice can still see a large, balloon-like penis etched into the desk's surface. She looks up at the whiteboard, as though expecting a teacher to be standing there.

"It's funny," she says. "The actual experience of being in a classroom hasn't changed a bit. Not since the school was invented. Isn't that funny?"

"I mean, it's not laugh-out-loud funny."

288

"Interesting, though. I wonder why it hasn't all been moved In World. Why not do that? Why go to the expense of building and maintaining a physical place, where you need to come to learn?"

"I dunno," says Peepsy. "I suppose if NSA wasn't here, Graves and Tooley wouldn't get their big desks and nice comfy chairs."

"True."

"And what about people like Mr Rosen? I don't know what he'd do if he wasn't here. People like him need it. Need the audience. I feel like… if he wasn't in a school… he'd die or something."

So wise, this boy! What *would* Tom Rosen do? Where would he belong? She tries to turn around in the chair. Its moulded plastic is stiff and unyielding. Peepsy's face is a hazy blue orb in the darkness.

"Would you want to be a teacher, Alex?"

"Ugh. No way. Why would I want to go back to school?"

"Is it that bad?"

"Just boring."

"I saw your Goal Setting class."

"Goal Setting—" he starts to enumerate on his fingers "—IPRs, Pre-VACs, VACs, leadership training. Stupid *mindfulness* sessions."

"Doesn't sound like a huge amount of fun."

"Didn't you have to do any of this? No VACs or anything?"

Alice turns her whole chair around. "We had the option. But we didn't have to. Our school was always slow to pick up these things anyway. I went to Catholic girls' school."

"Oh my God, you *are* weird."

She smiles. "It's closed now. My year was the last one."

"It's like you've escaped from a cult or something."

"That's not miles from the truth."

"But you could choose what you wanted to do?"

"Mostly, yes."

"And you chose digging?"

"It's called archaeology, Alex. It's not *just* digging."

"Are you sure?"

"I think so…"

"Why did you choose it?"

Alice Nowacki considers this for some time. She gets out of her seat and looks at a curling piece of homework tacked to the wall. Very carefully she levers the drawing pins out of each corner, peels it from its sugar-paper backing and brings it to where Peepsy's sitting on his desk.

"What's this?" she says.

"It's a book review."

"Okay. What does it tell us?"

He squints at the paper. "Well, for starters, Simon Feinberg can't spell 'review'."

"What else?"

"He was pretty lukewarm about *When Hitler Stole Pink Rabbit*."

"Go on."

Peepsy shrugs.

"Well, we know he could read," says Alice. "He could write. He was educated, at the age of eleven. He was part of a class of people who were also able to read and write. Girls and boys, schooled together. That's interesting. What about his name. Feinberg. Jewish, presumably. We see him sharing the wall display with a Jeevan Singh, a Rahil Mohammed, a Viktoria Alexandrovich. What does *that* tell us? We get to know what he likes and dislikes. We learn a bit about his values. And look at his handwriting – so small, so cramped. He's almost torn the page with the pressure of his pen. Anxious about something, perhaps. He read the book on holiday, he says. Abroad. So he was probably from a wealthy family. I mean, I'm making some very broad assumptions here, but we get to *know* Simon from this one very small artefact. And it provokes us to ask questions about the things we don't know. It makes connections with all the other things in Simon's life. Who were his classmates? Who was his teacher? Why did he have to read this book at all? Was this a normal task for a boy of his age? Who created the book? How many copies were created? How was it made? Who made the paper? How was the paper transported to his school? That's what my job is all about. Trying to understand who we are through the marks we leave on the world. How we interact with the world. *Materially.* How we navigate all the stuff that's around us." She pauses. She's losing him. Lost him, a while ago. "So there you go. There's your answer. Stuff. I like looking at other people's stuff."

"Uh-huh." Peepsy is drawing a detailed diagram of a sniper rifle in the dust on his desk.

"Sad to think you and your friends won't leave anything like this behind."

He rubs out the picture and looks up. "What? That's not true. You'll be able to see everything I ever did. NSA track everything I do at school, and Alpha Omega will have saved all my In World data somewhere."

"That's not the same thing, though. Where's the hard evidence? Stuff like this?"

She wobbles Simon Feinberg's book review.

"Saved on the MNet somewhere. They keep permanent records for everyone."

"Are later generations going to stumble across the NSA's servers at some point and single out the 'Alex Pepys' folder to browse through? Having your life filed away along with every other person in the school isn't really making your *mark* on the world, is it? It's not like that data actually *exists*, does it?"

"What are you talking about? Of course it exists. It's there. My mum and dad can ask for it if they want. Where's it coming from if it doesn't exist?"

"I think I mean a different kind of existence. Something a bit more tangible. It's like when you or I play Alpha Omega. We don't really *exist* In World, do we? It's just a load of information."

"The information is real, though. Whether it's In World or Out of World. Like... everything's information, isn't it?"

"Yes, but..." But what? Her brain grinds to a halt. Why doesn't he get it? Why can't he see what the difference is? There has to be a difference, or she can't live with herself, after the things she's done.

"Oh!" Peepsy makes a noise that sounds like he's had an epiphany.

"What?"

"Talking of real." He nods behind her. "There he is."

She turns around. In the blackness of the open door there is another boy, much larger than Peepsy. He's not wearing anything. There's a little purple hole in the middle of his head.

"See? It's because you've got his bones," says Peepsy.

Alice, for some reason, waves. "Hi," she murmurs.

"He won't talk to you."

The boy's face is expressionless and, Alice thinks, slightly transparent. It's the strangest thing, particularly after the conversation she's just had with Alex: like he is both there and not there. He opens his mouth and his neck swells a little. The air in the classroom fills with a shapeless hiss.

"What?" she says. "What is it?"

"I told you. I told you I wasn't insane. It's a curse, see?"

The phantom raises a finger to its forehead and taps once between his eyebrows.

Zootopia Golf Safari! v.2.2.1.5

Loading landscapes
Loading textures
Loading NPCs
Calibrating VR hardware
Testing connection

Player D_Graves_MBA joined
Player [unnamed] joined

[unnamed] – I have to admit, I haven't played this one before. Are you much of a golfer?

D_Graves_MBA – I just like looking at the animals.

[unnamed] – Oh yes. It's a beautiful space. I love it. I get so little time to actually use Alpha as it's intended these days. It's quite sad to think how many millions of environments and scenarios I'll never get to experience. Even if I started now and never went Out of World for my entire life, I'd still never get to play them all.

D_Graves_MBA – There's a lion over there.

[unnamed] – Yep, I see it! Well, like I say, I suspect I won't give you the best game you've ever had, but I'll do my best. Looks like you're teeing off first.

D_Graves_MBA – Yes.

[unnamed] – So, I just wanted to thank you again for your coopera-tion in this project going forward, we really are so excited to be working with your students, and the students of so many great institutions.

D_Graves_MBA – You're welcome.

[unnamed] – I feel like we're on the cusp of something really exciting with this generation. A huge step forward. And without you and the

293

NSA and others it really wouldn't be possible, so thank you. Thank you, so much. Wow, great shot!

D_Graves_MBA – I hope we can both achieve the results we want.

[unnamed] – I'm sure we can. Speaking of which, the first portion of the funds has been transferred, and the rest we can get to you once we have the names and details of the subjects. I think it's going to be super-interesting comparing your data with ours. Really fascinating correlating In World behaviour with Out of World outcomes.

D_Graves_MBA – Your turn.

[unnamed] – Right. So what do I do? Like this?

D_Graves_MBA – Yes.

[unnamed] – I hit a flamingo, is that good?

D_Graves_MBA – No. You should also avoid the waterfall.

[unnamed] – Oh man, this isn't going to go well, is it? So, our analysts can't wait to get their hands on your data sets. They're practically drooling! Are the subjects pretty much finalised?

D_Graves_MBA – Yes.

[unnamed] – Did you consider the suggestion I made last time we spoke?

D_Graves_MBA – I did.

[unnamed] – Like I said, obviously there's only so much that we – and you – can monitor remotely, as it were. If we could also observe one of the subjects more directly, that would be… well, a total dream come true. With their consent, of course.

D_Graves_MBA – It will be possible.

[unnamed] – If you don't mind, we've had a look through some of the players' In World histories, and there's one name that stands out.

D_Graves_MBA – Yes?

16.30

GABRIEL HAS twenty-five more seconds to kill another ten students, over all four floors of NSA. They're glowing red on his mini-map, and he's plotted his route from room to room, but even so, a headshot every two seconds is pushing it. There is a tingling in his groin and his forehead.

Rooms 7C, 7E, 7F, a rifle round fired into each, three children's heads explode with a satisfying watermelon *pop*. Then up the stairs, onto the Analytics corridor. Twenty-one seconds to go, and he's ahead of schedule. A girl in room 14A, a boy in 14B, someone from his class who he lent his PAD charger to in Year 8. Ola something-or-other? He can't remember, but he didn't get the charger back. There are three more in the presentation suite at the end of the corridor: the first two drop immediately, a spherical red haze about their shoulders; the last one takes a bullet to the chest, buckles over and takes another two in the neck before the Game registers her as a verified kill. Ten seconds, two to go. Up two flights of stairs. They both emerge simultaneously from one of the T-rooms. The reload animation takes four seconds. Wait. He can do this in style. He selects the assault rifle's secondary function, and as the clock ticks noisily to zero he launches a single grenade between the two of them. One is thrown into the wall, the other into the lockers. Their bodies loll on the floor.

Perhaps they're still alive? Perhaps he wasn't good enough.

COMPLETED! says his head-up display. *SECRET UNLOCKED!* The tingling in his groin turns to gushing relief.

A new objective appears on his map, flashing concentric circles around one corner of the NSA's ground floor. Gabriel heads straight back down the stairs to collect his reward. The going is slow. Something needs resetting somewhere. The school's corridors are increasingly cluttered with the bodies of students and teachers, around which the remainder of the school's residents – children, naked women, tentacled alien folk and the occasional Nazi left over from a previous scenario – are trying to navigate. In the few classrooms that Gabriel hasn't bothered to interrupt, lessons continue as normal. The end-of-class siren still sounds every fifty minutes.

He forges ahead through the mayhem to the targeted location, which, he realises, is the SMT suite. When he rounds the corner, the faceless man is waiting for him in front of the Headmaster's office.

"Gabriel. How are we feeling?"

"Okay."

"Just okay? You seem to be doing better than that. Great work on the challenges. We're really pleased for you."

"What do you want?"

"To show you what you've unlocked. It's pretty exciting."

The faceless man is blocking Gabriel from advancing any further into the lobby area of the Headmaster's office. The sudden restriction in his movement brings Gabriel out in prickles of cold sweat.

"I wish you wouldn't keep interrupting. I thought you said I could do what I want. But it ruins everything when you turn up. I don't want you here."

"We totally understand. I'll leave you alone after this. But first, I just want to show you this new scenario."

Gabriel says nothing. He trains his rifle on the colourless oval where the man's face should be.

"Remember earlier, Gabe, when you were talking about going home? Well, truth is, you *can* go home. This is a scenario we've been working on for a while now. We just weren't sure if it was ready for testing. But you've really impressed us, so we thought we'd reward you. It's awesome, I promise. Come on in. Have a look."

The faceless man steps to one side and the door to the Headmaster's office opens of its own accord. On the other side is not an office at all, but a room that looks much more familiar. Gabriel steps through, and the sudden change in light and sound feels like he's plunged feet-first into a cold pool.

He is standing in a bedroom, his bedroom, or at least an almost perfect replica of the one he's been hidden away in ever since he turned thirteen. Everything's in its right place, TV, PC, Alpha console and VR kit, his samurai swords in their display cabinet, his posters, tacked to his walls in the usual places, including the one of Princess Alissa, stuck to the ceiling to encourage him to dream of her when he goes to sleep. His clothes are strewn on the floor. Used tissues, also. The level of detail is like nothing he's seen before. The only thing that's different is the smell, or lack of it. There's just the faint fizzle of ozone that's been in his nose since he went In World, instead of the thick, sweet odour of sweat and deodorant and old pizza that he associates with his personal domain.

"What do you think?" The faceless man is standing in the corner of the room, looking like a hat stand.

"Where am I?" he says, stupidly, because of course he knows where he is. There's nowhere he knows better.

"Pretty cool, right? Gabriel, you're no longer in VR. This is RR. Double-R, we call it, so we don't sound like pirates!"

It's the kind of joke some of the teachers at NSA used to make, and Gabriel doesn't laugh.

"Double-R?"

"It stands for Replicated Reality."

"You mean Augmented Reality."

"Nope. This is a 100% like-for-like simulacrum of the real world, built from the ground up, so to speak. You can interact with and manipulate every aspect of it, just like you can in Sandbox." There's a strange click of saliva that suggests the faceless man is smiling. "Out of World is now In World. Or at least it will be, once we're out of Beta."

"How did you do this?"

The faceless man pauses as though the question makes no sense.

"You can answer that, can't you, Gabriel? It's nothing new. Mapping data from satellites has been in the public domain for years. Same with shared media – photos and videos and such. With private premises we can buy the CCTV footage, but these days everyone wants an In World replica of their site for promotional reasons, so most people are quite happy to give us the textural and structural information we need. Now, everyone'll have their own copy of the world."

"But this is my bedroom. I don't remember giving you information about this. And I'm pretty sure I've never taken any photos of it."

"We can map domestic interiors with the Alpha consoles. This room is, I think, duplicated from a scan that took place last Sunday, while you were In World. We update as often as we can, but it looks like Mr Carnoso has already disconnected your machine."

Gabriel's bedroom door, which usually opens onto the hallway, instead looks back into the corridor of his personalised NSA.

"What about the rest of the house?"

"We're working on that. Living room and kitchen are mapped, I think. But there are still a few nooks we've not got enough data to reproduce faithfully. They're coming, though. This is just a taster."

There's something missing, Gabriel knows, but he won't admit it to himself. A presence that should be there, not in the room but somewhere outside.

"It's funny that we've ended up here," the faceless man continues. "We're starting to realise that when people play Alpha Omega, they don't actually want escapism at all. They don't want the tropical beach resort. What they want is the world they already know, but with a just a little more control over it. They want it to fit more with their feelings and their desires and their goals. I can see, Gabriel, you're already happier just for being in an environment you recognise."

That doesn't make sense. "What do you mean you can *see* I'm happier?"

"And it's about to get even better. Bear with us a moment."

The faceless man disappears and Gabriel is left to survey the artefacts of his previous life. He is calmer, for sure, but he's not sure he actually likes that. And the missing thing. He doesn't know whether he wants to see and feel it, or whether he's afraid that he will.

On cue, the missing thing appears.

"Hello Gabe!"

His mum appears in the space left by the faceless man, illuminated in a shaft of intensely pink light, recognisable and unrecognisable at the same time. Her skin is youthful, her hair thick and unbound. She is wearing a loose red dress, cut lower than anything Gabriel can remember his mum owning. The strangest thing, though, is the ease with which she moves. Nothing tentative or nervous about it, no groping for orientation.

"Hello Gabe!" she repeats in identical intonation. There's a slight oscillation in her words that suggests her voice has been reconstituted from disparate and fragmented recordings. She's looking straight at him, her eyes clear and porcelain-sharp. "Are you ready for school?"

"What the hell is this?" Gabriel says out loud.

When she steps towards him, she has the same big-hipped, wiggling

299

gait of the AI girls who have been colonising his In World experience ever since he arrived.

"Hold on a second." The faceless man's voice sizzles in his ears for a moment, and then goes silent again.

"Time to get ready for school," his mum says, sounding like a come-on.

"What the *fuck*." Gabriel edges around the bedroom. He wants to throw up.

"Time to get ready. You're a big boy."

"Stop it. Get me out."

White noise that suggests the faceless man is listening in. No reply, though.

"Hello?"

"Big boy." His mum extends her hand.

"*Hello?*"

"You can put it anywhere you want."

Gabriel raises his arms above waist height for the first time in two days and his heart protests with a series of aching palpitations. He gropes around his temples and the control gloves *clack* against the smooth, cool plastic of the VR headset. The band of elastic is too tight to fit his fingers underneath, so he has to grab the hardware from the front. The picture of his bedroom and his mother glistens and distorts. An intense sickness pushes at the back of his eyeballs, and for a moment he thinks he might be dying.

"Gabriel, wait."

The faceless man's voice is distant and unreal. As he lifts the headset off his eyes, he can feel something snagging on his forehead – not on it, *behind* it, he realises as he tugs harder. It's like there's a fishhook in the front of his brain.

"Gabe, stop."

Filtered air seeps in around the neoprene seal and stings the surface of his eyes. They flood with hot, viscous tears, blurring the edges of all he can see. Still the sensation of a thread being pulled from between his eyebrows.

When the headset finally clatters too loudly to the floor, the room beyond holds all the dark, formless menace of a nightmare.

17.00

WHEN TOM ROSEN wakes up, he thinks he's in the bedroom he grew up in, and wonders why his TV isn't there, why the door is so far away, why someone has left the lights on. In fact, this has happened to him every time he's woken up since he was eighteen and left home for university.

It takes a couple of minutes for him to remember where he is, why he's there, and another couple to realise that he's been unceremoniously abandoned by Alice Nowacki. On top of that she's taken the kid with her, in some sort of proleptic enactment of how their marriage (which he's still considering, on and off) might pan out.

He rolls onto his side. The ProSustain has left him hollowed and strangely rigid on the outside, like he's a fibreglass model of himself. Bits of him snap as he stands up straight. The pair of runaways have left no clues as to where they've gone. He shouts into the darkness.

"Alice? Hello?"

There's no echo. The piles of trash absorb the sound completely, so his voice only projects a few metres in front of him, making the basement feel much smaller than it actually is. He tries the door again. Locked, obviously.

A dull *clang* reaches Tom's ears from the opposite end of the

Dungeons, back where they found Peepsy. He picks up his tattered jacket, which he was using as a blanket, and shuffles at not-quite jogging pace towards the source of the sound.

Around the corner he sees that the segmented metal shutter separating the waste disposal area from the rest of the Dungeons has been opened by hand, and in the gap stands one of the support staff in dirt-coloured overalls.

"Aha!" says Tom. "Hi. Hello. Amazing. You opened it. Is there a way out at this end?"

The man's eyes narrow slightly, as though he's trying to work out if Tom is real or not. He sucks his teeth and says nothing.

"Yes? No?" Tom scans the man's uniform. The name "Dennis" is embroidered on his left chest pocket. The named overalls are a new development in the terms and conditions of their employment, an attempt at appeasement by the NSA after receiving complaints about the support staff's treatment.

The man jerks his chin in a way that could either suggest "come with me" or "get out of here". Tom takes it to mean the former and slips through the gap between the shutter and the wall. Straight away he's hit by the heat of the incinerator again. Dennis hauls the whole thing closed.

"You haven't seen two other people, have you?" he asks Dennis's curved back. He'd probably be a couple of feet taller than Tom if he wasn't so stooped. "A woman and a boy?"

Dennis waits until the partition is fully sealed before turning around, and even then he doesn't look at Tom.

"No," he says, and lopes past him, neck stuck out in front like a vulture.

That, Tom realises, is the first time a member of the support staff has ever exchanged any words with him in fifteen years.

"No? Oh. Well. Can I go back through there? I should probably look for them."

"No," Dennis says again.

"But there's no way out of the Dungeons, is there? Not if the door's locked."

"No."

"So… we should probably go and find them, right?"

Dennis takes about five or six steps to fully come to a halt, like a ship stopping mid-ocean. By now he's next to the piles of waste where they first found the filthy Alex Pepys. He twists his head over his shoulder.

"We don't go in there. And we don't *want* to go in there."

Then his engines fire up again and he's on his way.

Behind the incinerator and the three mountainous piles of recyclable and non-recyclable waste is a service elevator, which is apparently still operational. Waiting inside are half a dozen more support staff, overalls camouflaged against the dirty steel and aluminium sides. They all watch in silence as Dennis embarks, followed by Tom. Somebody hits a button with their palm, and the grille across the front of the elevator closes, screaming.

"Where does this come out?" asks Tom. The support staff look at him like he's speaking in a foreign language. Dennis tugs at the cuffs of his overalls. He seems embarrassed.

Tom watches the scrolling brickwork of the lift shaft. For all its grinding and rattling, the service elevator only seems to go up one floor. The cage opens into another passageway that's so dark Tom can't see his hand in front of his face. The support staff seem to know their way from one end to the other via extrasensory perception. Next to him, Tom can hear Dennis breathing, and feels the heavy sway of his torso. He guides Tom like a metronome.

303

The bodily sounds of the other men and women are steadily drowned out by a pervasive harmony of digital and mechanical noises. There are several frequencies of insect-like buzzing, the growl of something that sounds like a very powerful motorbike engine, and beneath everything the slow pulse of a turbine.

Around the second corner there's a pair of double doors that aren't closed completely flush, and out of the crack is seeping a light the colour of mustard gas. Dennis pushes through head first.

Tom has heard rumours that the support staff are supposed to live on-site. The idea wasn't completely unbelievable, but he's never seen the accommodation itself. He assumed that they were housed in the flats owned by NutriStart, along with the new teachers. In fact, they all seem to be living here, in this yellow haze, in hundreds of bunk-beds arranged like a field hospital. The ceiling is very low, so low that the people in the top bunks can't sit up straight without hitting their heads. At regular intervals the rows of beds are broken by large pieces of machinery – generators, boilers, air-conditioning units, all the other engines that power the buildings overhead. The combined noise is unbearable. It shakes Tom's atoms apart. Tubes and cables snake from ceiling to floor and from wall to wall, sometimes winding themselves around bedposts and under mattresses. The support staff hang their spare clothes from them like washing lines.

A hundred faces look at him briefly, with disinterest, as one might notice a fly entering a room. They are from a wide variety of ethnic backgrounds, but the light, or whatever it is that's in the air, gives everyone a uniformly poisoned-looking complexion.

"My God. Is this where they put you all?"

Perhaps Dennis can't hear him through the soup of sound, or he's just being his usual incommunicative self, but he doesn't reply.

He leads Tom from one end of the dormitory to the other, through another set of flimsy double doors, and up some steps to an entry point that looks like a spaceship's airlock. Dennis nods to a polished black infrared scanner.

"It's locked," says Dennis.

"This one too?"

"Use that." Dennis points at Tom's lanyard.

"It won't work, though."

"Use it."

Tom waves it around in front of the scanner. As expected, nothing happens.

"You're a teacher here," says Dennis.

"Not anymore, actually. They've disabled my pass."

Dennis sucks his teeth again, and trudges back down the steps to the dormitory. Again Tom follows him, weaving through the rows until they arrive at what is apparently Dennis's own bunk. Dennis turns, lowers himself slowly onto the mattress, and closes his eyes. It's soon clear that he's not going to open them again. His chest rises and falls steadily under his overalls.

Tom stands awkwardly among the other support staff, though he needn't really feel awkward since nobody is paying attention to him. About half of the whole workforce is down here, he estimates. Some are perched on the edges of their beds, shaving or picking at their fingernails or staring into the dirty ether. A few are down to their underwear, brushing their teeth and spitting into mugs at their bedside. Some are coughing violently. He was half expecting to meet Alice and the boy in here. Part of him is worried for them; part of him is still furious that they wandered off without him.

"Does anyone know what's going on?" he says, loud enough for the nearest few rows to hear him. Nothing. An old man spits out his toothpaste. A thin, birdlike woman raises her bedsheet over her face and lies there like a cadaver.

Tom goes to see if he can find a bunk of his own.

18.00

THE FIRST thing to come fully into focus is Gabriel's own body, his flesh off-yellow in the half-light. The colour of his complexion is made all the more noticeable by the whiteness of the telemetry pads stuck to his chest and back and head, many of which he can't see, but knows are there from the tug of the wires when he turns in his seat. Below his navel he has a towel around his waist, stiff and coarse against his skin. A tube emerges from its folds, thicker than the others. He's on a drip, too.

Gabriel squirms against the smooth upholstery of the chair, which is segmented and reclined like a dentist's, whimpering as the pads come unstuck. Although he can breathe perfectly well, the sensation feels strangely like drowning, ensnared in fibrous weeds. The worst is the catheter, which snags and burns as it's withdrawn, enough to make him start weeping again. He mouths "Mum" involuntarily. The faceless man continues to mutter at him from the floor, where the headset is lying.

Once he's free of the wiring, he composes himself and sits upright. His cubicle is about ten feet in each direction, barely lit by a neon disc embedded in the ceiling. The floor is a rubbery mirror, showing a few smears from the last time it was mopped. Various pieces of sophisticated-looking medical equipment are stacked in a tower next to the dentist's chair, topped by a black Alpha Omega console. Everything is plugged into everything else, and hums soothingly.

He doesn't remember being put here. He remembers getting into the DV outside his estate, settling into the passenger seat, and then somehow that experience was elided with his experiences In World.

He has to use his arms to manoeuvre his legs off the chair, and he hangs the dead weights of his feet above the floor for a moment. When he tries to stand up, he immediately collapses, feeling nothing in his knees when they strike the hard vinyl. He lies on the cushion of his right cheek for several minutes, inhaling the chemical tang of the floor cleaner. Eventually he crawls to the cubicle's glass door and hauls himself up on its handle, his free hand clasping his towel, which is wrapped around his thighs and waist like a giant nappy. The door opens inwards, a challenge of balance and coordination he's not quite ready for, and he clings to the handles on both sides like they're the mast of a sinking ship, before propelling himself into the corridor beyond.

As it turns out, Gabriel is in cubicle 88 of at least 100. There's a Perspex sign on the wall that says so. He wanders past another five doors, 89–93, behind which are three children of about his age, and an older man and woman. They're all practically naked, their heads concealed with VR equipment, gloved hands twitching. Sometimes he rests and pushes his nose to the glass, watching them. It reminds him of the tropical house in the zoo his mum took him to once. It's about as warm, too, now he's left his own air-conditioned cubicle.

Someone is coming from the other end. Wordless, urgent footsteps. Gabriel zigzags from one side of the corridor to the other and stumbles into a bathroom opposite the VR suites. He goes to the sinks for a drink of water, passes his hand under the tap to activate it, and then becomes suddenly, paralysingly anxious about the prospect of putting anything in his mouth, about drinking, eating, sleeping, doing anything besides sitting completely still, in this bathroom, on his own. The water runs and runs. Gabriel looks up at his reflection in the mirror. His appearance as a whole is horrifying under the unforgiving lights, but one thing in particular chills him. Above his eyes is a red, winking hole, like someone has popped the world's biggest spot in the middle of his forehead.

21.30

THE SPONGE filling of the crash mat is soft and water-logged and feels like quicksand to lie on, but Peepsy's stubbornly dragged it all the way to the classroom from the piles of PE equipment and now feels obliged to make use of it as a matter of pride. He wriggles around, listening to the sounds of seepage under his shoulders and head. It smells like pond water.

"Oh yes," he says. "This is great. Very good. Very comfortable. I'll get a good night's sleep on this."

Dr Nowacki's bed is a nest of old tracksuits. She's sitting bolt upright in the middle of it, staring at her PAD. Ever since the boy came and went she's been very quiet. Peepsy has been doing his best to fill the silences with his own noise, but it's getting a little tiring. His stomach gurgles in the silence.

"Sorry," says Dr Nowacki, roused suddenly. "You must be starving."

"I shouldn't have thrown that orange away."

"I've got a sandwich in here," she says, reaching for her rucksack. "And some raisins. I was planning on rationing them."

She unwraps a package of foil and hands him half. He sniffs at the filling.

"Houmous," she says.

He nods, folds up the corners, then puts the entire thing in his mouth.

"Anything new?" he says, with difficulty.

"Nope. No WiFi, no nothing. Here." She hands him a flask of water. "Be a bit more sparing with that, we don't have a lot."

He takes two tiny sips.

"Where do you think Mr Rosen is?" he asks.

"Probably sleeping where we left him. Or he came looking for us and now is just as lost."

"Do you think he'll be okay?"

"As okay as we are."

"And are we okay?"

She shrugs. "I suppose."

Peepsy reclines on his mat and stares up at the ceiling, its panelling pocked and cratered like the moon.

"Who do you think he is?"

"Who?"

"The boy."

"He's just another student. Don't know what he's doing down here. Playing a prank or something."

"Oh come on, Professor. I thought we were agreed on the curse. How'd he just disappear like that?"

"It's pretty easy to disappear down here, isn't it? We've managed it."

"So you don't think he's a Druid?"

"I think he's a kid from your school. Don't you recognise him?"

"Nope."

Peepsy makes a reticule out of his finger and thumb and pretends he's scanning the planetary surface for minerals, or perhaps preparing for some sort of orbital bombardment.

"Wouldn't you rather it was a ghost, though?" he says when Dr Nowacki falls silent again. "Isn't that why you really got into archaeology? For all this supernatural stuff? Holy Grail. Sword in the Stone. All of that."

Dr Nowacki laughs. "Guilty. That's why we all do it. Forget everything I said before."

"Maybe I'll be an archaeologist, then. You don't get curses and ghosts in data analysis."

Dr Nowacki puts down her PAD and turns to him. "Really?"

"Sure. Why not. When we get out of here, get me an internship at your place."

He's just saying that, of course. He'd never follow it through. His parents would be so disappointed in him, and they've already endured enough disappointment to last them a lifetime.

THURSDAY

7.00

THE CROWD outside the NSA has been growing steadily through the night, and now, with the sun just coming up, it's large and loud enough to probably be classed as a mob. Stephanie Bäcker is trapped, and her SeeingStick has been largely useless in the confusion. It has been gently but firmly reminding her of the danger since about midnight, repeating the words "Multiple moving obstacles detected, return to a place of safety" over and over again in its Irish lilt, the only pause coming when one of the other mothers nearby inquired after the stick, and then addressed the stick directly, and then started flirting with the stick for an incredibly embarrassing few minutes. The NSA's promotional video has also been playing non-stop. Stephanie reckons she could now sing all six minutes of the backing track, note-perfect, from memory.

The parents are tired and angry. Stephanie can hear the windows and doors of the school being attacked with feet and fists and heavy objects, to no avail, and every so often a particularly confident dad's voice will ring out – "Let *me* try!" – and there will be grunts of exertion, followed by a stream of swearing and excuses. The NSA, it seems, is quite impregnable. Incommunicado, too. There have been no messages to parents, no press releases, no updates to the school's In World Hub. The only attempts at assuaging the crowd are being made through the brain-numbing promotional video, and the man, who claims to have a son at the school but is obviously affiliated with its management team in some way, still circulating among the parents and loudly affirming the NSA's "outstanding track record for pastoral care".

Once every half hour or so someone suggests messaging the fire service, but there's not a single person present who is willing to call whatever fire service they're a member of, because it means their insurance contributions will go through the roof. At some point during the night, somebody turned up with power tools and tried to drill and saw their way into the building, but the doors, windows and cladding proved indestructible.

Some members of the press are here now, as well.

"And you haven't seen your daughter for how long?"

"Must be, what, thirty-six hours?"

"Going on that way."

"And how worried are you?"

"Really, very worried."

"Extremely worried."

"Extremely."

"Is your daughter on Alpha Omega?"

"Yes, of course."

"I don't suppose you could show me her profile?"

"Sure. She just uploaded a whole new photo reel, I think…"

"Oh. Oh dear. God, no. That's no good at all."

"There are better photos though, hold on…"

"She's tiny!"

"Please…"

"No, she won't do at all." The journalist raises his voice. "Anybody else got a missing daughter? Sixteen or over, ideally. Five-foot-nine or thereabouts."

As well as the human journalists, who all sound like they are themselves in their teens, Stephanie can also hear the zoom of the news drones strafing the crowd. Sometimes they stop and hover, a steady whir of fans meaning they've found something or someone to focus on.

Stephanie knows that she and her SeeingStick will act like a beacon for newsfeeds who want a heart-tugging human-interest story.

Throw in the scandal of Gabriel's expulsion, and the tragedy of his disappearance, and they'll be swarming all over her. She tries to make her way out of earshot of the drones and the journalists' questions, and ends up squatting in a flower bed at the bottom of the steps.

Besides the crush of indignant parents, there's something else that's kept her here all night. It's the strangest feeling, but she knows, *knows* that Gabriel is in the school. She keeps thinking she can hear his voice. He feels so close she could cry. Perhaps it's just nostalgia, a psychic imprint from happier (if not actually *happy*) days when her son went to school like everybody else, and made a few friends, had his lunch, did his homework, and came home with the clean smell of sweat and washing powder about him instead of the rancid, pubescent stench that comes from his bedroom now. Perhaps there's also the fear that if she went home she would have nothing to do, apart from listen to the humming of that box under the stairs, and wait for the call from Safeway Security Ltd.

"Does anyone here know Gabriel Bäcker?" she says in a low voice, hoping the journalists won't hear her.

No reply apart from the shuffling of feet.

"Anyone? Gabriel Bäcker?"

"Explosives," comes the new suggestion. "We need to make some explosives. Blow the windows out."

It's *exactly* what her husband would have suggested.

7.15

GABRIEL WAKES UP in a kitchen with no memory of how he got there. He's at the bottom of a laundry bin, piled high with dirty napkins and aprons and chefs' whites. Not a bad hiding place, he congratulates his past self, but the smell of old, dried food is making him nauseous and he's forced to come up for air regardless of who might see him. The kitchen's empty, thankfully, and dark. The only light is coming from blueish UV tubes overhead that remind him of the nightclubs In World. He slithers over the edge of the bin like an egg yolk and plops onto the floor, where he lies for a few moments. The middle of his head is still stinging.

Before he goes looking for a way out, he rummages in the bin and finds a shirt and some trousers that are almost his size and aren't too badly stained. The trousers are checked black and white and look slightly clownish, but they're better than the oversized nappy he's been wearing up until now.

Outside the kitchen he climbs some stairs that lead up through three, maybe four storeys. The floor has a rubbery coating, like a hospital's floor. Perhaps he *is* in a hospital, thinks Gabriel, until he reaches a frosted glass door with a huge decal of the Alpha Omega logo, the Greek letters, one inside the other. A private clinic for employees of the Game? If it is, why wasn't he told he was being brought here?

Gabriel squints. On the other side of the door it doesn't look much like a ward. There's a riot of colour and indistinct shapes through the blur of the glass. It looks like it could be a children's play area. With one hand hitching up his chef's trousers, he leans on the door and pushes through.

It is, technically, an office, though this word doesn't do the place justice. It's very bright and open plan, scattered with men and women in armchairs and swings and beanbags. None of them notice Gabriel's entrance because they all have their own VR headsets on and wouldn't have seen or heard him if he'd burst through the door at the head of a marching band. The office has a carousel, a ball pit, three slides, an ice-cream van and something that looks like a replica pirate ship right at the back. There's also a rubber dinghy ride that meanders its way between the workstations, which Gabriel nearly tumbles into. The ride gives the whole place a tropical humidity.

It feels safer on the floor, and when he's low down the hole in his forehead doesn't throb so much. Gabriel goes on his hands and knees to a man sitting in a tiny model airplane. The man's head is bowed as though in prayer, lips slightly parted. He's manipulating something delicately with his gloved and wired fingers. Perched on the nose of the model airplane is a PAD, and some sort of compartmentalised cheese-dip snack box. Gabriel takes both and crawls into the corner, where he hides in the ball pit.

Gabriel opens up the PAD's home screen. As well as the Alpha Omega logo, there's also a picture of a sausage dog, winking and smiling and saying, "Good day!" Those two words aren't just a cute bit of dialogue, they're the name of the brand itself: Good Day are Care's biggest rival. They nearly moved to a Good Day estate when his dad left.

The PAD's owner is, luckily, still logged in. He's also synced his current Alpha session, so Gabriel can view exactly what the developer is doing in a live-streaming thumbnail video in the top right-hand corner. It all looks quite mundane – he seems to be putting the finishing touches to a rendering of someone's bathroom, the environment covered in the fibrous, skeletal frame and numbered coordinates that only show up in "design mode". The developer is selecting the correct colour and texture for a shower cap.

It takes Gabriel a while to give himself administrator privileges. The process is exactly the same as when he hacked the NSA MNet, and is simple but time-consuming. He swipes at the PAD screen with one hand while the other dips in and out of the synthetic cheese goo. After so long not eating anything, it's electrifyingly salty.

Somebody shouts from the other side of the room. Gabriel freezes. It's a few seconds before he realises it's a recorded message from the ice-cream truck.

Once he has access to the root, Gabriel searches the directories for his own name. There are hundreds of thousands of results. He gets a vertiginous surge of adrenaline. He decides to finish the cheese dip before taking the next step, scooping every last little bit out of the corners of its compartment. He nestles a little lower into the coloured balls.

The first folder he opens is labelled "Bäcker, G., IW Data". There is an icon that says "Live" and another that says "Historic". "Live" takes him to a streamed video of the scenario he tore himself from the previous night. His mother's avatar is still wandering in front of the first-person view, looking seductive but a little lost. "Historic" takes him to hundreds, thousands of video clips, arranged by day. They play when he hovers his finger over them. The most recent are from his test-play – he can see himself charging around the NSA, exploring the beach, meeting the faceless man for the first time – but the older records go back years into his playing history. He can see the co-op missions he used to do with Alex Pepys, the first time he visited the Party, aged twelve, the hours he put into harassing teachers In World when he joined the NSA in Year 7. His early forays into Meninist territory, before he learned to cover his tracks.

Another document is named "Bäcker, G., Biometrics". This opens up a chart that seems to be updating live – a clock blinks in the top corner – monitoring heart rate, blood sugar, adrenaline, serotonin, dopamine, cortisol. There are acronyms appended to the graph's lines: SSRI, SNRI, TCA, TeCA. All of these are flat-lining as of about 1800hrs the previous night, but in the hours and days before that the data makes a rich and colourful landscape.

Then he notices the name of the directory containing all of this information. "NSA/Good Day" it reads at the top of all of the search results. He zooms out. There are hundreds of "IW Data" folders, initialled and surnamed. Many of the names he recognises from when he was at school. Not friends, as such, but they ring bells. He dips in and out of them, greased, cheesy fingers quivering. He searches "NSA". He searches "Good Day". He searches "David Graves". He reads and absorbs, the stinging in his forehead becoming more and more acute.

He's suddenly aware of another man in the ball pit with him.

"Hi there, Gabe."

The faceless man's voice sounds strange Out of World, sloppy at the edges, almost drunken. He's reclining opposite Gabriel like he's in the bath. The faceless man has a face after all, but it's almost as blank as the one he has In World. It's round and pale and textureless. His auburn hair is so heavily gelled it looks like a toupee. All of his features are of precisely average size and shape, as though they themselves have been algorithmically created, the exact median of a human face.

"What are you doing down here?"

Gabriel sits perfectly still, as though this might make him invisible.

"We'd really like it if you could carry on the test-play. We thought you were doing brilliantly."

Gabriel burps, his cover blown. "I don't want to."

"Why not? Aren't you happy In World? If you're not, you can always change it. You're in charge here."

"No, I'm not. I'm not testing the Game at all. You're testing me."

The faceless man performs a masklike frown, and Jesus Christ, thinks Gabriel, doesn't it look like one of the preset expressions used In World.

"No one's *testing* you, Gabriel. We're getting feedback, that's all. We want the Alpha experience to be as good as it possibly can be, for you, for everyone."

"I've seen what you're doing." Gabriel shows him the PAD screen he's just been looking at. "I don't need curing."

At that, the faceless man's face returns to neutral, and he leans forward. The plastic balls rattle between them.

"Okay Gabe—"

"Don't *call* me that."

"Gabriel. Perhaps we could have been a bit clearer from the start. We didn't want to put you off, that was all." He taps him on his thigh. "Your game isn't just any normal test-play. It's a piece of research with much wider reaching implications. Alpha Omega isn't just about entertainment. It's about happiness. The data we're getting from you and our other volunteers is going to help you and millions, maybe *billions* of people live happier, healthier lives."

"Is this going to help me live a happier life?" Gabriel points to the hole above his eyes.

The faceless man interlaces his fingers. "Think bigger picture, Gabe. Do you have any idea how miserable your classmates are? Because I do. I've seen the data. What about your parents? What about everyone? It's an epidemic. Do you know what I mean when I say epidemic?"

Gabriel clasps the PAD to his chest.

"The amazing thing about In World Therapy is that it can automatically diagnose mental health problems that people don't even *know* they have, just from the way they behave In World, and then treat them through tailored environments and scenarios."

"And medication."

"Medication?"

"How much are Good Day paying you and NSA to diagnose all of us?"

"Oh my goodness." The faceless man laughs. "Gabriel. I'm so sorry. There's been a misunderstanding here."

"It's more than a misunderstanding."

"No, Gabriel, I need to clear this up. Oh man!" He laughs again. "You're not like everyone else. I've told you that, right? You're not flying coach class here. You're in the executive lounge." He shakes his head. "The deal we made with Good Day is old news. Yes, Alpha's been working with a whole load of schools to try and get a fuller picture of kids' mental health. The original plan was that we all – Alpha and the schools and Good Day – work together to get you guys feeling happier and more effective, et cetera, et cetera. But you're so *right*, Gabe. What you said earlier. You don't need curing. And meds are dirty things. I realised, before the trial had even started, we've been coming at it from the wrong direction. Let's make sure kids are happy in the first place! Prevention rather than cure, right? That is precisely where you come in, buddy. I'll let you in on a secret: Good Day is on the way out. Pharma is on the way out. Why swallow a bunch of chemicals if you can just feel better by playing a game? It's cheaper, it's safer, and you feel *genuine* happiness. It's *you* that's producing the chemicals."

"Until you leave the game."

"Well, there's an obvious solution to that, I think."

The faceless man makes a strange, helpless shrug.

"But you're still running the test on the others. With Good Day."

"I know – it's a pain in the ass – but a contract's a contract. I mean... you know that better than most."

"I didn't sign a contract."

"I did say, Gabe, you didn't have to sign anything."

"Then who did?"

The faceless man ignores him. "Everyone deserves to be happy, don't they, Gabriel? That's not too outrageous a statement, is it? If it's within our grasp, surely it would be unethical *not* to do what we're doing? If you stop the trial now, you'll be setting everything back considerably. Your own treatment included."

"I don't need treatment."

"Your behavioural data would beg to differ. Your mum would beg to differ."

"My mum?"

"Your school would beg to differ, too. Don't think for one moment that you were expelled because you misbehaved, Gabe. It's hardly wise for an academy like NSA – which, I don't know if you're aware, is absolutely *on the brink* financially speaking – to lose the revenue from a student for a simple matter of misbehaviour. They let you go because you were ill."

"I don't want to go back In World."

"Again, I'm sorry to break it to you, Gabe, but your biometrics suggest otherwise. All our data points to the fact that you were very happy in the scenarios we were creating for you. Not we. You. That you were creating for yourself. The inclusion of your mother was an oversight, I'll admit that. We got ahead of ourselves."

"My mum," says Gabriel again. He is conscious, suddenly, of the infantile sound of the word. When he speaks it, his mouth makes the same shape it made when he was just out of the womb. And here he is in a ball pit, in his big elasticated trousers, unable to swallow solids, still a baby.

"She wants you to get better more than anyone."

"I want to talk to her."

"Let's get you back In World, first."

"No."

"Gabe."

"No."

"I didn't want it to come down to this, but you are contractually obliged, I'm afraid. Do you know what that means? It means it's the law."

The man's face interchanges about four different expressions, as if he's unsure of which is the correct one for this situation.

"Tell you what," he continues when he doesn't get a response from Gabriel. "Let's get you something to eat and drink. You can video call home if you like, talk to mum, and then we can get on with things when you're feeling ready. How does that sound?"

Gabriel thinks, then nods.

"Good going," says the man. He half swims, half crawls to the edge of the ball pit and climbs out. Gabriel wades after him, the employee's PAD in one hand, the cheese snack pot in the other. He stands in front of the faceless man, scratching at the spot on his right forearm where one of the intravenous tubes was attached. He's surprised to find he's taller than him.

"You ever had ice cream for breakfast?"

Gabriel shakes his head.

"Well, it's something else! Say, want to give me that PAD?"

Gabriel shakes his head again.

"Gabe?"

Gabriel swings the PAD with as much strength as he can summon, and the corner connects with the man's temple. Again he seems unsure of which expression best suits what's happening, and he settles on something that conveys not so much pain as disappointment. He staggers to one side and trips back into the pit. Gabriel clutches at his waistband and runs.

He lumbers between the swings and slides and tubs of brightly coloured bricks. Out of World, his movements are nightmarishly slow. Along the way, the developers are woken from the Game. Their heads rise and droop and rise again, but none of them removes their mask. The ice-cream van is singing to him again.

At the far side of the room he tumbles through another set of glass doors into a corridor lined with elevators. He summons the nearest one, thumps a button, and collapses in the corner. He can't catch his breath. His heart feels like an overfilled waterbed.

The elevator takes him up to the ground floor. Ahead of him is more of an avenue than a corridor, the ceiling so high he could be outdoors. On either side are windows like shopfronts, and down the centre are benches and fountains and topiaried bushes. Among them, the employees of Alpha Omega are going about their business. It looks like a carefully designed "market scene" from a stage musical.

Gabriel spills out of the elevator into the avenue. The marketgoers stop and stare, unsure of what it is they're looking at. Nobody seems to want to stop him. He stumbles onwards, peering through the windows. Through the glass on the right there's a yoga lesson. About fifty people are lying on their backs and clasping their knees to their chest. They roll around like eggs. Some women are watching it from a balcony, neon-coloured coffee cups in their hands. They're laughing. Beyond the yoga studio is a conference room where some suits – he can't see how many – are sitting in darkness watching a video of a baby dressed as a 1950s private detective. They're laughing too. Everyone's laughing.

When Gabriel looks behind him to see if he's being followed, he's thrown over the bonnet of a car, a very small DV which someone is apparently driving indoors. "Oh my God," he hears the man behind the wheel say, but thinks nothing of it, thinks nothing of anything, and gets to his feet and carries on to the end of the avenue.

His path arrives at a large chrome-and-glass atrium. Its centrepiece is a three-dimensional rendering of the Alpha Omega logo, perhaps thirty feet high, transparent and prismatic, casting coloured light into all corners of the space. Beyond it, Gabriel can see he is at street level. He can see the foyers and ground floors of other buildings. He can see traffic, and a few pedestrians. It looks like an alien planet.

Everyone in the atrium is just watching him, their faces a mixture of curiosity and amusement and nothing at all. He's aware of footsteps behind him. Someone offers him some sparkling water.

Gabriel runs for the door, which turns out not to be a door. It doesn't budge. He presses himself against the glass, like a goldfish on the edge of its bowl, while the people in the street point and stare and film him steadily on their PADs.

9.30

"TODAY'S MY BIRTHDAY."

Alice turns to Peepsy, who's stopped in the middle of the tunnel, his white T-shirt a smudge in the darkness. They've been hiking through the tunnels for half an hour. Still no sign of a way out.

"What?"

"Today," he says again. "It's my birthday. I forgot."

"You forgot?"

He shrugs.

"Well," Alice says, bringing him into focus with the PAD light. "Happy birthday. I haven't got you a card or anything."

"That's alright."

"How old are you then?"

"Thirteen."

"Wow. An official teenager. I feel like we need to do something. To celebrate."

"Like what?"

"I don't know. What would you normally be doing on your birthday?"

"Not a lot." He fiddles with his fringe. The quiff has long since collapsed, and now he's taken to twisting it into a single, long, stiff tusk that protrudes from his forehead. "It's not like we have a big blowout on my birthday. Mum and Dad aren't super rich."

"Really? I thought NSA was one of the more expensive academies?"

"It is. That's why we're not super rich. And the academy my sister has to go to is even more expensive."

"I didn't know you have a sister. What does she do?"

"Dribbles a lot. Wets herself. Screams in the middle of the night. Usual big sister stuff."

His blue-lit face looks older than it should. She knows he's not joking, but wishes he was.

"I'm sorry."

"Why?"

"I didn't mean to bring it up."

"Ha."

"What's so funny?"

"*Bring it up*. Everyone always talks about her like she's a dirty secret. It's fine. We can talk about her. It wouldn't be very nice to pretend she doesn't exist."

"Can I ask what's wrong with her?"

"Yep. Someone drilled a hole in her head."

"Oh my."

"I mean, she asked to have it done. She used to go to NSA. Every-one thought she was going to be Brand Ambassador – she came top in her VAC exams, captain of the netball team, everything. When she was doing her internship in Year 12 she kept missing her targets, so she went to get the trepanning thing done. To improve her concen-tration. It was all legit – like, she didn't have it done in some back alley somewhere. But anyway, something went wrong, they went too deep or something, and now she's just a vegetable. Can't walk or speak or anything. Ho hum."

"Oh Alex." She puts a hand on his shoulder. He stiffens and she takes it back.

"So, actually, that's what I'm usually doing on my birthday. Look-ing after her."

"Well. When we get out, I'm taking you somewhere nice. Pizza and chips, or whatever kids eat these days."

"When we get out?"

"Yes, when."

"Okay." He gobbles up another couple of glucose tablets and pockets the wrapper. "I hope it's soon, because I'm down to my last packet of these and I think I've burned off that sandwich."

"We'll find a way. Don't worry."

On they go, into the abyss. Alice is, in fact, quietly terrified that they haven't found an exit, haven't even found their way back to where they left Tom, despite trying to retrace their steps. There's the business with the "ghost", too. She didn't sleep at all, and they're down to the dregs of her water bottle.

They pass more classrooms, bathrooms, changing rooms. A whole other school compressed and fossilised beneath the NSA. This deep into the Dungeons, nothing is horizontal or perpendicular to anything else, so it's impossible to keep track of one's bearings. The whole structure seems to pitch and yaw, imperceptibly, like a slowly sinking ship.

Along the way they find an open store cupboard piled with musical instruments, trumpets and saxophones and violins stacked in their cases, triangles and tambourines, a plastic bucket full of recorders. Peepsy selects one of these and blows a spider out of the mouthpiece. He mournfully intones "Happy Birthday" in rhythm with their footsteps, and it's only after about ten attempts that he gets all the right notes.

"Have you asked for a present from your parents?" This question is mostly just to get him to stop tootling.

"Sort of. I just asked for them to transfer some Bits to my Alpha profile. Then I can buy some stuff In World."

"Stuff." She smiles.

"It's not really a proper present, I know."

"Okay, after we've had pizza and chips, I'll get you a proper present."

"Like what?"

"I don't know. Whatever you're into. A football or something. Do you and your friends still play football?"

"Of course we still play football. What do you think we are?"

"Yes. Of course. Sorry."

"And we still go outside. And we talk to each other *in real life*."

"I'm sure you do."

"We're not completely retarded."

"You can't say that, Alex."

"But we're not."

"I mean that *word*."

"Yes, I can. I'm allowed to because of my sister."

"That's not how it works…"

"I'm just saying: we're not stupid. We don't need you to tell us that spending loads of time on Alpha is going to turn our brains to mush. Like, we *get* it. It's just difficult not to spend loads of time on it. That's what it's designed for. And it's *really* fun. The most fun." He blows into the recorder as hard as he can and it screams like it's injured. Then: "You know that, don't you? You must be on Alpha. Everyone is."

A terrible silence. Alice looks at her hands. There's no way of explaining to Peepsy that, yes, she does have a profile on Alpha Omega, and for years now it's been her primary source of income. No way of explaining how she's at the Party almost every night; how the Party has developed, almost without anyone noticing, from a fairly innocuous dating app into the world's most extensive platform for amateur pornography; how, partly to make more money, partly as a weird joke with herself, Alice has recently been committing herself to the most absurd and horrifying scenarios she and her fellow users can dream up, involving illnesses, foodstuffs, livestock, etc., getting a friend to mock them all up in an animation and video editing suite in return for a cut of her "tips"; how she's retained the name "Clodia" to give her exploits a slightly intellectual veneer, and at least pretend that the joke is on the *users* rather than on her. There is no way of explaining this to Peepsy, or to anyone. Not even Henry.

"I am," she says. "I hardly go on it, though."

"Sure, that's what everybody says. That's what *I* say. But it's never true."

Peepsy plays "Happy Birthday" once more, this time with a jaunty, samba-type feel to it. Alice blows on her hands. The air is significantly colder now.

"Do you think we're still under the school?" Peepsy asks. "Feels like we've walked for miles."

"Honestly? I have no idea. I don't even know if we're the right way up anymore."

"Do you have any reception? WiFi?"

Alice checks the top of her PAD again. Sad faces across the board. She wonders if Henry is still trying to contact her, or if she's given up.

"No connection," she says. "And running out of battery as well."

Peepsy gulps. He twists his single spike of hair again. Then his face lights up.

"Look!" He points behind her. "Fire exit."

Above her head is a green-and-white glass box, with an arrow and an angular figure of a man running. At the end of the collapsing corridor are two double doors with a push bar.

"Worth a shot."

They get to the doors at the same time and push together. Alice gasps. Peepsy makes a noise like "Ay". On the other side they're met with the coldness and emptiness of deep space.

10.00

IT'S THE SAME dream Tom Rosen's been having since Alice Nowacki returned from the grave, the one that visited him in the single, hallucinatory hour of sleep he managed to snatch on Tuesday night, and again when he was curled up on the floor in the Dungeons. Now it's back for a third time. It is dusk. A cold, end-of-the-world feel. He's on his way to a grand party, the kind of party he's never been to, in the grounds of an enormous house, with butlers carrying canapés, and pyramids of champagne glasses, and a hedge-maze, and peacocks mingling with the guests. He knows that this is what the party is like, even though he's not actually at the party yet. He is both there and not there. He is excited about it, and has a woman in tow – he's excited to impress her, too. The woman is sometimes Alice Nowacki, sometimes Bernice Potter, sometimes Maggie O'Brien. Sometimes all three of them are there, following him up the broad, darkened driveway and laughing. When they finally reach the house, Tom finds he's been approaching from the rear – he can hear the sounds of the other guests floating over the back wall. He makes his way around the whole perimeter of the house, but there doesn't seem to be an entrance anywhere. The Nowacki/Potter/O'Brien composite starts to get restless. Still he can hear the music and laughter and clink of glasses from inside. "It's fine, I know the way," says Tom, but already the company is starting to recede, and he can hear Maggie telling him he's pathetic, and he just keeps wandering in circles around the place. Even though he'd like the dream to end there, it doesn't, because in an unexpected twist he *does* find a way into the party, only to discover that the house is his parents' house, and that the party is modest and quiet and sad, and he spends the rest of the evening apologising to his dear old mum and dad for not bringing a date, they patiently hushing him like a child.

He's woken by a change in the frequency of the dormitory's noise. There's an urgent buzzing that sounds like one of the machines is broken. The air in the basement has left a salty rime on his eyelids, and he has to lick his fingertips and run them along his lashes before he can blink comfortably. On the other side of the room, through the complex mesh of bunks, wires and piping, he can see a small group of support staff gathered around three turbines built into the wall. Two of the fans are still spinning, one has stopped, and someone, possibly Dennis, is poking at it with a broom handle. When he first arrived, Tom assumed the fans' purpose was to recycle the air in the basement, but now he wonders whether they're actually pumping fumes *in*, whether this might, in fact, be the outlet for the rest of the school's air-con.

Tom gets out of his bed and performs some rudimentary stretches. His hands touch the ceiling when he reaches up. Attached to each bunk is a metal cage with a name tag, containing the bunk's owner's personal effects. Amongst the toiletries of "M. Da Santos Martinez", who hasn't returned all night, is a half-full bottle of forest fruits flavoured protein water. Tom takes a swig and goes over to speak with Dennis.

The jammed turbine is still humming. He approaches and peers over the shoulders of the assembled support staff. In the six o'clock position, mangled between the fan's blade and a criss-crossed metal grille, is a smart black brogue. This is the offending item that Dennis is trying to dislodge with the broom. In the darkness on the other side of the turbine, though, something is emerging from the brogue; a sports sock, a pale, bare leg, with a child on the end of it.

"What are you doing?"

Dennis and the others' faces seem impassive at first glance, but when Tom really studies them he sees something much more complex underneath. Their indifference is a mask, a tough callous that has developed to hide something else.

"What are you *doing*?" Tom says again, feeling himself flush and sweat along his hairline. "That's a kid! Shut the thing down, it's going to take his foot off!"

The shoe is at a truly grotesque angle, its rubber sole twisted like a dog's chew-toy. Dennis lowers his broom handle and stares at Tom like he's an idiot. Tom doesn't push the matter, but he does go to the panel at the side of the turbines and punch several buttons until the other two slowly spin to a halt.

"You're not supposed to shut them down," says Dennis. "Some-one'll get fired."

Nobody helps Tom as he pulls at the edges of the metal grille, hauling with his full bodyweight until it shudders and clangs and begins to peel away from its attachments. Once he's able to get an arm through, he levers the whole thing up and the grille pops off like an enormous bottle top. He grabs the boy's leg above the ankle – below looks too much like it's turned to pulp – and his thin body slithers out of the vent and onto the floor.

He thought he could smell something savoury underneath the acrid chemical fog in the basement, and now he knows why. Small Paul seems to have lost about 30% of his bodyweight. He looks almost mummified, like a piece of dried fruit. The drying process has apparently intensified his distinctive odour. He isn't dead, but his breathing is very quick and very shallow, and he's grinding his bloodstained teeth.

Tom picks him up and carries him to the nearest bunk.

"Can someone get some water?"

"Not allowed to interact with the students," says one of the support staff, her hair tied back in a bun so tight it looks like it's about to pull her scalp off.

"What? Come on, help him!"

There's a general murmuring, in which Tom can make out the words "responsibility" and "allergy" amongst others. It's not their fault. They're bound by the handbook as much as he was. He goes all the way back to the other side of the room, gets the flavoured water from M. Da Santos Martinez's bunk, returns to the panting Paul Winkler and pours a little over his mouth. It leaves a clean patch around his lips that looks like a clown's make-up, or rather the reverse of it.

"Are you alright, Paul?" Tom says, stupidly, and he can imagine Alice laughing at him. "Can you hear me?"

The boy's tiny arms are outstretched, vertically from the bed, his hands curling and uncurling as though grasping at something unseen. Tom gives him a little more from the water bottle. Dennis's long shadow falls over them both.

"He's not allowed to be here."

"I know. I get that. But he's here now and he's not well so you need to look after him."

"We're nothing to do with the student body," Dennis asserts. "Not supposed to get involved."

"I think you can ignore the handbook, Dennis, in the circumstances. Just keep an eye on him. If he got down here through the vent, then we can probably get up the same way." Small Paul makes a clicking sound out of the side of his mouth. "I'm going to go up and see if I can find out what's happening. And I'll try and get this place opened up."

Most of the support staff have drifted back to their bunks by now. Dennis stands at Small Paul's side and looks into the boy's face as though it is a puzzle to be solved. Tom worries for the moment that Paul will be classified as an anomaly by the support staff, as unrecyclable waste, and dealt with accordingly. He considers staying, but then there's no chance of him getting any worthwhile help if someone doesn't get the school unlocked.

"Unless," Tom suggests, "I look after him and you go up?"

Dennis looks up and shakes his head. "I'm not maintenance. I'm not allowed in the vents."

"Right. Well. Take care of him then." Mr Rosen met Small Paul's mother and father once, for a parents' online consultation session, and they'd seemed equally small and frail and fretful, disorientated by the video call, more like his grandparents than his parents. The loss of their only child, he suspects, would be ruinous. "Wish me luck."

No one's even watching when he climbs into the opening of the vent. The metal tube is just high enough for him to walk in, though he's bent double, his back and shoulders pressed against its curved roof and making a soft, rhythmic thump against the joins. After a few awkward steps he's already in pitch darkness and uses his PAD to light the way ahead.

Tom worms blindly through the substructure of the school, left, right, up. At the end of a long, unbroken stretch of the vent, he sees a soft, buttery pool of light coming from a hole in the bottom. He approaches on hands and knees, his spine hot and creaking from stooping so much.

The hole is a perfect circle, housing a stationary turbine and covered with a metal grille, like the one he entered through. He peers down and finds he's above the school kitchens, or at least part of them. The vent is designed to suck up the thick vapours expelled by the dish-washing machines. He can also hear a shuffle of feet and somebody "shushing" somebody else.

He sits on the edge of the circle and kicks down hard on the mesh. The first attempt sends his groin into more spasms. He curses and changes legs, and after four more strikes with his heel it falls to the floor below. He can hear more muttering. Then he dangles his lower half through the hole and slips onto the top of the dishwasher, its stainless-steel casement booming like a timpani drum.

Once he's climbed to the floor, he barely has time to look at the kitchen's residents before something black and heavy and circular arcs from the right of his vision and connects with the side of his head. There are a few moments before the pain really explodes when he thinks, very clearly, that being hit with a frying pan feels exactly like how it is depicted in the cartoons, his entire body reverberating like a tuning fork. Someone else hits him below the ribs with what he assumes is another kitchen utensil, and a third attacker goes for his legs.

He's curled up on the tiles, head clasped in his hands, when someone calls out:

"Oh my God! Stop! It's Mr Rosen!"

There's a break in the assault. Panting.

"Careful. He might be just like the kids."

"He's a teacher. The teachers are fine."

"Not true! What about Briggsy?"

"Briggsy was broken *ages* ago."

"But look at his face."

Tom feels the soft edge of a loafer prod at his cheek. He bats it away and rolls himself supine. He can hear the mob backing cautiously away.

"What the hell was that for?" he says, feeling around his right eyebrow, which is smooth and taut like the skin of a plum. The lump from Monday's head-smashing incident still hasn't subsided either. The shape of his face is fairly monstrous at the moment.

No one answers. He sits up and looks around. About ten people are looking at him, a mixture of teachers and students, tired and drawn and stained with blood and other things.

"What is this? What are you all doing here?"

A man steps forward, one of the young teachers Tom was watching in the briefing on Tuesday morning. He's lost his top hat, but his monocle is still dangling from his breast pocket.

"Sorry, Mr Rosen, we thought you were Paul. Or one of the others."

"One of the other what?"

"The kids."

"And why would you need to beat the shit out of me if I was one of the kids?" His eye is so swollen now he can hardly see out of it.

"Haven't you seen them?"

"I met Paul on the way up here. There's hardly anything left of him."

"Paul Winkler's not the only one."

The young teacher – what's his name? Swinton? Swinson? Swainson? – looks at him seriously, then offers him his hand. Tom grasps it to haul himself up. The other man squeezes a little too hard, a tiny display of physical dominance.

"Can you just tell me what's going on? I've been locked in the Dungeons for the whole night."

"We don't know what's going on either."

"But the kids…"

"It's bad."

"*What's* bad?"

The man looks at him.

"Come and have a seat."

The other teachers and children start to wander off, congregating in two distinct groups on either side of the room. Neither group seems to know how to act around the other. As they part, Tom is given a view of the full length of the kitchen, its walls lined with refrigerators and ovens and microwaves big enough for a man to stand up in, along with more complicated machinery for food preparation and processing. It looks more like a car production line than a kitchen. There are more people, besides those in the circle, including the catering staff themselves, who aren't socialising with each other or anyone else. They're tucked into nooks among the machinery or sitting on the floor in twos and threes. They could be refugees.

Swinton leads him to one of the steel worksurfaces, where the kitchen's residents have collated the food they've foraged. A Year 10 girl is plucking cubes of NutriStart branded frozen tofu out of a torn plastic bag.

"Help yourself," says Swinton.

The younger teacher is obviously enjoying keeping Tom in suspense. Tom rummages among the bags and selects a can of beans. The girl skulks away, eying him warily with a solid block of bean curd tucked into one cheek.

"Is there a can opener down here?" he asks.

"It's not just the Dungeons that are locked," Mr Swinton begins, ignoring Tom's question. "Everything is. Internal and external doors. The whole school's been in lockdown, as of midday yesterday, when the new security system came online. And all the doors and windows are reinforced as per Graves's instructions last year, so you can't break them. Believe me, I tried."

Swinton nods to himself. Tom studies the rim of his can of beans.

"And the kids?" he says.

"No one knows what's happened to them. Half of them still seem alright. The other half – most of them are running around like Winkler. Some are passed out. There's a corner of the library where they're all just screaming. Must be a hundred of them. You can hear them through the glass."

Tom nods. He decides to keep all his own intel to himself, all the evidence that he and Maggie found. It gives him a little private glow of superiority.

"Everyone's locked in their rooms. We've got parents and media gathered outside the main entrance. Us lot are all the staff and students who weren't in lessons when the school was shut down, and we've all just gravitated here. Everyone had the same idea, I guess. Came for the food, when it was obvious we weren't getting out. And it's a bit hidden away."

He polishes his monocle absentmindedly. There's a long period of silence, while Tom takes it all in.

"What about SMT? What've they been doing this whole time?"

"Tooley's still sending out internal messages. Or at least his office is."

Swinton points at an LCD screen above the serving hatch, which is playing the NSA promotional video, over which is stencilled the message:

Please remain in your rooms and follow procedure for "lockdown" as detailed in staff handbook. Have a good day. Mr R.M. Tooley (Principal Deputy Head).

Tom's laugh is so loud and coarse it hurts his throat.

"I see. Looks like he has the whole thing under control, then. Can he even get out of his office?"

Mr Swinton shrugs. "There's nothing we can do. We'll just have to wait."

"And what about all the kids locked in their rooms? And the support staff?"

"Like I say. There's nothing we can do."

Tom thinks of Alice and Peepsy, alone in the darkness. He's still flip-flopping about whether he's worried or not. He's worried for *one* of them at least.

"You haven't seen Alex Pepys, have you?" he asks.

"You were with Alex Pepys?"

"I was with him in the Dungeons. Me and him and a friend of mine."

"You're not allowed in the Dungeons."

"For crying out loud. Have you *seen* him?"

"No. But he was with you at midday?" Mr Swinton already has his PAD out and his fingers patter over the screen.

"Yes." Tom pauses. "Are you updating your register? You are, aren't you?"

The younger man doesn't reply. He frowns momentarily at Tom before completing his task.

"Good," he says at last.

"Good?"

"Listen. I know you're worried. We all are." He puts a hand on Tom's shoulder. Tom looks at his beans again. "But just stay put. We're safe here, we've got enough to eat and drink. WiFi signal is pretty good."

"Oh excellent."

"Just don't open the walk-in freezer."

"Why not?"

"Just don't."

Tom weighs the can in his hand, considers hurling it at someone.

"Can you at least tell me how to open this?"

"Don't know. Ask Maggie. She's rooted out most of the things around here."

Tom's heart contracts unpleasantly at the mention of her name. He didn't like how things were left between them, and Mr Tooley's accusations, however untrue, have made him anxious. He doesn't know what he's going to say, but it's too late, anyway. She's there, in front of him, as bedraggled as ever but completely unflustered by the circumstances. Of course she was out of lessons when the security system came on. When was she ever *in* lessons?

"Hello, sir," she says, leaning on the worksurface.

"Hi, Maggie."

She laughs at him. "Jesus. You look bloody awful."

"Nice to see you too."

She seems to have forgotten all about their last meeting.

"I left the can opener down the other end," she says. Then she leans in to whisper in his ear. "Say, you want to see what's in the freezer?"

12.00

GABRIEL IS hunkered down behind the roots of a gum tree in an artificial bayou. He doesn't know why the offices of Alpha Omega should need a bayou at all, but he found it, after blundering around the lobby and taking another three trips in three different elevators. There was a roped walkway he was meant to stick to, but he quickly and deliberately got himself lost in the undergrowth.

He's sitting in about six inches of pleasantly warm water, hidden by foliage. The air smells green and mossy. The remains of butterflies are smeared across the screen of the PAD he stole. They keep getting attracted by the lights and the colours, and he keeps having to swat them so he can see what he's doing. There's a rumble of an alligator somewhere downstream, which he assumes is just a recording to add a bit of authenticity.

It's getting difficult to concentrate. What he's trying to do is get all the information off the PAD and into the world. Or rather, Out of World. There's no point in him broadcasting everything on Alpha Omega, because they'll just delete it, at his end, at the recipient's end, and no one will be any the wiser. To make matters more difficult still, they keep trying to lock him out of the PAD. Every few minutes he has to create another profile for himself and circumvent the new security protocols they've put in place, in what is becoming quite a tiresome game of cat and mouse. His current strategy is to forward the incriminating data through various cloned identities and eventually land it in the inbox of someone who is affiliated with the NSA but not with Alpha Omega. There's one particular person who springs to mind, one of the few members of staff who Gabriel quite liked, despite, or maybe because of, his backwardness. There's also his mum.

The bayou has been cultivated under a domed glass roof, which is magnifying the midday sun and making everything unbearably hot. The PAD has trouble registering the strokes of his fingers, there's so much condensation on it. He's getting sleepy. A purple fuzz has started to creep in at the edges of things. There goes the alligator again.

The faceless man appears soundlessly, and Gabriel has no idea how, since he's had to slosh through ten feet of water to get to his hiding place behind the gum tree. He's already concealed the bruise on the side of his head with make-up, it looks like. Or Gabriel just didn't hit him that hard in the first place.

"This is quite an expensive ecosystem you've ruined, Gabe," he says. "I can't let you stay here. It's for employee well-being only."

Gabriel tries to get up but can't get any purchase in the mud. He can't tell where his legs end and the water begins.

"Come on. On your feet, soldier." He's about to try and lift Gabriel by the armpit, and Gabriel wafts a hand at him, like he's one of the butterflies. The faceless man shrugs. "Still just trying to help," he says.

Gabriel rolls onto his front and tries crawling away. The PAD disappears into the brown water. His chef's trousers are slipping from his waist, but he's past caring. A flat groan escapes from him.

"Where exactly are you trying to get to, Gabe?"

"I'm going to tell everyone."

"If that's what would make you happy, then you're more than welcome to."

Gabriel crawls another few feet.

"That's what I've been trying to tell you. Whatever you want, that's what *we* want. You want to tell the world, we can set that up. You want vengeance, we can set that up, too."

Two or three other figures appear from the bushes. The centre of Gabriel's forehead starts stinging again.

"Is that what you want?"

He's too tired to speak, now.

"Gabe?"

Delivered by AIM.

Dear Jared,

Have you tried NutriStart's Delicious Hair Removal Spread? 100% natural, 100% delicious!

Thank you for your suggestions. Finalised list of names is below.

ADDY	W	BULLEN	G	DURAND	C
AHUJA	K	CANN	S	DUVALL	O
ALLEN	C	CANTRELL	E	EDMUND	Y
ALLYN	J	CHEEK	O	ENSIGN	D
ANTONIO	L	CIRCLE	G	ERSKINE	M
APPLEGATE	U	COMMITTEE	F	EWART	P
APRILLE	H	CONGDON	C	FARIQ	A
ARRIS	D	COOKSON	J	FARNUM	D
ASHER	W	COTTAGE	Z	FENNELL	E
AUBREY	N	COURTENAY	N	FINN	R
BABB	M	CREWS	J	FONTAINE	T
BÄCKER	G**	CUBA	P	GALVIN	F
BALLS	E	CULBERTSON	P	GRICE	M
BATTEN	I	DAN	Y	HADFIELD	A
BEEKMAN	S	DARE	H	HARTER	N
BEMIS	R	DARNELL	F	HAZLITT	C
BLANC	B	DAVID	O	HELL	W
BLUNDELL	E	DAVIDS	R	HINDLE	R
BORLAND	Z	DILLON	R	HOFFMANN	F
BRAINARD	A	DOBBINS	D	HOLLY	F
BRILL	T	DOLLARD	B	HOPWOOD	F
BROWN	S	DOLLARD	W	HOUCK	I

HOUSER	L	MORRISSEY	S	RUSS	H
IDA	Y	MOTOR	E	SABIR	N
IRON	A	MUSGRAVE	R	SACKETT	Y
KATE	F	NEVILLE	H	SAMPLE	E
KEANE	D	NIMMO	P	SCHULZ	R
KRAUS	B	NIX	Y	SHERLOCK	E
LANDER	W	O'BRIEN	M	SHUTTLEWORTH	K
LAYCOCK	R	OLDER	J	SLOANE	F
LE MAITRE-BRIDGE	C	ONABOLU	A	SMEDLEY	E
LEVER	C	PAINE	A	SNOOK	S
LITCHFIELD	A	PASTOR	G	SOUTHARD	S
LO	Y	PEET	S	STANSFIELD	G
LOEB	D	PICKUP	T	STIMSON	E
LOWTHER	I	PLATE	W	STONE	T
LUSK	F	PRINCE	R	STRAUS	A
LYNDE	K	PROVOST	K	TA	W
MAHAN	R	QUINLAN	V	TALLEY	V
MAHMOOD	A	QUIRK	F	TANAKA	T
MANNERS	F	RACE	H	TAPLIN	M
MARVIN	U	RAFFI	H	TIFFANY	K
MATT	R	RAINES	U	TOPPING	D
MC GRAW	J	RAINEY	B	TOWLE	L
MC KNIGHT	E	REALTY	J	TULLEY	T
MCBRIDE	J	REPUBLIC-CHASE	H	TURK	Y
MCCARTY	E	ROBIN	T	VARLEY	V
MCFEAT	S	ROCHESTER	T	VEITCH	S
MCKENNA	L	RODMAN	B	VERE	O
MESSER	H	RONALD	R	VERNON	C
METHODIST	J	ROUND	D	VINSON	G
MORAN	J	RUFF	G	WAGGONER	G

WAGGONER	U	WASSERMAN	J	WINDSOR	W
WAGSTAFF	G	WEIR	B	WOODALL	K
WANAMAKER	M	WHEREAS	R	WRIGLEY	P
WANTED	I	WHITFORD	W		
WARFIELD	N	WINKLER	P		

IPRs, dietary history and dietary plans for new year should also be accessible now. I will be in touch re: timings with Bäcker, parental consent, etc.

Regards

David

12.25

MR_RED_PILL CAREFULLY loads three large plastic drums into the driver's seat, passenger seat and boot of the DV. No one else has turned up today, so he has to struggle with each tub by himself, in full knowledge of how volatile the contents are. He's terrified of dropping them on the garage's concrete floor, even though he does his dumbbells at least every other day. His mum hears his grunts of exhaustion and twice asks if he would like any help, which he declines.

He's furious with the others for their desertion. And they called themselves real men! He's most disappointed in Captain Gumbo, who has gone completely off-radar, even though he was the one who came up with the idea in the first place. All talk, just as Mr_Red_Pill expected. But then what else should he have expected from a teenager? The kid probably just prefers blowing things up in Alpha and doesn't have the cojones to take it Out of World. The Captain was also meant to provide a schematic of the school to show them exactly where they could cause the most meaningful damage, but he hasn't delivered on that either. Not that it probably matters, with all these explosives in the car.

He closes the doors very gently, then turns his PAD on. At least the GPS is working now. He looks at the screen and sees the view from the dashboard camera, pointing at the shelves of paint and tools and hoses on the rear wall of the garage. It's all straightforward from now on. He'll be able to watch the whole thing while he's eating his breakfast.

12.30

MR BRIGGS is squatting among a pile of boxes labelled "Breaded Cod-style Lozenges", his eyeballs frozen in a kind of totemic stare. Frost glitters on the shoulders of his suit jacket, the tops of his knees, the tip of his nose. Occasionally a puff of condensation drifts from his blue, half-parted lips, the only thing that suggests he is, in fact, still alive.

"How long's he been in there?" Tom asks Maggie. She's opened the door to the walk-in freezer just wide enough to fit their faces in, one above the other.

"Since yesterday evening. He spent all afternoon sitting in the corner of the kitchen, totally silent, not saying anything. And his face getting redder, all the time, till it went purple, like a steak, and he gets up, and he starts telling everyone to get back, throwing pans around and calling for backup into his PAD like it's a walkie-talkie, and he's crying too – big fella like that, crying and swinging his fists – and it took about ten of us to get a hold of him and throw him in there. Mr Swinton didn't help at all, obviously."

"Is he okay like that?"

"Seems alright, doesn't he? Not causing anyone any bother."

"I mean… won't he freeze to death?"

"Nah. Look – Mr Briggs!" she shouts. "You cold?"

The huge, frozen golem doesn't move or speak.

"See?" Maggie says. "He's fine."

She withdraws her head from the gap in the door and Tom does likewise, and they seal him into his icy tomb. At first he feels sorry for poor damaged Lt Dan Briggs, ex-marines, but then he thinks that the freezer is not far from being a sensory deprivation tank, and might be exactly the kind of treatment he requires.

Back in the kitchen, Maggie turns and appraises him.

"They got you good with that frying pan. What a shiner! You look like the Elephant Man."

Tom takes the insult, enjoys it, would be happy to take another. "Thank you, Maggie," he says.

"Oh, you wanted your beans opening, didn't you? Right this way, sir, let me show you to your table."

She leads him down the length of the kitchen, and he can see the other students watching her with reverence. He wants to say something about how they parted last time, to apologise, but realises that he's also afraid of her, afraid of reminding her, of breaking the fragile truce that she seems to have engineered entirely by herself.

At the far end of the kitchen they turn right into the storage area, piled high with drums and tins and boxes containing substances that presumably have some kind of nutritional value.

"So, what's been happening up here?" he asks.

"Oh, this and that." Maggie whirls about. "I can't believe, of all the people to be stuck with in an apocalyptic, locked down, nuclear-bunker-type situation, I get (a)—" she counts on her thumb and forefinger "—Mr Swinton, who hates me and can't understand my accent, and (b) bloody *Clara Benning*, who's not even in my class, but still dobbed me in for missing the Alpha Omega INSET course at the beginning of term."

"Has anyone been in touch with the outside world?"

"Are you joking?"

"What?"

"This whole situation is basically the only thing anyone's talking about on Alpha. Everyone's posting videos all the time. A boy in Year 7 found a way around the PAD restrictions."

"Then why isn't anyone helping?"

349

NICHOLAS BOWLING

"Because no one can get in. Doesn't matter how many people know. Graves spent all the fees on making NSA indestructible, didn't he?" Maggie goes back to searching for the can opener. "I left it here somewhere. I was trying to open one of those big tins of cream. The cutting bit wasn't big enough, though. The wheel thing. In fact, I might have broken it. Sorry. Ach! Where the fuck did I put it?"

"Maggie..."

"I know, I know, I'm cursing, but it's not exactly business as usual round here, is it?"

"No, not that. I just wanted to say sorry. For before. Whenever it was. Tuesday. Can barely remember now."

"Sorry for what?"

"For not helping you. For taking advantage of you. I was planning on helping you out, I promise."

She shrugs her broad shoulders, her jumper slumping and settling slowly like chainmail. "Doesn't matter anymore, does it? Not like I'm going to carry on at NSA after all this. They'll have to close it down, won't they? How are they going to explain all of this in the weekly newsletter? Can you imagine?"

She turns to him and laughs. He laughs with her. Then he remembers his meeting with Tooley, the threat of the legal team, the two witnesses. Alice Nowacki's inquiring face also returns to him and he has to mentally swat it away like a fly.

"Maggie," he says, "did you tell Mr Tooley about us?"

Her smile disappears and reappears, altered. "Us? What is 'us', Mr Rosen?"

"Just about... you know. What I've been asking you to do."

She barks another laugh. "Jesus, sir, don't ever represent yourself in court. You're making it sound a lot worse than it is."

350

Again that violent rattle from his heart. "You know what I mean. I just wondered if you'd mentioned anything to anyone."

"Nope. 'Just between us.' That was what you said, wasn't it, you big creep?"

Tom cringes. He finds *himself* skin-crawling. How is that possible? He looks around the storeroom to avoid meeting her eyes. Shelves and shelves of branded boxes, vacuum-packed meats, meat substitutes, meat powders, meat-flavoured vegan loaf, whey cutlets, corn paste, wheat paste, rice paste, soy-based gels, seed mixes. He swallows hard.

"Just joking, sir," says Maggie. "Sir?"

Tom doesn't reply because he's looking at something else. In the corner of one of the shelves he can see a robust plastic box that doesn't have a product description on it. It does have a brand logo, though: a grinning sausage dog like the design on his packet of ProSustain, and on the socks of the man he couldn't see in Mr Graves's office.

"What is that?" He pushes past Maggie.

"Hey!"

"Why is this in the kitchen?"

"Do you want your beans open or not?"

He examines the box, which is solid but with rounded edges, and has two locked clasps on its lid. It reminds him of the kind of thing they use to transport organs for transplants. He traces his fingers over the graphic on the top.

"I've seen this before."

"It's Good Day. They make all the vitamin supplements. It's probably additives for our delicious school meals. You should see the stuff they try and feed me these days. Bottom of the class, lowest scores in PE. They basically just give me a big bowl of steroids now. Ha ha!"

351

Tom considers this for a moment. Given her physique and her general disposition, it might not be far from the truth. "Good Day don't just make vitamin supplements."

"Well sure."

"Are you still feeling alright, Maggie?"

She rolls her eyes. "Oh grand, sir, just grand."

"But no nosebleeds or anything?"

"No. I'd kill for a bit of human flesh, though."

"I'm serious."

"That's always been your problem, sir."

There's a shout from around the corner. It's distant, controlled, like a teacher disciplining a child. A second time around it becomes more desperate, and is joined by more voices, young and old. Something metal is knocked to the ground. There is the clatter of the serving hatches opening. Shouts turn to screams.

Tom freezes. It's Maggie who rushes to the kitchen first, and after a few moments he unwillingly follows. There are more children in there now. They're running and scuttling and loping like wounded animals. Some of them are still on two feet, talking with such speed and force they are preceded by a fine spray of pink saliva. One of the quicker ones has already seized Mr Swinton. She's dragged him to the floor and is chewing on the fingers of his left hand. He knows her, Tom does: Aaliya something. He gave her a revision session before her pre-VACs. The other residents of the kitchen are fleeing in all directions, or fending off attackers with utensils, or in some cases trying to talk rationally to their classmates, to remind them who and where they are, but all without success.

"Jesus, Mary and Joseph," says Maggie.

"We need to go," says Tom.

"Can't we help them?"

"No. Not now." He grabs her hand.

"Ach, get off me!" she says and wriggles her fingers out from between his.

"Sorry."

"What are you doing?"

"Getting you out of here."

"Ha ha!"

"What?"

"You're just funny, sir."

The deranged children are spilling in through the serving hatches and wriggling like eels over the counter. They're starting to make their way down to Tom and Maggie's end of the kitchen.

"Why am I funny?"

"You just are."

"But why?"

"I thought you were getting me out of here."

He looks at her for a moment. Funny is better than pathetic, at least. He resists grabbing her by the hand again, turns, heads to the door at the back of the storeroom. Maggie goes in the opposite direction.

"What are you doing?" she says. "Doors are all locked, dummy."

Maggie goes up to the serving hatch nearest them, thumps two of the intruders in their faces, and heaves them back through the hole. Then she dives after them, into the dining hall beyond.

"Come on, sir!" she yells from the other side.

Tom has trouble getting his legs up onto the counter. His trousers are too tight, and he's not very athletic anyway. Something snags in his groin again, a feeling like a metal spring being forcefully uncoiled. Clumsily he rolls out of the kitchen and flops onto the floor on the other side, feeling nothing like the hero he would like to be.

13.30

PEEPSY IS ALL out of glucose tablets. He's very cold, very hungry. By now his footsteps have a delirious momentum which makes him reluctant to stop and rest, in case he can't get started again. He can taste blood in the back of his mouth, because he's plugged his nostrils with balls of used tissue and the blood has nowhere to go but back on itself.

His thoughts rise and fall in time with his walking. His parents and his sister come up regularly, but they're distant and two-dimensional, as though they are characters in a game or TV show he used to be interested in but probably won't return to.

He follows the pale oblong of Dr Nowacki's PAD like a will o' the wisp. The darkness in all directions is absolute. The path isn't concrete or linoleum anymore, but something loose and stony, and either side could be rock walls or a sheer drop or flat desert. There's no way of knowing. Such questions about his immediate surroundings have the same abstractness as the thoughts about his family. He just doesn't consider them particularly pressing anymore, and neither does Dr Nowacki, it seems.

Onwards through the abyss. Occasionally he glimpses the outline of Nowacki's rucksack, recognises the contours of its contents, thinks he can see the hollow eyes of the dead boy staring back at him. This is his mission objective. His goal. He is *goal-oriented*, as his teachers always used to say. He'll achieve his goal, return the remains to their resting place, lift the curse, because it *is* a curse, whatever Nowacki has to say on the matter. But then what? It's not like he'll just go back to the NSA after all this. Maybe this is the end of everything.

Another gush of hot iron in the back of his throat makes him gag. Dr Nowacki stops and turns.

"Are you alright, Alex? Holding up okay?"

He nods and gives two thumbs up.

"Good show. Raisin?"

"Alright." It's the first thing he's said in a couple of hours, and the word is phlegmy and foul-tasting.

She taps a couple into his palm and offers him the last of the water.

"One mouthful each," she says.

"Sure?"

"Sure. I reckon it won't be much further. Feel that?"

He can't feel anything apart from a throb in the top of his nose, and the slow squirm of his stomach.

"There's a draught. This'll come out somewhere. Don't know where. But somewhere."

"Where do you think we are now?" Peepsy says.

"I literally have no idea."

"Under the school?"

"We've come too far, I think."

"Then where?"

"Don't know."

"Are we dead?"

Dr Nowacki's laugh doesn't echo, just like when they were in the Dungeons. "I don't think so. I feel halfway there, but, no, I've still got a pulse."

"Okay. I don't think so either. But if we do die, I just want to say I've had quite a fun couple of days. So, thanks. And sorry, I suppose, because I got you into this in the first place."

"No apology necessary. I've had fun too."

Peepsy can't tell if she's lying.

"Wait a sec." He sits on the ground. It's damp and silty like a dried-up riverbed. He takes a few deep breaths and swallows. "Professor?"

"Yes?"

"Can I carry the bag for a bit?"

"If you want."

She slips the straps from her shoulders and carefully hands him the rucksack. Peepsy checks the items. The phosphorescent dome of the skull shines back at him from the depths of the bag.

"It's strange to think I've got one of these under my face," he says, probing his own cheekbones. "Isn't it?"

"Yes. I think that myself sometimes. Happens a lot when you're looking at dead people every day."

"Funny, really." He raps his knuckles on the top of his head. "Hello? Anyone there?"

No reply.

Nowacki watches him. He can't read her expression. He rests for another couple of minutes in the darkness, then gets to his feet and hoists the bag onto his back. The burden feels good.

They trudge on in silence for an indeterminate amount of time. Peepsy goes back to thinking about his family, thinking about whether they have missed him, whether they've even realised he hasn't come home from school. Perhaps not. Perhaps he seems as distant and fictional to them as they do to him. He thinks about his sister. When this becomes too difficult, he thinks about the pizza that Dr Nowacki promised him, but under the circumstances the concept of "pizza" also seems very remote.

At some point Dr Nowacki stops. Peepsy is some way behind her but can see in the PAD light that the ground at her feet is bulbous and volcanic. It's not until he's directly behind her shoulder that he realises the strange balloon-like protrusions are not the earth itself, but more blackened human skulls.

"Goodness." Dr Nowacki steps forward carefully, shining the PAD from left to right. "We must be beneath the burial complex. I've seen all this on the site report." She shakes her head, still picking her way between the bodies. "It's incredible. It's unlike anything I've ever seen."

"What is it? Who are they?"

"You might have been right about the Druid thing, Alex. Look at how they're arranged."

"There's a rumour at school that they bury the kids who fail their exams down here."

"Ha."

Her laugh sounds very flat again.

"Can I borrow that?" Peepsy takes the PAD from her and squats down. The heads all have holes in them, like the one he found. "Spooky."

They both stand and look at each other. Dr Nowacki looks like she's afraid to say something. She squints in the beam of the torch, and then her face disappears. A picture of an empty battery flashes urgently on the PAD's screen. Then Peepsy sees nothing at all.

14.10

TOM DECIDES that a visit to the ICT Department might prove useful, and after some persuading, Maggie agrees to go with him. They take the same route Tom took on Monday after his meeting with Tooley, only now the corridors of the NSA are a gauntlet of mindless, errant children. Some are more aggressive than others. Some ignore them completely. Most have their shirts or blouses or bare chests speckled with something unpleasant. Tom finds himself creeping around corners and dashing from one piece of cover to the next like every FPS game he used to play when he was a teenager. It's sort of fun.

The Guild are safely locked in their turret, though. Maggie says "I told you so" ten different ways. Tom can see the receptionist, asleep on one of the waiting-room sofas in her dragon costume. He knocks and Maggie shouts through the glass, but the dragon doesn't hear them and doesn't wake up.

"Look at that," says Maggie, pointing down into the car park.

From up here they can see the crowds crawling around the bottom of the school. There are hundreds of people, maybe thousands. Parents, reporters, influencers, health and security personnel. Among them are DVs, drones, mobile routers, generators, temporary bathrooms, a few street-food vans and pop-up restaurants. There's almost a festival atmosphere.

"Shall we go down there?" Tom asks

"I dunno."

"I think we should go down there. Try and talk with them."

"Whatever you say, boss."

"I'm going to call in on Tooley and Graves on the way."

"This is some rescue mission, sir!"

"What?"

"I'm getting you out of here," she says, in a not very flattering impersonation of Tom. "Ha ha!"

He ignores her. They return to the ground floor and navigate their way around three sides of the NSA's hexagon. Tom passes the EMM office and sees a pale-faced Mr Barren peering through the porthole. He's rapping weakly on the other side of the door. Tom doesn't stop.

Around the third corner is the SMT suite. There's a rhythmic, pneumatic sound coming from inside. Maggie runs ahead into the lobby area.

"Oh my God. Sir, look at this. *Sir.*"

Tom follows her. She's up on tiptoes, looking inside the Deputy Headmaster's office.

"He's lost it!"

Mr Tooley is atop his mechanical rodeo bull, gazing at his knuckles. It's on its tamest setting, pitching forwards and backwards very slowly. Tom knocks on the door.

"Mr Tooley?"

The Deputy Head doesn't look up. He clings stiffly to the front of the saddle and doesn't move an inch.

"What's he doing?" says Maggie.

"I think he's thinking," says Tom.

"Why's he even *got* one of those?"

"It was a present."

"Who from?"

Tom doesn't answer. He tries knocking again, to no avail.

A boy suddenly pops up from behind the coffee table. It's Ben Weir, who was nearly expelled in Year 7 on account of his mild Asperger's. He grasps wildly at Maggie, shouting something about the trigonometry of the office. There's blood on his teeth and clear fluid coming from his ears. Maggie tears herself away and runs out of the lobby, into the corridor, and Tom follows eventually, staying long enough to throw a tea urn at their pursuer. Across the way is the Headmaster's antechamber. In they go, hauling a sofa and a desk across the doorway. Ben Weir hammers on it with his fists, yelling about "sine" this and "cosine" the other.

The door through to the Headmaster's office is, of course, locked.

The secretary has abandoned her post. Tom and Maggie sit cross-legged on the deep carpet. They're in exactly the same spot where Tom saw the man with the sausage dog socks, and Mr Graves with his tray of cocktails. A celebration of their ongoing partnership, no doubt. Where's the proof, though? What are the *specifics*?

As if the universe has heard and responded, Tom's PAD makes its customary *ping*. He hasn't heard it for so long it makes him jump. He looks at the screen.

"Who the hell is Peter Van Den Hoonaard?" he says.

"I don't know," says Maggie. "I'm hungry."

"He's just sent me a message."

"Parent?"

"Don't think so. He's not sent it via AIM. It's come straight to this specific PAD. A good old-fashioned email."

He tries to get back onto the MNet to check the name, but he doesn't have the credentials since his sacking. Van Den Hoonaard. Doesn't ring any bells. And it's a pretty unusual name.

He opens the message. There's no title or text, but it has a huge bundle of data attached to it. An attachment! Tom hasn't seen one of those in years.

The vibrations from his PAD intensify when he tries to open it. Slowly the screen fills with the names of students from NSA, some he recognises, some he doesn't. It's not long before he realises that the students he's familiar with are the same ones from the list Maggie drew up for him. He doesn't need to study it particularly closely to get the gist of what's been going on.

Outside the barricade, Ben Weir is still pacing around, occasionally drumming on the desk. His name is on the list. Inside, Maggie is chatting happily to herself about what she thinks the Headmaster is up to. Her name is on the list, too.

Tom doesn't know what to say. He feels a few things. Vindicated. Depressed. Ashamed. But not surprised. No, not surprised at all.

14.45

AS IF THEY didn't have enough problems, the air-conditioning in the ICT Department has broken, and The Guild are now sitting at their monitors in their underwear. Their sweat is presenting them with several functional problems. It's difficult to get purchase on their VR control sticks. One or two keep sliding completely out of their chairs.

Anne Brant can't make sense of anything on her screen anymore. Yesterday evening they were all patting themselves on the back for having the foresight to install both soda and jellybean machines in the break-out room, but after twenty-four hours all that sugar has made her hot and irritable and fuzzy-headed. She's run diagnostics on the whole network, reinstalled four previous versions of the old security system, even attempted the equivalent of "on and off at the wall". Everything's completely unresponsive. The main problem is that no one can really get under the bonnet of the new software. The source code is safely under lock and key somewhere in the People's Republic of China. Of the members of The Guild who are still awake, half of them still refuse to believe that they don't have the power to correct the error themselves, and the other half are lost in the labyrinth of TASCO's In World customer service centre.

Anne is now at the point where the characters in front of her have ceased to mean anything. They look like runes, or alien glyphs. The only thing she keeps coming back to, which several people have suggested, is simply shutting off the power to the whole site, but no one knows how to do that. Even if there was some kind of power cut, the NSA has backup generators for precisely that eventuality.

She sits back in her chair. She'd love something savoury right now.

"I give up," she says.

Behind her one of the DAs is mesmerised by the footage from the CCTV cameras. He's watching what's happening in the corridor on the fourth floor.

"Look at them," he says. "It's like they're possessed."

Anne can see a ripple of skinny bodies beneath the camera. Some of them are trying to climb the walls vertically. Even from where she's sitting she can see the smears they're leaving on the brickwork.

"You know Scroll of Mayhem?" says the DA.

Nobody replies, but they all know *exactly* what he's talking about. Anne's just glad her kids were too stupid to pass the entrance exam.

14.48

AMIDST THE raging parents now literally throwing themselves at the school's doors; amidst the explosions of hysteria when vague shapes appear at the windows on the upper floors, and a hundred people all claim they can see their son or daughter; amidst the influencers streaming their tearful thought-pieces or pranking the parents or creating parodies of the NSA promotional video; amidst the hollers of the private security personnel, who have been summoned by a few wealthy parents, and by the school itself, and sound like they're quite tribal in their attitude to one another's employers: Stephanie Bäcker receives a message.

For the first time that afternoon, the people around her notice that she's there.

"What was that?"

"Was that mine?"

"Yours doesn't make that noise."

"Then whose *was* it?"

"Is it from the Head?"

"Is it from the children?"

Stephanie finds herself suddenly surrounded by bodies. She can feel their heat and smell their breath. One or two of them are already grasping at her PAD.

"What does it say? Is it from Joshua?"

"There's no reason why it would be from Joshua."

Stephanie reaches into her bag for her headphones.

"Let me listen to it," she says quietly. "It might not be anything."

"We haven't got *time* to wait for you to listen to it!"

"Just give it here."

"I'll read it."

"*I'll* read it."

"Who's Mr Van Den Hoonaard? Isn't he SMT?"

"I lose track, there's so many of them."

"Oh my God."

"What?"

"*What?*"

Then there's an uncanny silence. Someone is obviously reading the message very carefully.

14.50

MAGGIE IS hammering on the door to Mr Graves's office with her hands, knees and sometimes her head. Her swearing is so loud and lyrical it almost sounds like she's singing. At first Tom is worried that Good Day's medication has undone her, but when she turns around her wide, green eyes are quite lucid.

"How could they?"

Tom shakes his head.

"I mean, how *could* they?"

"The school was in debt. People pay a lot for data."

"Is that it? I'm just *data*?"

"I don't know what to say."

He really doesn't. He couldn't even tell her outright. He had to hand her the PAD and ask her to read Peter Van Den Hoonaard's email for herself.

Maggie curses and goes back to thundering against the locked door for another few minutes.

"We should try and get you out of here," says Tom. "Before…"

"Before?"

"Before things get worse."

"Worse! Jesus Christ! How are they going to get worse?"

"You're not like *him* yet."

He jerks his head in the direction of the doorway. Maggie stops her assault on the door and frowns at Tom. They both listen carefully. There's still muttering coming from outside, but it isn't Ben Weir. It's somebody else, and they're talking quite calmly and rationally.

"Excuse me, please," says the new voice. "Excuse me."

Tom gets up from sitting cross-legged on the floor and peers through the gap between the desk and the sofa they're using as a barricade. Gerald Liu's face is perfectly framed between the sofa's legs. He's looks the same as the last time Tom saw him, his blazer and tie immaculate, a slight sheen of perspiration on his brow the only sign that he's experienced any discomfort.

"Gerald! Are you alright?"

"So sorry, Mr Rosen. Very sorry."

"Get in here!"

"Excuse me. Very sorry."

"Help me with this, Maggie."

"Really? Gerry? We're not inviting him in, are we?"

"Be nice, Maggie."

She huffs and helps Tom dismantle the barricade. Gerald wanders in with his suitcase, panting slightly. It's lost one of its wheels, and the axle keeps digging into the carpet.

Maggie hauls the desk and sofa back in front of the doorway. She appraises the boy, front and back.

"What's he doing here?"

"I don't know," says Tom. "Gerald? Were you looking for me?"

"Very sorry."

"What are you apologising for? Catch your breath."

"Yes."

"Yes?"

"I have been looking for you. Yesterday and today, everywhere. I went around and around. I thought maybe you have left the school, but then the teachers said that you are still here. Miss Potter said that you visited her. She said that you were very strange."

"Did she?"

Tom wonders where Bernice Potter is, but only briefly. She's probably still locked in her room with Amir and Alysa and their Goal Setting presentations. And what of Alice Nowacki? He dismisses her, too. She was the one who abandoned *him*, this time. They're even now.

"The whole school is broken. All the doors are closed." Gerald shakes his head. "But I have found you, Mr Rosen, and now I must say: I am *very* sorry."

"What *for,* Gerald? You don't need to say sorry for anything."

"I followed you, like Mr Barren says. I tell him where you go. I tell him what you do. Then I tell Mr Tooley. Very important man. I have to help him because I don't want to go back to Beijing. In Beijing it is very hard work. It is very dirty. You maybe will get very sick. My father cannot keep me in Beijing. So I work very hard here, and I help my teachers, and I tell Mr Tooley what I see, because he asks me to. If I don't he will tell my father. And maybe I have to go back to him. But then, I see—" Gerald's mouth makes a perfect circle of surprise "—Mr Rosen is in trouble, and Mr Rosen is not a teacher at NSA anymore, and maybe because I saw him with his friend." He turns to Maggie. They both do. Maggie's mouth is half-open, her eyes slightly narrowed, as though she's having trouble keeping up with what Gerald Liu is saying. "And now I think Mr Rosen is maybe sad, because he is not a teacher anymore, and, maybe, he has to go to another school. And so, Mr Rosen, I say, you are my *very* good friend, and I am *very* sorry."

So Tooley and Barren *did* put him up to it! No surprises there, either. Tom puts his hand out, grasps the boy's little paw, gives it a squeeze.

"You're a good man, Gerald Liu. You're not the one that needs to apologise."

Gerald's face returns to a default expression of comfortable incomprehension.

"You got any food, Gerry?" Maggie asks.

He unzips a corner of his suitcase and starts tugging out its contents one by one. Dog-eared textbooks flop onto the carpet, along with pieces of scrap paper covered in diagrams and formulae whose meanings and significance are known to Gerald and Gerald alone. In the few months that Tom has taught him, this situation has occurred at least once a week, when, as Gerald searches for some vital piece of information, the entire suitcase has exploded onto the floor of his classroom. Tom usually ends up helping him to repack everything, so he's not late for his next lesson. Gerald has textbooks and worksheets for subjects that aren't even taught at NSA, his father having prepared him for every possible academic eventuality, and after a year at the school he still insists on carrying the whole collection with him in case they might come in handy. There's stationery in there, too: scissors, staplers, something that could be a nail gun. There are mathematical instruments, coloured pencils, brushes, tubes of paint.

Gerald finally produces two small, circular cakes wrapped in tissue paper and hands them over carefully, one to Tom, one to Maggie. Tom takes a bite. He can't put his finger on what the filling is – something between nuts and fruit and glue. Right now it's the most delicious thing he's ever eaten.

"Thank you, Gerald," he says.

"You are welcome, Mr Rosen!"

Gerald nods and smiles. His face is so open and affectless, it seems to Tom to express some medieval ideal of virtue.

"So what do we do now?" says Maggie.

"Main entrance?"

"No," says Gerald. "It is locked."

"Well, looks like we're here for the night again," says Maggie, dusting off her hands and getting to her feet. "I guess we build a fire, sing a few songs. Gerald, you know any good ones from the motherland?"

His face lights up.

"Many!" he says.

16.00

IT'S TOO DARK to go forwards or backwards. The bone-strewn ground is uneven and slick like the shallows of a great, black lake. Alice has lost her balance so many times that she can't tell which direction she's facing anymore. The only thing that helps her orientate herself is Peepsy. His breath is nervous and quick beside her. They grip each other's hands like mother and son.

"This is rubbish," says Peepsy, on the verge of tears.

"I know," is all she can say.

"Why can't we go back?"

"I don't know which way is back."

The earth booms dully with the sound of machinery far, far above them. Peepsy trips again and swears.

"It's my birthday. My fucking *birthday*."

"Try to stay calm, Alex. We'll get out soon enough. Slow and steady wins the race, and all that. I can still feel the draught from somewhere up there."

"Maybe Mr Rosen has got out and gone to find help? A search party or something?"

"Maybe," she says, although that kind of affirmative action doesn't sound like Tom at all. "Don't worry. Someone out there will be looking for us. Kids don't just disappear without anyone noticing."

That may not be entirely true, she admits to herself. She's not even sure what she means by "someone out there". They may as well be the last living souls in an empty universe. They may as well be outside of space and time altogether. Not In World; not Out of World; not living; not dead. Some kind of limbo. Perhaps that other lost boy could have told them.

"I think we should put the bones back here, now, with the others," says Peepsy, suddenly, after a long silence.

"Why?"

"Maybe then our luck will improve. Maybe it'll break the curse."

After everything that has happened, after all her cynicism, the gesture feels right in the circumstances. An offering to the primeval darkness. A good old apotropaic ritual. It's not as though her rationalism has come up with anything worthwhile in the last few days.

"Good idea," she says.

She hears Peepsy sling the bag down from his shoulder, loosen the drawstring and place its contents on the ground. He spends a couple of minutes burrowing with his hands in the wet earth.

"You know the Celts thought the head was the seat of the soul," says Alice.

Peepsy's still digging.

"They preserved the heads of their ancestors," she continues. "Kept them in boxes, sometimes."

"D'you think that's why someone drilled a hole in this one?"

"I'm sure that's part of it. Perhaps they were trying to let the soul out."

"No way," says Peepsy, out of breath now. "Opposite. I reckon they were trying to get in. The soul's in there, and they were trying to get a sneaky peek at it."

Alice waits for a moment, pondering this new bit of wisdom in the darkness. Peepsy smooths over the last bit of mud and stands up. He mutters something under his breath. It might be a prayer, but she has the presence of mind not to ask him.

"Right, all done," he says at last. "Sorry about that."

"Don't worry about it," says Alice.

"I was talking to the bones."

17.00

GABRIEL'S DV whines along the London O2 Orbital. He's flanked by hundreds of identical vehicles moving at identical speeds, which sometimes gives the impression that he and his fellow passengers are in fact stationary, with the rest of the world being rolled past them like the backdrop in an old Western movie. They move like a shoal of fish, slowing and accelerating at the same time, handfuls of them peeling off at the exit ramps. Gabriel's DV forges ahead in the centre lane. He's about half an hour from his destination.

His insides are still fluttering from the drama in the Alpha Omega offices. Oh man, the faceless man got what was coming to him! Slow and difficult, that's how Gabriel likes it. He can remember the snag of the guy's flesh on the blade, the weight of it. His rifle and his machete are on the back seat. He's glad he found his clothes, too. His favourite outfit: black trench coat, black combat trousers, stormtrooper boots, sunglasses, black fingerless gloves. He balls his fists every few seconds to feel the leather tighten around his knuckles.

With the faceless man taken care of, Gabriel is heading back to the NSA. Whether his messages got through or not, he's determined to deliver his revelations in person. The whole conspiracy laid bare. He's also looking forward to confronting Mr Graves. Perhaps he'll perform some kind of public execution. It'll be ten times worse than what happened to the faceless man. He can see it now, the crowds gathering around him, calling for Graves's gigantic head on a platter. He'll pronounce his judgement, and the axe will fall, and they'll all rue the day they ever decided to make an enemy of Captain Gumbo. What a show it's going to be!

The vehicle shifts itself left and leaves the Orbital. At the first junction another DV pulls up alongside him, and he sees its passenger is a woman, and her breasts are exposed. She's completely naked from head to toe. She winks at him, but Gabriel thinks nothing of it.

17.05

GERALD LIU, having missed the irony in Maggie's suggestion, is now nearly halfway through his performance of *The Peach Blossom Fan*. Maggie herself, having watched incredulously for the first five or six scenes, has decided that if there's to be no escape she may as well join in. Now she's providing a beat and backing vocals for Gerald's singing, even though it's obvious that the opera requires neither.

Tom is sat on the floor again, reading Peter Van Den Hoonaard's email for the twentieth time. Even though he's played no part in the horrid business, there's a cold, black shame he can't shake off. Every time he tunes in to Gerald and Maggie's duet he wants to cry, though he hasn't cried, he thinks, since he was Gerald's age, and he has to swallow his rising heart back into his chest.

He's shared the information as widely as he can on the school MNet. He hopes that's enough. He was considering asking Maggie or Gerald to post the thing on Alpha Omega, but probably wouldn't have got very far since the scandal involves Alpha Omega itself. He couldn't even use AIM, the instant messaging service, because Alpha owns that, too. This is all a moot point anyway. Tooley's new restrictions won't allow the students to use their PADs for anything like that.

Gerald eventually reaches the end of his song, and Maggie applauds. He coughs drily.

"My neck hurts."

"Your throat?"

"My throat hurts," he corrects himself. "Is it okay if I stop now?"

"Ah, come on Gerry, I'm just getting into it!" says Maggie.

"Of course, Gerald," says Tom. "Don't do yourself an injury."

Gerald goes to his suitcase, opens yet another hidden pocket and produces a stainless-steel bottle of water. He unscrews the top, glugs at it, offers it to Maggie. She's humming the last song that Gerald was performing, though she's making it sound more melodic than the original. She also drinks, then hands it to Tom. Tom looks at the bottle. A logo's been lasered into the metal, five capital letters: TASCO.

"You know Mr Tooley won't take kindly to this," he says. "Very off-brand."

Gerald looks mortified. "It is my father's!"

"I'm only joking," says Tom. He's about to laugh, to reassure Gerald, but stops. "Your dad works for TASCO?"

"TASCO is my family business. A very important business. My grandfather, he wants to keep people safe. In China, in the UK, all over the world."

"Wait: you *own* TASCO?"

"My father is the—" and Gerald at this point closes his eyes to ensure perfect recall "—chief, executive, office."

"He's CEO? Of the company that's built this security system? Gerald, I feel like you could have told us this earlier!"

"Very sorry, Mr Rosen. Very, *very* sorry."

He starts flicking through one of his geography textbooks, but obviously isn't reading anything on any of the pages.

"Well?" says Maggie. "Can't you have a word with your dad? Doesn't he know how to fix this thing?"

He shakes his head.

"Listen, Gerry. I love singing with you. But I need to get out of here.

I'm not just going to sit and wait for my head to explode." She says it as a joke, but Tom can hear she's frightened. Her voice is just a touch too loud. "Not just me. A *lot* of people need to get out of here."

"No," says Gerald, still shaking vigorously. "I am working very hard. I want no trouble for my father."

"But would he be able to help?"

"No trouble," he says again. "It will make him very angry."

"Why?"

"No trouble. Mr Graves said I can come to the school but must not cause trouble. He made a very good deal."

"Mr Graves made a deal with your father?"

He nods.

"Gerald, how did you do in the NSA entrance examination?"

"It was a very good deal. Everybody was very happy."

"What do you mean by a deal?"

"My father helped Mr Graves. Mr Graves lets me learn at the best school, number one."

"Did Mr Graves let you come here in return for a discount on the TASCO system?"

"I always work hard. I promise to work hard. No trouble at all."

Whether or not Tom has guessed the specifics correctly, he doesn't need to know anymore. A discount! He can't imagine anything grubbier. And poor Gerald, failing in every subject, making no friends, struggling to understand half of what's being said to him.

"Listen to me, Gerald," says Tom, and suddenly he's appalled by how easily he has slipped back into Mr Rosen. "I'm sure your father will understand. Your classmates are very ill, it's very dangerous for them to all be locked in here."

The boy sags in his blazer.

"Don't you want to help your friends?"

His brow wrinkles softly. He nods.

"So can you contact him?"

Gerald fishes his PAD out of his suitcase. He stands up and walks to the corner of the room, where he turns and faces the wall. All he needs is a dunce's cap, thinks Tom. He hangs his head, mutters something under his breath, and begins typing.

17.30

WHEN GABRIEL arrives at the NSA, everyone's waiting for him, just as he expected. Staff and students grin and applaud and pat him on the back.

"Great job, Gabriel!" they say.

"You did it!"

"You're the man, Gabe!"

He leaves his DV outside the main entrance, tools up, then makes his way to the Headmaster's office. He's overcome by the sight of the school, and all the supporters that have come out to greet him. There are so many of them. He's never used the word "beautiful", but it is, that's how he'd describe it. And that sunset!

17.33

THE NEWS has passed through the crowd like a shot of adrenaline. Stephanie has now heard it shouted, whispered, exaggerated, down-played, and misinterpreted so many times she's lost her grasp of what the original message might have actually said. With the frenzy gathering a new momentum and moving away from her back towards the school buildings, Stephanie retreats to her flower bed to listen to the PAD properly for the first time.

She recognises some of the names from a long time ago, from the new parents' social evenings. Mrs Aprille: she was a bastard, she remembers. Kept flirting outrageously with her husband, right in front of Stephanie, as though she was deaf as well as blind. Gabriel's name comes up number eleven on the list. She asks the PAD to open the attachment and read her its contents. Numbers, acronyms, occasional long-form notes: *Responded well to scenario 5.1. Signs of withdrawal, but within accepted pre-defined limits. Climate control of minimal relevance to end results.* The timings of the most recent data suggest that he was still under observation when she went to the Alpha Omega headquarters. So is he in the school, or isn't he? If he's not here, where is he? She still has the indescribable sensation that he's within earshot.

She only wanted to help him. She would have done anything to bring him back from the abyss. No doubt it's the same with all those parents who, among the torrents of loud indignance, have fallen strangely quiet. It wasn't meant to be anything like this. No one said anything about medication, or monitoring, or intravenous this, that and other. But there's still no escaping those last three words, articulated brightly in the PAD's transatlantic accent, which she just hopes Gabriel didn't see: *parental consent given.*

18.00

—HELLO FATHER.

—Son? It's two o'clock in the morning.

—I know. I'm sorry.

—Is there a problem?

—Sort of.

—What have you done?

—I haven't done anything. Everything's going well. With my studies, I mean.

—Well? I'm busy, Jie.

—It's not a problem with me, it's a problem with the school.

—Jie! You can't just pass off your failings as the failings of the school. You can't blame the teachers if you're not getting the grades you should.

—No, there's a problem with the school *itself*. With the buildings. The remote security platform has gone online, but it's not working properly. Everything's locked. Everything's broken. No one can get out.

—TASCO products don't just break. It must have been installed incorrectly. Why are you telling me, anyway? This isn't your responsibility. You can't just go over the heads of the staff because you happen to know me. This is very disappointing, Jie.

—They asked me to! One of the teachers found out about you, and he told me I had to contact you. To ask for help. He wouldn't take no for an answer.

—I don't believe you.

—He's right here. Mr Rosen.

Liu Jie takes a photo of him and sends it to his father. Mr Rosen looks up, confused, then goes back to his conversation with the loud girl.

—Is he really a teacher? He looks like a homeless man.

—He is, really.

—Just what am I supposed to do?

—I don't know. I thought you could talk to the technical team and ask them to unlock the system. There's nothing we can do at this end.

A slight delay before his father's next message.

—How long has the system been locked?

—Nearly two days.

—Two days! Jie, why didn't you tell me earlier?

—You told me not to contact you!

—But this is very bad. Catastrophic. Oh my God.

A very long delay this time.

—What is it, Father?

—I'm watching the newsfeed.

—Can you help?

—Looks like I don't have a choice, does it? Why didn't you tell me earlier, Jie?

—You said I should only contact you if there was an emergency.

—Do you not think this is an emergency?

—I didn't want to bother you. I'm sorry.

—This is very disappointing.

—Mr Rosen said I was good man today, Father.

—I need to talk with the technical team right away.

Liu Jie's father goes offline and his icon disappears. He looks up. The loud girl is talking at the other end of the office's foyer. She speaks so fast, and her accent is so odd, he only understands about one in three words. Mr Rosen is listening to her, frowning. Liu Jie doesn't know what they're talking about, but then he's not really concentrating, because he's been distracted by the new arrival.

Standing in the middle of the office is a boy. It's the one who made friends with him when he first arrived in the country. A very good coder, but a bad student, he later found out. He didn't tell his dad about him, for that reason. They had some good times In World, the two of them – he even let the boy use a cloned version of his Shi Mo account. If anyone back home had found that out, Liu Jie probably could have been imprisoned; but the boy had demanded to be friends with him, so he didn't really have a choice. The boy always said he didn't want to meet up in school, and he'd be very angry if Liu Jie tried to track him down. But Liu Jie also has a talent for coding, and even more of a talent for not being seen. It was simple enough to work out the boy's age, and the location he played from most often, and cross reference with the school's MNet. When he finally traced Gabriel Out of World he was more than a little disappointed by what he found, and was happy to uphold his end of the bargain. He never approached him, never even acknowledged him when they passed each other in the corridors in the weeks that followed.

And now he's here, not a stitch on him.

"Gerald?" says Mr Rosen. "What is it?"

Liu Jie knows he doesn't have the words to convey exactly what he's seeing, not even in his own language, so he holds his tongue.

FRIDAY

7.00

THE AIR feels different when Peepsy opens his eyes. It's less still, less dead. His nose feels clearer, too, and he takes a full breath for the first time in days.

Dr Nowacki is shaking his shoulder.

"Alex. Sun's up. Look, you can see the light through there. I think we made it. We should have just kept going."

He rolls over on the shelf of dirt where he fell asleep the previous night. The earth has sucked the heat from his bones. He is so completely numb that he has the sensation of being only mentally present, without a body at all.

Nowacki lifts him to his feet. "Looks like it's pizza and chips for breakfast," she says. "What do you reckon?"

Peepsy's heart labours for a few moments as he tries to get his balance, and the weight of his flesh seems to return to him all at once. He blinks. Behind Nowacki there is a low crescent of grey-violet daylight.

There's a wariness in how they approach it, as though after so long in the wilderness it might be a mirage. But it is really there, a horizontal cleft between earth and rock, big enough to slither under on their bellies. Dr Nowacki lets him go first.

Peepsy flattens the half-empty rucksack and pushes it through ahead of him. He goes through feet first, and Dr Nowacki follows him. They stand and look upon the half-lit world. Everything seems new to Peepsy, like they are Adam and Eve surveying things as yet unnamed.

They're somewhere out beyond the boundaries of the NSA, at the base of a low sandstone cliff. Orderly rows of young trees stretch before them, the grass delineated by almost invisible seams, which suggests this area was part of the green belt "regreening initiative" a few years ago. He remembers it being an added woe for his mum and dad – there'd been talk of levelling his entire estate to re-turf the area. In the dawn light, though, everything looks ashen rather than green. Somewhere not far away is the *hush, hush* of traffic on the Orbital. There is something about the noise that makes him think of his parents in their beds, warm but red-eyed, kept up most of the night by his sister.

Peepsy tries to imagine what it would be like to go home now, to his own bed, but still thinks of it as something not even possible, let alone desirable. He sees himself getting up the following Monday morning, going to the NSA, wandering from one climate-controlled classroom to the next, returning home in darkness to a tense dinner table, followed by two hours In World and another two of sleeplessness. Another day, another set of Objectives to work through, another lunchtime eating nutritionally calibrated mush and trying to convince Hugo Raffi that Mr De Souza really does have a vestigial tail, and that's why his suit jacket is so big, and why he never takes it off. It's all so distant, so other. He's not even sure he wants to play Binball again. It's like he's grown up ten years in a week, and yet he feels almost no nostalgia for his old life.

"Alright?" asks Nowacki.

"I feel weird," says Peepsy.

"I know what you mean. Where do you think we are?"

"Green belt. I reckon the NSA will be over there." He points to the top of the bluff.

"Right-o. Shall we head back?"

Peepsy rubs his bare arms and starts tramping up the slope to the top of the bluff. From there he can see the construction site of the NSA's perimeter, and beyond that the school's grounds, the stadium and the geometric hulk of the main building, looking like a space station that never made it into orbit. The LED screen of the main entrance is a lighthouse penetrating the fog of the early morning. Beneath it, drenched in its glow, the school is besieged by thousands of people.

Dr Nowacki catches him up. "See. I told you someone would notice if a student went missing."

"Who are they all?"

"I don't know. Fans of yours?"

"What do you think's happened?"

Not for the first time, Peepsy assumes that he's somehow to blame.

7.52

ANNE BRANT is woken very suddenly to find the side of her face in a pool of spilled Dr Pepper, and her right earbud pushed so far into her ear canal that she knows she'll need tweezers to get it out again. It sounds like there's a very small Chinese man trapped inside her skull. He's talking steadily to her and her colleagues. When she sits up, she sees that the monitors are displaying an operating system that she doesn't recognise. Someone is selecting options and entering passwords, but it's no one in their department. Everyone is very still, very alert, watching the operation closely like it's a magic trick.

7.55

EVERY ONE of the NSA's locked doors open at the same time, and the building shivers like some great bird preening itself. The door to Mr

Graves's inner office swings outwards and nearly hits Tom Rosen full in the face. Maggie sits upright on the sofa where she's been sleeping, even though it was supposed to be part of their barricade, and it was supposed to be her turn to keep watch.

"Holy shit," she says. "Gerry, you did it!"

Gerald looks tired and wretched. He hasn't slept at all, as far as Tom is aware. Neither of them have.

"How are you feeling, Gerald?"

He gives an unconvincing thumbs-up.

"If that was your dad, thank him."

"I will thank him when I see him," he says. "When I go home."

"Home?"

"Would you look at that!" Maggie interrupts. She points through the door that's just opened. Tom turns and gets to his feet.

The smell from the Headmaster's office is a vile, sewage-y miasma that he practically has to wade through to get to the man himself. David Graves (MBA) has not moved from the spot where he and Alice found him on Wednesday morning, nor has he seen to any of his most basic bodily needs. His lips are blue, his fingers still twitching on the VR controls at his side. It is nearly impossible to tell if he is alive or dead.

7.56

A GREAT roar goes up from the assembled forces outside the NSA as the revolving door of the main entrance clicks and whirs and starts admitting parents into the foyer. Stephanie can hear them forcing themselves through the aperture, too many at a time.

"Take it *easy*!"

"You're *not* keeping me from my child, thank you."

"There's too many of us."

"You're just going to break the door again!"

"So my son is less important than yours, is that right?"

"Put your shoulder into it, darling!"

"You're crushing my *hand*. Oh God. Oh *God*."

And so on and so forth.

She can hear the interwoven frequencies of the drones, which have all, dozens of them, immediately descended upon this new development in the story.

She can also hear the sound of a DV somewhere, its electric engine far more powerful than a conventional people-carrier, travelling at a speed that is in no way appropriate for a school pick-up point.

7.58

THE DV'S trajectory is clear from the moment Alice sees it, just outside the construction workers' encampment, giving the whole sequence a horrifying, slow-motion inevitability. It disappears and reappears and disappears again behind the enormous black stanchions of the half-built wall, arrowing for the NSA's main entrance. Even from this distance the Meninist insignia on its rear doors is unmistakable – not so different from the old circular "Ban the Bomb" sign, but with the vertical line converted into an erect phallus, drawn just as crudely as the one she saw etched into the school desk in the underground.

7.59

TOM AND Maggie and Gerald Liu join the surge of bodies all heading towards the exit, students and teachers all tired and dirty and faintly hysterical. Some are carrying their limp, unconscious classmates on makeshift stretchers. The corridor's screens are still showing the NSA's weekly targets, profiles of successful alumni, adverts for milkshakes promoting concentration, muscle mass, hair regrowth. The coloured light isn't doing anyone's complexion any favours.

"Tom!"

He turns to see Bernice Potter forging through the crowds. He pretends he hasn't heard his name, puts an arm around Gerald and Maggie, and pushes them towards freedom.

8.00

THE EXPLOSION is perfect, as far as Peepsy is concerned. It's like the ones you get in Alpha when you use the nuke-launcher. It is doubly impressive for being mirrored in the glass and the cladding. A white-hot sphere that brings the world fleetingly and beautifully to life before swallowing itself and leaving a shadow as dark as the explosion was bright. The sound is incredibly loud, and leaves his ears and head feeling strangely, pleasantly clean inside.

"Don't look," says Dr Nowacki, but he can't not.

The flames skid weirdly up the sides of the building. The people gathered outside are running and shrieking, if they're not already curled like leaves on the floor. There's a wide, mangled path leading up to the entrance, where the DV drove through the crowds before impact, and the bodies on either side have unfamiliar shapes.

They watch together for a few minutes. Peepsy feels like he's at the cinema with his mum.

8.13

WHEN TOM ROSEN comes round, the world is all heat and fumes and high-pitched silence. The sleeve of his tweed jacket has finally detached itself fully from the shoulder. He sits up and spends a couple of minutes focusing intently on this new development, wondering whether to keep it as a kind of removable sheath, or to discard the jacket once and for all, because looking at his sleeve means he doesn't have to look at the rest of the foyer and the people strewn around it. He tests his limbs. They all work. There's a throb in his shoulder from where he was thrown to the ground. His face cracks and prickles like he's been out in the sun too long. Aside from that, everything seems to be in order.

His deafness starts to subside, and he wishes it wouldn't, because now he can hear the sounds of the students and the teachers who were too close to the entrance when the vehicle struck. It must have been loaded with some sort of high explosive because nothing remains of the DV itself apart from two of its wheels, which are now lying on different sides of the foyer. It's blown a hole in the side of the NSA about twice the size of the revolving door, and the heat has done unique and fascinating things to whatever supposedly impervious material the walls and windows are made of. The edge of the hole, and the people closest to the hole, are black. They get progressively less charred and noisier the further back he looks. Just behind him,

Maggie O'Brien isn't moving. Next to her, Gerald Liu is sitting surrounded by the scattered contents of his suitcase, blinking hard.

Tom goes and checks Maggie's pulse. She moans.

"You're okay," he says. "We're okay."

Should he check the pulse of everyone else? He's been on five or six of the NSA's first-aid training courses since he joined the school, and the thrust of them was always to simply contact someone else who is better trained than you. He wishes he knew what to do. There are a hundred pulses he could check. He rotates on the spot. He imagines Alice Nowacki shouting at him for not being decisive enough.

Tom is still spinning and pulling his sleeve on and off when Nutri-Start's fire and ambulance servicemen emerge through the smoke, the "N" logo of their helmets, white on red, visible before any other part of them. They pick their way quietly and meticulously through the debris. The sight of them frightens him, inexplicably.

"Up you get, Maggie," he says. "Gerald? Everything alright? Can you help?"

Gerald springs to attention. The boy is indestructible. Maggie groans and swears as they try to lift her by the armpits. The NutriStart paramedics see them and shout an instruction that Tom can't hear from under their breathing apparatus.

"Come on. You're okay."

"My head," Maggie says. "My eyes. Fuck."

Tom lifts her in both arms, with the medics and firemen still shouting at him, probably to advise him that it's a bad idea to move an injured child, let alone hoist her like a bag of laundry, but he knows what he needs to do, and no one else can tell him otherwise. Gerald stays at his right elbow, blowing on Maggie's face.

She's heavier than expected, and the way is strewn with horrifying obstacles, so the walk to the exit takes longer than expected. When they emerge onto the NSA's steps he finds as much carnage on the exterior of the building; more, in fact. Lots of the crowd have come forward to help however they can, lots more are simply looking on, or looking at each other in glazed paralysis. Drones bob and swoop and gobble up the footage.

He stands for a moment, framed by the black hole, Maggie in his arms, Gerald at his side. Somewhere in the back of his mind he's disappointed by the lack of applause. Parents and the security services rush up to meet him. He declines their offers to help and carries his burden – because it is *his* burden, no one else's, he's sure of that – through the noise and the tears and the chatter that's so garbled it sounds like it's being played in reverse. In the DV pick-up area there's a sleek-looking Care ambulance, the driver hovering anxiously at its open door. He looks at Tom, then at Maggie, then at the expensively equipped interior of the ambulance, then back at Tom. They're surrounded by parents now, pressing him for information on their children. Tom sets Maggie down on the floor of the ambulance. He can't hear what the driver is saying at first.

"She's not breathing right," shouts Tom over the clamour. "Pulse is slow, I think. She says her eyes are hurting."

"...she with?"

"What?"

"Who's she with?"

"What do you mean?"

"Who's her insurer?"

"I don't know. Does that really matter?"

The driver peers at Maggie's face and gives an apologetic smile. "If she's not with Care we can't treat her."

A father grabs Tom by the detachable sleeve and it comes off and disappears into the crowd. Someone shouts so loudly in his ear it seems to pass straight through his brain and emerge amplified from the ear on the other side.

"Are you serious?" says Tom.

"Really sorry."

"You're serious."

"Yeah. Really sorry."

"Well, maybe she is with Care. I don't know." She should have a wallet on her somewhere, with her medical insurance card in it. Unless it was in her huge sports bag that she used to lug around with her? He fumbles around her jacket, and then trousers, and then hears a drone hovering overhead and realises how weird this must look. "I'm looking for her wallet," he says out loud, to no one specifically, to justify what he's doing. Maggie groans again. The driver wrings his hands.

While he's searching, he's aware that the turmoil around him has subsided. A circle of tense space has formed at the back of the ambulance.

"Mr Rosen?"

Tom turns around to see two members of the NSA's private security firm standing on the fringes of the crowd. They're dressed like a SWAT team, saddled with vastly complex utility belts of radios, handcuffs, sprays, electric batons, tasers. Their forearms twitch in anticipation of Tom's misbehaviour.

"Can you just hold on *one minute*," Tom says. "Can you not see I'm trying to help this girl?"

"Sure you are."

"What's that?"

"Helping her."

Tom looks at the pair of them dumbly. The one who's not talking is chewing gum with a slack-jawed, couldn't-give-a-shit attitude that suggests he might not even be aware of what's just happened at the school.

"Don't even start," he says.

"Step away from her, Mr Rosen," says the first man.

"Don't even *start*."

"We've been alerted to some improper conduct between yourself and Miss O'Brien by the Head of Safeguarding, Mr Tooley. We'd like to ask you a few questions."

"Improper conduct."

"Given how things currently look, I'd say it's in your own interests to step away from the girl."

Tom glances at the drone hovering between the two security men, recording the whole scene patiently, indifferently. Some of the parents are muttering to each other.

"Really? You want to do this now? Maggie is *injured*. She needs help."

"We can see that she's looked after, Mr Rosen. For the time being, we'd like you to come with us."

Tom turns his back on them again. "I'm not leaving her," he says.

"Mr Rosen."

He hears them step forward. Then there's another noise, a collective *whoop* from somewhere near the destroyed entrance, but drunken and unsteady. Everyone looks around. Here come the rest of the students, ill and unhappy boys and girls, their small and undeveloped bodies running on Good Day's unlicensed medication, hooting and babbling and adding an inconceivable extra layer of chaos to the situation. Cries of relief and elation from parents turn suddenly to dismay.

Tom is glad of the distraction. He lifts Maggie and puts her over his shoulder, then runs through the thinning crowd to a waiting Driverless Vehicle. He can hear Gerald panting behind him.

"Mr Rosen! Mr Rosen!"

He scans his DV pass and the car opens its doors and welcomes him into the driver's seat. Maggie gets dumped in the back, wheezing. Gerald gets in on the passenger side. He puts on his seat belt straight away.

Tom selects "manual" instead of "driverless" from the touchscreen, takes the steering wheel in both hands, and eases down the accelerator. The DV's recorded warning patiently advises the surrounding parents and journalists and street-food vendors to move out of the way. He takes the exact reverse of the route that the Meninists' vehicle took half an hour earlier.

Once he's free of the throng, he accelerates out of the NSA's grounds and into the morning traffic, which has all but stopped to watch the developing situation in the school. Tom picks the gaps and threads his escape, destination unknown.

8.45

ALICE HAS lost Peepsy. He was with her all the way until they got to the edge of the crowd, but then he saw someone he knew, and now he's disappeared. Now Alice is alone on the edge of the DV parking area, listening to various security personnel argue over which colour tape they should use to cordon off the site. The problem, it seems, is that each private security firm has its own branded tape, and overuse of a particular colour would make it look like one firm is more in control of the situation than another, and no one wants to miss out on this unique PR opportunity.

Around her are sporadic eruptions of disorder as children who were thought to be tranquilised return dramatically to life. They thrash like fish out of water. Almost all of them have bloodied noses like Peepsy did. No one will give her a straight answer as to what has happened to them. At the moment, Peepsy's curse is the best explanation she's got.

She spies him, all of a sudden, over the other side of the security tape. He's talking with another student, Josh, the tanned boy who'd approached her and Tom in the corridor.

Tom! Surely he's not still down there? She thinks of him, curled up asleep in the basement. She can't work out if she's glad he's safely out of harm's way, or disappointed that he is, as per usual, absent in a time of crisis.

She makes her way around the debris until she's behind the two boys. It's not really a conversation. It's more that Josh is talking *at* Peepsy, and Peepsy is gazing into space like a man whose own death has just been prophesised to him.

"Please don't go running off like that," she says.

Josh clams up, and neither of them turn around. That's it, then, she thinks. He's back amongst his own people.

"Hello, Josh."

"Hi."

"Are you alright?"

He nods.

"Have you found your parents?"

"Mum's coming. She hasn't stopped messaging me since Wednesday. Dad's in Greenland."

She turns to Peepsy, who's really getting into his thousand-yard stare now.

"Alex? What about you?"

"I've seen them," Josh answers for him. "They're here somewhere. Don't know where."

"Then let's go and find them! Alex?"

"I don't get it," he says. "My grades weren't even that bad."

"I mean, it's nothing compared to Bäcker," says Josh.

"Wait," says Alice. "What do you mean? Your grades?"

He goes quiet again. Josh obliges her.

"I've just told him about the testing."

"Testing?"

"The Good Day, Alpha Omega testing thing. Didn't you get it? Haven't you checked your PAD?"

"My PAD ran out of battery."

"Oh. Well. Here."

He hands Alice his own device and directs her to a message that's been posted on the NSA's internal network. It's been forwarded by none other than Mr Tom Rosen. That's not the only thing that catches her eye. Its original author was someone called Peter Van Den Hoonaard. That name. Where does she know that name from?

Then she remembers, and almost passes out from the sensation of two or three or four of her worlds colliding.

9.45

STEPHANIE IS in the back of one of Care's ambulances while a pair of doctors test her hearing and, stupidly, her sight. A third is somewhere nearby, typing on a touchscreen.

"You've got a son at this school, right?" says the one who's typing.

"Yes." She pauses. "No. I don't know."

There's a baffled silence.

"Right. Is he covered by your policy?"

"Yes, of course he is."

"And have you seen him?"

The strangest thing is, she feels like she has.

"No," she says, to save them more confusion.

"But he's on the premises?"

"I don't know."

"Would you like us to check?"

"I don't think you'll have any luck."

"You stay there." A hand on her arm that feels firmer than it should. "We'll check."

He leaves, and she remains in the back of the ambulance while the other two doctors prod her and rub creams on her and breathe in her face when they ask her questions.

"You're Stephanie Bäcker?" someone else says. There's another woman in the ambulance with her, on an adjacent bed.

"Please respect the privacy of our patients," says one of the doctors.

"Oh shut up. Are you?"

"Yes," says Stephanie.

"Is your son Gabriel?"

"That's right."

"Captain Gumbo."

"That's the name he uses online. In his game. In World."

"I've seen him."

Stephanie sits up, and some tubes pop out of her arm, tubes she didn't even know were there. One of the doctors tries to manhandle her back into the bed.

"What? Where?"

"Everyone's seen him."

"*Please* respect the privacy of our patients," says the doctor again.

"Everyone?"

"The boy in the window."

"What's the boy in the window?"

"You haven't seen it?"

"No."

"*Really?*"

"No!"

There's a lot of rolling around in the bed next to her, as though the other woman is trying to retrieve something from the floor. A video starts playing. Street noises, as far as Stephanie can make out. Footfall and chatter and then gasps and laughter.

"Someone filmed it the other day, outside the Alpha headquarters. Watch this bit! Watch this bit! Where he flattens his belly on the glass! Ha ha!"

Stephanie can feel an intense pressure being exerted on the sides of her skull, like she's sinking into very deep water. She knows it's him, without even seeing the footage.

"Are you sure it's Gabriel?"

"Captain Gumbo?"

"His name is Gabriel."

"It's definitely him. One of the other kids here recognised him and tagged him. He's famous! Look! Where he tries to run away! Ha ha!"

10.00

WHEN ALICE finally finds somewhere to charge her PAD, she has 1,228 unread messages. Thirty-five of these are from Henry. They chart a steady trajectory from annoyance, to professional concern, to personal concern, to something much more surprising. One of the latest messages ends with the words, "I don't know what I'd do without you."

From Henry, of all people! She laughs out loud and looks around to see if anyone has noticed. The sound of laughter isn't exactly appropriate in the circumstances.

Another thirty are from other members of the BIA, asking her where she is, why she's not replying, whether she thinks her position on the team is tenable if she can't respond to a simple question within twenty-four hours.

The most recent message is from HBO, asking if they might talk to her with regards to a feature film that they're investing in, having obtained the rights to the events at NSA from a Mr R.M. Tooley, despite the fact that the scandal only came to light an hour and a half ago.

All the rest are redirects from her Alpha Omega profile, sent to a special encrypted folder, demanding "Clodia" to upload new scenarios or lose their subscriptions.

A huge, shuddering breath. There's no point trying to keep the tears back, now. She looks again at Henry's message. Then at the Clodia messages. She cycles between the two.

"I don't know what I'd do without you."

10.05

ALEX "PEEPSY" PEPYS can't breathe properly. His face is crushed into his father's armpit. His feelings of relief are only slightly marred by the fact that his father obviously hasn't showered for the last three days.

"You're okay," he says, over and over. "You're okay."

It's sort of convenient that the armpit is stopping Peepsy from nodding or agreeing with his father out loud.

10.10

THE SIRENS of the security service cars are so steady and so constant that, after nearly an hour of pursuit, Tom is starting to find their blaring and flashing strangely hypnotic. His chin is nearly resting on the steering wheel.

On the back seat, Maggie O'Brien burbles something. Tom shifts around in his seat and watches her for a few moments. Her nose is bleeding now, but it doesn't look like she's in pain. She just looks like she's sleeping. Thank God he managed to get her out of there in time.

"There are many cars on this road," says Gerald from between his legs. He has adopted the brace position.

"I know," says Tom.

"It is very dangerous," says Gerald.

"I know," says Tom again.

He turns back to the road and watches the speedometer creep up, 90mph, 100mph, 110mph.

When he was at school, as a student, Tom used to imagine running away all the time. It was an implicit threat to the world: if it pushed him too much, he would be gone, never to return. Then they'd miss him. He pictured himself living a self-sufficient life somewhere in the Shetlands, far from civilisation, watching – somehow – as his friends and family and teachers fretted over his disappearance and regretted their mistreatment of him and begged him to come back. It was like the reason he never made any decisions was that all his energy was being stored up for this one *ultimate* decision, to remove himself from the world completely. When it came down to it, he knew, he could be more devastatingly decisive than anyone. And now it has come down to it. His whole life hinging on this choice.

10.12

"WE CAN ONLY take you to one of our Care facilities," says the doctor. "Or we can take you home. Otherwise you invalidate your policy."

Stephanie tries to leap from the bed again. The doctor makes a noise like he's trying to calm a horse.

"Please stay seated, Mrs Bäcker," he says.

"I need to get my son."

"You're in shock, Mrs Bäcker. Let us look after you."

"I want to go to the Alpha headquarters."

"Good luck with that!" says the other woman. Since their last exchange Stephanie has discovered that she's not even a parent. She's a graphic designer with some spare time on her hands who's come to see what all the fuss is about. She heard about it on Alpha and travelled down from Leeds the previous afternoon.

"Gabriel's still in there."

"Then he's staying in there. They're not letting anyone in or out, since everyone found out about all this. Whole place is shut down. Alpha just says they're preparing a statement. Look."

Not for the first time, she tries to show Stephanie her PAD. The doctor intervenes.

"Like I say, Mrs Bäcker: we can only take you to a Care facility, or to your home, where we can monitor you properly."

"Then take me home. Now."

"We still have a few tests to—"

"*Now.*"

10.54

ON THE DV'S dashboard display, a blue light signifying "empty battery" flashes with what Tom thinks is a curious lack of urgency. The Shetlands are still a long way away.

10.55

WHILE SHE'S trying to compose a reply to Henry, Alice receives yet another message. It's from Tom Rosen. He wants to know if she has a car he could borrow. He says it's urgent. It can wait, she decides, and goes back to thinking of a good joke.

11.35

STEPHANIE DOESN'T realise the package has arrived until she collides with it in the hallway. She goes shins-first into the side of it, and her yelp of pain stirs Mr Carnoso on the floor above.

It's not like the other one. This one's a battered old cardboard box, bound with erratic strips of parcel tape. She tears off the top with her nails. Her pulse is like a hummingbird's, her blood white-hot. She feels inhumanly strong.

"Another pressie!" says Mr Carnoso, coming down the stairs.

She doesn't reply.

"Says it's for Gabriel. I hope you don't mind me bringing it in!"

She reaches into the box.

"Any word from him yet?"

Inside is a large plastic tub. She runs her fingers around its surface. She can feel the raised edges of a triangle, and a warning message in braille. She has to re-read it a couple of times.

"Stephanie?"

The tub contains explosives.

"Steph?"

Explosives, for Gabriel.

"Was he at the Alpha headquarters?"

There isn't the same confusion as last time. She doesn't even stop to question why it's there, why Gabriel might have wanted it. Perhaps he foresaw the whole thing? She can see the way ahead quite clearly, now. She stands and finally answers Mr Carnoso, who's hovering at her shoulder, his nose whistling in her ear.

"He's still there," she says. "I need to go back there. To pick him up."

"Ah."

"I have to bring him something."

"I see."

"Could you help me lift this box into the car?"

12.20

THE WEIRDEST thing about coming home is that it feels like returning from any other day at school. Peepsy throws his filthy rucksack – the Professor's rucksack – on the sofa, pours himself a glass of juice, runs upstairs. He can feel his parents' eyes on him all the way, like they're expecting him to lapse into a psychotic episode at any moment. As soon as he's out of sight he can hear them murmuring.

He calls in on his sister on the way to his bedroom. He kisses her on the forehead, just above the scar, pushes a strand of hair out of her eyes.

"You wouldn't believe the week I've had."

His sister coos softly.

"The best part, though: I think I found you a boyfriend."

He decides he wants her company for a bit, so he makes himself comfortable on her bed, while she's strapped upright in her chair. Her interest in him comes and goes.

He tells her everything that's happened in the last five days, swiping around his PAD, scouring the newsfeeds, re-reading the messages from the whistle-blower. There are pictures and videos of at least five confused Peter Van Den Hoonaards, none of whom know anything about the NSA or the scandal.

There's one thing Peepsy hasn't checked yet. He opens up the list of names submitted by Mr Graves for the Good Day trials. Scrolls down to P. Then to Q. Then back up to O.

His name isn't there.

15.57

GABRIEL BÄCKER is taking a leisurely stroll through the NSA's organic garden. The leaves are coppered by the evening sunlight. He can't stop smiling.

"You're the man, Gabe!" says one of the students.

Gabriel nods and stops. What's that? Thunder? An earthquake? No one seems to have noticed but him. His skin shivers and contracts, like he's being vacuum-packed. He can smell smoke, chemical-tinged. He can feel heat too, and then, despite the glorious sunset, freezing rain on his bare head, and a siren that sounds like it's summoning him to lessons.

ACKNOWLEDGEMENTS

THIS BOOK has been a very long time coming, and a number of people have helped to keep the thing on track (despite my best efforts). Thanks to my editor Sophie Robinson, for inviting me aboard the good ship Titan and turning the manuscript into something that actually made sense; to Davi Lancett for invaluable help with both the style and the sci-fi bits; to Dan Coxon for his meticulous copy-editing; to my agent Jane Willis for enduring that repulsive first draft and for sticking with it regardless; to Sophie Churcher for helping to get the manuscript out and about, and for the coup of the audiobook; to Verity Smith, Sophie Lynas, Stephanie Melvin, Melissa Neckar and Ben Ward who all read it in various early and late incarnations and offered generous criticism and encouragement; to James Bowling for advice on some of the technical bits; to Will, Jancis and Nick Lander for letting me write and edit in your lovely house; to anyone else who has just generally been interested and supportive, whose names now escape me. Especial thanks to all the brilliant young people I've had the privilege of teaching over the years, who've kept me sane and happy and inspired. I promise you, none of you made it into the book.

ZERO BOMB
BY M.T. HILL

The near future. Following the death of his daughter Martha, Remi flees the north of England for London. Here he tries to rebuild his life as a cycle courier, delivering subversive documents under the nose of an all-seeing state.

But when a driverless car attempts to run him over, Remi soon discovers that his old life will not let him move on so easily. Someone is leaving coded messages for Remi across the city, and they seem to suggest that Martha is not dead at all.

Unsure what to believe, and increasingly unable to trust his memory, Remi is slowly drawn into the web of a dangerous radical whose '70s sci-fi novel is now a manifesto for direct action against automation, technology, and England itself.

The deal? Remi can see Martha again – if he joins the cause.

"Fresh, insightful and powerful." *Locus*

"Arguably the finest post-singularity escapade since Matthew de Abaitua's sci-fi novel *If Then*." *The New Scientist*

TITANBOOKS.COM

THE BREACH
BY M.T. HILL

Freya Medlock, a reporter at her local paper, is down on her luck and chasing a break. When she's assigned to cover the death of a young climber named Stephen, she might just have the story she needs. Digging into Stephen's life, Freya uncovers a strange photo uploaded to an urban exploration forum not long before he died. It seems to show a weird nest, yet the caption below suggests there's more to it.

Freya believes this nest – discovering what it really is and where it's hidden – could be the key to understanding the mysteries surrounding Stephen's death.

Soon she meets Shep, a trainee steeplejack with his own secret life. When Shep's not working up chimneys, he's also into urban exploration – undertaking dangerous 'missions' into abandoned and restricted sites. As Shep draws Freya deeper into the urbex scene, the circumstances of Stephen's death become increasingly unsettling – and Freya finds herself risking more and more to get the answers she wants.

But neither Freya nor Shep realise that some dark corners are better left unlit.

HOPE ISLAND
BY TIM MAJOR

Workaholic TV producer Nina Scaife is determined to fight for what remains of her family after her partner walks out on her. She takes her daughter, Laurie, to the beautiful but remote Hope Island, to prove to her that she's still a part of her life. But as the behaviour of the islanders becomes strange, Nina struggles to reconnect with Laurie, and the silent island children begin to lure her away.

Meanwhile, Nina finds herself drawn to a recently unearthed archaeological site… and then she discovers the first of the dead bodies.

"*Hope Island* is a masterfully tense tale, building a looming sense of dread and growing uncertainty. Disturbing and original, surprising and shocking, it's an excellent novel from a unique voice in the genre."
Tim Lebbon, author of *Eden* and *The Silence*

"*Hope Island* is a deliciously creepy mystery. Prepare to be unnerved."
D. K. Fields, author of *Widow's Welcome*

For more fantastic fiction, author events,
exclusive excerpts, competitions, limited editions and more

VISIT OUR WEBSITE
titanbooks.com

LIKE US ON FACEBOOK
facebook.com/titanbooks

FOLLOW US ON TWITTER AND INSTAGRAM
@TitanBooks

EMAIL US
readerfeedback@titanemail.com